He tasted her

"The cop was still here," Cooper growled against her lips. "I didn't want him suspicious."

He was kissing her for a cover.

Had she moaned? She'd definitely sunk her nails into his shoulders. She'd even arched against him.

"I...I know," she lied. Their mouths were barely an inch apart. "The kiss was a good idea."

A car cranked. The engine growled.

"I'm guessing that's him," Gabrielle said as she kept her hands on Cooper. But she did retract her nails. "Pulling away?"

He nodded. "I'm not letting you go until he's gone."

He tasted her. He claimed. He—

THE GIRL NEXT DOOR

BY
CYNTHIA EDEN

Published in Great Britain 2014
by Mills & Boon, an imprint of Harlequin (UK) Limited,
Eton House, 18-24 Paradise Road, Richmond, Surrey, TW9 1SR

© 2014 Cindy Roussos

ISBN: 978 0 263 91351 4

46-0314

Harlequin (UK) Limited's policy is to use papers that are natural, renewable and recyclable products and made from wood grown in sustainable forests. The logging and manufacturing processes conform to the legal environmental regulations of the country of origin.

Printed and bound in Spain
by Blackprint CPI, Barcelona

New York Times and *USA TODAY* bestselling author **Cynthia Eden** writes tales of romantic suspense and paranormal romance. Her books have received starred reviews from *Publishers Weekly,* and she has received a RITA® Award nomination for best romantic suspense novel. Cynthia lives in the Deep South, loves horror movies and has an addiction to chocolate. More information about Cynthia may be found on her website, www.cynthiaeden.com, or you can follow her on Twitter (www.twitter.com/cynthiaeden).

Thank you so much to the fabulous staff
at Harlequin Books. Working with you is a pleasure!

Chapter One

Cooper Marshall burst into the apartment, gun ready as his gaze swept the dim interior of the room that waited for him. "Lockwood!"

There was no response to his call, but the stench in the air—that unmistakable odor of death and blood—told Cooper that he'd arrived too late.

Again.

Damn it.

Cooper rushed deeper into that darkened apartment. He'd gotten his orders from the top. He'd been assigned to track down Keith Lockwood, an ex–Elite Operations Division agent. Cooper was supposed to confirm that the other man was alive and well. He'd fallen off the EOD's radar, and that had sure raised a red flag in the mind of Cooper's boss.

Especially since other EOD agents had recently turned up dead.

Cooper rounded a corner in the narrow hallway. The scent of blood was stronger. He headed toward what he suspected was the bedroom. His eyes had already adjusted to the darkness, so it was easy for him to see the body slumped on the floor just a few feet from him.

He knelt, and his gloved fingers turned the body just

slightly. Cooper pulled out his penlight and shone it on the dead man's face.

Keith Lockwood. Cooper had never worked with the man on a mission, but he'd seen Lockwood's photos.

Lockwood's throat had been slit. An up-close kill.

Considering that Lockwood was a former navy SEAL, the man shouldn't have been caught off guard.

But he had been.

Because the killer isn't your average thug off the streets.

The killer was also an agent with the EOD, and the killer was trained just as well as Lockwood had been.

No, trained *better*.

Because the killer had been able to get the drop on the SEAL.

Cooper's breath eased out in a rough sigh just as a knock sounded on the front door.

The front door that Cooper had just smashed open moments before.

He leapt to his feet.

"Mr. Lockwood?" A feminine voice called out. "Mr. Lockwood…i-is everything all right?"

No, things were far from *all right*. The broken door *should* have been a dead giveaway on that point.

"It's Gabrielle Harper!" The voice called out. "We were supposed to meet…"

His back teeth clenched. Talk about extremely bad timing. He knew Gabrielle Harper, and the trouble that the woman was about to bring his way was just going to make the situation even more of a tangled mess.

Cooper holstered his weapon. He had to get out of that apartment. *Before* Gabrielle saw him and asked questions that he couldn't answer for her.

He rose and stalked toward the bedroom window. His

footsteps were silent. After all of his training, they should have been.

Gabrielle's steps—and her high heels—tapped across the hardwood floor as she came inside the apartment.

Of course, Gabrielle wasn't just going to wait outside. She was a reporter, no doubt on the scent of a story.

And she must have scented the blood.

She was following that scent, and if he didn't move, fast, she'd follow it straight to him.

Cooper opened the window then glanced down below. Three floors up. But there were bricks on the side of the building, with crevices in between them. If he held on just right, he could spider-crawl his way down.

The floor in the hallway creaked as Gabrielle paused.

She should have called for help by now. At the first sign of that smashed door, Gabrielle should have dialed 911. But, with Gabrielle what she *should* do and what she actually *did*—well, those could be very different things.

If she wasn't careful, the woman was going to walk into real trouble one day—the kind that she wouldn't be able to walk away from.

He slid through the window. Since it was after midnight, Cooper knew he'd virtually disappear into the darkness when he climbed down the back side of the building.

He'd make it out of there, undetected, provided he didn't fall and break his neck.

He eased to the side, his feet resting against the window's narrow ledge. He pulled the window back down and took a deep breath.

"Mr. Lockwood!" Gabrielle's horror-filled scream broke loud and clear through the night.

She'd found the body.

Jaw locking, Cooper made his way down that building. Gabrielle had just stumbled into an extremely dangerous situation. Now he'd have to do some serious recon in order to keep her out of the cross fire.

IT WASN'T HER first dead body.

Gabrielle Harper stood behind the patrol car, her gaze on the apartment building. The cops had rolled in quickly after her call then they'd pushed her *out*.

They hadn't needed to push her so far. She knew better than to contaminate the scene. They didn't have to worry about her destroying evidence.

Not my first dead body. But the sight of Lockwood's slit throat had still made nausea rise within her.

"Tell me again," Detective Lane Carmichael said as he leaned back against the patrol car and studied her with an assessing gaze, "just why you were at Keith Lockwood's house in the middle of the night?"

A crowd had already gathered.

Her gaze slid away from Lane's and toward the apartment's entrance. The body was being wheeled out through the double doors. Lockwood had been zipped up in a black bag. Bagged, tagged and taken away.

She swallowed.

"Gabrielle."

The snap of her name jerked her attention back to Lane. His suit was wrinkled, his dark hair was tousled and his face was set in grim, I'm-sure-not-pleased-with-you lines.

That was typically the way Lane looked at her. Even when they'd been dating—briefly—he'd often given her that same look.

She worked the crime beat in Washington, D.C., covering stories for the *Inquisitor*—both the paper and its online subscriber base. Since Lane was a homicide detective, their paths crossed plenty.

That crossing had been good when they were dating. Now that they weren't—not so good.

"Lockwood called me," she began.

"Dead men don't make phone calls." His arms were crossed over his chest—his interrogation stance. "The ME estimates that he's been dead for over seven hours. Try again."

Seven hours. She filed that helpful detail away for later. "He called me around eight a.m. The guy left a voice message for me, saying he had some info to share about a story I'd covered."

Lane's head tilted. "Just what story would that be?"

Gabrielle pushed back her hair. It was summer in D.C., and she was sweating. "The unsolved murder of Kylie Archer." A woman whose body had been discovered in her apartment months ago. Kylie's throat had been slit.

Just like Lockwood's.

Even in the summer heat goose bumps rose on her arms.

"I need everything you've got on Lockwood, Gabby," Lane told her, his voice grim. "Everything."

But she could only shake her head. The body had been loaded into the coroner's van. Uniforms began to walk back into the apartment building. "I don't have anything to give you. He called *me.* Left a message for me to meet him at this address after midnight. He mentioned Kylie's name and said he had more information for me." She was trying to cooperate, didn't Lane get that? "I'd just run a piece on the web, highlighting Kylie's unsolved murder, so I figured that Lockwood had seen it and he had a lead to share with me."

Once a month, she featured an unsolved crime in her column. Thanks to those features, she'd helped close three cold cases.

Lane should thank her for that help.

His glare said he wouldn't be thanking her anytime soon.

"What if the killer had still been inside that apartment?" he demanded. "What if he'd come at you with that knife?"

She had mace in her bag. Not much as a weapon, but it was *something*. "No one was there when I arrived."

"You sure about that?"

Pretty sure since she'd gone through every room in that place. "I—"

"Gabrielle?" A surprised voice. Male. Rough. Very distinct.

When a woman heard a voice like that—so deep and hard and rumbling—she didn't forget it.

She fantasized about it. She enjoyed it.

She didn't forget.

"What's going on?" That voice continued, and then a warm, strong hand closed over her shoulder. "Is somebody hurt?"

She turned and faced the owner of that sexy voice— Cooper Marshall. Tall, gorgeous and with a smile that had made her heart skip a beat the first time she met him.

In other words—trouble.

"Someone's dead," Lane said before she could respond to Cooper. "And if Gabrielle doesn't learn to be more careful, she could wind up the same way."

Cooper's fingers tightened on her shoulder. "Dead?"

"You need to clear out of here," Lane said, speaking to her and giving another of his firm nods. Lane liked his firm nods. "There's no way any civilians are going to get near that crime scene tonight."

That was not what Gabrielle wanted to hear. She had definite plans to explore that apartment, because she suspected that Lockwood had been in possession of some evidence that she could use.

"Catch the train, Gabby," Lane advised her as he turned away, "and call it a night."

A police car pulled away.

Cooper kept holding her. His touch sure felt warm.

She glanced at him again. Cooper was wearing black—a black T-shirt and pants, and the guy actually seemed to blend with the night. For such a big guy, she'd found that he blended easily.

But then again, he'd told her that he was a P.I. Private investigators were supposed to be extremely good at blending.

"What did you stumble on this time?" Cooper asked her, the growl kicking up in his words.

"Oh, the usual." She tried to keep the tremble from her voice. *Failed.* "A witness who was murdered before he could talk to me."

Cooper swore.

Yes, yes, that was how she felt, too.

"Forget the train. I'll take you home." Then he was pulling her with him and away from the crowd that had gathered on the street. "I was on my way home when I saw the lights. I thought I'd stop by and see what was happening." He spared her a glance. "A dead man, Gabrielle?"

Yes, well, finding Lockwood dead hadn't exactly been on her agenda.

Cooper's motorcycle waited at the side of the road. He climbed on then tossed her the helmet. "Just hold on tight, and I'll have you home soon."

She caught the helmet, but hesitated.

"What?" The light from the streetlamp fell on his face. It glinted off his dark blond hair and made him look even more handsome—and dangerous. "Don't you trust me for a little ride? Come on, we're neighbors. It's not like the trip is out of my way."

He was right. They were neighbors. They shared a brownstone—just the two of them.

When she'd moved in four months ago, she hadn't been sure what to expect from her male neighbor. Her landlord had told her that Cooper regularly worked out of the country, that she probably wouldn't hear a peep from him.

She'd heard some peeps. And so far, he hadn't been out of the country.

On her first day in the apartment, she'd baked him chocolate chip cookies. She had a thing about baking— it soothed her. So she'd strolled down with her cookies to say hello.

She'd gotten a good look at him, standing in the door- way, tall and sexy, and she'd almost dropped those cook- ies.

"Gabrielle?"

She shoved on her helmet and climbed onto the motor- cycle behind Cooper.

He laughed. "You're going to have to sit a little closer than that. And put your arms around me."

She'd put her arms *behind* herself and was currently gripping the back of the seat.

He revved the engine. The bike kicked to life and when it shot forward, her hands flew up and wrapped around Cooper.

She gripped him as tightly as she could.

All muscle.

She could feel his rock-hard abs beneath her hands. No big surprise. She'd heard him working out before. Boxing. The guy loved to punch.

She'd seen him sporting an assortment of bruises since she'd met him, so she figured he must do more than just hit his punching bag. The guy probably fought at a local ring. The image of Cooper, bare-chested, fighting...well, that was an image that had sure floated in her mind before.

The motorcycle zoomed through the city, flying through intersections, cutting closely around corners. At one point, Gabrielle had to squeeze her eyes shut because she was pretty certain they were going to crash and become nothing but a mangled pile of limbs.

"We're here."

Her eyes cracked open. Sure enough, they'd made it to the brownstone. Located off the main streets and nestled in one of the few, quiet corners of D.C., the brownstone stood with its porch lights blazing.

She loved that place.

"You can...um, release that grip on me now," Cooper told her.

Gabrielle realized that her nails were digging into his shirt—into him. "Sorry," she muttered and jumped from the bike. "I'm not exactly a motorcycle fan."

He shoved down the kickstand, and then took his time rising from the bike. "Really? And here I thought you liked to live on the wild side."

What? Since when?

"Coming in at all hours of the night," he murmured as he brushed past her and headed up the steps that would take them inside the brownstone. "Covering the most dangerous cases in the city. You sure seem like a woman who enjoys living on the edge."

She wasn't going to touch that one.

As they paused on the narrow porch, the wind chime that she'd hung up a few days before pealed softly. The sound soothed her, at least a little bit.

Gabrielle followed him inside. A large, curving bannister led to the apartment upstairs. Her place was up there. His apartment was downstairs, right below hers. They both had a key to the main door, and she watched as he secured that door.

He'd gotten her home, so this was where they should part ways. Only she found herself hesitant to leave him. Maybe it was the image she still had of poor Keith Lockwood. *I can still smell the blood.* No, she wasn't in a hurry to rush up those stairs and spend the night all by herself.

Gabrielle already knew sleep wouldn't come easily. She'd be too busy remembering the sight of that body.

So she lingered at the foot of the stairs, studying Cooper.

He turned toward her and cocked his head. Then his eyes, a shade of a blue that electrified her, narrowed. "You're scared." He stalked toward her.

Gabrielle stiffened at the accusation. "I'm a little shaken. I found a dead body. I *get* to be shaken."

He stopped less than a foot from her. "I'm sorry you had to see that."

"Yes, well, I'm sorry that Mr. Lockwood is dead. Maybe if we'd met earlier, if I'd just gone by his place sooner instead of waiting for our meeting time—"

"Then you might be dead, too," he said, cutting through her words.

Gabrielle pushed back her hair. "He asked me to meet him. He called and said that he had a tip for me." *So much blood.* "I guess someone wanted to make sure he never got the chance to deliver that tip."

He took her hand.

Her breath rushed out. In four months, he hadn't touched her. Until tonight. He'd touched her at the crime scene, and now he was touching her here.

She hadn't expected his touch to unsettle her so much.

But it did. Awareness pulsed through her as she stared into his eyes.

"Come with me," he invited softly. "You shouldn't be alone after what happened."

"I'm always alone."

He frowned.

Wait, those words had come out wrong. That was her problem. She was good at *writing*. When she was talking, Gabrielle had a tendency to say the wrong thing. She cleared her throat and tried again, "What I meant was that I don't mind being alone. It's late, and I should be getting upstairs."

He used his grip on her hand to tug her toward him. "It's late all right, but I'm betting you've got so much adrenaline pumping through your body that sleep is the last thing on your mind." His eyes glittered down at her. The guy easily topped six foot two, maybe six foot three, and he had the wide, broad shoulders that a football player would envy.

When she looked up at him then, she didn't see the danger that she normally perceived.

She saw strength. Safety.

"I know a thing or two about adrenaline rushes. I can help you ride it out."

He didn't mean that sexually, did he? Because they were nowhere close to having a sexual relationship. No matter what a few heated dreams might have told her.

"Come on." He guided her toward his door. She'd never actually been past the threshold of his place, so curiosity stirred within her.

Curiosity. It had been her downfall since she was a kid.

He opened the door. The alarm immediately began to beep, and he quickly punched in a code to reset the system.

"Why don't you have a seat on the couch?" Cooper offered. "I'll grab us both a drink."

Her gaze shifted around the room. Ah…there was the punching bag hanging from the ceiling in what looked like a workout room that branched from the living area.

The hardwood floor gleamed in the apartment. A leather couch and armchair were centered around a very large TV. Typical. What wasn't so typical…

She didn't see a single family photograph. Actually, there were no photographs at all in the place.

The walls were bare and painted a light brown.

A small hallway snaked off to the left, and she found herself leaning forward to peer down that dark corridor.

"My bedroom is back that way. The guest room, too." His breath blew against her ear and Gabrielle gave a little jump. She hadn't even heard him approach. "There something in particular you're hoping to see?" Cooper asked

"Ah, no, nothing." She pasted a fake smile on her face and turned toward him. "I don't know why I came in here. I should let you get some rest."

"I don't sleep much." He lifted his right hand. His tanned fingers had curved around a clear glass. "For you."

"Thanks." She put it to her lips and nearly choked when she took a gulp.

Whiskey.

"A few sips might help you to calm your nerves."

Uh, *no.*

He downed his own glass in seemingly one swallow. "It's been one hell of a night," he muttered as he set his glass down on the nearby end table.

She put her glass down, too. The whiskey was burning her throat. When it came to drinking, she was way too much of a lightweight.

"You don't want to take the edge off?" Cooper asked her, frowning slightly.

She sank into the couch. *I should be heading for the door.* "I don't mix so well with whiskey."

"I can make you something else…"

"No." The leather was supple beneath her fingers. Tension still held her body tight, and she kept thinking—

"It doesn't do any good to keep picturing the dead." Cooper sat next to her. His thighs brushed against hers. "Turn around."

"Wh-what?" Now that was just sad. He was making her so nervous that she was actually stuttering.

"You're so stiff you're driving *me* crazy," he said.

She turned around. His hands reached for her shoulders. Oh, no, there was no way those fighting fists were going to give any kind of relaxing massage—

His fingers began to knead her flesh.

Gabrielle's eyes nearly rolled back in her head. She was wrong. So very wrong. His fingers were magic.

"I can help you to relax. Just breathe. Don't picture him. Get that image out of your head."

The man was way too good with his hands. "Is this… how you usually deal with adrenaline?"

A soft laugh. "No, I usually use sex."

The tension snapped right back in her shoulders.

"Relax," Cooper ordered, "that wasn't an offer."

Oh, right.

"Unless you want it to be…"

Trouble. She'd known that the guy was serious trouble from day one.

"What cold case are you working on?" He asked before she could do more than suck in a shocked gasp of air. "I know you told me that you were starting to profile them."

She had told him that, during one of their brief two-minute conversations when their paths occasionally crossed. "Kylie Archer. Her case isn't as old as the others, but the cops don't have any leads, so I thought I could try digging."

"That digging led you to the body?"

"Keith Lockwood," she whispered. The image of his body tried to push into her mind again, but she shoved it back.

He kept rubbing her shoulders. His broad fingers were sliding down her back.

Her thighs shifted restlessly.

"He knew who killed the woman?"

"I don't know." She would find out. As soon as the cops backed off, Gabrielle would be making her way back inside that apartment.

Her eyes drifted closed as he kept caressing her skin. His fingers skimmed over the edge of her arms. Then he returned his attention to her shoulders, started working down. Down...

He pushed lightly against her lower back.

Gabrielle had to bite back a moan. That felt so *good*.

But...was a massage supposed to turn a girl on?

This one is. No, correction...he is.

"You didn't see any sign of anyone else in that place?"

"The door was open when I went inside. Someone had shattered the lock. When I saw that, I knew something was wrong."

His fingers stilled. "You knew something was wrong, and you *still* went rushing in? You should have called the cops first!"

"Lockwood could've been hurt. That's why I went in. As soon as I saw the body, I called 911."

"Next time," his deep voice rumbled as he started his

massage once more, "do me a favor, okay? Call the cops before you rush in and find yourself facing a killer."

She wanted to melt into a puddle. His hands were heaven. The tension was gone. Well, all but the sexual tension. The sensual awareness she felt was heating up.

And that's my sign to leave.

His fingers were very close to her hips. And she was arching against his touch like a cat.

Get a grip, Gabrielle. It's just a massage. It's not love-making.

But she almost wished that it was.

Gabrielle jerked away from his touch. "I have to go." She jumped to her feet.

He stared up at her.

"Thanks for the ride home. And the drink. And the massage." She was rambling. "Good night." Then she scrambled for the door.

"Gabrielle."

His voice stopped her just as her fingers closed around the doorknob.

"If you get scared, if you need someone to talk to, I'm here."

Good to know. She tossed him a quick, nervous smile, then she fled. No other word for it.

A smart woman ran from trouble.

THE WOMAN WAS going to be trouble.

He'd known that, of course, the minute she moved in.

Long, black hair, golden skin, dark eyes… And a body that sure made him want to sin.

Gabrielle Harper was the last person he'd expected to find in his life. A reporter, right upstairs?

Fate had a twisted sense of humor.

If Gabrielle ever found out what he really did for a

living, if she found out about the secret government group known as the EOD—

Can't happen.

There were only a few civilians with clearance to possess intel about the Elite Operations Division. Too-pretty and too-tempting Gabrielle couldn't learn about his group.

Secrecy meant survival for the EOD agents. He would do anything to secure that survival.

Anything necessary. Those were his orders, after all. They'd come straight down from the top—from the director of the EOD, Bruce Mercer.

And anything necessary…well, that included a little breaking and entering.

Cooper had waited a few hours, until he was sure that Gabrielle had finally drifted into slumber. Then he'd commenced his B&E routine.

It was ridiculously easy to get inside Gabrielle's place. Since *he'd* installed the locks right before she moved in, Cooper had a key to her apartment.

He also knew her security code.

Again, because *he'd* installed the system.

She'd left a light on in her hallway. The faint glow spilled into the living area.

Her place was an exact copy of his. Only instead of a workout area, Gabrielle had an office in that side space.

The office was his destination. But first, he had to make sure that he wouldn't be disturbed.

He crept toward her bedroom. Cooper pushed the door open just a few inches.

Another light was on in there. A closet light this time.

Gabrielle didn't like the darkness. Odd, considering that her job sent her right into the dark path of criminals every day.

The glow fell on the bed, on her.

She'd kicked away her covers, and she lay on her side. Gabrielle wore a pair of jogging shorts and a faded college T-shirt. Her legs were long and bare and perfect.

Killer legs. Truly killer.

Her eyes were closed. Her right hand curled, palm up, on the edge of the bed. Sexy and vulnerable—a dangerous combination.

He took a deep breath and smelled her. A light scent. Lilac. He knew it only because she *always* smelled that way. He'd had to figure out the scent because it was driving him crazy.

The first day he'd met her, she'd come to him, a sweet smile on her face and a tray of chocolate chip cookies in her hands.

He'd gobbled up the cookies. He'd wanted to gobble *her* up. He still did.

Focus on the job.

Carefully, Cooper backed away from the door. Then he made his way to the office. Booting up her computer was easy. Figuring out her password was a bit harder. Luckily, he'd had some help from the EOD on that end.

Another agent, Sydney Sloan Ortez, had created a program that let him bypass most security walls on systems like Gabrielle's.

It took sixty seconds, and he was in.

He found Gabrielle's files on Lockwood. With a few clicks, he transferred copies of those files to his flash drive.

Then… *Sorry, sweetheart, I hate to do it but…* He uploaded a virus to her computer.

The EOD didn't want Gabrielle getting involved in Lockwood's murder. Mercer had given him an order to throw her off the killer's scent.

Now they had her case notes. Her files.

She'd have to start over from scratch once again. That would buy him some time.

Enough time to hunt a killer.

WELL, WELL, WELL...

It seemed that Cooper Marshall was the agent on his trail.

He'd seen Cooper in the crowd outside of Lockwood's place. He'd known the reporter was going to meet Keith, so figuring out that the police would be called after midnight hadn't been exactly hard.

He'd watched the scene with interest.

He certainly hadn't expected to see Cooper Marshall rush through the crowd and go straight to the reporter's side.

Then to *leave* with the woman...

Interesting.

Perhaps Gabrielle Harper was more important than he'd originally thought.

He would learn more about her. Then he would determine...was she valuable enough to bring into his game?

Or was she a pawn that could be eliminated?

Chapter Two

Gabrielle slid under the yellow police tape that blocked the entrance to Keith Lockwood's apartment. The cops had tried to repair the lock on his door, but their attempt hadn't been exactly successful.

That lack of success made getting in much easier for her.

She'd waited for night to fall once more. Waited to make sure all the cops had cleared out of the place.

She wasn't waiting any longer.

Gabrielle tiptoed into the apartment. She didn't turn on any lights. Lights would be seen from the street below, and she wasn't about to advertise her B&E stint.

So instead of turning on the overhead lights, Gabrielle pulled out a small flashlight. She crept carefully through the apartment. Her first stop was the desk near the kitchen. She opened the top drawer.

Empty.

The second drawer—

Empty.

The third—

Totally cleaned out.

Her eyes narrowed. There had been a computer on that desk last night. It was gone now, so she'd have to check in with Lane to see if the cops had confiscated it. No doubt, they had. Their tech department would search it and when they were finished, she'd just call in a favor from said tech department and get them to spill their results to her.

She turned away from the desk. There were other places to search.

Like the room where she'd found the body.

Her shoulders squared as she headed down the hallway. The scent of death still hung in the air. She hated that smell.

Her foot pressed down on the wooden floor. The long, low creak made her stiffen, but she kept going.

Then she was in the bedroom. Her flashlight illuminated the floor and the outline of the body. The blood had stained the wood.

So much blood.

Gabrielle exhaled. She hoped that Lockwood had died quickly. No one deserved to suffer.

She forced herself to look away from that outline. Her gaze and her light darted around the room. She could see a chest of drawers, a dresser and a nightstand. No photographs. *Just like Cooper's place.*

That wasn't normal. She edged closer to the nightstand positioned to the right of the bed. People usually kept photographs of family and friends in their homes. Light touches to personalize the place.

At the edge of the bed, her foot stepped down on something hard.

She heard the crunch of glass.

Gabrielle winced—*so much for being good at crime scenes*—and she bent down. She'd stepped on a frame. One that had dropped to the floor and slipped under the edge of the bed.

So Lockwood did have at least one picture.

She turned the frame over. Pieces of broken glass fell onto the bed.

Her light scanned over that photo. Her breath came faster. Her heart raced.

The picture was of Keith Lockwood. He was smiling in the picture, and he had his arm around a pretty, blonde woman.

Gabrielle easily recognized Kylie Archer. She'd seen plenty of pictures of that woman before.

What were you going to tell me about her? What? Gabrielle sure wished the dead could talk.

She backed away from the bed, still studying the photo. Backed away and backed *into* someone.

Someone big and strong.

Gabrielle opened her mouth to scream.

The scream never escaped because a hard hand covered her mouth. And even as that hand covered her mouth, an arm rose around Gabrielle and jerked her closer to—

"Easy," that familiar deep voice told her, as Cooper's breath blew against the shell of her ear. "I'm not going to hurt you, and a scream would just send the neighbors rushing to call the police."

Because he'd scared her, Gabrielle elbowed him in the ribs. He let her go with a grunt.

Gabrielle whirled to confront him. "What are you doing here? This is a crime scene!" She aimed her light right at his face.

He winced. "Trying to blind me?"

She thought that might only be fair since he'd just tried to scare her to death.

"And, yes, I know it's a crime scene," he said, sounding aggrieved. "That's why I wondered what the hell you were doing in here."

"You followed me?" Her voice was a whisper. He must have followed her. There was no other explanation. But why?

He shrugged. "After last night, maybe I was a little worried about you."

Oh. Wait. That was...nice.

The sneaking up on her part? *Not so nice.* "I didn't even hear you." Not so much as a sound.

"I'm used to sneaking in and out of places."

His comment sounded a bit sinister.

"And speaking of *out,* we need to go." But he was frowning now. "What are you holding?"

Her right hand gripped the flashlight. Her left still held the picture frame.

She took the light off his face and let it fall on the photo. "See how close they are? The way his hand is wrapped around her? I think Lockwood and Kylie Archer were involved." Lovers. Their bodies rested so easily against each other. "And, judging by the way they were killed—with their throats slit and with no sign of defensive wounds on their bodies—I'm also suspecting that the same person killed them both."

Silence.

She'd expected more after her big reveal. Gabrielle cleared her throat.

"How do you know there were no defensive wounds?" Cooper asked.

"Because I had time to check Lockwood's body before the cops got here." She also knew exactly what to look for regarding those types of wounds. "The thing that doesn't fit for me is the broken lock. Kylie's home didn't have a broken lock. Her door was locked, from the inside, and the cops were the ones to break their way inside."

Again...more silence. She wasn't really used to working with someone else on her stories, but she expected him to say something.

"Uh, Cooper?"

"Leave the picture. We need to go *now*."

"But I want to search some more. I need to—"

"When I parked, I saw a cop car coming down the street. I double-timed it up here to you, because I was worried the officer might be coming in for a sweep."

Her eyes widened. She dropped the photo to the floor. Mostly in the same spot. "We need to go *now*."

She grabbed his hand and rushed down the hallway.

She dodged the squeaky floorboard.

So did he.

She paused. He hadn't stepped on the squeaky floorboard when he'd first come in the apartment, either. The squeak would have alerted her to his presence. "How did you—"

"Hurry."

She kept going. She slid under the police tape, hustled into the hallway.

And heard footsteps.

Gabrielle darted to the edge of the stairs, and she saw the cop. Lucky for her, he was looking down, not up, so he didn't see her.

Cooper wrapped his arm around her waist and hauled her back. "Come on." He pulled her with him.

Lockwood's apartment was the only one on that floor. There weren't exactly a ton of places for them to hide.

"Storage," he muttered, moving toward a narrow, white door.

She hadn't even *seen* that door at first.

He opened it and pushed her inside.

It was the size of a closet. A very small, very overstuffed closet. Her body plastered against his.

"Not a sound," Cooper barely breathed the words.

She gave a jerky nod. Gabrielle could hear the footsteps then. The cop going to the apartment, going right past the storage closet.

But what if he comes back?

The closet smelled of ammonia. It had to be where the cleaning supplies were kept for the building. It was pitch-dark in there, so she couldn't see anything, and Gabrielle wasn't about to turn on her light.

There was silence in the hallway.

She figured the silence meant that the cop had entered the apartment.

If Cooper hadn't gotten me out of there, the cop would have walked right in on me.

Explaining her way out of that situation wouldn't have been easy.

Cooper still had his arm around her. Her hips and derriere pressed against him. Her back was to his chest. She could feel the steady rhythm of his breaths.

He didn't seem shaken. Not even a little.

Meanwhile her own breath seemed to heave out far too loudly.

She didn't move, didn't try to ease away from Cooper. She was too afraid she'd stumble onto another piece of flooring that would creak and give away their position.

After a seeming eternity, the cop's footsteps sounded in the hallway again.

The footsteps faded away as he descended the stairs.

Her shoulders slumped. She tried to pull away from Cooper.

"Not yet. Let's give him a chance to get good and gone."

She stilled. Tight, dark spaces weren't so high up on her list of favorite things. Actually, they were dead last on that list. But she wasn't alone right then. That was something.

Cooper. Why did she feel so safe with him? A man she barely knew?

Because he just saved you and you're going to owe him now.

"Can you try…" He whispered in her ear. She shivered as he continued, "Can you try to avoid committing any more crimes for the next few days?"

"No promises," she whispered back. "My computer crashed, and I'm back to square one on this case." Not totally true. She had backup files.

Not an amateur.

His hold eased. "I think we've waited long enough. Let's just head out, nice and slow, okay? Follow my lead."

Right. She could do that.

He opened the door, looked to the left and the right. He went down the stairs first. Cooper kept a tight hold on her hand when they escaped from that building.

Then they were outside. The night air was muggy and thick, and it felt like heaven after the ammonia-filled confines of that closet.

"Thanks," she began with a weary smile, "I needed your—"

His eyes had been over her shoulder, on the street, but he suddenly grabbed her and yanked her close.

Cooper kissed her.

It wasn't some easy, getting-to-know-you kiss. Not tentative. Not light.

It was hot. Hard. Openmouthed.

Toe-curling.

Fantastic.

His arms wrapped around her. He lifted her up against him, and Gabrielle's toes barely skimmed the ground.

His tongue licked across her bottom lip then thrust into her mouth. He tasted her. He claimed. He—

"The cop was still here," Cooper growled against her lips. "I didn't want him suspicious."

He was kissing her for a cover.

Had she moaned? She'd definitely sunk her nails into his shoulders. She'd even arched against him.

"I—I know," she lied. Their mouths were barely an inch apart. "The kiss was a good idea."

A car cranked. The engine growled.

"I'm guessing that's him," Gabrielle said as she kept her hands on Cooper. But she did retract her nails. "Pulling away?"

He nodded. "I'm not letting you go until he's gone."

His body was so warm.

The kiss had been a fake.

Humiliating. Maybe she'd played it off, though. Maybe.

They stood there, embracing, mouths so incredibly close, and in that moment, Gabrielle realized a very important fact.

Cooper was aroused.

If she hadn't been so distracted a moment before, she would have been keyed in to that situation sooner. She was so focused on the hot feel of his mouth she hadn't realized until now that the hips thrusting against her—

He freed her.

Gabrielle stopped feeling quite so humiliated. He had been affected by the kiss. Mr. Dangerous had gotten just as caught up as she had in the heat of the moment.

"We need to get home," he said in that deep rumble of his. "Come on, my bike's waiting."

Her phone vibrated, jerking in her pocket. She'd turned the ringer off before her little stint of B&E. "Hold on," Gabrielle told him. She yanked out her phone and recognized her boss's number at the *Inquisitor.*

"Gabrielle..." Cooper gritted out.

"It's my boss. Calling after midnight. I have to take this." Because there was only one reason Hugh Peters would call her this late.

A story.

"What is it, Hugh?"

"I just heard on the police scanner…" Excitement thickened his voice. "They got another vic. A female. Same MO as Archer."

Her fingers tightened around the phone. "Where."

He rattled off the address.

The address was close, just a few blocks away. She could jog there.

She *would* jog there.

"You get there and you find out what the hell is happening, got it?" Hugh said. Before she could answer, he continued, "Three kills? This mess is starting to look like the work of a serial."

His words chilled her. "We can't know that, not yet."

Cooper's gaze was on her.

"Get there and find out," Hugh ordered.

She shoved the phone back into her pocket. "Thanks for the offer of the ride, but my night's not over yet."

No wonder the cop had rushed away. She tilted her head and heard the wail of sirens in the distance.

Cooper stiffened. "What's happened?"

"Another woman has been found with her throat cut." She spun away from him. It was a good thing she jogged regularly. "I'll see you later, Cooper. Thanks for the help!"

He grabbed her wrist. "You're racing to a murder scene?"

"It's what I do." He was slowing her down.

Cooper shook his head. "Going on foot isn't the way. I can get you there faster." He pointed to his waiting motorcycle. "Just give me the address, and I'm there."

She didn't want to waste time arguing. She called out the address even as she climbed onto the bike. Seconds later they were racing away.

"IT LOOKS LIKE the same MO," Cooper said into his phone. He'd backed away from the crowd, found the best cover of shadows, and now he watched the chaotic scene with a careful gaze. "One of the cops said that the victim was a woman named Melanie Farrell."

"She's not one of ours," the clipped voice on the other end of the line responded. That voice belonged to Bruce Mercer. Cooper's boss. A man who knew where every single secret was buried in D.C.

Mostly because his job was to bury those secrets.

"You sure about that?" Cooper pressed. "She was found in her apartment, with the doors locked. Her throat was slit, and there were no signs of a struggle."

A low whistle. "You sure learned a lot on this one, fast."

His gaze tracked over to Gabrielle. She was currently talking quickly to a uniformed cop. The cop looked nervous. Since Gabrielle was grilling him, the guy should be nervous. "I had a little help." She'd been the one to get all of those details.

"The reporter." A long sigh slipped from Mercer. "I thought you had her contained."

Containing Gabrielle was a bit of a challenge. It was a good thing that he liked challenges. "I can use her. The cops tell her more in a few minutes than they would ever reveal to me." He had the P.I. cover for a reason, but Gabrielle's resources were proving to be far more useful.

Gabrielle eased away from the cop and gazed up at the building.

Trying to find a way inside, aren't you?

She edged toward the left, moving near the alley that he knew snaked behind those apartments.

"Melanie Farrell is *not* one of our agents." Mercer was adamant. "She shouldn't be targeted by our rogue."

The rogue—the EOD agent that Cooper was hunting.

"Kylie Archer wasn't an agent, either," Cooper said, going with his gut.

"Who?"

"She was killed a few months ago. Again, same damn MO."

"Our guy has been busy." Anger heated Mercer's words.

Our guy. Because they did think it was one of their own. One who'd tried to attack Mercer by going after his daughter and now…

"I found out that Kylie was romantically involved with Keith." Well, Gabrielle had found that out.

He couldn't see her now. Cooper's body tensed.

"The guy tried to get at you by taking away the one person who mattered," Cooper said.

Mercer's daughter.

"He couldn't get her, so maybe he decided to attack other agents by going after the people they valued." It was a theory that he was just developing, but so far, the pieces fit.

"That idea only plays," Mercer said slowly, "if we can link Melanie to an EOD agent."

"Sydney can find a link." If anyone could, it would be here. Sydney Sloan Ortez was in charge of information retrieval for the EOD. When it came to computers, no one was better. She could dig into any person's life with her machines. Could, and had.

"I'll get her started," Mercer promised. "In the meantime, you keep tracking this rogue. He knows our agents, he knows us, but I'll be damned if he's going to get away with these attacks on my watch."

Mercer hung up. Cooper pushed the phone into his back pocket. Gabrielle had slipped into the alley, and she'd never glanced back to see if anyone was watching her.

She should learn to pay attention to what—*who*—was behind her.

He'd sure gotten the drop on her easily enough in that apartment. If he *had* been the killer, she would have died.

His back teeth ground together as he stalked toward the alley. He'd had no idea that his neighbor was so drawn to danger.

Just like me. But he knew why he liked the thrill that came from danger. That burst of adrenaline made him feel alive.

What drew Gabrielle into the darkness?

THE FIRE ESCAPE led all the way up the side of the building. Gabrielle studied that fire escape, considering the options. It would sure be easy enough for the killer to slide through a window in the victim's apartment then flee down the fire escape.

Was that why the front door was locked? Did you get out this way?

She slipped deeper into the alley. The voices were muted here. Her shoe brushed over a discarded aluminum can. The acrid odor of rotten garbage was strong in that alley.

Gabrielle glanced to the left. A green garbage container sat to the side. The alley snaked away a bit then opened to another street.

Since there were no lights in that area, it would have been easy enough for the killer to hide down there.

"You're in the wrong place."

The whisper drifted to her. When the words sank in, Gabrielle froze.

"You shouldn't be here, all alone..."

She whirled around. That voice was coming from the shadows near the garbage container. "Who's there? Show yourself!"

Laughter. Low and chilling. "Not yet...not yet..."

Goose bumps rose on her arms.

"Gabrielle!"

That was Cooper. A shout had never sounded more wonderful.

Before she could call out to him, something—someone—grabbed her and shoved her into the brick wall of the alley. Her head hit the bricks, hard, and her body slumped.

"Not yet..." That whisper told her once more.

Then she didn't hear anything else.

She hadn't answered him.

Cooper rushed forward, running fast. She'd just been out of his sight for a few minutes. The cops were close by. Gabrielle couldn't just vanish.

A crumpled form lay curled near a garbage container. *Gabrielle*.

He didn't realize that he'd bellowed her name. But in the next instant, he was on his knees beside her, frantically searching for a pulse at the base of her throat.

The pulse beat slow, steady, beneath his fingers.

He brushed back her hair. Her head slumped weakly against his hold.

What in the hell had happened?

His gaze flew around the alley. It was too dark to see much.

And he didn't hear anyone.

"Gabrielle?" His fingers shifted through her hair. When he found the bump on the side of her head, he swore.

Then he stood, holding her carefully in his arms. She needed help.

"Freeze!" a male's voice shouted.

He wasn't in the mood to freeze. He was in the mood to get Gabrielle help.

Light from a flashlight hit him in the face. That light was so blinding that it made viewing the person connected to that voice hard. The man was little more than a shadow.

"Gabrielle?" The guy's voice roughened. "What the hell did you do to her?"

"Nothing," Cooper growled. "When I found her, she was unconscious. I'm trying to help her." *And you're slowing me down.*

The light came closer.

"I'm not armed," Cooper told him. That wasn't true, but the man wouldn't notice the weapons he carried. They were too well concealed. "We need to get her help."

He could see the man's face now. It was the detective from the other night, Lane Carmichael.

"I remember you," Carmichael said, obviously placing him. "You were at the other crime scene, too."

Great. *Not* the connection Cooper wanted the detective to make. If he wasn't careful, the cops would start looking at him for the kills.

He wasn't sure his P.I. cover could stand up to their perusal.

Carmichael yanked out his radio and called for backup—and an EMT.

A moan slipped from Gabrielle's lips. Under the flashlight, her lashes began to flutter. She blinked a few times then seemed to focus on him. "C-Cooper?"

"It's all right," he tried to reassure her. "I've got you."

A faint smile curved her lips. "S-saving me…again? You're making a h-habit of it…"

Yes, he was.

The EMT ran toward him. The man reached for Gabrielle.

For an instant, Cooper had the crazy urge to keep holding her. *I don't want to let her go.*

But he never got too close to anyone or anything. That was the way he wanted his life to be. The way it had always been.

He let her go.

As she was taken away from him, Cooper's shoulders tensed. He was going to find out exactly what had happened to Gabrielle in that alley.

Once more, his gaze swept the area, but he didn't see anything out of the ordinary.

With this killer, I wouldn't.

The ambulance's siren blared, and Cooper found himself hurrying toward that sound.

HE HADN'T BEEN able to resist. The woman had been right there. All alone.

She was the one who kept digging into his life.

So he'd thought it would only be fair that he started to play with *her* life.

The fact that she was connected to Cooper Marshall was just bonus. The connection made things even more interesting.

I can use her.

But not yet. She didn't matter enough. Not yet.

He whistled as he walked down the street. Plenty of tourists were still out. Even this late, the streets were full of people.

It was easy to blend with those people. To walk right past the overworked cops.

Cooper had climbed into the ambulance. He was playing hero. That wasn't a role well suited to the man.

He and Cooper were a lot alike. That was why Mercer had Cooper hunting him.

Darkness clung to them both. They were loners. Killers.

In the end, though, only one of them would survive this game.

It wouldn't be Cooper.

Pity. He'd once called the man friend.

Now, he just thought of Cooper Marshall as a target.

Chapter Three

Gabrielle took a deep breath. She squared her shoulders, smoothed her skirt. Then she lifted her hand and knocked soundly on Cooper's door.

She had a proposition for him, one that she very much hoped he'd accept. She wanted—

The door swung open. Only Cooper wasn't the person standing on the other side of that door.

A very pretty woman with glass-sharp cheekbones and shoulder-length black hair stared back at Gabrielle.

A date. He's on a date. The kiss—the one she ridiculously thought about far too much—had been fake. As good-looking as Cooper was, *of course,* the guy had a pretty girlfriend.

"Can I help you with something?" The woman asked. Her voice was smooth. Friendly. Her smile was a little uncertain.

"I was looking for Cooper."

"He's in the shower—"

The floor could truly open up and swallow her. She'd been indulging in some serious fantasy time with Cooper, and he'd been...busy...with this lady.

"—but you're welcome to come in and wait for him, if you'd like." The woman backed up, pulling the door open a few more inches. "You're his neighbor, right? The reporter?"

She didn't want to cross that threshold. She didn't want to, but Gabrielle still needed Cooper's help. "Yes. I am." She offered her hand. "Gabrielle Harper."

The woman's shake was firm and warm. "I'm Rachel."

You weren't supposed to dislike people you didn't know. She'd just met pretty Rachel. Rachel seemed friendly. Rachel also seemed to be eyeing her with a gaze that was a little too assessing.

Then Cooper appeared. He strode down the hallway, a pair of jeans hanging low on his hips. No shirt. His hair was wet. *Fresh from the shower.*

When he saw Gabrielle, he came to a very fast and hard stop.

"Company," Rachel murmured as she dropped Gabrielle's hand. A faint smile curled her lips. "I was just getting acquainted with your nice neighbor."

Cooper's blue gaze narrowed. Then he started walking again, a determined stride that carried him right to Gabrielle. "How's your head?" His hands lifted, as if he'd touch her head. "I'm sorry I left you at the hospital—I'm not family, so the doctors wouldn't let me stay with you."

She caught his hands, flushed. "I'm fine. My dad always did say that I had a hard head."

He didn't smile. "You were unconscious in that alley. When I first saw you, I was afraid that you were dead."

She was still holding his hands in front of his girlfriend. This scene was so awkward. She stepped back. "I didn't mean to interrupt when you had company. I can come back later." She sidled toward the door. "It was, uh, nice to meet you, Rachel." *Total lie.*

Cooper gave a rough bark of laughter. "Rachel isn't

company. She's—" But then he broke off, frowning. "Wait, who do you think she is?"

That was a weird question, but Gabrielle blurted, "Girl-friend?"

Rachel was the one to laugh then. "He should be so lucky." She bent and scooped up a designer bag. "We're just friends. No worries on that score." She winked at Gabrielle. "Maybe that makes it nicer to meet me?"

It did.

Rachel inclined her head toward Cooper. "And maybe you can meet up with me and Dylan later? I know he'd love to get an update on you."

Cooper gave a quick nod. "Will do."

It had to be her imagination, but Gabrielle could have sworn the enthusiasm in his voice was faked.

Rachel slipped away a few moments later, and Cooper locked the door behind her.

Gabrielle's hands twisted in front of her. It had been almost two days since she'd last seen him. She'd thought about him plenty during that time.

Especially when the flowers arrived at the hospital—lilacs, her favorite. There hadn't been a card, just the flowers.

"You sure that you're okay?" He took her elbow and guided her to the couch.

She'd be better—less distracted—if he put on a shirt, but Gabrielle nodded. "I needed to thank you, both for finding me in that alley and for the flowers. I, um, lilacs are my favorite." She wore a lilac-scented body lotion, because she loved the smell so much.

His blond brows lifted. "How do you know they were from me?"

She blinked. Embarrassment burned through her. Since

she wasn't dating anyone, she'd just assumed they were from him. "I—"

He laughed. "You sure are pretty when you blush. And, yes, they were from me." His fingers brushed back a lock of her hair. "I'm glad you liked them."

She had those lilacs upstairs, sitting in a vase on her kitchen table. Every time she looked at them, she smiled.

But you're here on business. Don't get distracted. Gabrielle cleared her throat. "I need to ask you a few questions."

His hand lowered. She was hyperconscious of the strength of his body next to hers. "Sure. Give me just a minute, okay?" He rose and disappeared down the hallway.

She didn't move. She wanted to move. She wanted to pry and search—

Hold that curiosity back.

She stayed locked to the couch. He returned quickly, pulling a black T-shirt over his head. The man certainly seemed to enjoy wearing black.

"I was about to make some dinner. Want something?"

Gabrielle shook her head.

A half smile lifted his lips. "Come on, I make a mean spaghetti. It's a recipe I stole from Rachel. Her family's Italian, and *no one* does spaghetti better."

Her stomach growled.

"I'll take that as a yes," he murmured.

Then he headed into the kitchen. She heard pots and pans clanking. Gabrielle rose and followed after him. "I didn't come here so that you would fix me dinner."

He already had the water set to boil. Tomatoes were spread out on the counter.

"That's right," he said easily. "You came here to ask me questions. So ask."

While he cooked? She'd expected something a little more...businesslike.

"Ask." He sliced the tomatoes. Fast and with almost fanatical skill. She'd never seen anyone be so good with a knife.

"I...um..." She exhaled slowly. *Stop being frazzled with him.* "Did you see anyone else in that alley with me?"

He stopped slicing. He glanced at her, held her gaze. "It was dark. I could only see you."

That didn't mean that no one else had been there. "Did you hear anything?" Gabrielle asked carefully.

He dropped the pasta then came toward her while the sauce simmered. "No, I didn't hear anything." He propped against the counter and studied her. "Why?"

"Because I don't remember falling."

"After a head injury like yours, I know it's common to forget—"

"What I do remember," she said, speaking quickly and cutting through his words, "is a man's voice."

"What?"

"I told Lane—Detective Carmichael, but he said the alley was searched thoroughly, both before and after my 'accident,' and there was no sign of anyone else there. Anyone else other than you, anyway."

Lane wasn't exactly a fan of Cooper's. In fact, he seemed pretty suspicious of Cooper. But then, Lane was suspicious of most folks. That was his nature.

"If you're trying to ask me if I slipped into the alley and slammed your head against a wall..." She saw Cooper's knuckles whiten as he clenched the edge of the countertop. "The answer is *no*, I didn't do that."

Gabrielle quickly shook her head. "That wasn't the question I was asking. I know you didn't do it. You're the guy who keeps rushing in to save me, not hurt me."

He blinked. A furrow appeared between his brows. "That's a whole lot of trust to give someone. You don't know me that well."

"I know you well enough to realize you aren't a killer."

He gazed steadily back at her. "Do you?"

What kind of response was that? It almost sounded as if he were trying to scare her. "Look, it wasn't your voice."

Cooper held up a hand. "You've lost me."

"I remember hearing a man's voice. It wasn't your voice."

Now there was doubt in his blue eyes. Lane had looked at her with the same doubt when she'd tried to explain this situation to him.

His hand fell back to his side. "There was a lot going on that night. It would be easy to get confused. Especially with that bump on your head."

"A minor concussion." She waved it away.

He stepped from the counter and caught her hand. "You don't shrug away an injury like that. Head injuries can be dangerous."

When he touched her, her heart beat faster. An electric current seemed to run through her body. *Just from a touch.* "That's why I stayed in the hospital. To make sure everything was okay." And because her boss at the paper had insisted on it. Hugh had told her she either stayed or she looked for a new job.

He didn't take kindly to his reporters being hurt.

She didn't take kindly to *being* hurt. "I know what I heard."

His gaze turned guarded. "Then tell me."

"A man grabbed me in that alley. He told me that I was

in the wrong place." The memory of that rasping voice rolled through her mind. "And then he said...*not yet.*"

A muscle flexed in his jaw. "You don't remember his face?"

"I remember the feel of his hands grabbing me. I remember the rasp of his voice, but his face?" *If only.* "No, I don't remember that. I'm not even sure if I saw him. I was hoping that maybe you'd seen something."

"You were the only thing I saw."

He turned away from her. Cooper spent a few moments in silence as he finished preparing their meal.

"It could've been a mugger," she said to his back, as he reached for some plates. "I didn't have a purse with me, so maybe that's why he ran after I passed out."

"It could have been." He shut the cabinets with a rough motion of his hands.

"It could also have been the killer." That was her fear. Her suspicion. "I think he escaped the apartment by climbing down the fire escape. He fled through that alley. Maybe he dropped something. Maybe he had to go back for it." She followed him to the table. "Or maybe he was just one of those guys who enjoys going back to the scene of the crime. Someone who likes to watch the cops spin their wheels and come up with nothing."

He pulled out a chair for her. "Is that what the cops have?"

She eased into the seat. "Lane says there aren't any suspects. No prints, DNA or any other evidence was left at the scenes."

He sat across from her. He picked up his fork.

"I went back to all the crime scenes—" Gabrielle began.

The fork clattered against his plate.

"I didn't break in," she rushed to clarify, realizing how

he must have interpreted her words. "I looked behind the buildings. Kylie Archer's place had a fire escape, too. The killer could easily have escaped on it."

"Lockwood didn't have a fire escape."

"No, he didn't." The spaghetti smelled fabulous. "But then again, maybe that's the reason why Lockwood's front door was smashed in. The attacker didn't have any other way to get inside, so he had to use force there."

Cooper ate in silence.

She took a bite of the spaghetti. He hadn't been lying. It was fantastic. "I'll have to make you one of my cherry pies," she said, sending him a nervous smile. "You did dinner, so I can do dessert."

His head tilted. His eyes heated, the blue getting even brighter. "Sounds like a date."

"I—" She nearly choked on the spaghetti. "I have a proposition for you."

That half smile flashed again. Did he have a dimple in his cheek? It looked like he did.

Sexy.

"I'd love to hear the proposition."

He made it sound…hot. It wasn't. She put her fork down. "I want us to work together." She tried not to let the words come out as desperate.

He kept eating.

"I think we could make a good team. We could keep investigating the cases and find the killer—"

"I'm not in the market for a partner."

Okay. He was going to make her lay everything out for him. She'd have to show that desperation, after all. "But I am in the market for some protection." Because she was afraid, and Gabrielle didn't want to let the fear stop her from doing her job. "I think someone has been watching me. I think *he* has been watching me."

"TELL ME AGAIN…" Dylan Foxx began as he narrowed his eyes on Rachel Mancini. "Why is Cooper having a cozy dinner with the reporter? He's supposed to be keeping her out of this mess and not—"

"—seducing her?" Rachel finished. She'd seen the way Cooper looked at the other woman. She knew exactly what was on his mind.

Dylan shut the door of his office. They were in the EOD headquarters, a place most civilians would never visit. Actually, most civilians would never even know of its existence.

The EOD was a hybrid organization, one composed of former members of various military branches. The EOD had been founded and was still led by Bruce Mercer. The EOD was far off the books, and the agents took jobs that no one else could handle.

Jobs that often ended in violence. Death.

The EOD agents were the ones who went out after the hostages that *couldn't* be rescued. They were the ones who eliminated the most dangerous threats in the world.

Right now, unfortunately, one of those threats came from within.

A rogue agent.

Suspicion was rampant in the EOD. Trust, the cornerstone of the agency's success, was being shattered. If you couldn't trust the agent who had your back in the field, how were you supposed to complete the mission?

Rachel sank into the chair near Dylan's desk. She trusted him 100 percent. But she wasn't ready to extend that trust to all of the agents at the EOD.

They all knew how to kill, lie and keep secrets.

Someone was using those deadly skills.

"I could see them through the window," Rachel murmured. Not that she enjoyed the Peeping-Tom bit. "They went into the kitchen and the guy cooked."

"Cooper?" Dylan's dark brows shot up.

She nodded. "Maybe he's just trying to get under her guard. The lady has proven to be pretty resourceful."

"The lady's dangerous." He threw himself into the chair near her. Leather groaned. "I ran down her bio. She's got a trail of awards behind her and a reputation for being a real bulldog when it comes to her stories. She's latched on to our killer, and I don't see her just backing away now."

Not even after a trip to the hospital.

"The more time she spends with Cooper, the more likely she is to discover that his cover is a lie." Dylan ran a hand through his black hair. "The last thing we need is her trying to air a story on the EOD."

"We aren't on her radar." Rachel had done her own research on Gabrielle Harper. "She works to help victims. She's not even thinking about us."

"Not yet, she isn't. But if she's used to uncovering secrets, how long do you think it will be before she senses Cooper is hiding something from her?"

"Well that depends," Rachel said as her gaze held his, "on just how good Cooper is at lying. It's been my experience that some men are extremely talented when it comes to deceit."

There was a sharp rap at the door.

Dylan held her gaze for a moment longer. "You *know* you can trust me."

Yes, she did, as a partner, as a friend.

As a lover?

No, she couldn't risk that. She'd gone down the wrong path with a lover before. She still had the scars to prove it—scars that marked her on the inside and out.

She cleared her throat and called, "Come in!"

The door swung open. Aaron "Deuce" Porter stood on the other side of the threshold. His green gaze swept between them. "Didn't mean to interrupt anything." His voice was low.

"You're not," Rachel said flatly.

Deuce's lips twisted a bit. Deuce had been with the EOD for years—long before Rachel had come aboard. She'd worked several missions with him and learned quickly why the brown-haired agent had earned the moniker of Deuce.

The man could blend like no other. Undercover missions were his specialty. He often joked that he hadn't been born with just one face—but two.

Deuce. He could be two people in an instant, and had been, on missions in Rio, South Africa and the Middle East. He could drop an accent, change his walk, even change all of his mannerisms in an instant.

Two men—in one lethal body.

"Mercer briefed me on the case," he said as he came inside. He closed the door behind him. "I'm supposed to provide backup for your team." His smile faded. "Seems a reporter is getting a little too close on this one."

"Yes…" Dylan sighed out his answer. "But Cooper is working on her."

Now Deuce did laugh. "Well, Cooper has always had a way with the ladies."

Rachel's eyes narrowed.

"Love 'em and leave 'em," Deuce said. "If anyone can get the reporter under control, I'm sure it will be him."

Rachel's hands clenched into fists. "I think you're underestimating this woman. A little seduction isn't going to put her off track."

"Well, if that doesn't work—" Deuce's shoulders straightened "—option number two is a whole lot less pleasant for her. According to Mercer, the woman isn't to interfere in EOD business. Stopping her is a priority, even if we have to use containment."

Containment? On a civilian?

Mercer must really be worried. They hadn't crossed that line, not since—

Rachel cut off the thought. She didn't want to go into the darkness of her past. Not then.

But Dylan was staring straight at her, and she knew that she'd given herself away.

Sometimes she worried that Dylan was coming to know her too well.

And that scared her to death.

"SOMEONE'S BEEN WATCHING YOU?" Cooper repeated carefully. He made sure his expression reflected surprise. "Are you sure about that?"

"Yes, I am," she told him. "You think I don't know when I'm being tailed? I could feel someone following me for the past day, shadowing me. But every time I turned around…" Her breath blew out. "No one was there."

He made himself say, "Maybe because no one *was* there."

She shot to her feet. "Look, I'm trying to hire you, okay? You don't have to believe me in order to take the case."

"I thought you wanted us to be partners—"

Her dark eyes flashed at him. "I'm going to *pay* my partner for protection."

She was really afraid. He rose to his feet, slowly uncurling his body until he towered over her. "Are you sure nothing else has happened?"

Her lips pressed together then she said, "I think he was in my apartment."

Hell.

"My computer... At first I thought it was just some kind of glitch, but I had a tech I know take a look at it. He said my files were deliberately corrupted."

"Maybe you got a virus—"

"I've got top-of-the-line virus protection software. Whatever was done to my system, it was done by a professional."

Sydney definitely counted as a professional.

"All of the data that I'd had on that computer, all of the files on Archer and Lockwood—they were destroyed." She lifted her chin and her gaze glinted. "It's a good thing I had backups, because if I hadn't, I'd be in serious trouble with my boss."

His fingers locked around her shoulders. "You have backup files?"

For a second, she almost looked insulted. No, she *did* look insulted. "I'm not an amateur. This is what I do. I work these cases. I help *solve* the crimes that cops have to let go cold."

Why?

"Someone was in my place," she said again, dogged. "I know he was there."

"*How?* Did your alarm go off—"

"No, but my computer...it was moved. Just a few inches, but I could tell."

It figured she'd be that observant.

Gabrielle pulled away from him. "Look, if you won't help me, fine. I'll find someone else who will." Then she marched toward the door.

He stared up at the ceiling. This was so tangled. This was so—

The door opened.

In a flash, he rushed across the room and slammed the door shut. "I'll be your guard."

"Partner."

He turned her in his arms. "If that's the way you want to play it."

Gabrielle nodded. His body was flush against hers. Those kissable lips of hers were just inches away.

Focus.

The problem was that he *was* focusing, way too much on her.

"What will I owe you?"

His back teeth clenched. "My standard rate is five hundred a day." He totally pulled that number right out of the air.

Her eyes widened.

Too high.

"But I'll work out a deal with you," he rushed to say, because maybe this could work. If he stayed close to her—and he was planning to stay as close as he could possibly get—then he wouldn't have to worry about sneaking into her place again and destroying any more files. He'd be able to retrieve every bit of intel at the same time she did.

Even better, he'd be able to control the intel that she received.

"Deal?" Gabrielle whispered and she licked her lips.

His whole body stiffened. "Yeah, maybe I'll get my name mentioned in the byline of your story." Right. That would be the *last* thing he wanted.

He put his hands on either side of her head, flattening his palms against the door. He wanted her mouth beneath his. That one kiss hadn't been nearly enough to satisfy him.

It had just made him hungry for more.

"Of course, there is one other thing you can give me,"

Cooper said, aware that his voice had roughened even more than normal.

Her breath rushed out. Her hands rose to his chest even as bright flags of color stained her cheeks. "I am not—" she began angrily.

"Pie," he cut in. "I do believe there was a promise of cherry pie on the table." And if her cherry pie was half as good as her chocolate chip cookies had been, then he'd sure be one very lucky man.

She stopped pushing him. Her hands rested over his chest and seemed to burn right through the fabric of his T-shirt. "Oh. Right. Of course."

He smiled at her. She was so cute.

But dangerous.

Kiss her.

Instead, he dropped his hands and stepped away from her. "When does this partnership start?"

She glanced over his shoulder at the clock on the wall. "I'm really glad you agreed to my deal." Her head tilted. "Just how good are you at blending into the shadows?"

His lips twitched. "I get by." If she only knew.

"Good," Gabrielle said decisively, "because I've got a lead for us to follow and our partnership starts right now."

His OLD FRIEND let him right inside the apartment. But then, he'd expected an easy entrance.

He'd also expected to see the haggard lines of grief on Van McAdams's face.

"Did you hear?" Van asked as he turned away. The guy left the door wide-open.

Van had better training than that. Much, much better.

"I saw the story on the news." His gloved fingers closed over the doorknob, and he pulled the door shut.

He turned the lock quickly. There could be no time for any disturbances.

Van's shoulders were slumped as he headed toward the den. "What am I supposed to do now? Without Melanie, I don't have *anything*."

He pulled out his weapon. Slipped silently right up behind the man who mistakenly thought they were friends. "I guess you can join her. You can die."

Before Van could even turn to face him, it was too late. He'd attacked.

Van's body hit the floor seconds later.

The killer smiled. So easy. So incredibly—

Voices rose in the hallway. And one of those voices was familiar.

Cooper Marshall.

He stared down at the bloody knife in his hand and considered his options.

Chapter Four

"You're not coming in with me," Gabrielle said as she glanced over her shoulder. She kept her voice firm, authoritative. In this partnership, she was the one doing the paying, so it seemed fair that she got to be the one giving orders. Right? "You're to stay out here." She gestured toward him, then toward the small hallway. "Lurk. Make sure that no one else comes up here and tries to get in this apartment."

Because she was following a red-hot lead—one that she wasn't about to lose.

Kylie Archer had been murdered, and her boyfriend had also been killed in the same manner.

Now that Melanie Farrell was dead, would her boyfriend also follow suit? If the killer acted on the same time line, he could wait months to kill Melanie's lover.

That means I have time to talk to him, to warn him.

To save him?

Cooper didn't follow her lurk order. He stepped closer to her. "You need to tell me why we're here."

"I *did*." On the motorcycle ride over, she'd yelled to him—*twice*—that she was following up on a lead. Her hand lifted and rapped against the apartment's door. She'd called and said she was coming by. The guy had been home an hour ago.

"A boyfriend," he said.

Still not lurking.

"I talked to Melanie's friend at work. Melanie's family didn't know about the guy, but if you're in deep with someone, the best friend *always* knows." It was a woman's rule. "Melanie called once and had Trish pick her up from this place. I did a little dot connecting, and I found the single guy in the apartment building who fit his description." A guy who was still not answering the door. "And voilà, I got him!"

"You got him," Cooper repeated, voice roughening.

She nodded but froze when she heard the distinct sound of glass shattering. That sound had come from *inside* the apartment.

Her fingers curled around the doorknob and she jerked, hard. "Mr. McAdams!"

Cooper stiffened.

"Van McAdams!" Gabrielle yelled. "It's Gabrielle Harper. We spoke earlier! Please, open up."

Cooper grabbed her shoulders and pushed her away from the door. In the next instant, he had a gun in his hands.

He'd just yanked that thing right out of his ankle holster, and he had it aimed at the door.

"What are you doing?" Gabrielle whispered, horrified. Her gaze flew down the hallway. "You can't just pull out a gun!"

"Two dead bodies, that's what I've found since I've been hanging out with you. I'm not in the mood for body number three." He squared his shoulders and called out, "Van, open the damn door, or I will bust my way inside."

The door didn't open.

Gabrielle started counting in her head. *One, two, thr—*

Cooper kicked the door open and rushed inside. He'd only taken about five steps when he froze—then dropped to the floor.

Because there was a man on the floor, a man sprawled in a pool of blood.

"Call an ambulance!" Cooper barked. He grabbed for the man, rolled him over.

Gabrielle flinched when she saw the man's neck. Fumbling, she yanked out her phone and managed to dial 911.

"Don't do this," Cooper growled. *"Don't."* Blood poured through his fingers as he tried to staunch the wound on the man's neck.

The man—Van McAdams?—his eyelids twitched.

He's still alive.

"What is the nature of your emergency?" the cool voice on the other end of the line asked Gabrielle.

"A man's been attacked! He's dying, please, get help here, now!" She threw out the address even as she tried to get closer to Cooper. His head had bent. His ear was right above the wounded man's mouth.

Surely McAdams couldn't talk with that kind of wound.

"We have an ambulance en route, ma'am," the operator told her.

"Get more than an ambulance!" She fired back. "Call Detective Lane Carmichael! He needs to get here, too."

"Gabrielle!" Cooper snapped out her name.

She blinked.

"I need you to put pressure on the wound." A muscle jerked in his jaw. "I have to search the apartment. The SOB who did this…he could still be here."

The breaking glass… Her gaze flew to the floor. There was no glass around McAdams. Someone else had made that sound.

"Gabrielle!" he snapped again.

She jumped to his side.

He positioned her hands. "Keep the pressure on him. Van, you look at her, okay? You stay with her."

Van wasn't looking at her. He wasn't looking at anyone.

Cooper surged to his feet. He had his gun with him as he ran down the hallway.

"It's okay," Gabrielle lied to the man who didn't even seem to be breathing. "Help's coming. You're going to make it. Just keep fighting. Stay with me."

Blood. So much blood.

It reminded her of another night.

No, don't go there. All of the scenes had reminded her—too much—of her past.

But…this scene… Her eyes were on the blood. Her breath froze in her lungs. Had Van…written something in the blood? It looked as if he had. An *E*. An *O*.

She squinted as she tried to make out the last letter. *D?*

What in the world was an EOD?

"Van, please, stay with me," she whispered to him as her hands pressed against his wound.

She leaned toward him, and felt something press into her knee. Her gaze darted from Van's pale face to the pool of blood.

Metal was there. Glinting. Rectangular in shape.

A dog tag?

A military dog tag. Its chain was broken.

When the killer cut his neck, he cut Van's dog tag right off him.

"Stay with me," she said again, but this time, she was begging because this man—he was the key. He could tell her the identity of the killer. He could solve all the crimes.

If he just lived.

THE BEDROOM WINDOW had been smashed. The shattered glass had fallen—a bit inside the room, but most had flown outside.

Cooper tried to lift the window.

Stuck.

So the killer had just improvised. When he heard Gabrielle at the door, he'd busted his way to freedom.

Cooper shoved his head outside and glanced below. There was no sign of the killer. He'd gotten away.

Again.

Van McAdams. They'd worked a case together over in Paris. Van was a good guy, quick to smile, slow to anger. Always cool under fire.

And now he's dying.

"Cooper!" Gabrielle yelled.

He knew what that yell meant. Cooper raced down the hallway as fast as he could, but he was too late. He'd been too late from the beginning. By the time that the glass shattered, the killer had done his work.

Gabrielle looked up at him, tears glinting in her beautiful eyes. She was crying for a man she'd never met before that night.

His guts were tearing open because he *knew* Van. They'd laughed together, talked about their lives, women.

Van had been hoping to…

Marry. He'd had a girl that he'd been seeing for years.

Cooper put his hands on Van. He worked frantically to try and bring the guy back.

My girl…she hated all the traveling that I did, the secrecy. But things are going to change. I'm gettin' out of the EOD. I'm going to have a life. With her. Van's Mississippi drawl had rolled through the words and so had his determination to have his happiness.

But he hadn't gotten his life and that happily-ever-after dream.

"She was his girlfriend, wasn't she?" Cooper asked, his voice flat. He hadn't been able to find a link between Melanie Farrell and the EOD, because there wasn't a link. Not anymore.

Van had left the organization for her. So no one at the EOD had known about her.

His gaze fell on the message that had been written in blood. Every muscle in his body stiffened.

No, someone at the EOD knew. Someone damn well knew.

His boot slid out, smearing the blood and hiding the final message that Van had left behind.

Footsteps thundered outside of the apartment.

Help had finally arrived.

Too late.

"You don't look like a killer."

Gabrielle's head whipped up at Detective Lane Carmichael's low voice. She was at the police station, in the *interrogation* room of all places.

She'd been the one to call Lane, but when he'd swung in with his cavalry, she'd found herself in police custody.

"You *know* I'm not a killer, Lane."

His lips compressed. "Maybe I don't know nearly as much about you as I thought, and I certainly don't know anything about the new guy you've got with you."

Lane had separated her from Cooper as soon as they arrived at the station. "Where is he?" Gabrielle demanded instead of responding to Lane's jibe.

Lane pulled up a chair and stared back at her. "Van McAdams is in the morgue, but you knew that, right? He was dead when you called for help."

Bile rose in her throat. "He wasn't dead then. He was trying to talk." An impossible task, considering what had been done to him.

"Giving you a last-minute message, was he?" Lane asked.

She thought of the letters that she'd seen in the blood. Her eyes squeezed closed. "Look, I know you saw what he wrote. Despite this crazy act right now, you're a decent cop." Actually, a good cop. Maybe he was jealous. She didn't really know what his deal was. But there'd been a definite edge in his voice when he referred to the "new guy." "You're a—"

He grabbed her arm. "What are you talking about? What did McAdams write?"

Her eyes flew open. "I-in the blood. He tried to write a message. If you didn't see it, if one of the techs didn't, your guys are just getting sloppy."

He glared at her. "There was no message in the blood."

"Yes," she said, voice adamant, "there was." There had been no missing it.

"Then tell me...what did it say?"

Gabrielle licked her too dry lips. "There were three letters. I think...I think it was an *E*, an *O* and a *D*."

His brows shot up. "What is that supposed to mean?"

She didn't know, but Gabrielle intended to find out. "They could be the killer's initials or perhaps even the first three letters in his name." *Maybe you need to do your job and figure it out.*

But he just shook his head grimly. "You report the stories, Gabrielle. You aren't supposed to get in the middle of them. I told you this before. What you're doing is too dangerous."

Yes, he had told her that before: same song and dance, different day. The fact that he kept trying to control what she did…no, the fact that he kept trying to change her and make her into someone else—a girl who played things safely—*that* had been why their short-lived relationship had crashed and burned.

Lane exhaled slowly. "If you aren't careful, you could find yourself caught in the sights of a killer."

Then he shoved away from the table, stalked to the door, and he left her there.

Just…left her.

But the image of Van McAdams stayed with her, tightening her stomach and seeming to squeeze her heart. *I'm so sorry. I wish that I'd arrived sooner.*

Because seeing him like that, actually still alive—it was just like the night she'd found her father.

He'd been alive, too, when she first burst into her home. He'd been hurt so badly. She'd wanted to save him.

She'd only been able to watch him die.

A tear slid down her cheek as her shoulders hunched.

THE INTERROGATION WAS a joke. Like *this* was supposed to intimidate him? Being shut in a twelve-by-nine-foot room with a cup of water and air blowing on him, all nice and cool and comfortable?

This was like a vacation for him.

The door opened. The detective stalked inside. Lane Carmichael.

Carmichael's face was tight and angry, his eyes snapping. Ah, bad cop at his finest.

If Cooper hadn't been mourning McAdams, he could have appreciated the detective's performance. As it was, he felt annoyed. And he was ready to leave.

I need to meet up with my team.

"What was in the blood?" Detective Carmichael fired at him.

Cooper shook his head.

"Gabrielle said the victim wrote a final message in his own blood." Carmichael slapped his hands on the table and leaned toward Cooper. "What was the message?"

"I didn't see a message." He had a job to do. He'd sworn to protect the EOD. *I'm sorry, Gabrielle.*

"So Gabrielle is imagining things?" Carmichael asked. "Is that what you're saying?"

"I'm saying I didn't see anything." He'd hoped that she hadn't seen those letters. But maybe she hadn't been able to make them out clearly, and even if she had, Gabrielle wouldn't understand the message that McAdams had left behind.

"I don't trust you," Carmichael growled out the words. Red stained his cheeks. "I've been looking into your background, and you know what—"

The door flew open behind the detective. It banged against the wall with a thud. "Orders just came down," a sharp voice barked. "Marshall is free to go."

Carmichael's mouth dropped open in shock. Then he whirled and sputtered, "But, Captain, I was just—"

"Orders came down," the captain said, her voice brooking no argument. "He's free to go."

Cooper pushed back his chair. The captain glanced over his way, and her gray eyes narrowed. "You must know plenty of secrets about this city, Mr. Marshall," she murmured, "seeing as how the DA personally called me and said that you needed to be released."

Because his boss had no doubt made a fast call to the DA. Cooper inclined his head toward the captain. "When I leave, I'll be taking Ms. Harper with me."

But Carmichael was already shaking his head. "I've got more questions for Gabrielle."

"Then you can ask them tomorrow," Cooper responded,

his own voice roughening. He could remember the glimmer of tears in Gabrielle's eyes. She'd been hurting and—*she needs me.* "She's been through hell, and I'm taking her home." He wasn't looking for permission from the cops. He was telling them what would happen.

If they wanted to discover just how much pull he had in D.C., then they'd try to stop him from taking Gabrielle out of that station.

After a brief hesitation, the captain inclined her head. The lights glinted off the dark red color. "Of course, Ms. Harper is free to go. Detective Carmichael will follow up with her tomorrow."

The detective's eyes were angry slits.

"Thank you," Cooper said as he marched through the open doorway. Then he turned to the left. He'd seen the other interrogation room when he'd been so…firmly… escorted into the station.

He shoved open that door.

Gabrielle was wiping at her cheeks. *Wiping away tears.* His chest ached. "It's time to go."

She glanced up at him.

When she cried, her face should have gone all splotchy. She shouldn't have looked even more beautiful with her gleaming eyes and trembling lips.

But she did.

He opened his hand to her.

Gabrielle pushed back her chair and nearly ran to him. "I didn't want him to die! I didn't—"

"It's okay," he said, trying to soothe her.

The soothing didn't work. Gabrielle shook her head. "I told McAdams that he could be in danger. I warned him that the killer could be targeting him next." Her gaze searched his. "Why didn't he listen?"

Because he trusted the wrong person.

That was what the man's final message had been about. He'd opened the door to another EOD agent. Someone he'd thought he could safely admit to his apartment as a colleague or a friend.

But when McAdams had turned his back, that friend had attacked him.

Cooper wrapped his arm around Gabrielle and turned for the door.

He wasn't particularly surprised to see Carmichael blocking the exit. As usual, the detective was glaring.

"Gabrielle told me that you both heard the sound of glass shattering…" Carmichael began.

Cooper nodded. He could confirm that part.

"You kicked in the door," Carmichael continued, pointing at Cooper, "and when you searched the place, you realized that the perp had broken the window and escaped?"

"Yes," Cooper snapped.

"Tell me how the hell he did that," Carmichael demanded. "He was four floors up. There was no fire escape. Am I supposed to believe the guy flew out of there?"

Cooper's hold tightened on Gabrielle. "The bricks were rough on that side of the building. Just as they were thrusting out a little too much at Lockwood's place. For a man with the right skills, getting out would almost be too easy. Scaling down would be just like rock climbing."

The detective stepped aside.

"Let's go," Cooper said into Gabrielle's ear. She was too pale.

They'd taken two steps past the detective when Carmichael mused, "The right skills… Tell me, Marshall, do you happen to possess those skills?"

Yes. "I'm not your killer, and you know it. Gabrielle's my alibi—"

"And you're hers, yes, I *know* that. But I wasn't asking

if you killed the man. I was asking if you *could* have gotten out of that apartment the same way that the killer did."

Gabrielle had stopped walking. She stared up at Cooper, waiting.

There was no point in lying. "Yes, I could have. I would have been down that wall and away from the scene in less than a minute. *Just like the perp was.*"

Then, before the cop could ask him any other questions, Cooper took Gabrielle toward the front of the station.

His motorcycle wasn't around—one of his teammates would take care of it for him—so he directed Gabrielle into the first cab that he saw.

They raced away from the station.

He glanced back and wasn't surprised to see a dark SUV slip behind the cab. He knew that his boss had been the one pulling the strings to get him out of the station, and Mercer would want an accounting of the night's activities right away.

But Mercer would have to wait.

Because there was someone else who needed him first.

His arms tightened around Gabrielle.

So much blood.

Before she'd been escorted to the interrogation room at the station, she'd washed and washed her hands, but Gabrielle swore that she could still feel the blood on her skin.

She'd watched Van McAdams die, and she hadn't been able to do *anything* to help him.

Just like before.

"It's not your fault."

They were in front of the brownstone. The cab's wheels rolled away, leaving them alone out there. The night was hot, stifling, and Gabrielle thought she could still smell the overwhelming scent of blood.

He opened the door and led her inside.

When he paused, she didn't stop. Gabrielle headed straight for the stairs.

But Cooper caught her hand, stilling her on the second step. "You think I don't know what you're doing?"

Right then, she was trying to run. "Can't be in fighting form all the time," she murmured. "Sometimes…sometimes we all need to crash." That was exactly what she wanted to do. She wanted to get inside her apartment where she could fall apart and no one would see her break.

He put his foot on the bottom stair. "Whatever you need, I can give you."

She shook her head.

Cooper turned her back to face him. His hand lifted, and his fingers curled around her chin as he stared into her eyes. "I can keep you safe. You can crash, you can fall, and I'll be there to pick you right back up."

Her lips trembled. She caught her lower lip between her teeth because she didn't want him seeing that weakness.

Just hold it together a little longer.

But McAdams—those last, terrible moments—had stirred up memories of her own past that she just couldn't shut out any longer.

There was a reason she took the cold cases. A reason she tried so hard to find justice for the ones who had been forgotten.

"Fall into me," he told her again. "I'm here."

When had anyone else ever said something like that to her? She'd stood on her own for so long, Gabrielle couldn't remember what it was like to have someone else there when the storm hit.

She found herself nodding. "Come…upstairs with me?" So she wouldn't be alone when the crash hit.

Then Gabrielle turned. She headed slowly up that staircase, and Cooper was right behind her. She could feel the reassuring heat and strength of his body following hers.

She opened the door to her apartment, flipped on the lights, reached for the alarm—

And realized that her place had been trashed.

Couch cushions were cut. Furniture overturned. Her files were scattered across the floor.

"Get back!" Cooper's low snarl. He didn't wait for her to comply. He grabbed her shoulders and pushed her back behind him.

He had his gun in his hand again. She didn't even remember him getting that weapon back from the cops at the precinct. While he pushed her back, Cooper stepped inside her place.

No. She grabbed his arm. "He could still be here." Wasn't that what they'd feared at McAdams's place? That the killer was there?

"I hope he is," Cooper whispered back.

Then he advanced.

Fear twisted within her, but she wasn't about to stay in that hallway by herself. Maybe *that* was the killer's plan. Divide and conquer. So when Cooper stalked forward, she leapt right after him.

Her hands fisted around her keys—and the mace attached to that keychain. Having her own weapon made her feel a little bit better.

Until they got to her bedroom.

And she saw the clothing that had been slashed. The other room…it had almost looked as if someone was searching for something in her den. But this—this was just destruction.

Her pillows had been slit open. Feathers covered the floor. Her sheets were cut, her mattresses sliced.

Her dresser mirror was smashed.

All of her drawers had been yanked out and tossed. Her breath heaved in at the sight.

Rage. She could feel it in the room.

Cooper's body stiffened, but he didn't speak. He kept searching her home—checking the closets, the bathroom.

No one was there.

The intruder was long gone.

Gabrielle found herself standing in the living room, gazing around with dazed eyes. *Everything* that she'd valued was gone.

Cooper was on his phone. Probably calling the police for her. *Again.*

She rubbed chilled arms. The cold wasn't just on the surface, though, it went bone deep.

Cooper shoved his phone back into his pocket. He'd already holstered his weapon.

You can fall into me. She wanted to fall right then, but Gabrielle was afraid that if she did, she'd never be able to get up again.

"I told you," she said and was surprised by how eerily calm her voice sounded. "Someone was watching me."

"You were right." His eyes blazed with a barely banked fury. She should be feeling a similar fury, but she wasn't. That coldness seemed to be cloaking all of her emotions.

"I called in a favor," he told her. She couldn't look away from his eyes. She didn't want to look anywhere else. *Everything is gone.* "I've got a team coming over here. If the SOB left any prints, any evidence, we'll find him."

That seemed...odd to her. "You didn't call Carmichael?"

"He'll be informed." His fingers curled around her arms. "Right now, I want you to come downstairs with me. You're going to be staying at my place tonight."

His place. Her eyes widened. "What if—what if he did this to your apartment, too?"

"I don't think—"

She pushed past him and ran down the stairs. Cooper was working with her now. What if the intruder had realized that? What if he'd destroyed Cooper's place, too?

Breath heaving, she staggered to a stop at Cooper's door. He was beside her. Always, moving so fast. He unlocked his door. Hit the lights.

Untouched.

The intruder had just gone after her. He'd just destroyed *her* home.

"I'm glad," she whispered as her shoulders slumped. "I didn't want him hurting you…because I pulled you into this mess."

He swore and tugged her closer to him.

"I know it's related, it has to be," she said. She wasn't going to ignore the facts, even though they terrified her. "It's him. The killer. He knows I was at McAdams's place. He could have been there, watching us from the outside when the police arrived." A crowd of people had gathered on the street.

He could have been right there.

Her heart pounded in a double-time rhythm. "He knows who I am, where I live. And getting hauled into the station by Carmichael tonight…" She swallowed. "That just might have saved my life."

Because maybe the perp's knife wouldn't have just been used on her furniture and clothes.

He could have used it on me.

Chapter Five

Cooper shut his apartment door. Gabrielle was inside, showering, and he had a few minutes to spare.

Rachel and Dylan Foxx were already waiting outside for him—along with a sweeper crew. He jerked his head, and the crew hurried upstairs. If the killer had left evidence behind, they'd find it.

"The local cops?" he asked. Because Carmichael would find out about tonight's events, sooner or later.

The EOD wanted that discovery to be *later*.

"Our team won't leave evidence behind. The detective will be called in once we're finished," Rachel said smoothly.

Because before the local authorities took over, they had to make sure nothing had been left to implicate the EOD.

His hands clenched into fists as his gaze met Dylan's stare. "He's targeting her."

"That doesn't fit." It was Rachel who replied. "He's going after EOD agents—"

"Their girlfriends," Cooper said flatly. "He kills the girlfriends, the lovers, first. Then he goes after the agents." It was the rogue's pattern. "He knows these men, knows them better than we do." *Because he was hiding behind the mask of a friend*. "And maybe he thinks that Gabrielle saw something, that she knows *something* about him, because that SOB destroyed her home."

He wouldn't even allow himself to think about what might have happened if Gabrielle had *been* home when the rogue attacked.

"Are you sure," Dylan asked, voice quiet and gaze steady, "that she doesn't know more? She was the one who found out about Van, right? Long before anyone in-house knew he was connected to Melanie Farrell."

"Someone in-house knew." He hadn't been given a chance to reveal this yet. "The last thing Van did was leave a message for me, in his own blood. *EOD*. That's what he wrote." McAdams had just been confirming what they already knew—

The killer terrorizing D.C. was one of their own.

"Did the cops see that message?" Dylan demanded as his face tensed.

"No, I took care of it." And that didn't sit well with him. He'd destroyed evidence. "But Gabrielle saw it."

Rachel and Dylan shared a long look.

"What?" Cooper snapped.

"She's a reporter," Rachel reminded him with a raised brow.

"I *know* what she is."

"She's not going to forget what she saw. That woman will dig and dig until she figures out what the EOD truly is."

Not possible.

"You have to stop her." Dylan's firm order. Dylan was the team leader on this case. The former SEAL had been working with the EOD much longer than Cooper had. "Throw her off the scent, give her another lead, but stop her from focusing on the EOD."

Easier said than done. "Right now, my goal is to keep

her safe." Even as he said the words, he realized they were true. It wasn't about finding out what Gabrielle knew any longer. Not about getting close to any intel that she might possess.

He wanted to make sure that she didn't get hurt. That the rogue didn't come within ten feet of her again.

And I want to make sure that if she ever does fall, I'm right there to catch her.

The thought rushed through him.

Changed him.

Then he heard the rustle of footsteps behind him. "She's coming," he whispered. Gabrielle would be looking for him, and she'd want to know what was happening upstairs.

The door opened behind him bare seconds later. He glanced over his shoulder.

Her long hair was wet. Slicked back, it accentuated her high cheekbones and her wide, dark eyes.

She'd put on one of his old T-shirts. It seemed to swallow her delicate shoulders, and she'd worked some kind of magic to get a very faded pair of his running shorts to fit her.

Her bare toes—adorned with bright red polish—curled against the hard wood floor. "I hope you don't mind," Gabrielle said softly, "but I didn't have anything else to wear."

Because the rogue had destroyed everything she had.

Bastard.

"I don't mind at all." The words came out too gruff. Too rough. He cleared his throat and tried again, saying, "I can go out and get some more clothes for you, if you tell me your size."

Actually, he already knew her size. It was in the nice, tidy dossier that the EOD had given him.

"Why don't you let me make a run?" Rachel interrupted.

Gabrielle's gaze slid to her.

"Most of the stores will be opening in a few hours," Rachel added. "I can get the clothes for you, no problem."

Gabrielle hesitated. Then she cocked her head as her gaze slid between Rachel and Dylan, and the top of the stairs. "I'm sorry…what are you all doing here? I thought the cops were coming to investigate."

"My name's Dylan Foxx, and I am the cops, sort of," Dylan said as he offered his hand to her.

Gabrielle took his hand. "Sort of?"

"I work for the government," Dylan explained. Cooper was surprised by that truth. But then Dylan continued, twisting fact and fiction as he explained, "I have a crew that specializes in crime scene investigation for Uncle Sam. They're upstairs now, and as soon as they're done, I'll be turning the results over to—" he glanced at Cooper as if for confirmation "—a Detective Carmichael?"

Cooper realized that Dylan was still holding Gabrielle's hand. What was up with that? He maneuvered her away from Dylan. Dylan had a tendency to be a little too slick with the ladies.

"Do you work for the government, too?" Gabrielle asked Rachel.

Rachel nodded. "I'm Dylan's associate."

Gabrielle fiddled with the bottom of Cooper's shirt. "By any chance, have either of you ever heard of the EOD?"

Cooper's heart slammed into his chest.

Rachel frowned. "The what?"

At the same moment, Dylan shook his head. "No, can't say that I have. Why? What is it?"

Gabrielle turned toward Cooper. "It was written in the blood at the crime scene. You saw it, didn't you?"

He *hated* to do it, but Cooper shook his head. "No, sweetheart, I didn't."

She blinked. "But…it was there. Carmichael said he didn't see it, but you had to—"

"I didn't," he made himself say again.

Her gaze fell. "I saw it," she said softly, determinedly. "*EOD*. Clear as day. That was McAdams's last message, and I'm going to figure out what it means."

No, you can't find out.

Her gaze touched his once more. "I'm going to call my editor at the *Inquisitor*. I want to publish an account of everything that happened. Somewhere out there, someone knows either who or what the EOD is."

That couldn't happen. There was no way that he could let her publish what she'd seen.

Dylan's gaze met Cooper's. He easily read the order in the other man's eyes.

Cooper inclined his head.

"When your team finishes," Cooper said, "give us a report."

"Of course," Dylan agreed. His attention shifted to Gabrielle. "I'm sorry we had to meet under these circumstances."

"So am I." Her lips twisted into a weak smile. "But if you and your team can help me to find the man who broke into my place, I'd sure appreciate it."

"We'll do everything we can," Dylan told her. He backed away.

Rachel lingered. There were shadows in her eyes as she studied Gabrielle. "It doesn't seem safe," Rachel suddenly blurted.

Dylan frowned at her.

"The story that you're following…all of the people that are winding up dead." Rachel exhaled on a shaky breath.

"Do you have family who live outside of D.C.? Friends? Maybe you should leave until the police catch this guy."

"His first victim was killed four months ago," Gabrielle said. "Four months. The police haven't caught him yet, and I'm not the type to run and hide and just *hope* that things change."

"Even if staying puts you in harm's way?" Rachel pressed.

Gabrielle's shoulder brushed against Cooper. "I've got my own bodyguard. I trust him to keep me safe."

Don't put so much trust in me.

The mission had started so easily.

But right then, he hated the lies that he'd told to Gabrielle.

Rachel got the sizes for Gabrielle's clothes and she promised to be back first thing in the morning with the items. When she started to leave, Gabrielle reached out and gave the other woman a quick hug.

Surprise rippled across Rachel's face.

"Thank you," Gabrielle told her as she eased back. "After what happened, just knowing that clothes are coming—" This time, her smile was full and real. "It may sound crazy, but it means a lot to me. Actually, it means everything. This guy isn't going to stop me. He won't intimidate me. I'm going to get justice for his victims."

Because that was what Gabrielle did, Cooper realized. She didn't go after the criminals because she wanted attention or glory. She did it for the victims.

So they wouldn't be forgotten.

Gabrielle slipped back into the apartment.

He turned to follow her, but stopped when he saw Rachel glaring at him.

That glare would have melted a lesser man.

He leaned toward Rachel, acting as if he were giving her a hug. "What is it?" Cooper whispered.

Her body was stiff and tense against his. "She deserves better than this," Rachel hissed.

Better than you.

Yes, she did. Jaw locking, he followed Gabrielle inside his apartment, and he wondered just what he'd have to do in order to stop her from telling the world about the EOD.

BRUCE MERCER SAT in his office. His fingers tapped on his desk, a slow, steady rhythm as he listened to Dylan Foxx's update.

The agent was rambling, unusual for him. That rambling meant—

"You found nothing in the reporter's place," Bruce said.

Finally, Dylan stopped his ramble about fingerprint dusting and DNA analysis. Dylan gave a quick nod. "The fact that they didn't find anything is significant, sir."

No, it wasn't. "We already knew one of ours was behind the kills. It only stands to reason that if he didn't leave a trace at the other scenes then he'd be just as careful at Gabrielle Harper's place." The EOD agents were the deadliest and the most covert in the U.S.

Some in his unit were even called Shadow Agents—men and women who were so good at infiltrating enemy camps and carrying out their dangerous missions that they more closely resembled shadows than humans.

You didn't hear a shadow, didn't feel it. Didn't even realize it was there—until it was too late.

"Cooper stopped the cops from seeing that Van had written *EOD* as an identifier for his killer," Dylan said. "But he was too late to prevent Gabrielle from seeing the message. She told us that she was going to print that info in the *Inquisitor*."

"No, she isn't." Even if he had to shut that place down, he'd make sure her report never saw the light of day. He wasn't going to risk the lives of innocent agents. Not that it wouldn't come to that point. He had faith in one man. "Cooper will stop her. He'll find a way to convince her that isn't the right tactic to use."

"You sound awful certain…"

"I am." Bruce's attention turned to the fat stack of manila folders in front of him. "I've called in a profiler." One that he'd handpicked from the FBI. He didn't usually let the Bureau nose around his cases, but this was a different situation.

Right then, the EOD could actually *use* someone from the outside. A fresh pair of eyes, an unbiased observer, was exactly what he needed.

He had high hopes for Noelle Evers.

She'd better not disappoint him.

"Do you know," Mercer asked the other man, curious, "how many agents we've had at the EOD in the past fifteen years?"

Dylan shook his head.

Of course, he didn't know. That intel was classified.

"When agents leave, we do our best to keep tabs on them, but the truth of the matter is this…they leave because they want to vanish. They want to start new lives and not be hunted by their enemies."

They tried to make their pasts disappear.

"But these men and women aren't like everyone else. They're the deadliest foes you could ever cross. I trained them. I brought them into this life." His fisted hand slammed down on the files. "So that means I'm the one responsible for this killer—a man who started on this dark path because he wanted to hurt *me*."

They'd first become aware of the rogue months back, when inside information on Mercer had been leaked to one of his oldest and most powerful enemies. Anton Devast had learned about Mercer's daughter. He'd tried to kill her in order to get revenge on Mercer.

A life for a life.

In the end, Devast had been the one to die.

With Devast's death, the rogue had spiraled even more out of control. The deaths had started then. More than just what the press knew about. More than just what the intrepid Gabrielle Harper had discovered.

With Van's death, they'd now lost four agents.

Four.

All within the past six months.

"Profilers are supposed to tell which men and women are killers," Dylan spoke slowly, bringing Mercer's attention back to him. "But here, that's what we all are."

Mercer shook his head. "No, Foxx, you've got that wrong. You're soldiers. You're heroes. The profiler is looking for a monster, someone pretending to be just like you." Someone adept at hiding his true self.

Mercer pushed back in his chair. His gaze cut to the right, to the window that overlooked D.C. "I never thought the biggest threat I'd face would come from within the organization that *I* made." With blood, sweat, tears. He'd sacrificed so much for the EOD. Even his family.

I'm sorry, Marguerite. His wife had been one of the first that he lost—the first, and the one that still made him feel like he was missing half of his heart.

How much longer? It wasn't the first time he'd wondered that question. How much longer could he truly sit at the helm of the EOD?

Maybe he was getting too old for this mess. Maybe he should be the one looking for a way out.

I need someone else to take over the reins.

Because the idea of escape could sure tempt any agent.

But Mercer couldn't allow his legacy to be destroyed. "We'll find him," he vowed. He wasn't going out—not yet.

Not like this.

When he left, it would be on his terms. It wouldn't be due to some twisted killer who'd decided to put EOD agents on his hit list.

The EOD had survived attacks before. Hell, agents had been targeted before. When you were the best out there, plenty of enemies would come gunning for you.

We stopped them before. We'll stop this SOB, too.

COOPER MARSHALL HAD taken in the reporter. He'd brought her into his apartment so that they could spend the night together.

How cozy.

The watcher stood outside of the brownstone. Dawn hadn't come yet, and the darkness concealed him as he stared at the building.

Last night, he'd also learned that Marshall had called in his team—Rachel Mancini and Dylan Foxx.

They were on his list, too. Another pair that would be destroyed.

But first he had to deal with the reporter. She'd surprised him by getting too close, far closer than the EOD. He wouldn't underestimate her again.

He would use her.

A light was shining in Cooper's bedroom. He could see the shadows of two forms—Cooper and Gabrielle.

He smiled as he watched those shadows.

Oh, yes, Gabrielle would definitely be useful to him.

She would help him to destroy Cooper.

"YOU TAKE THE BED," Cooper said as he rolled back his shoulders and tried to keep his gaze off the long, golden expanse of Gabrielle's legs. "I'll bunk on the couch."

He turned away from her, away from those tempting legs.

"Sleep is going to be impossible, you know that, right?"

He glanced back over his shoulder at her. "You're exhausted. You've been up most of the night." *And been terrified the majority of that time.* "You need rest."

"And every time I even *think* about closing my eyes, guess what I see?" Those dark chocolate eyes were wide and on him. "It's not exactly an image that makes me want to hit the dream circuit."

Her fingers were trembling. Her body held too tightly, too stiffly.

He faced her once more. "The rush. You still have adrenaline spiking through you."

Her hands fisted. "The shower didn't exactly stop that. It didn't do anything to calm me down."

No. He took a step toward her. "I told you before, I can help with that." Adrenaline still coursed through his own blood—adrenaline and fury. *The rogue had gone after her.*

Gabrielle shook her head. "I don't want a drink. The whiskey didn't work for me last time."

Her lips were red and full, and that little quiver of her bottom lip made him want to kiss her, to feel that quiver beneath his own mouth. "Forget the drink," he said, voice rumbling, "I've got something else in mind."

Something that he'd needed, wanted…

He took another step toward her. She didn't back away.

But her gaze did drop to his mouth.

"Cooper…"

He loved the way she said his name. Not with fear or hesitation but with need, a yearning to match his own.

His fingers slid under her chin. He tipped her head back. "Once wasn't enough." One kiss had done nothing but stir his appetite for her.

They were alone. Safe. Adrenaline could be turned into passion so easily.

His head lowered.

She rose onto her toes and her hands—now unclenched—pressed to his chest.

The first touch of his lips against hers was tentative. Easy. A hard task when the desire pumping through him was dark and demanding.

He wanted her on the bed. He wanted her naked. He wanted to hear her scream his name.

One step at a time.

Because before he got what he wanted, Cooper needed to seduce her.

Her mouth parted beneath his.

He took the kiss deeper. Swept his tongue past her lips and tasted her. Sweet. So sweet. She could easily become an addiction to him.

The kiss grew harder as the desire beat in his blood. His hand slipped from her chin and sank into the rich fullness of her hair.

The bed is so close.

He found himself backing her toward the bed. Still kissing her, only now the kiss was deep and hard and it still wasn't enough.

He wasn't sure he could get enough from her.

His mouth pulled from hers, and he began to kiss her neck. Her scent filled his nostrils. *Lilacs.* His aroused flesh pressed hard against the front of his jeans.

"I don't…do this…" Her voice was husky. Her nails bit

through the fabric of his shirt. "I don't…I don't just jump into bed with men I don't know."

He stilled at that and looked at her. "You know me."

"I've lived upstairs from you for months." She licked her lips.

Need sharpened within him.

"But I don't *know* you. Who were you before you came here? You have secrets, Cooper. Sometimes, I can all but feel them between us."

He kissed her again, helpless to do anything else. He kissed her, took her mouth and wanted to take *her*.

The desire he felt for her was stronger than anything he'd experienced before. Cooper had enjoyed more than his share of lovers. He should be able to hold on to his control easily.

Instead, he could feel it shredding.

Because of her.

"There's nothing between us," he said, whispering the words against her mouth. "Right now, there's me and there's you, and nothing else matters."

Not the killer hunting them.

Not his secrets.

"Trust me," he told her. "I won't hurt you. You can count on me."

Her lashes lifted. Her eyes were so beautiful and deep. There were flecks of gold in the darkness of her eyes. As he looked into her eyes, he had the odd feeling that she was seeing into him. Seeing past the mask he wore for others and straight into his soul.

His chest ached.

She's not like the others.

Cooper kissed her once more, because he had to do it. Kissed her deep and savored her.

Then he stepped back. "When you do trust me enough,

you let me know." The words were low, growling from him. "Because you will reach that point. You'll see that you can count on me, and I'll be here. When you're ready, I'll be here," he said again.

She stared back at him. Her lips were flushed, slightly swollen from his kiss. Her cheeks were stained red.

So. Beautiful.

He forced himself to offer her a smile. "And by here," he said quietly, "I mean the couch. Because I think you need some time." *Before you become mine.*

Once they crossed that line, there would be no going back.

She'd changed the rules for him. He didn't think Gabrielle realized just how intense things could become.

Before his control broke, Cooper headed for the door. His fingers curled around the knob.

"I've had one lover."

That stopped him.

"When I said that I didn't jump into bed, I meant it." Her words tumbled out. "I'm not looking to be a flavor of the week with you. I—"

"Sweetheart," he said this without glancing back at her. His control was barely hanging on. "You'd never be that." She was in a class all her own. "When we are together..." *Hell, yes, they would be.* "It's not going to be about anyone else. No one from your past, no one from mine. It's only going to be about us. About pleasure." He opened the door. "You'll trust me soon enough."

He left her, because if he stayed even a few moments more, they would be on the bed.

WHEN THE DOOR shut behind Cooper, Gabrielle's breath wheezed out.

Wow. She was...

Her eyes closed. She didn't think she was ready to handle Cooper Marshall.

She had the feeling that he was the kind of guy who just might be able to ruin her for all others.

When he'd been kissing her, when his big, strong hands had been on her, she'd wanted him to ruin her. She'd wanted him to do all kinds of things to her.

It hadn't been about the adrenaline. It had been about good, old-fashioned lust.

The only thing that had held her back? *Fear.*

She wasn't physically afraid of Cooper. Actually, she was sure he wouldn't hurt her like that at all.

Gabrielle was afraid of the way he made her feel. Out of control. Edgy. Wild.

Those feelings were dangerous.

Cooper Marshall was dangerous.

THE KILLER WATCHED as the light in Cooper's bedroom finally shut off. For a while there, those two shadows had gotten close.

Intimately close.

But then one form had left. Cooper.

Playing the gentleman. What a lie.

He was sure Cooper wouldn't keep up the act for long.

In his experience, Cooper wasn't exactly a man known for his patience. When Cooper saw something he wanted, he took it.

Just like I do.

He and Cooper had quite a great deal in common. That similarity was why they had worked well together in the field.

They'd battled side by side.

Cooper had even saved his life.

He should have let me die.

That had been Cooper's mistake. Now, death would come again. Only this time, Cooper would be the one to wind up in the pine box.

Chapter Six

"You can't do this," Cooper's voice rumbled as he leaned over Gabrielle's shoulder and glared at the computer screen. "If you publish this, it will be like waving a red flag right at the killer!"

Gabrielle glanced up and found him just inches away from her. Close enough to kiss.

No, no, do not go there.

She jerked her gaze away from his lips. "Other reporters have already scooped me on this case! I can't sit on the story any longer."

It was just past 9:00 a.m. She'd given up on the whole concept of sleep quickly enough, and when Rachel had appeared with fresh clothes—Gabrielle seriously owed that woman—she'd wasted no time in rushing down to the *Inquisitor*'s main office.

Her home computer might have been smashed, but she still had data on file at her workstation.

"No one else," he said slowly, seeming to force the words out as he glared at her, "is even mentioning anything about a message being written in blood. You can't—"

"I can," she cut him off. "I will."

His eyes narrowed to blue slits. "You're baiting the killer. You want him to come after you again, is that it?"

"I don't have a death wish." She hit Send on the file

it would be on her boss's computer instantly. With a story this big, she had to get Hugh's permission to publish. Hugh lived for breaking the big news. He'd probably give her the okay in five minutes flat.

"He was in your home."

Like she needed the reminder. "I want him stopped." She pushed to her feet.

He straightened and kept that hot, bright stare on her. "You think using yourself as bait is going to do that?"

"I'm not—"

"Harper!" Hugh's bellowing voice cut across the room. "My office. Now."

Wow. That hadn't even been two full minutes. The boss did like his stories. She brushed by Cooper, slid out of her cubicle, and hightailed it to Hugh's office. She heard Cooper following behind her, and she saw Penelope Finn's gaze cut appreciatively to him. Penelope was the lead entertainment reporter, and the woman was always, *always,* styled to perfection.

Penelope leapt to her feet as they passed her desk. She was wearing a body-hugging dress that matched her golden eyes, and she zeroed in on Cooper—literally blocking him with her body. "I don't think we've met," she said.

Gabrielle rolled her eyes. Typical Penelope. Gabrielle didn't slow down to rescue Cooper. He was a big boy; he could rescue himself. Besides, her boss stood in the doorway, glaring at her.

Hugh was wearing a stark white shirt that emphasized his coffee-cream skin. Hugh considered himself a master of style, and the guy had been known to charm his way into any and every closed-door meeting in D.C.

But, beneath the charm, a real bulldog lurked.

She loved that about him. After all, Hugh had been the one to teach her everything that she knew about reporting.

"No, we haven't met," Gabrielle heard Cooper say flatly to Penelope. "Sorry, but excuse me."

Then, before she could reach Hugh, Cooper's fingers closed around her shoulder.

Gabrielle glanced back.

"You can't go live with that story," he told her.

"No," Hugh said, voice still a bellow even though they were about five feet from him. "She can't."

The charm certainly wasn't in effect then.

Jaw dropping in surprise, Gabrielle whirled back toward her boss. "You're not serious."

"Dead serious." He jerked his thumb over his shoulder. "My office, Harper, now."

Definitely no charm.

She stumbled into his office.

Cooper tried to come with her.

Hugh stepped in his path. Cooper was at least a head taller and probably seventy-five pounds heavier than her boss, but Hugh still doggedly blocked his entrance as he studied the younger man.

"Who are you?" Hugh demanded. "And why are you in my newsroom?"

"I'm her partner," Cooper shot right back. "Where she goes, I go."

"Is that so?" Hugh let him in the office. His dark, assessing gaze raked over Cooper. "Protection, huh? A bodyguard?" He shut the door behind Cooper, sealing them all inside. "Good." He stomped toward his computer. "After what I just read, she can't be safe enough."

"Uh, *she* is right here!" Gabrielle barely managed to keep the words below a shout. "And what do you mean, Hugh? I can't publish the story? It's a *huge* story."

Hugh exhaled loudly. "When are you going to realize, there are more important things than stories? Your *life* is on the line here." He shook his dark head. "No, no, I'm not doing it. I'm not going to let you tell the killer you were minutes behind him last night—"

Gabrielle had to laugh at that. "He already knows. Why do you think he broke into my place?"

"Because you're the next target on his list?"

Hugh's words made her skin chill. "I'm not."

"You're smarter than that. You just don't want to admit it, because if you do, then you'll realize that you're neck deep in danger." He ran a hand over his chin. "We'll keep some of the article. The parts that *don't* yell 'Come and get me' to the killer."

Her article did not yell that.

"Get a confirmation from Carmichael that we're dealing with a serial, and we can lead with that. We'll give him a name, something flashy and scary like the City Stalker, and we'll—"

She could see red. Literally. "It's not about making this guy into a celebrity. It's about catching him!"

Hugh crossed his arms over his chest. "For me, it's about keeping my reporter safe. Change the story. Take out the part about the message that was written in blood—hell, the cops probably want that kept off the record anyway."

"But someone out there could know what the message means!" This was insane. And this was not *Hugh Peters*. Not Hugh Print-It-All Peters.

"In its current form, this story will *not* be published at the *Inquisitor*." His eyes, a shade darker than her own, pinned her. "This isn't your first rewrite, so just get back to your desk and take care of business."

She was missing something. "You've never backed down from a story before."

He swallowed. His gaze cut to a silent Cooper.

"Did someone…did someone contact you?" she asked.

Crazy but…Hugh truly didn't back down from stories. "Hugh, do you know what the EOD actually is?"

"Bodyguard," Hugh muttered, "I'm going to insist that you step out of the room, right now."

"I'm not moving," Cooper said.

Her heart was about to burst out of her chest. *Hugh knows.* "Cooper, I want to talk to Hugh. It's just the two of us here. We'll be perfectly safe."

The faint lines near Cooper's eyes tightened.

"I'm the paying partner, remember?" she managed.

Uh-oh. *Wrong* thing to say. His eyes went glacial. "How could I forget?" He turned for the door. "I'll just go play watchdog from outside."

She hadn't meant to make him angry. She'd apologize, mend fences and do whatever. *After* she found out what Hugh was holding back from her.

The door clicked closed behind Cooper.

"Spill," she demanded.

Beads of sweat lined Hugh's forehead. "Are you sure your guard won't try to listen in?"

No, she wasn't sure of that at all. Actually, she expected him to at least attempt some good eavesdropping. Gabrielle would be rather disappointed in him if he didn't.

"What do you know? Tell me, Hugh. After what I've been through, I think I deserve to know."

He crooked his finger, motioning for her to come closer.

Frowning, she maneuvered toward him.

"You're in over your head," he whispered.

No way would Cooper be able to eavesdrop on that whisper.

"I've dealt with killers before." She tried to sound confident. Like fear wasn't a tight knot in her gut.

"If the killer is working with the EOD, then he's like no one you've ever faced before."

He knew.

"EOD...it's a business?" That hadn't been the initials for a person's name, but something else.

"No." He licked his lips. His gaze darted toward the shut door. "I've only heard whispers, because that's all anyone ever hears. No facts. No proof. Nothing that will ever make it into the press."

"Hugh." Impatience hardened his name. "You're talking in circles, and you're telling me nothing."

"The government."

Hugh had conspiracy theories—a lot of them. She sighed. So much for getting the truth—

"The EOD is a covert unit that works for Uncle Sam. Trained killers. Brutal, cold."

The killer who'd gone after Lockwood and the others had certainly been brutal. His prey hadn't even had time to fight back.

"I've never heard of the EOD." She'd been in Washington for seven years. She'd graduated college, then come to the big city.

"You wouldn't. They're so far off the radar, most civilians never know about them."

"But you heard whispers." An EOD agent. If the killer was as well trained as Hugh was saying, then scaling the side of the apartment should've been easy for him. Cooper had said that a man with the right skills would have no problem climbing down those bricks.

The right skills.

"A man came to me with a story once." Again, his gaze shifted to the door, and he kept his voice low. "He'd been kidnapped off some speck of an island in the Caribbean. He thought for sure his captors would kill him, but then rescue came."

"This story sounds like it had a happy ending—"

"All seven of his captors died. They were taken out by *one* man. One. An EOD agent. The guy said the agent moved like a shadow, faster than anything he'd ever seen. Before his captors could fire their weapons, they were dead on the ground." He sucked in a deep breath. "That's what they are. Death."

"It sounds like the agent was saving him—"

"I did some poking around after that case. A message was delivered to me." His fingers shook. "One that convinced me I wanted to stay away from anything involving the EOD."

Hugh had been scared. No, he was *still* scared.

"I'm delivering the same message to you. You're one hell of a reporter. You're got more grit and determination than anyone else who's walked through the doors of the *Inquisitor.*" His shoulders thrust back. "But I don't want to see you disappear, and the EOD can do that. They can make you vanish."

Her fingernails bit into her palms as her hands curled tightly. "The last thing Van McAdams did was leave that bloody message. You're telling me that the EOD had him killed? Killed his girlfriend? Killed Lockwood and Kylie Archer?"

"I'm saying that if *you* want to stay alive, then you need to forget about the EOD."

Like that was going to happen.

"I don't want you putting any more of a target on yourself. Your life isn't worth a headline."

Hugh was a good man. Sure, he blustered, he bulldozed, but he cared about the people who worked for him. He—

"If I have to, I'll bench you," he threatened. "I'll pull you off the crime beat and get you to help Penelope with the gala coming up at the White House."

"You wouldn't."

"To keep you alive, I would."

Hugh had an evil streak. She'd worked for him ever since she'd come to the city. First, she'd been a barely paid intern, but she'd climbed up the ladder. She'd proved herself.

And she was *not* going to get benched into doing entertainment pieces. "I'll take out the EOD reference," Gabrielle promised.

Relief slackened his features.

"But I am *not* giving this killer a name—"

Hugh waved that away. "You don't have to. I already did." He heaved down into his chair and started tapping away at his computer. "Didn't you hear me? City Stalker. No, wait, maybe D.C. Stalker—that gets it more specific, don't you think?" He snapped his fingers together. "I've got it now! The D.C. Striker!"

Her temples were pounding.

She turned away from him. There were other leads to follow. Actually, Hugh had just given her the best lead possible. She might not be able to print the story about the EOD—not yet, anyway—but now she knew where to start digging.

She just needed to get the right shovel and to dig in the right place.

There were plenty of skeletons buried in D.C. Skeletons and secrets. Time to unearth them.

"We have a problem," Cooper said, voice low, as he held his phone in a too-tight grip. "Hugh Peters knows about the EOD. He's in a closed-door meeting with Gabrielle right now, and he's telling her about us."

The line was quiet. Dead silent. "I'll take care of Peters," Mercer finally said. There was a lethal menace in the director's voice.

"What about Gabrielle?"

"Find out how much he's told her. Then we'll see if containment is necessary."

Containment? *No.* "She's just trying to help," Cooper heard himself saying. "She wants justice for the victims. She's not trying to take down the organization."

"Marshall..." Now curiosity had entered Mercer's voice. Emotion of any kind in Mercer's tone was unusual. "Just how close are you getting to the reporter?"

Not close enough.

Cooper glanced up then because he heard the sound of approaching footsteps. The curvy blonde, Penelope, was strolling toward him with a wide smile. He bit back a curse. Like he needed this now. "I'll update you ASAP." Then he ended the call. Mercer would make sure that Hugh didn't spread any more stories, and as for Gabrielle—

Over Penelope's shoulder, Cooper saw Hugh's office door open. Gabrielle stood on the threshold.

"Hello, again," Penelope said. Penelope Finn. He'd glanced down at the nameplate on her desk when he'd been trailing Gabrielle into Hugh's office.

Penelope lifted her hand toward him. "I didn't catch your name before."

Because he hadn't thrown it at her. He'd been too concentrated on Gabrielle. *And I still am.* "Cooper." Quickly, he shook her hand. Then he tried to step around her so that he could catch Gabrielle's attention.

Penelope sidestepped, keeping her body in front of his. "I was about to cut out for an early lunch. Want to join me?"

Just then, Gabrielle glanced his way. Gabrielle frowned when she saw just how close he was standing to Penelope. He was pretty sure that Gabrielle shook her head in disgust, right before she turned away and headed for the door that led to the stairwell.

"Wait!" Cooper called out.

"Oh, I'll definitely wait for you," Penelope promised him.

She couldn't be serious.

"I'm with Gabrielle," he said flatly, because that was all he needed say. "Enjoy your lunch."

Her jaw dropped, but then she gave a little laugh. "Good, *very* good response."

He didn't have the time to try to figure out that woman. He just skirted right around her. He rushed across the room and caught the stairwell door just as it was swinging closed.

He heard the clatter of Gabrielle's footsteps. Rachel had brought her a pair of high heels that morning, and it sounded like Gabrielle was trying to race away in them. He jumped down the stairs and caught her, locking his fingers around her wrist. *"Partner—"* he stressed the word "—just where are you going?"

"Digging," she mumbled. "Going to find my shovel and *dig.*"

What? He pulled her closer, positioning them into the shadows under the stairs. As far as privacy went, this place was their best bet. "I want to know what your boss told you."

She bit her lower lip.

I want to bite it.

He shoved the thought back into the darkness of his mind. Later, he could try to get that delectable mouth beneath his again. At that moment, he had to find out if the EOD agents had been compromised.

Gabrielle shook her head. "I don't want to risk you. This thing…it's bigger than I thought. If possible, even more dangerous." She tugged her arm free from him. "The partnership was a bad idea."

Oh, no. This could not happen. He held his body perfectly still. "I thought the partnership had saved your hide a few times. Your boss was the one just saying you needed a bodyguard."

"But who protects the bodyguard?" Gabrielle asked, voice sad and a little lost. "I didn't think about the risk to you. I was only concerned with myself. I can't do that anymore. I can't put you in jeopardy."

She was *protecting* him? He hadn't needed protection, not since he'd been a kid.

A scared teenager, clinging tightly to his mother's hand and begging her not to leave him. The memory flashed through his mind. There had been tears in his mother's eyes. She'd promised him, *promised,* that no matter what, she'd always be with him.

His mother had lied. Before night had fallen, she'd been gone.

He'd been alone. No father. No grandparents.

Alone.

"I'm sorry, Cooper," Gabrielle told him. "But this is where we end. I'll pay you for the time you helped me."

Back to payment? A growl rose in his throat.

"You can't work with me any longer. There are things that you're better off not knowing about at this point." She headed down the stairs.

He stared after her a moment. She was seriously trying to protect him, *him,* from the EOD.

Right now, he hated his job.

The secrets between them weighed heavily on his shoulders, but he knew he couldn't let things end like this.

Despite what she'd said, they weren't even *close* to an end.

He stalked after her. Just as she was about to reach for the door that would take her to the ground floor, his hand lifted, and he shoved his palm against that door, making sure she couldn't open it.

Her scent—so sweet and light, not like the cloying scent of Penelope's perfume—teased his nose.

He bent his head closer to hers, following that tempting scent. "I'm not the kind of man who gets frightened by a little danger."

"It's not little." She turned her head, met his gaze. "And I can't let you take this risk for me."

She was being honest. Brave. *Caring.* She was ripping his guts apart. He stared into her eyes, and he wanted her.

Yet the truth was that she was so far out of his league it wasn't even funny.

She deserved someone who was just as honest as she was, someone who wasn't working a second agenda.

Someone who might not have to *contain* her.

But he'd be damned if he'd step aside and let anyone else get close to her.

Cooper brushed his lips over hers. He fought to keep the kiss light, but it was a losing battle. He needed her, desperately, and he wasn't sure that he'd be able to hold back with her much longer.

Her taste drove him wild. Made him need and want— *only her.*

"Cooper…" She breathed his name.

He took that breath, drinking it from her lips. He turned her in his arms, held her close.

He wanted to give her something real. Not a lie. The desire wasn't a deception. It was as real as he could get.

She kissed him back, her response tentative at first, then stronger. Her fingers sank into his hair. Her body arched against his.

I won't give her up.

He just had to find a way to stay at her side, because there was no other place that he'd rather be.

When I'm with Gabrielle, I don't feel alone.

He felt alone when he was with other people. Alone at the EOD. Alone on his missions, even when other teammates were with him.

He'd worked with another agent a while back, a man who seemed to have ice flowing through his veins. Drew Lancaster had been an untouchable agent. The guy had cared only about his job. No family. Few friends.

I'm just like him.

But something had changed for Drew. No, someone had changed Drew. The little doc who took care of the agents at the EOD. She'd gotten under Drew's skin and thawed his ice.

Cooper was afraid that Gabrielle was doing the same thing to him. Getting past the defenses he'd erected.

The way she made him feel could be dangerous.

He hadn't let himself care about anyone in a very, very long time. Already the force of his desire for her was so strong—

She pulled her mouth from his. He didn't let her go. His body brushed against hers.

"I won't tell you," Gabrielle said, lifting her chin, "what Hugh revealed to me in that office. So trying to seduce the information out of me just won't work."

For an instant, he saw red. His pushed her back, caging her against the wall with his body. "We need to get a few things straight," he gritted out.

Her eyes widened.

"I'm not going to be seducing you for information." Was that what the other agents at the EOD thought he was doing? "I'm kissing you and touching you…because

I want you. I want you so much that I want to strip you right here and take you in this damn stairwell."

Gabrielle swallowed.

His hips were pressed against her, so she had to feel the proof of his words.

"I'm not seducing you for information—" his voice was low and hard and anger bit through each word "—I just *want you*."

Her gaze searched his.

"And you want me," he added. "This isn't about information. It's not about anything but us."

After a brief hesitation, Gabrielle nodded.

That little nod wasn't good enough.

"You aren't going to ditch me. You're not going to make me run by saying there's danger around. Sweetheart, I've been handling danger all my life." He'd lived on the rush for years. *It's what made me feel alive.* "I can take any threat. I'm not going to run and leave you alone."

Leaving her alone was the last thing on his mind.

"I'm not running, and I *will* have you." He thought it was better to be clear about his intentions. "And when you're under me in bed, it's not going to be about seducing you for intel. It's going to be about seducing you for the sheer, hot pleasure that we can bring to each other."

Because on that point, at least, there would be no deception.

He started to step back.

Her hands flew up and curled around his shoulders. "My turn," she said, surprising him.

Cooper's brows climbed.

"I'm not seducing you so that you'll protect me from that killer out there."

She wasn't—

"When I'm with you, it's going to be because that's

where I want to be. Because I *want* you." Her voice dropped, got even huskier, seemed to stroke right over his skin as she added, "And I do want you, Cooper. I want you more than I've ever wanted another man."

She was going to bring him to his knees.

"But I am *not*," Gabrielle continued in the next instant, "going to tell you anything about the EOD. So I figure we have two choices. We can continue working as partners, but you don't get to ask me about the EOD again. You just *don't*. Hugh's afraid of the group, and if Hugh is afraid, then I am, too. I won't do anything to put you in their sights."

His teeth were clenched so tightly together that his jaw ached.

"Or we can go with option two," she said, her voice like sin. "We can forget being partners, just be lovers—and there will be no more questions asked from either of us."

His heart slammed into his chest. The blood in his veins heated and seemed to pump even faster, harder.

"There's another option," Cooper forced himself to say. "Option three. We stay partners and we become lovers." He paused, long enough to let those words sink in. "That's the option I want."

She wet her lips. "Me, too…"

Then that was the option they would take. And, maybe…maybe Gabrielle never had to learn the truth about him. If he could keep her away from the EOD, then Gabrielle could keep believing he was just a P.I. who lived in her brownstone.

They could keep being partners…and lovers.

He backed away from her. *For now.* She skirted toward the door and stepped into the lobby. But then she paused. Her hand reached for his. Her fingers curled around his.

The touch was so innocent and light. An ache grew in

his chest. "Gabrielle," he began, but then Cooper saw the man rushing toward him. The man with a badge clipped on his belt and a burning glare on his face.

Detective Carmichael had just joined the party.

"Lane?" Gabrielle didn't release Cooper's hand. "Do you have news? Did you find out about—"

The detective braked to a hard stop right in front of her. "Why didn't you call me?" He *pulled* Gabrielle away from Cooper. "I just heard about the break-in! Damn it, Gabby, you should have let me know right away! I would have rushed over!"

And Cooper realized that all along, the detective had responded a little too personally to Gabrielle.

I've had one lover.

Jealousy thickened within Cooper. He had the feeling he was looking at Gabrielle's ex. He should have seen it before.

"You're homicide," Gabrielle said as she glanced around the lobby. They'd attracted a few stares. "This was a B&E. Cooper said he had friends who could help and they—"

Carmichael sent a withering glare Cooper's way. "I'm sure he has plenty of *friends*. Just like the friend who managed to get him hauled out of my precinct last night."

Cooper gave him a grim smile. *Get your hands off her, cop.*

Carmichael maneuvered Gabrielle to the right, getting them in a private corner. Cooper followed right with him.

"You and I are both connecting the dots, Gabby," Carmichael said.

Cooper hated the way the other man said *Gabby*. Her name was Gabrielle. A beautiful name for a beautiful woman.

"It's no simple B&E. You know it. The guy is after

you." He rolled back his shoulders and finally let her go. "I want you to consider moving into a safe house."

"No." Her immediate response. "I have my own guard—my partner." Her gaze darted to Cooper. "I'm safer with him than I'd be anywhere else."

"With *anyone* else," Cooper clarified. Because the cop wasn't going to keep Gabrielle safe. Cooper was.

You're an ex for a reason, buddy.

Cooper was suddenly determined to find out that reason.

"What do you really know about him?" Carmichael demanded as he rounded to glare at Cooper. "Because I've been digging into your past, Marshall."

Cooper stared levelly back at the man. Was he supposed to be worried? He knew that his service records were shielded, courtesy of the EOD.

"You were in a boarding school until you were eighteen. Then…somehow…even though your mother was dead and you had no other relatives, you got a paid ride from an unknown benefactor. Four years at Yale."

The detective *had* been digging. But he still hadn't discovered anything particularly impressive.

"Four years, then you vanished. Not a blip on the radar until a year ago when you came back to D.C. and started working as a P.I."

He hadn't vanished. He'd enlisted. And unless Carmichael got a whole lot more authorization, he wouldn't ever see Cooper's records. Cooper exhaled slowly. Carmichael was an annoyance, nothing more. "Perhaps you should spend less time looking into my past and a little more time looking for the killer. The city would be safer then."

Carmichael lunged toward him.

Gabrielle put herself between Cooper and the detective. Carmichael kept glaring. In turn, Cooper kept his faint smile in place.

The smile hid the fact that *I'm really starting to hate that cop*.

"Cooper isn't a threat to me. He and I are the ones that are giving you leads, so you need to back off," Gabrielle's voice was fierce.

Carmichael didn't look like he was ready to back anyplace.

"I don't think you should trust him," Carmichael muttered.

"I do, though. Because he's had my back every step of the way."

No, he hadn't. Shame twisted with the jealousy inside of him.

"And speaking of leads…" Gabrielle said as she pushed back her hair. "We have to follow one now." She put her hand on Cooper's arm, but her stare was on the cop's face. "If we find out anything you can use, I'll contact you. Just like always—*before* I put anything in the paper."

So that was part of their relationship. Carmichael had been busting lots of perps in the past six months, earning commendations…with Gabrielle's help?

"I've got my phone on me," she added. "You can call me if you need to reach me, Lane."

The detective leaned toward her. "And if you need me, anytime or anyplace, you call. Don't let me find out about a break-in the next day, got it? I…care about you. Remember that."

Then he was gone, storming toward the lobby's doors.

Cooper didn't move. Emotion had been thick in the cop's voice.

"I really do have a lead for us to follow," Gabrielle said, sighing. "That wasn't just me trying to get rid of him."

He turned his head. Found her eyes on him. "You were the one to break things off."

Gabrielle winced. "You think you figured us out. Just after that little chat?"

He thought he wanted to know everything about the cop right then. Carmichael had torn into his past—turnabout would only be fair.

"No, not yet." He would though.

For now, he took her hand, threaded his fingers through hers. Even though his hand was so much bigger than hers, they seemed to fit. "So...where's this lead?"

She gave him a half smile. "Hope you don't mind a little trip to jail. Because that's exactly where we're headed."

Chapter Seven

She was burning through her favors at an insanely fast rate.

Gabrielle walked through the Department of Corrections, her heels clicking lightly on the floor. She'd had to use two favors just to get in the DOC—and to get access to Johnny Zacks.

Johnny was awaiting sentencing for a heist he'd done a month ago. Another jewelry store break-in, his fourth. Only this time, Johnny had gotten shot by a security guard.

Johnny Zacks had been breaking into jewelry stores for the last few months. He was usually in and out without a trace.

Except for this time…

Johnny was already waiting in the room for her. He was cuffed to the table, and a bored-looking guard stood in the corner, watching him.

"Thanks, Quent," Gabrielle said to the guard. He'd been the one to first connect her to Johnny. Quent might look like he didn't give a damn, but he did. The man had a giant heart.

Quent's head barely inclined at her words.

Johnny, young, tan, with blond hair that was too long

and wide blue eyes, glanced suspiciously at Cooper. "Who's the muscle?"

"My partner." Saying that was getting easier and easier. "He's helping me to look for your sister's killer."

She felt, more than saw, Cooper's surprise.

"Y-you've got news on Kylie?" Johnny asked.

Johnny was actually Kylie's half brother. He'd been out of the country when she was killed, and when he'd come back and discovered that his sister had been murdered, the guy had broken apart.

And gone on a robbery spree.

It seemed that Johnny was the wild child in the family. Kylie had been his strength. Without her, he was still floundering.

"I believe that the man who killed your sister has taken three more lives."

Johnny's hands fisted.

"He's still in the city, the cops are looking for him now—"

"Because more people are dead." Disgust tightened Johnny's face. "They should've been looking for him before! They shouldn't have given up on Kylie!"

"I'm not giving up on her," Gabrielle said softly. "You know that. I gave you my word."

Johnny sucked in a ragged breath and nodded.

"I need to ask you a few more questions about your sister's boyfriend—"

"Fiancé," Johnny cut in, straightening. "They were getting married. She called me and told me that she was marrying Keith. She was so excited." His voice softened. "That was the last time I talked with her. I try to remember her that way, happy, you know?"

"I know," she told him, her heart aching.

Cooper pulled up a chair and sat down next to her at the table.

Gabrielle cleared her throat. "Johnny, you told me that you met Keith a few times. Was there…anything about the guy that set off alarms for you?"

"Alarms?" His head cocked and his face scrunched.

Wait, wrong word. Treading more carefully, Gabrielle said, "It's hard for me to find a lot of information on him. He's—"

"He was ex-military," Johnny said at once, then he jerked his head toward Cooper. "Like him."

Her body tensed. "How do you know that?" She hadn't found any enlistment records for Keith Lockwood.

Johnny smiled. When he smiled, he looked even younger than his twenty-two years. "I can always spot 'em. Me and Kylie, we grew up bouncing around military bases. Our dad commanded one…'til he died." His shoulders rolled back. "It's in the walk. The posture." He tapped his temple. "I can always tell." He pointed at Cooper. "I pegged you the minute you walked in."

Cooper didn't respond.

"Did Lockwood *say* he was in the military?" Gabrielle pressed. She didn't want to tell Johnny that she doubted his word, but—

"Kylie told me," he replied. "Her guy would have nightmares. Maybe flashbacks, I don't know what they were exactly. He'd wake up, screaming about his team, about someone getting left behind."

Excitement had her hands trembling. "Did your sister ever mention if Lockwood worked for a specific unit?"

Johnny shook his head. "It was some kind of black ops deal, I know that much. Kylie told me that whenever she asked Keith about it, he said he *couldn't* tell her, and that man…hell, he usually told her everything. But he was walking away. They were going to start fresh." He blinked and seemed to see the past. "Kylie was happy. Did I tell you that? When she called me, she was happy."

Gabrielle swallowed the knot in her throat. "You did."

He nodded. "Kylie liked pretty things. Things that sparkled." His dimples flashed again. "I gave Kylie pretty things. She needed them, you know? I wanted her to go to heaven with them. So she'd sparkle up there——"

"Johnny." She said his name deliberately, to bring him back. The grief still got to him. Still hurt him. "I am going to find her killer. I told you I wouldn't give up, and I won't."

His head bowed. "Thank you."

"But you have to keep your promise, too, remember?"

Cooper was watching them, so quiet and intense.

"You take the plea deal, you get some counseling and you don't ever steal again."

He looked up at her. "I don't need to steal. I gave Kylie what she wanted." His eyes narrowed. "And you'll give her what she needs. Justice."

"I will."

A buzzer sounded then, and Quent stepped forward. "I've got to take Johnny back now."

"Thank you." Gabrielle rose. There were more questions she wanted to ask, but Johnny had already confirmed her growing suspicions.

She didn't speak again until Johnny and Quent were gone. Then she focused on Cooper. She started to tell him about her new theory, but then she hesitated. "Was he right?" Gabrielle found herself asking instead. "Are you ex-military?"

Emotion vanished from his eyes. Strange, she could actually see the mask slipping into place. Why hadn't she noticed that before?

Just when she thought he wasn't going to answer her, Cooper said, "I was."

"Those missing years," she murmured. "The years Carmichael couldn't find in your past. You were on active duty."

He inclined his head. "Guilty."

"What branch?"

"I joined the Air Force." There was a brief pause, then, "I was a PJ—a pararescue jumper."

Her eyes widened. "You jumped out of the planes." It wasn't the jumping out that was the danger—it was what he jumped *into* that could be so terrifying.

"I did my job," Cooper said simply.

Talk about a major understatement. She'd read reports on PJs before. Those guys jumped into infernos, into war zones and even into the paths of hurricanes.

She rocked back on her heels. "No wonder you were used to the adrenaline rushes."

"Told you," he said as his eyes glinted, "I've got plenty of experience with them."

"Why'd you give it up?" Gabrielle asked him. "What made you turn away from that life?"

"Because I got a better offer." He shrugged, as if the change didn't matter. "I get to make my rules now, and I'm still helping people."

She smiled at him. "Yes, you are." She headed for the door. "Johnny gave us a real lead in there." They cleared the guard areas and headed back outside. "I already know that Van McAdams was in the military."

"How are you so sure?"

The sun glared down on them in the parking lot as they paused near his motorcycle.

"The killer sliced his neck open." She pulled in a deep breath. "And he sliced through the dog tags that were around Van's throat. I saw the dog tags in the blood near him." She gave a firm nod. "That's two men dead, both men who were in the military—"

"Plenty of people were in the military." He didn't seem to be jumping on board with her idea.

Maybe he needed more of a push. Shading her eyes, she told him, "I want to find out what, where and when they served. If Lockwood and McAdams were together, if they knew each other...*that* could lead us to the killer."

Thunder rumbled in the distance. A storm would be hitting that night. But that still left them with plenty of time to follow up on more leads.

"We're getting closer," Gabrielle whispered. "I can feel it. I—" She broke off when her phone began to ring. Gabrielle yanked it out of her bag and she frowned when she saw *Blocked* on the caller ID.

"Is it Carmichael?" Cooper asked as he pressed closer. "Has he found something new?"

She swiped her finger across the screen so she could take the call. "Harper," she said.

"He's not who you think..." The voice was low, rasping, and she had to strain to hear the words.

Gabrielle put her hand over her left ear, trying to drown out the noise from the lot and the street as she focused on the call. "I can't hear you—say that again."

"Cooper Marshall isn't who you think..." The voice was still low, still rasping, as if the caller were trying to disguise his voice.

But this time, she clearly understood his words. Her gaze flew to Cooper. He frowned back at her.

"He's right there, in front of you, and he's lying to you." A rough laugh. "Lying right to your face."

Her stare slid away from Cooper and she scanned the lot. "You're watching me."

More laughter. "You interest me. You shouldn't have even been in the game, yet here you are, leading the race."

"I didn't realize we were playing a game." There was no accent to his voice, at least, not one that she could detect.

"Of course, winner kills all—"

Fear had her voice cracking as she said, "People's lives aren't part of a game!" Then she mouthed *It's him* to Cooper.

Cooper immediately tried to reach for the phone, but she backed away from him.

"Good, good," the voice in her ear praised her. "Don't let him get too close. That's what he's trying to do. Get close to you. Lie to you. Use you."

Like she was going to believe a killer.

"He's not who you think...don't trust the wrong man. Doing that will just get you killed."

Then the line went dead.

For a moment, she didn't move at all. *Where is he?*

"Gabrielle?" Cooper touched her arm.

She flinched. "He's here. He's watching us." She spun around, her gaze searching all around the area.

Cooper took the phone from her. He tried to do a call return.

"You can't," she said, her eyes still scanning the area. "He blocked the call."

Cooper pulled her back toward the shelter of the building. Cars were in front of them. The heavy stone of the building behind them. As far as protection went, it sure seemed like a good spot to her.

Cooper put his phone to his ear. A few seconds later, he said, "Rachel, the SOB just called Gabrielle. See if... if Sydney," he said as his gaze fell away from Gabrielle's, "can hack into the system and find him."

She figured Sydney must be another one of his useful friends. Those friends were sure coming in handy.

"She says that he's watching us," Cooper continued. "We're at the DOC. Yeah, yeah, I want a search."

A search for the killer sounded like an excellent plan to her.

"I'm going now. I'm sending Gabrielle back in with the guards."

Whoa, he was benching her?

He ended the call and secured the phone back in his pocket. His stare leveled on her. "Get inside. Stay there until I come for you."

"While you face him alone?" That sounded like a horrible plan.

His smile was grim. "You don't need to worry about me. I've got this."

He was cold and deadly and he didn't show even a hint of fear.

He's not who you think.

"Get inside," Cooper ordered her.

Now she knew why he seemed to be so good at giving orders. That was the military in him, coming out.

Only she wasn't so good at following orders. Especially in a *partnership*. "I'll call Carmichael."

His jaw hardened. "Do what you need to do."

Uh, calling the cops *counted* as doing what she needed to do.

"I have to know that you're safe, Gabrielle, or I can't look for him. Every minute we waste…he could be getting away."

She managed a nod, but she sure wasn't happy about him racing out alone. Then she was inside and he just—gone in an instant. She glanced around, looking through the window, but she could find no trace of him.

A chill settled over her as she kept staring outside.

Don't trust the wrong man. Doing that will just get you killed.

She didn't plan on dying.

"THE KILLER JUST made contact with Gabrielle Harper," Bruce Mercer said as he lowered the phone back onto his desk. His gaze lifted and locked on Noelle Evers.

The FBI profiler had arrived less than an hour ago. She'd come right to him so that he could begin briefing her on the hell they faced.

Outsiders didn't normally get this close to the EOD. Noelle Evers had passed one very thorough background check in order to get her insider access.

But he trusted Noelle—mostly because he knew her secrets.

Behind her glasses, Noelle's eyes widened. She'd pulled the glasses out a few moments before to begin reading the files that he'd gathered for her.

"That's a very dangerous sign," she said.

He didn't need to be told that.

"But...that's also something we can use," Noelle continued. "If the reporter can draw the killer out, then the authorities will have a better chance of catching him—"

"The local cops aren't catching him. The EOD is containing him."

Her head cocked. "He *is* the EOD." Her fingers curled around the files in her lap. Files on Lockwood and McAdams. And on the other two agents who'd been killed—Frank Malone and Jessica Flintwood. "These agents were highly trained. They could kill in an instant, yet they never had the chance to fight back against their attacker. He's a man they trust implicitly." She squared her shoulders. "I know you told me that my access would be limited, but I need to see the files of every agent they worked with on their missions."

He was already shaking his head before she finished speaking.

Her delicate jaw hardened even as her hazel eyes narrowed on him. "Lockwood and McAdams let the killer in because they trusted him. You trust a man or a woman who has protected your back in the field. They let him in, just as Malone and Flintwood did."

"I can't give you access to the files of existing agents."

"You are tying my hands!"

He rose. "Then find a way to untie them. You're here to work up the profile so that I can see which of my agents might best fit it. You can build the profile without digging into confidential records."

Noelle rose, too. She was a tall woman, skirting close to five foot nine, and she had on high heels that gave her an additional two inches. "If I can't talk to the agents, what about the reporter?"

He smiled. "Of course, but don't let her know about us."

"Of course," she muttered right back.

Mercer headed for the door. Noelle wasn't the only one who wanted to question that reporter. He needed to find out exactly what the rogue had said to her.

"He may have made similar contact with the other victims," Noelle said, her words making him pause near the door.

Mercer glanced back at her.

"I figure we have two options with him. Either this is part of his MO—he calls his victims, he taunts them, and then he kills them…"

Mercer waited.

"Or else he's contacting Gabrielle Harper *because* she's a reporter. He wants the attention that she can give him."

"He wants to expose the EOD."

Noelle nodded. The light glinted off the lenses of her glasses. "He's killing agents—"

"*Punishing* the EOD," Mercer said. He'd done his share of profiling over the years, too.

"So why not take it one step further? Show the world just how dangerous the EOD truly is."

That couldn't happen. Too many lives were on the line.

"I'll arrange a meeting between you and the reporter." He just had to pull a few strings.

Then they had to figure out…was Gabrielle Harper becoming the killer's target? Or did the rogue think she could be another weapon to use against the EOD?

THE SOB HAD actually *called* her. Rage still beat in Cooper's blood. Hours had passed since that phone call. He'd searched the area near the DOC but had found no trace of the killer.

He'd taken Gabrielle back to the brownstone. The cops had finally cleared out, but Gabrielle hadn't shown any interest in going upstairs to her place.

She'd gone straight for his apartment instead.

The storm that had been threatening all day had finally erupted. He heard the clatter of thunder as the pelting drops of rain fell outside.

Gabrielle was on his couch. She'd kicked off her shoes and tucked her feet under her body. She looked small—delicate.

And scared.

Her fear pissed him off.

He stalked toward her. His knees brushed the couch. "He's not going to hurt you."

She looked up at him. He hadn't been able to hear the caller's words, not clearly, and he hadn't wanted to push her for more information with so many eyes and ears around. She'd talked with Carmichael about the call, but the cop had pulled her away from Cooper for that little chat.

He forced his jaw to unlock as he stared down at her. "I need to know what he said."

Because Mercer had already called him—twice—demanding details.

"He...he told me that you weren't who I thought you were." Her arms wrapped around her stomach. "He told me that you were lying to me."

His heartbeat seemed to echo in his ears.

"He knew your name," she continued without looking away from him. "And he told me that you weren't who I thought."

Bastard. "He's trying to shake you up. To make you afraid."

"I *am* afraid."

"Don't stop trusting me." He reached down, caught her hands and pulled her up so that she stood beside him. "He wants you to turn away from me so that you'll be on your own, vulnerable."

I won't have that. The rogue wasn't going to take Gabrielle's life. Cooper didn't plan to walk into an apartment and smell her blood.

Or find her lying on the floor, motionless.

"Cooper?" Gabrielle frowned at him. "Are you all right?"

No, he wasn't. His heart wasn't drumming in his ears any longer. It didn't seem to be beating at all. His body felt cold, like ice that sank through skin and bone. "I won't do it."

Her head tilted toward him. Her dark hair slid over

her shoulder. The move exposed the golden column of her neck.

Sliced open, bleeding out...

"Do what?" Gabrielle asked him as she searched his gaze.

"I won't find you dead. It's not happening." He knew what the cold was in that instant—fear. Fear didn't burn, it chilled, and it was freezing him from the inside, out.

He pulled Gabrielle close and put his mouth against hers.

The rogue couldn't get her. The killer wasn't going to drive a wedge between Cooper and Gabrielle, and the guy *wasn't* going to kill her.

The kiss was hard, too rough. But Cooper wasn't in control then. The ice had to melt. He had to get closer to Gabrielle, had to make sure that she was safe.

His hands wrapped around her body. Her mouth was open, so sweet and hot. He drove his tongue past her lips and tasted.

Took.

He lifted her into his arms.

There would be no stopping this time. He couldn't.

Cooper carried her back to the bedroom, kissing her the entire time.

Desire pulsed within him, growing stronger with every step, tangling with the fear and the fury within him.

Lightning flashed. Thunder shook the windowpanes.

He lowered her to her feet, letting her bare toes skim the hardwood, positioning her near the edge of the bed. Light from the lamp spilled over the bed.

Cooper stepped back from her. He couldn't give her honesty about all parts of his life, but in this moment, he would give her everything that he could.

"I want you." His voice was gravel rough with desire. "Trust that. Trust *me*."

Her gaze held his. He could see her need shining in her gaze. "I do," she said softly.

That broke him. The last of his control vanished.

She started to lift up the edge of her shirt. His fingers caught hers. He wound up throwing that shirt across the room.

His hands stroked her, caressed. Her skin was softer than silk, smooth and perfect.

She wore a black, lacy bra. A temptation that was going to force him to his knees.

But then her hand went to her jeans. She shimmied out of her jeans. Long, tan legs were bared to him. Those legs—and the matching scrap of black lace panties that covered her hips.

Don't pounce. Because he wanted to pounce. He wanted to take and take and take and let the pleasure drive out the last of the chill that clung to his skin.

Instead, he lowered her onto the bed. He kissed. He touched. Her bra joined her clothes when he tossed it to the floor. Her breasts were perfect, full with tight, pink tips. His tongue licked those taut peaks. She arched against him. Her nails dug into his back, pressing through the thin T-shirt that he wore.

Her hips pushed up against him. Her spread legs moved restlessly against his body.

His hands slid down to the front of her panties. Panties that had surely been designed to make a man go crazy. Carefully, he stroked her through the lace. She was hot and so ready for him.

He had to make this good for her. He wanted Gabrielle as wild and hungry as he was.

His fingers pushed into her. Her breath rushed out.

Then she was the one yanking up his T-shirt and trying to touch his skin.

But when she touched him...

I need her too much.

He pulled back and stripped in seconds. He reached into the nightstand and fumbled for the protection he'd put there.

Then he slowly removed the scrap of lace that covered her sex. He tried to be careful, but he wanted her so badly—the lace ripped.

Gabrielle just laughed. She lifted her hips toward him. "I don't want to wait anymore."

Her voice—her husky words—pushed him over the edge. His hands closed over her thighs. He parted them even more, making room for his body. He put his aroused flesh against her.

Their gazes locked.

He drove into her with one long, hard thrust.

Her breath gasped out. Her eyes darkened even more. Cooper stilled, worried that he was hurting her.

At his hesitation, her legs wrapped around his hips. She arched against him. "More," Gabrielle whispered.

He'd give her more. He'd give her all that he had.

His fingers threaded with hers. He withdrew then thrust harder, deeper, again and again. The moans she made urged him on. They were the sexiest sounds he'd ever heard. Pleasure waited, so close, so close. Her body felt amazing against his. Being *in* her, that hot, tight paradise of her body—it made the blood in his body seem to burn.

She cried out and he saw the pleasure on her face. Her cheeks flushed. Her eyes went blind.

She whispered his name.

He drove into her, not able to hold back. The headboard

thudded into the wall, and when the pleasure hit him, it was like nothing he'd felt before.

His body shuddered as he pumped into her. He held her with hands that were too tight, but he couldn't let go.

She was all he knew. The only thing he wanted.

The one thing that he wasn't going to give up.

His gaze met hers. Pleasure was a drug making him desperate, light-headed.

Gabrielle smiled up at him.

For Cooper, in that instant, *everything* changed.

THE RAIN FELL down in a hard, heavy torrent. The local forecasters had predicted that the storm would last for hours.

Cooper had taken the reporter home.

He'd called, given Gabrielle a warning that she should heed, but the woman had seemed to pay him no attention.

Her mistake.

She would learn the truth soon enough.

When you trusted the wrong person, you wound up dead.

Another woman had trusted Cooper once. She'd believed in him, just as Gabrielle believed in the man now.

That woman was buried in a cemetery thirty miles away.

Soon, Cooper would be buried, too.

The killer pulled up his coat and whistled as he turned away from the brownstone.

It was almost time for his next attack. Almost...

Chapter Eight

He didn't look nearly as fierce when he slept. Gabrielle turned her head, letting her gaze slide over Cooper's face. The danger was gone. The dark intensity vanished when he was unaware.

He looked younger but still as handsome.

Just not as deadly.

His blond hair was mussed. The brilliant blue of his eyes was hidden. His tanned skin looked even darker against the white of the sheets.

And, in the light, Gabrielle could see that Cooper had scars—a lot of them.

When they'd made love, her fingers had skimmed over his body. She'd been so far gone, though, that she hadn't recognized the rough outline of the scars for what they were.

Her stare drifted down his body. Since the sheet pooled at his hips, she had a great view of his truly impressive chest and abs.

And the seven scars there. She counted those scars again. Yes. Seven.

From gunshots? Knife wounds? Just what had happened to Cooper in his life? What made him so dangerous?

He's not who you think he is.

That dark voice wouldn't get out of her head.

She couldn't escape into sleep, not the way Cooper could. Maybe it was the storm. Storms always reminded her too much of her past.

It had been storming—a fierce, hard storm, just like this one—the night she'd found her father.

The thunder had cloaked the sound of the gunshot. None of her neighbors had even known that he was hurt.

By the time she'd gotten home, it had been too late.

Lightning flashed outside of the window.

Swallowing, Gabrielle lifted her hand. One of Cooper's arms had curled over her stomach. Carefully, she eased out from under that arm. Then she put his hand back down on the bed. Her gaze studied his face closely, but he didn't stir.

She pulled on his robe. It was there, so surely he wouldn't mind if she borrowed it, right?

Gabrielle tiptoed out of his bedroom. It was still early, barely past nine at night, and there was no way she could sleep.

Once back in the den, she hesitated.

The place just seemed so empty. Why didn't Cooper have any personal mementos there? His place...it was just like Van McAdams's.

Van and Keith had been in the military, and so had Cooper.

She glanced over her shoulder.

Why had Cooper been at the scene of Keith Lockwood's death that first night? She'd thought it was just coincidence at the time, but...

She found herself creeping toward the small desk in the corner. A laptop sat on the desk, closed, turned off. Her fingers slid over the laptop.

She'd just made love with a man—and she knew only the barest of details about his past.

Gabrielle leaned down. There were two drawers on the side of the desk. Neither showed signs of having a lock.

"What are you doing?"

Cooper's voice came from *right* behind her. She jumped, spun around then tried to suck in a deep gulp of air. "Cooper, you just scared five years of my life away!"

She hadn't even heard him approach. He'd snuck up on her the same way he had at Lockwood's apartment.

His eyes were narrowed as they raked her face. "You left me."

"I couldn't sleep." Thanks to that little scare, her heart raced in her chest. "I thought I'd get up and—"

"You were going into my desk."

What was up with his accusing tone? Talk about going from sensual to suspicion in sixty seconds flat. Her hands tightened on the robe. "No, I wasn't. I wouldn't do that to you." The accusation was an insult. "Look, just because I'm a reporter, it doesn't mean I snoop on my friends—"

His eyelids flickered. "Is that what we are?" His head tilted. "Because I thought we were lovers now."

He wore a pair of jeans that hung low on his hips. A line of stubble lined his jaw. He looked rough, tough and sexy.

Gabrielle wet her too-dry lips. "I think we can be both." She found herself leaning toward him, so she snapped her shoulders back. "But we need to be clear. You said I can trust you, and I want you to trust me, too."

He glanced away from her.

What was that about?

Gabrielle took a bracing breath and plowed on. "I want to know you. Who you were before you came to D.C. Who you are now." Because she didn't want her lover to be a stranger to her.

Thunder rumbled again. She flinched.

His brows pulled low. "Why does the storm scare you? I thought nothing scared you."

Gabrielle laughed at that. "You're so wrong. I'm just usually better at hiding my fear." His shoulders seemed so wide. He was strong and solid standing there, and he made her feel like she didn't need to fear.

He made her feel safe so perhaps that was why her words just kept flowing. "I found him during a storm like this one."

"Him?"

"My father. He was waiting for me at home. I was out late, at a football game with some friends. I came home sure he was going to get all over me for breaking curfew..." Gabrielle glanced toward the window. "But when I went in, our house was dead silent. Silent and so dark. My dad always left the light on for me. He'd sit in his chair and he'd watch TV until I came home." Her gaze drifted back to him.

Cooper didn't touch her. He just watched her as lightning lit up the room once more.

If she wanted to know about his past, it only seemed fair that she should reveal hers to him.

"He wasn't in his chair. He was on the floor lying on his back. I ran to him, I begged him to talk to me, but he was gone."

Her father's eyes had been so empty. As empty as Van McAdams's. The life had been completely gone from his stare. She'd never forget the sight of his empty gaze.

"What happened to him?"

"He was shot. One bullet, right in the heart." Her own heart hurt every time she remembered that night.

"I'm sorry." His arms reached for her. Cooper pulled her against his chest. At his touch, tears welled in her eyes. It had been over eight years, but she still missed her father.

He'd been her constant. Her hero.

Her mother had cut out on them when Gabrielle had just been a toddler. Run away with a married man and never looked back.

"The police said it was a robbery gone wrong. Some cash and electronics were taken, but…" She squeezed her eyes shut and pulled in a steadying breath when the thunder rolled once more. "But they never found the person who killed him. The trail went cold, and he was forgotten." Gabrielle forced herself to pull back so that she could gaze up into Cooper's eyes.

"That's why you do it," he said softly.

"That's why," she agreed. She'd never been able to give her father justice, and that knowledge ate away at her. "I give the other families what I can't get."

He shook his head. "You're not what I thought…"

His words made her stiffen. They were too similar to the killer's. "You're *exactly* what—who—I thought you were," she fired back fiercely. "You've had my back. You've risked your life. You—"

He kissed her.

You're one hell of a kisser. Because she'd thought he would be, from the first glimpse that she'd had of him. She'd almost dropped her chocolate chip cookies because she'd taken one look and gotten lost in his blue gaze.

His lips were firm and warm, and the things that man could do with his tongue…

Cooper eased away from her. "I'd risk my life for you in an instant. Know that. I'll protect you with every bit of power I have."

She believed him.

"Sometimes, I think all our pasts can do is hurt us." His words were a rumble. His right hand curled under her jaw. "It's the future that I like to think about. What can be."

But a past couldn't be forgotten, or completely buried, no matter how much you might wish it to be so.

Why wasn't Cooper telling her about himself?

She felt as if she'd just laid her soul bare for him.

Goose bumps rose on her skin. She backed away from him, hunching her shoulders a bit. When lightning flashed again, Gabrielle didn't flinch, and she was rather proud of that fact.

But she was also curious. About Cooper. Always—him. "What scares you?" Gabrielle whispered.

He didn't move. No, he did. A small movement. He *tensed*. "What makes you think anything does?"

Her lips lifted in a wan smile. "Everyone fears something. Even you, tough guy." Even the man who jumped into fires.

His eyes were on her, burning bright. "Maybe *you* scare me."

His response surprised her. "Why?"

A phone rang then, vibrating from its position on the couch. Cooper's lips thinned, but then he said, "Because I don't want you hurt."

Her lips parted in surprise, but he had already reached for the phone. He answered it, even as his eyes stayed on her. "Marshall." His eyelids flickered a bit. "Yes, she's here."

The call was about her?

He turned away from Gabrielle, showing her his broad back. "We're not coming out in the storm. Why? Because she doesn't like damn storms, that's why."

Her breath caught in her throat.

"When it's over, *that's* when we can talk," Cooper growled.

Another phone rang then—her phone. She instantly recognized the familiar beat of music that alerted her to the caller's identity. Gabrielle hurried across the room, vaguely aware that Cooper had ended his call and followed her.

Her fingers trembled a bit as she picked up her phone. She took the call saying, "Penelope, look, this isn't a good time for me—"

"Something is happening here," Penelope whispered.

"What?"

"After you left a man and a woman in suits—you know, the boring, government-type suits—came in to the *Inquisitor.* They went into Hugh's office. They closed the door, and now Hugh is about to leave town for a trip down to the Cayman Islands."

What? Hugh was heading off to the islands? That made zero sense to her.

"Get in here!" Penelope ordered.

Then the woman hung up on her.

After her day, Gabrielle really didn't need Penelope's drama.

Gabrielle hurriedly tried getting her boss on the line. Only he wasn't picking up. The guy *never* ignored a call from any of his reporters. And Hugh also didn't just rush out of town. In fact, he usually stayed at the *Inquisitor* until after midnight most nights.

What's going on?

She looked up. Cooper had his eyes on her. "My boss is leaving town." She rubbed the growing knot of tension in the back of her neck. "Some strange folks in suits came in, and Penelope was pretty much saying they've pressured him to leave." *Government-type suits.* "Feds," she muttered.

Cooper's brows climbed. "Uh, you think Feds are pressuring your boss to get out of D.C.?"

Her gaze cut to the window. "I have to get down to the *Inquisitor*."

"You just told me that you don't like storms."

"No, I don't," she agreed quickly. "They scare the ever-loving hell out of me. But I can't let fear stop me." She never had, never would.

She headed for the bedroom.

He blocked her path. "Maybe *we* should get out of town."

Her eyes widened. "What?" But, before he could reply, Gabrielle shook her head. "I can't! I have a story, people counting on me ..."

"You have a killer calling you, threatening you. You need to get out of sight and get some place safe." He gave a hard nod. "I can keep you safe. I can take you someplace that no one else would ever be able to find."

His words held an ominous ring that unsettled her. "I don't want to vanish. I'm not hiding." She brushed past him.

"Fine." That word was bitten off. "I'll take you to the *Inquisitor*."

Gabrielle stopped at the bedroom door and swung back to face him. "Uh, try that again." She motioned to the window. "I'm not getting on your motorcycle. We'll take a cab. My whole facing-your-fears bit only goes so far."

For an instant, she thought he'd smile at her.

But then he did that little trick of his—that trick where all emotion vanished from his face and eyes. "When you want to vanish, tell me. Remember that, okay? I can get you out of this game anytime."

"It's not a game."

"Isn't it?"

Life and death shouldn't be a game.

And Cooper's words shouldn't have reminded her of the killer.

But they did.

The killer's voice seemed to echo in her mind.

"Winner kills all."

HUGH'S COMPUTER WAS GONE. His files were boxed up.

And he was sweating.

Gabrielle stood in the doorway of his office, frowning. "Hugh?"

His head jerked up at her call.

"What happened here?"

He cleared his throat and gave a shrug. "Vacation time," he told her with a too-jovial tone in his voice. "Got some coming, so I thought I'd head out for a few days."

Bull. She glanced at Cooper. He shrugged. Raindrops clung to the sides of his hair.

Gabrielle marched into Hugh's office. "Come in and shut the door, Cooper." Because this conversation wasn't going further than the three of them.

She slapped her hands against the surface of Hugh's desk. His Adam's apple bobbed as he watched her.

"You don't run from anything," she told him. "And you taught me not to run."

"I'm not running." That false jovial air weakened. "It's a vacation, I told you that."

The door clicked shut.

"Who got to you? Did the cops put pressure on you because of that call I—"

He reached across the desk and grabbed her left hand. "You're in too deep."

Gabrielle shook her head. "I'm a reporter. You taught me that there can *never* be a 'too deep'—this is our job. To follow the truth, no matter where it might take us."

"What if it takes you to the grave?"

"Hugh…"

He freed her and rolled his shoulders. "Feds confiscated my computer. They told me they believed that the killer had hacked into the system here at the *Inquisitor*, that he'd been using my own intel to get close to you. That was how he knew where you lived, knew your phone number… The Feds said they traced him, they found evidence he'd been in your personnel file. Every bit of info I had on you…" He paused and his chin lifted. "The killer's got it now, too."

"How do they know that?" she demanded. "They can't know! They—"

"Were they just trying to come up with a reason to take my computer? My files? Maybe," Hugh allowed, "but they had a court order, so it wasn't like I could stop them from taking everything."

Cooper, standing just behind her, remained silent.

"Why the trip out of town?" Gabrielle asked.

Hugh's gaze slid away from hers. "I've made a lot of enemies with my stories over the years."

"And you never ran from any of those enemies."

His head inclined. "But I'd leave in an instant if it meant I could keep my people safe."

He's leaving for me. The knowledge was twisting her insides into knots. "What did they tell you?" Gabrielle demanded.

Hugh reached for his bag. His attention shifted to Cooper. "Should have realized it sooner," Hugh mumbled. "But maybe it's a good thing that you're here."

Her blood iced. *No, no, no.*

Hugh's smile stretched across his face. She knew that smile. It was his fake smile. One he gave when he was in the presence of an enemy.

She wasn't Hugh's enemy. That just left…Cooper.

"If anyone can keep her safe, I guess it will be you, bodyguard." Hugh walked around the desk, clutching his bag. He paused for just a moment beside Gabrielle. "I'll be seeing you again. You can count on it."

Her heart felt like it was about to burst from her chest.

Hugh didn't trust Cooper. She sure got the message he'd sent her—loud and clear—*should have realized it sooner*.

Hugh reached for her. He hugged her—and slipped a small flash drive into her hand.

Her fingers curled around the drive, concealing it completely.

He pulled away. This time his smile was real. It reached his eyes. "You know I can't turn away from a good story," he said.

No, he couldn't.

"I'll be back."

He strode toward the door. Cooper started to slide out of his path, but Hugh stopped him. Hugh slapped a hand down on Cooper's shoulder. "If Gabrielle gets so much as a bruise…"

Gabrielle slipped the flash drive into her back pocket.

"…you'll answer to me."

Then Hugh was gone.

Cooper glanced her way. "What the hell was that about?"

It was about Hugh not trusting him. About Hugh being forced out of D.C., but by whom?

Her money was on the EOD. She needed to access that flash drive, but Hugh had concealed it from Cooper for a reason, and she didn't want his eyes on it, not until she'd seen for herself just what material it contained.

"He's gone!" Penelope poked her pretty head in the doorway. "Actually gone—with a serial killer loose in the city! Am I crazy? Or is he?"

Gabrielle's heartbeat drummed so loudly she was sure that Cooper and Penelope had to hear it.

"And there's someone here," Penelope continued as she smoothed back her hair. "Some woman who said she's from the FBI." Her perfectly manicured index finger pointed to Gabrielle. "She keeps asking to see you."

The situation was going from bad to worse.

Cooper was frowning now as he glanced through the doorway.

Penelope smiled at him and she batted her lashes. "The FBI lady is right down the hall, second door on the left."

Cooper hurried out.

Gabrielle crept toward Penelope.

Penelope's smile vanished. "What is going *on?*"

"I'm not sure." She didn't want to mention the EOD to Penelope. Until she figured out more about what was happening, Gabrielle didn't want to risk the other woman's life.

Sure, Penelope was flighty, she was flirty, but she was also one of the few people that Gabrielle counted as a friend.

"What can I do?" Penelope asked. "Hugh's worried, I can tell, and when he worries…*I* worry."

Gabrielle eased out a slow breath. "I need to use your computer, and I need you to keep both Cooper and that FBI agent busy while I do it."

Penelope nodded. "Done." She started to walk away, but then stopped. "When this is all over, you'd better share your byline with me."

"I will," Gabrielle promised. She would have promised just about anything right then.

Penelope bustled away. "Oh, Cooper, the agent is this way, in the conference room…"

They only had one conference room. It was down the

hall, in a location a good thirty feet away from Penelope's desk.

Perfect.

Gabrielle all but ran for the empty desk.

AN FBI AGENT. What were the Feds thinking? To get involved in an EOD case like this just wasn't protocol. Mercer should have shut them out immediately.

"Right here," Penelope said, her perfume seeming to swirl in the air around him. She threw open the door. "Agent Noelle Evers, this is Cooper Marshall. He's—" Penelope broke off, tapping her chin thoughtfully. "I think he's working with Gabrielle," she murmured, sounding confused.

"I'm her partner." Cooper crossed the room and offered his hand to the slim redhead. He'd never seen the woman before. Her handshake was brief but solid, and he had the feeling the woman was assessing everything about him— probably because she was.

He glanced over his shoulder, expecting to see Gabrielle.

But Penelope was the only one there, and she was shutting the door.

He pulled away from Agent Evers. "Gabrielle…"

"Oh, she'll be right in. She just stopped by the restroom." Penelope lowered her voice to a conspiratorial whisper. "Talking with Hugh got her emotional. She hated to see the old guy go. He was like a father to her."

Her real father had left her too soon and with a fear of storms and a quest for justice that wouldn't end.

He headed for that door. If she was upset, he wanted to be with her.

Penelope blocked his path. She smiled at him, but her

gaze drifted to the FBI agent. "You're here about the D.C. Striker, aren't you?"

The D.C.—

"Yes," Agent Evers said, voice smooth, "I am."

Excitement lit Penelope's gaze. "He's a serial killer, isn't he? Hugh was right about that. You're here because that's what the FBI does. You hunt serials."

"It's one of the many things we do," Agent Evers said, still in that smooth voice that didn't give away any emotion. "We hunt them, and we try to figure out why they do the things that they do."

Her job was very different from his.

He didn't try to understand the killers. He just eliminated them.

GABRIELLE SANK INTO Penelope's chair. Her fingers were trembling as she pushed the flash drive into position.

A few clicks of the mouse, and she had that drive open.

There were two files stored there.

One was titled…*EOD*.

She clicked that one first.

Her gaze darted over the document that opened. It looked like it was a series of notes that Hugh had made.

Ex-military. Covert Ops. Specialize in hostage retrieval and unconventional warfare. Lockwood and McAdams… military records are sealed. Possible EOD agents.

Then Hugh had listed what appeared to be a series of locations and dates. Were those EOD missions?

A phone rang beside her, and Gabrielle jumped. She glanced up, made sure no one was watching her then she went back and clicked on that second file.

That file was labeled *Striker*.

She expected to find more notes within that file. Instead, she found data on—Cooper.

Military records. She had no idea how Hugh had gotten access to these files. Lane had tried and come up empty-handed.

Should have known Hugh would be more resourceful. Somehow, he'd managed to get access to sealed records. Hugh had contacts in all the right—and wrong—places.

She leaned forward as she read the service details. Cooper had joined the Air Force the day after he graduated from Yale. She scanned through the file, noting the commendations, the awards.

There'd been so much training for him. The notations were seemingly endless. Combat Dive School. Army Airborne certification. Military Free Fall Parachutist. He'd been on a special tactics team, and even gone in for Advanced Skills Training.

Her fingers trembled as she clicked the mouse. No wonder the guy could move so soundlessly. He was some kind of super soldier.

Then she saw that Cooper's service ended five years ago. Ended…with an annotation that said Cooper Marshall had been killed in the line of duty.

Her breath choked out.

Killed?

Of course, he hadn't been killed. He was alive and well, and right down the hall in the conference room.

But Hugh had scanned a death certificate. It was right there for her to see, plain as day.

According to those files—files that clearly had a "Confidential" stamp on top of each page, Cooper Marshall was a dead man. There was even a picture of him included. A younger version of Cooper, but definitely him.

She pulled the cursor down and reached the last page of the file.

Hugh had written a note to her.

According to my source, Cooper Marshall is a ghost. Watch your back with him. This story—these murders are all about the EOD.

You're the reporter covering the kills, and all of a sudden, Marshall is shadowing you. He lives in your building, he has access to you…

I think your "guard" knows a whole lot more than we do. Be careful with him.

He was connecting dots that she should have connected herself.

But she'd been blind.

Sometimes, you couldn't see the enemy that was right in front of your face.

Or in your bed.

She scrolled back up and read the details of his "death" one more time. Cooper Marshall had been attempting to rescue a downed pilot behind enemy lines in Afghanistan. He'd gotten that pilot to safety, but Cooper had sustained extensive injuries. He'd died before making it back to base.

Gabrielle's fingers rubbed together as she remembered the scars that marked Cooper's stomach and chest. He had been injured, grievously. But he hadn't died.

"Look, I get that you're into her," Penelope's sharp voice called out, "but give the woman a minute of privacy. I told you already that Gabrielle is going to join us—"

She shut the file and jerked out that flash drive. Her heart raced in her chest as Gabrielle shot up from the chair.

And came face-to-face with a dead man.

Chapter Nine

To be dead, he looked incredibly good. Damn him.

But she had to look shaken because Cooper frowned at her. His hand came up and skimmed her cheek. "What's wrong?"

Have you been lying to me?

She should have put the puzzle pieces together sooner. Gabrielle felt like a fool as she stared up at the man she'd made love with just hours before.

"Gabrielle?"

She slid around him.

Penelope was staring at her with wide eyes, and just behind the entertainment reporter, another woman was also watching her. This woman had dark red hair and a sharp gaze.

Gabrielle's stare swept over the redhead. With that suit, yes, she would've instantly pegged the lady as FBI.

"I have some questions for you," the redhead said.

"What a coincidence," Gabrielle muttered right back. "I've got my share of those, too."

She didn't glance at Cooper as she headed for the conference room. There were too many eyes and ears on them at that moment. It would be far better to have this conversation in private.

Penelope tried to follow them back into the conference

room, but the FBI agent firmly shut the door—well, pretty much in the other woman's face.

Gabrielle's eyes narrowed. "I didn't catch your name," she said to the lady.

"Noelle Evers." Noelle offered her a brief smile as she marched toward the conference table. Some folders and a notepad were already spread out there. "And I'm here to learn more about your recent phone call with—"

"The D.C. Striker?" Gabrielle finished for her.

"If that's what you want to call him," Noelle agreed, but she didn't sound impressed with the name.

"She's a profiler," Cooper said as he took the seat near Noelle. "She's here to help the cops catch this guy."

Gabrielle still stood. Her knees had locked on her, so she wasn't even sure that she could sit. "Have the two of you met before?" Suspicion made her ask that question.

And then it happened. Cooper immediately said, "No," but the agent's eyelids jerked, just a little bit. Noelle glanced quickly at Cooper, then away.

Gabrielle's back teeth clenched. A profiler should learn to be better at hiding her emotions.

But that little tell had convinced Gabrielle that she had to press a bit more. "It's all about the EOD."

No emotion crossed Cooper's face. *Oh, so that's when he does that.* The emotion vanished each time he kept a secret from her.

"I don't think I understand," Noelle began carefully. She motioned to the nearby chair. "Why don't you sit down? Then we can really talk."

Gabrielle felt like they were talking just fine. It wasn't like sitting improved a conversation. "Why isn't Detective Carmichael with you? If you're here investigating the killer, shouldn't the local cops be helping you?" But Lane hadn't even given her a heads-up about the profiler.

The whole scene felt wrong. Gabrielle wasn't going to ignore her instincts any longer.

Noelle glanced over at Cooper once more. *What is she doing?* It almost looked as if the profiler were waiting to follow Cooper's lead.

Cooper was staring straight back at Gabrielle. A faint furrow dipped between his brows.

"Right now," Noelle finally said, "the FBI is *assisting* the local authorities. It may become necessary for us to take over the investigation, but at this point, I'm just attempting to gather more data about our suspect."

The answer was smooth, and it sounded rehearsed.

"What did the suspect say, exactly, when he called you, Ms. Harper?" the profiler wanted to know.

"He told me not to trust Cooper. The guy said that Cooper wasn't who I thought."

There was still no expression in his eyes.

"He told me," Gabrielle continued, her chest aching now as she realized that she'd been played by a master, "that if I wasn't careful, I'd trust the wrong man and I'd wind up dead."

Cooper surged to his feet. "Gabrielle—"

"You're EOD." It made sense. So much sense and she felt herself flush. "*That's* why Van's last message was erased at the crime scene. You smeared the blood deliberately, didn't you? To keep your organization quiet. You destroyed evidence."

A muscle jerked in his jaw.

But he didn't deny being EOD. She'd actually expected a denial.

"I think—" Noelle spoke softly as she pulled her files a bit closer "—that we all need to calm down."

"I'm completely calm," Gabrielle said. She was. An eerie calm that she hadn't expected had settled over her.

Gabrielle pulled out her phone. She held it gripped in her hand. She tilted her head as she studied the profiler. "If I call Detective Carmichael right now, is he going to back up your story? Is he going to even know who you are?"

Noelle hesitated.

That was Gabrielle's answer. "He's not, because you aren't working with the local cops. They aren't the ones who sent you to me." She rolled back her shoulders and forced herself to meet Cooper's stare. "The team that you had searching my apartment—they were from the EOD, weren't they? This guy, this fellow doing the killing, he's one of your agents."

Cooper didn't speak, neither confirming nor denying her charge.

She'd wanted a denial. Crazy, of course, but she'd wanted one.

A woman didn't like to be that wrong about her lover. She was.

Gabrielle retreated from him and the FBI agent.

Noelle rose. "I really need to ask you more questions. It's imperative that I learn as much about this man as I can."

So that the EOD could catch one of their own?

"He's fixated on you," Noelle continued, as Gabrielle took another step back. "The fact that he's contacting you gives us an advantage. It means—"

"—that you think you can use me as some kind of bait." Her blinders were definitely off. No wonder Cooper had agreed to be her partner. He was letting her rush out and try to draw the killer's attention.

She'd been live bait in the EOD's trap, and she hadn't even realized it.

"Thanks, but no thanks." Gabrielle spun away and yanked open the door.

"Gabrielle!" Cooper called after her.

Her eyes were tearing up. Knowing that she'd just been a means to an end for him *hurt*.

"Gabrielle? Are you okay?" Penelope asked as she hurried toward her.

"I need to get away," she whispered back.

Penelope handed her a pair of keys. "My car's in the lot."

Then Penelope pushed her away—and rushed toward the conference room door. "Is it my turn for questions? Because I've got tons…."

Penelope was buying her some time by being a distraction. Perfect. Gabrielle gave up trying to look in control—the eerie calm had totally fled. She rushed for the elevator.

Once she slipped inside, she risked a glanced back and saw Cooper prying himself out of Penelope's grip.

There was emotion on his face right then.

Rage.

The doors slid closed, and Gabrielle sucked in a deep breath.

It looked like the killer had been right about Cooper.

THE BLUE CONVERTIBLE squealed out of the lot just as Cooper reached the parking garage. Damn it, damn it, *damn it!* That interview had gone horribly wrong.

And now Gabrielle was just gone.

How had she found out about him?

He yanked out his phone. Waited with gritted teeth as the phone rang once, twice, then— "What's wrong?" Dylan Foxx demanded.

What wasn't? A killer was on the loose. The SOB seemed to be going right after Gabrielle, and now, his lover of less than four hours—four hours!—had just run from him as if he were the very devil.

To her, maybe he was. So much for playing the role of the white knight.

"We need containment," he said, though he hated to utter those words. But there wasn't a choice. He couldn't let Gabrielle run from him.

Someone had tipped her off about him. He had to find out just how much she knew.

With the killer targeting her, Gabrielle couldn't just vanish.

He wouldn't let her.

"Gabrielle's on the move," he said, aware that his voice snapped with fury. "Heading west from the *Inquisitor*, driving a blue convertible." He gave Dylan the license plate number.

"Are you sure containment is what you want?" Dylan asked, his tone guarded.

"Those were my orders." If he'd become compromised, if Gabrielle was put in too much danger...

He swallowed and tried to choke back the emotions filling him. "Make sure, *absolutely sure*, that no one hurts her in any way."

He didn't want her to be hurt. He didn't want her to be afraid.

But, judging by the way she'd looked at him just before those elevator doors closed, Gabrielle was *already* both hurt and afraid.

She's scared of me.

Because she'd learned the truth about him.

He was just as much of a killer as the D.C. Striker.

WHERE WAS SHE supposed to go? Back to the brownstone? Retreating to that place really wasn't an option because Cooper lived there, too.

And she couldn't go back to work—he was already

waiting back at the *Inquisitor*. Scratch that safe spot from her list.

But she also just couldn't drive aimlessly around the city all night.

Gabrielle braked to a stop at a red light. She glanced in her rearview mirror and saw a pair of headlights approaching.

The red light changed. She turned left.

So did the car behind her.

Gabrielle took a right turn.

The car turned right.

Her fingers tightened their grip on the steering wheel. She accelerated. That car accelerated, too.

Fear began to thicken within her. Fury had driven her away from Cooper, and she'd foolishly ignored the threats around her. Gabrielle couldn't ignore those threats any longer.

Is it the killer? He'd been watching her before. Had he seen her leave the *Inquisitor*? Without Cooper at her side, the killer might think this was the perfect time for him to strike.

She fumbled and yanked out her phone. For an instant, she thought about calling Cooper.

But, instead, her index finger pushed the button to connect her to Lane. She held her breath. Another red light was up ahead. The light went green. Good. No stopping.

And Lane wasn't answering. Where the heck was he when she needed him?

The green light had turned yellow. In a flash, it went red. She didn't stop. She rushed forward and ran that light.

A horn blared as a truck came right at her. Screaming, she yanked the wheel to the side even as she slammed on the brakes.

The truck missed her by only inches.

Her breath heaved out. She'd dropped her phone. She fumbled, trying to find it.

Someone rapped on her window. "Ma'am?" A woman's voice called. "Ma'am, are you are all right?"

Gabrielle rolled down her window. "Yes, sorry, I—"

The woman wasn't alone. A man stood behind her. His posture was stiff, guarded, and when he shifted his stance a bit, she saw the holster under his arm.

"I'm afraid that you have to come with us, Ms. Harper." The woman's voice wasn't so concerned any longer. It was authoritative and flat.

The truck that had nearly hit Gabrielle moments before had also come to a stop. Two more men were climbing from that vehicle. They headed toward her.

"You're EOD," she said, understanding as a chill seemed to settle over her body.

The woman stared back at her. "There are two ways to do this," the woman said, voice soft.

"Let me guess," Gabrielle muttered as she climbed from the car. "Easy and hard?"

A nod.

The armed man came closer to Gabrielle. The light from the streetlamp glinted off his dark hair. "No one's going to hurt you, ma'am," he assured her. "We're here for your protection." He smiled at her and offered his hand. "My name's Deuce."

Hesitant now, she reached for that hand. "No way is Deuce your real name…"

He yanked her forward. His left hand came up in an instant. Too late, she saw the handcuffs. Before she could jerk away from him, one cuff snapped over her wrist.

"No, it isn't," he agreed softly as he pulled her into his arms. "It's a name for second chances. Maybe you'll give old Cooper one of those chances when this mess is over."

Then she was pretty much dragged into the waiting car. The doors slammed behind her, and the vehicle raced away.

Anger pulsed through her with every mile that passed. Second chance? *Hell, no.*

COOPER SHOVED OPEN the door to Bruce Mercer's office. *"Where is she?"* The door banged against the wall behind him. Judith Rogers, Mercer's assistant, let out a screech as she tried to jerk him back.

"I told you, Marshall," Judith snapped, sounding as furious as Cooper felt, "the boss is working! You can't just barge in there!"

Yeah, he could. He had.

Mercer glanced up from his computer. "If you're referring to Gabrielle Harper, she's here, of course. Where else would she be? Especially since *you're* the one who told us to pick her up."

Cooper's hands fisted. "I want to see her." He ignored Judith's attempts to pull him back. For a small woman, she was surprisingly strong. Just not strong enough.

Mercer glanced at his assistant. "It's okay, Judith. I needed to talk with Cooper anyway."

"Yes, well," Judith stopped trying to drag Cooper out and she gave an annoyed sniff, "he needs to learn how to *not* barge into an office."

She stomped away and slammed the door quite loudly on her way out.

Cooper didn't move. "Gabrielle." Ordering that containment on her had been the hardest thing he'd ever done. He knew she had to be furious, had to feel betrayed. He needed to get to her and try to explain what was happening.

"We have her on the fourth floor."

His eyes widened. They had prisoner rooms on that floor. "Tell me that she's not—"

"Easy." Mercer lifted his hands. "She's just in an interrogation room. Deuce is guarding the door."

Guarding the door? Right. More like he was guarding *her* in order to make sure that Gabrielle didn't try to escape.

"We don't have a lot of options here," Mercer said with a shake of his head. "I can't have a reporter exposing the EOD."

Cooper tried to keep his control in place. Hard, when he already knew it had fractured. Actually, his control had been weakening since the first moment he'd met Gabrielle. "Let me talk to her."

Mercer's brows rose. "Are you so sure she will want to talk with you? I think your charm might have run its course with the reporter."

The fractures grew deeper. "I shouldn't have made that a request," Cooper threw back. "I should have said...I'm *talking to her*."

Mercer stood then. He wasn't quite as tall as Cooper, and even though Mercer had to be pushing his late fifties, he was still in top shape. "I think you're forgetting a few things, Agent Marshall," Mercer told him.

"I'm not forgetting anything." He wasn't going to let the EOD hurt Gabrielle.

"Yes, you are." Mercer marched around the desk and came toward him. "It was the EOD who saved your hide in Afghanistan. My team who pulled *you* out. Otherwise, you really would have been dead. We went there to find you when you were being held captive. We got you out."

"So now I owe you." But what about Gabrielle? He owed her, so much.

She's changed me.

Mercer's eyes were narrowed as he studied Cooper. "You're not the same agent anymore."

He didn't want to argue with Mercer. He just wanted to get down to the fourth floor.

Mercer sighed. "You can all fall so fast, and you don't even see the danger until it's too late."

"She's not a danger. I can convince her to keep the news about the EOD quiet. Let me talk to her, explain things—" She'd been running away before. He hadn't known where she was going. He'd been worried that she might have other contacts in the press that she would talk with about her new discoveries.

He'd also been worried that the rogue would get her. Fear had burned like acid within him. Cooper hadn't been able to stand the thought that Gabrielle was in the killer's path, unprotected, vulnerable.

"I think you're compromised on this one," Mercer told him bluntly. "You aren't the best agent for the job."

"What?" There was no way he'd let Mercer bench him. "*I'm* the one who's been monitoring her. I'm the one who kept the EOD out of the news. I'm the one—"

"—who slept with the reporter."

Every muscle in Cooper's body locked down. "How the hell do you know that?"

"You think that you were the only agent I had keeping tabs on her? Deuce has been watching her place. My agents always have backup close by."

"Then I guess he got a real eyeful." His control wasn't fracturing. It was splintering.

While Mercer was his same old cold self. "Emotions cloud judgment. I know what I'm talking about here."

"You mean your daughter?" They were alone, so Cooper decided to cut right to the chase. He'd worked closely with Mercer before, and he knew the man's secrets. "You let your love for Cassidy compromise you—and you nearly got her killed."

"I *did* get my wife killed," Mercer shocked him by saying. Grief flickered in his eyes. "And when I realized how dangerous I was to those closest to me, I backed the hell off." Mercer's gaze turned shuttered once more as it drifted over Cooper's face. "I backed away from the only family that I had left because I wanted to protect them."

And what? He was supposed to follow in Mercer's footsteps? Hell, no. Cooper would make his own way in this world, and he'd make his own choices. "If you think I'm backing away from Gabrielle, you're dead wrong—"

"I backed away," Mercer's voice cut though his words, "because I thought I was protecting them. But it turns out, my leaving just meant that I wasn't there when they needed me the most."

Cooper blinked. Okay. Now *that* he hadn't been expecting. "I thought you were going to say I should stay away from her. You said emotions compromise agents."

"They do. So be aware of that danger, but, no, I'm not telling you to back away from her." Mercer turned away and paced toward the window. "I had a sister. She was younger than me—ten years younger. So beautiful and sweet. After I lost my wife, I didn't want to run the risk of losing her, too."

Mercer had *never* gotten this personal with him. As far as Cooper knew, Mercer didn't get personal with anyone.

"I didn't want one of my enemies to get close to my sister," Mercer said, gazing out of that window. "I had—still have—so many folks who'd love to hurt me, and they'd do it in an instant by taking out the ones I care about in this world."

Like a sister.

Mercer's shoulders were stiff and straight, his spine

tense. "But it wasn't an enemy who took her." Sadness deepened his tone. "Cancer did that. It came in an instant. It took her from me too soon. I blinked, and she was just—gone."

Cooper rubbed his chest, pushing at the ache that was always there when he remembered his mother. "I'm sorry. My...my mother died of cancer." He could understand the pain Mercer felt.

"Did she?" The sadness deepened in Mercer's voice. "I'm sorry for your loss, too, son. So sorry..." Mercer's voice trailed away. He didn't look back at Cooper, but stared straight ahead. Cooper could see Mercer's reflection in the window's glass. "We do our best in this world. We try to protect those we love. We try to make a difference, but, in the end, we can still fail. We can still hurt. And we can still lose...."

I don't want to lose Gabrielle.

"There's one lesson I've learned. If you want to be happy in this world, then you need to find the one thing that you care about the most. When you find it, you move heaven and hell and you do *anything* you can to protect that thing." Mercer finally turned toward him. "Do you understand what I'm saying to you?"

He did. Mercer wasn't pulling him from the case. He was clearing him to do anything necessary—*to protect Gabrielle.* He hadn't expected that response from Mercer. Cooper had thought that he'd have to fight in order to stay at her side.

"Go on, get down to that fourth floor. And remember, if you need anything...day or night, you call me. You can count on me to be there for you, Marshall."

Everyone was wrong about Mercer. He wasn't the cold, emotionless director.

Cooper spun for the door.

"Annalise should've had a different ending." Mercer's words were a low mumble.

Yet Cooper heard him clearly, and he froze. "How do you know my mother's name?"

Silence. Then, "Do you really think you'd get an offer to join the EOD without me reviewing every single detail of your life?"

So Mercer had already known about his mother's cancer *before* he'd told his own story. Maybe that was why the director had revealed his past to Cooper. *He knew I'd understand.*

"The fourth floor's waiting," Mercer reminded him.

Cooper didn't want Gabrielle waiting any longer.

THE DOOR CLICKED shut behind Cooper.

Mercer glanced down. His hands were shaking. When he'd been talking with Cooper, the old pain had come back. The hurt, for what he'd lost.

Annalise. He hadn't needed to dig into Cooper's past to learn about her.

He could just close his eyes and picture sweet Anna. That long blond hair. Her wide smile and glinting eyes—the same shade as Cooper's.

She should've had a perfect life. A long life.

"I'm doing my best to protect him," Mercer whispered. By staying away, he'd missed out on being close when Annalise needed him.

So he'd made sure to keep a good eye on Cooper. When the man had been taken in Afghanistan, Mercer immediately ordered his agents to sweep in for a rescue mission.

Cooper had a love of danger—a love that put him in too much jeopardy.

If Cooper could love something more than that wild rush of adrenaline, if he could love *someone* else more…

Then the man might actually have a chance of living the life Annalise would have wanted for him.

Cooper just had to feel a deep connection for someone else. He had to *need* someone more than he needed the next mission.

Judging by the rage and fear that Mercer had seen in his eyes, the reporter was making Cooper feel that connection, all right.

Now, the trick was going to be actually keeping her alive—and convincing Gabrielle Harper that Cooper deserved a second chance with her.

Luckily, Mercer had plenty of resources at his disposal.

Besides, if Cooper was anything like his mother had been, the boy should be able to work his charm.

Mercer would just see how that charm worked on Gabrielle.

THE DOOR SQUEAKED OPEN.

Gabrielle's head lifted. Her eyes locked on the man who'd just entered her little prison.

Betrayal stabbed in her gut. She jumped to her feet, but the cuff around her left wrist—the cuff that was currently attaching her to the table leg—prevented her from charging across the room at Cooper.

He stilled. "I didn't realize… I'll get that cuff off you."

He'd better do a whole lot more than just that.

Cooper turned back around toward the door. The dark-haired, green-eyed agent—the one who'd called himself Deuce—stood behind Cooper.

"Give me the keys," Cooper demanded.

Deuce whistled as he rocked back on his heels. "Are you sure that you want to do that, man? She's likely to go right for your throat."

"The keys," Cooper gritted, and he opened his hand.

Deuce tossed him the keys. "It's a good thing you had combat training." His stare swept toward Gabrielle. "I'll just…ah…leave you two alone." He backed out of the room.

Cooper hurried toward her.

She was so furious Gabrielle didn't even know where to start. She had to bite her lip to hold back the furious yells that wanted to erupt.

His fingers closed around her wrist. His touch was warm and solid and— "You really do look good for a dead man," she told him, her eyes angry slits.

The cuff clicked open. He didn't let her wrist go. Instead, he lightly rubbed the flesh. She knew he had to feel the frantic race of her pulse beneath his fingers.

"How did you find out?" While her voice had been heated, his was soft.

"Sources, Cooper. Sources. I have them, you know." She wasn't about to throw Hugh under the bus. It was a good thing she'd taken the liberty of hiding the flash drive in Penelope's car. Otherwise, she would've lost that evidence during her little confinement time. That flash drive was her ace in the hole. It was her—

"They found the flash drive," Cooper told her. "And, soon enough, I *will* have the name of your source."

Could the night get any worse? "I guess you like going through my things." She snatched her hand back from him. "I figured it out, you know, that mysterious crash of my computer days ago…that was you, right? You and your EOD buddies."

She wanted him to deny it. To tell her that she was wrong. He hadn't really snuck into her house and sabotaged her system.

But he nodded.

Gabrielle took a step away from him as she sucked in a deep gulp of air.

"Let me explain," Cooper began. To the right, a large mirror stretched along the wall and threw their reflections back at them. She looked tired and scared and angry.

And he, damn him, looked strong and determined and too handsome.

The fact that he looked so controlled just increased her fury. "Explain? I'm a prisoner! This shouldn't be happening to me. I've got rights, but those rights were ignored when your buddies dragged me in here." She tossed her hands into the air as she backed away from him. "I wasn't Mirandized—"

"—because you aren't charged with anything," he muttered, yanking a hand through his blond hair.

"This is kidnapping." She wondered if she could run past him and make a break out of the door. They'd blindfolded her before she was brought into this building. She had no idea where she was—or even *if* she was still in D.C. They'd seemed to drive around for hours in that car.

And she'd been terrified every moment.

Cooper exhaled. "Believe it or not, you're here for your protection."

A bitter laugh escaped her. "I'll go with the 'not' option on there. I'm here because I found out your secret and you don't want me telling the world what I know."

He stalked toward her.

Coward that she was, Gabrielle backed up even more. She backed up until there was no place left to go, and she hit the wall.

Cooper kept coming.

His hands rose and flattened on either side of her head, caging her between him and the hard wall. He wasn't touching her, a very good thing, because his touch just twisted things within her even more.

"This isn't about me," he said, staring deeply into her eyes. "It's about the agents in the field. About the work that they do that requires secrecy. You can't print what you've learned about the EOD. You do that, and you compromise their lives."

"And what if the EOD is killing? What then?" She threw her accusation at him. She wanted to hurt him as she was hurting. *I trusted you.* More, she'd started to fall for the guy when he'd just been playing her.

She and Lane hadn't worked out because he wanted to put her in a glass bubble and stop her from doing everything that she loved. They'd crashed and burned fast because she hadn't wanted to give up the person who she was in order to please him. The breakup had hurt, but—

With Cooper, the pain was worse. So much worse. She'd really thought that he'd been on her side. A true partner, an equal. She'd believed that he supported what she was doing.

When he'd been sabotaging her all along.

She swallowed and tried to calm her racing heart. "Van McAdams left a very clear message—"

"Van *was* EOD," Cooper revealed, voice rumbling. "So was Lockwood. Why do you think I'm on the case? They weren't active-duty EOD any longer, but they were still *ours*. I'm trying to find their killer, and I'm working to make sure that no more agents go down."

There was more there. She'd already figured the pieces out. When she'd been cuffed in this room, Gabrielle had been given plenty of time to think. "One of your own is killing. He scaled McAdams's building, right? He did it, the same way that you told Carmichael *you* could do it.

He got easy access to those men because they knew him. They trusted him. *He's one of yours.*"

And that terrified her. Because it sure sounded like EOD agents were trained killing machines.

"The killer is a rogue," Cooper said as he leaned in even closer. "He killed two other agents that you don't even know about. He took them out, then he started going after civilians."

Her breath caught. "Kylie Archer."

"From what we can tell, she was the first non–EOD agent." His face hardened. "The agents you don't know about yet were Jessica Flintwood and Frank Malone. They were partners, a team."

Just like she'd been partners with Cooper.

"He killed Jessica first. He slit her throat, just like with the others. Then he took out Frank a few weeks later."

Her eyelids flickered. "He kills a woman, then a man." But…with Kylie and Lockwood, they'd been a couple. So had Melanie and Van. Her gaze widened. "Were Jessica and—ah, Frank, were they involved?"

He frowned at her. "What?"

"Were they involved?" She could see the pattern, it was right there. "A couple. Just like the others."

"I don't know…" His head cocked to the right. "They worked together closely. Agents aren't supposed to cross that line, so if they were, they would've kept it quiet."

"But he found out." It made sense to her, but Cooper was still frowning. "He's targeting the women first, then going after their men." She didn't know why, but the killer had a pattern, a routine that he was following."

"Right now," his voice roughened, "I'm worried he's going after *you*." A grim pause, then Cooper said, "He's calling *you*, breaking into *your* house, targeting *you*."

His words made her afraid, but she wasn't about to give into fear then.

"But it's not going to happen," he promised her. "Because I am not going to let anyone hurt you."

Before she could say anything else, his head lowered, and his mouth pressed to hers.

NOELLE EVERS JOLTED. "That's it. That's why he does it!"

Deuce Porter glanced at her. "Ma'am, that's a kiss." His smile was wide. "Maybe we should step out of observation and give those two some privacy."

Mercer had sent her down to watch the interaction between Cooper and Gabrielle, because he'd thought Gabrielle might speak more freely to that agent.

Mercer had been right.

But what she'd learned, the profile that was developing before her, it wasn't what she'd expected. "I have to see Mercer."

Deuce's brows climbed. "I thought you'd be talking to all of us. You know…figuring out which one of us has snapped and gone crazy." He shrugged. "Though you'll no doubt have a hard time picking just one candidate. I think we're all a little crazy."

"I know what he's doing," she said, excitement growing within her. "*Why* he's doing it." The why was the most important part. Once you understood a killer's motivation, that made the perp vulnerable. You could manipulate him then.

Trap him.

She hurried for the door.

"Why?" Deuce asked, the question a growl. "I'd like to know why he killed my friend. Lockwood and I—we worked plenty of missions together. He was a good man. He didn't deserve to go down like that."

She couldn't tell the agent why. She was only supposed to talk with Mercer. Just him.

Noelle opened the door and hurried into the hallway. She was in such a hurry to get to Mercer that she slammed straight into the man standing there.

Big, strong, with midnight-black hair and dark, golden eyes, the fellow caught her in an instant and held her in a steady grip.

"Dragon, you don't want to be getting too close to her…" Deuce warned from behind her. "She's Mercer's profiler. She's here to find out which one of us has gone psychotic."

Dragon?

The man before her slowly released his hold on her.

"Of course, after what happened to you on that last mission, maybe *you* should be talking to her," Deuce mused. "How many of your captors did you kill? And all without even a single weapon."

She shouldn't be hearing this. She should be rushing for the elevator and hurrying up to see Mercer.

Instead, Noelle found it hard to look away from that man's golden eyes. She frowned at him, a pulse of recognition stirring within her. "Have we met before, agent?"

His lips curved in the faintest of smiles. "I've seen you, but I don't think you've seen me, Doctor."

Then he turned around and headed down the hallway. His movements were absolutely soundless, and he moved with an easy, catlike grace.

Deuce came to her side. "Be careful with him," he murmured. "I mean it, Agent Evers. I've never seen a more deadly agent, and I've been here for almost seven years now. That guy doesn't get close to anyone, and when he kills…" His breath rushed out. "We're supposed to have remorse, aren't we? We're supposed to be more than just machines, following orders." His hands shoved into his pockets. "People should matter more than just mission orders."

Yes, they should.

She cleared her throat and hurried for the elevator. Noelle slipped inside.

She wasn't in that elevator alone.

The man Deuce had called "Dragon" was there. He didn't speak as they rode up that elevator together.

Goose bumps rose on her arms.

There was something about him.

One look, and he'd scared her.

One look, and he'd—

The elevator chimed. The doors opened. Noelle nearly tripped as she rushed out and toward the desk of Mercer's assistant.

Before she could even ask to see the director, he was there, frowning at her. "What's wrong? What happened?"

It wasn't what *had* already happened that made her fear so much.

They went back into Mercer's office. He closed the door, sealing them inside. She tried to calm her racing heartbeat. "Kylie Archer was involved with Keith Lockwood."

His brow furrowed. "I already told you—"

"Your rogue killed her in order to get at Lockwood. She was the easy kill, the one who wouldn't expect his attack. Then, while Lockwood was grieving, while he was weak with his loss, the killer went after him."

The pairs made so much sense to her now. Once she'd realized that the first two victims were also intimately connected, she understood why the rogue was taking out the women first. *Because he wants the men to suffer more. He wants them to mourn for what they've lost.*

Mercer's expression tightened. "He did the same thing with Melanie and Van."

Yes, he had. "He's killing the women, almost executing them, and I think he is doing it just to make their lovers suffer. He wants them to hurt, to grieve. When they're broken, then he goes in—"

"—for the kill," Mercer finished.

"He's doing it again. It's already in motion. I can see it now." Her words were coming out too fast, so she tried to slow them down. "Gabrielle Harper. He's not talking to her because she's the reporter investigating his kills. He's focused on her because of her relationship to Cooper." A very personal relationship, judging by what she'd just seen in that interrogation room. "He's already told us—we just didn't realize—Gabrielle is his next target. And, once she's dead…"

His voice and face grim, Mercer said, "He'll go after Cooper."

Chapter Ten

He shouldn't be kissing her. He should be taking things slower, trying to soothe her. Trying to mend the fences that he'd destroyed.

But he needed her. So much.

His body pressed against hers, and Cooper knew that Gabrielle had to feel the force of his arousal. For her.

Everything was for her.

Her hands flew up and grabbed his shoulders. He tensed, expecting her to push him away.

Then her mouth parted beneath his. Her tongue met his. She kissed him back with the same raw, wild need that he felt.

In that moment, she nearly brought him to his knees.

Everything was going to be all right. Gabrielle understood why he'd kept his true identity secret. They could go back to the way things had been before.

Her taste made him light-headed, desperate for more.

His hands locked around her. He pulled her against him, holding the curve of her hips.

But then she shoved against him. "No." Her voice was husky but brimming with anger. "Just because I want you, you *aren't* going to get away with what you've done to me."

Tears glittered in her gorgeous eyes. Actual tears.

"I trusted you. You broke into my home. You destroyed evidence."

"I was following orders." Those words seemed hollow to his ears.

She edged away from him. "That's what you're still doing. Let me guess…whoever runs this place told you to come in here and charm me again?"

He wasn't touching that one.

She laughed, and the sound wasn't like her at all. Gabrielle wasn't that bitter. Gabrielle was open, happy.

"This isn't going to work. *We* aren't going to work." She headed for the door.

He had to stop her. Cooper hated to do it, but he stepped into her path.

Her head tilted back as she stared up at him. "What are you going to do?" Gabrielle asked him as she swiped a hand over her cheek. "Handcuff me again?"

"No." *Stay calm. Stay calm.* But it was hard because he felt like his world was unraveling before his eyes. "I'm going to make sure that you're free to go, but in return, you have to do something for me."

"I get to just walk out of here?" Doubt was plain on her face.

"We have your flash drive. You don't know anything else about the EOD, nothing concrete. And if you try to cover the story, you *will* put lives at risk." He crossed his arms over his chest and studied her. "That's not who you are. You bring justice to families. You don't go out and try to hurt anyone."

"You actually sound as if you know me."

"I do." Better than he'd known any other lover.

"I wish I could say the same about you."

Hit. The woman was lethal with her words.

"But I don't know you," Gabrielle continued on fiercely. "I feel like I'm staring straight at a stranger."

"You're staring at your lover." She wasn't going to deny that—deny *them*.

She gave a hard shake of her head. "I'm staring at an EOD agent who's done nothing but lie to me."

"I'm the one who got you out of Lockwood's place so the cops wouldn't find you there. I'm the one who's been helping you." She might not want to see the truth now, but sooner or later, she'd have to look past her rage.

I want sooner.

"We can keep helping each other," he told her, trying to keep the desperate edge out of his words. "We make a good team, Gabrielle, and that doesn't have to end. Agree to drop any inquiries into the EOD, and I'll talk to my boss. I'll get you out of here."

Her eyelashes flickered. "Why did I get dragged into this place? If I already had an EOD agent with me day *and* night, then why did I—" She broke off as her eyes widened. *"You."*

Hell. This was about to go from bad to worse.

"*You* were chasing after me. I ran from you, and you called in your backup, didn't you?"

His back teeth had locked. "A killer is out there. After *you*. What was I supposed to do? Let you run straight into danger?"

"You don't even know that he's after me—"

The door opened behind Cooper.

"Yes," Bruce Mercer's distinct voice said clearly. "We do know that the killer is after you, Ms. Harper. And if you want to keep living, then I would suggest that you calm down and get used to the idea of working with the EOD."

THE PROFILER WAS too damn good.

She'd been poking her head in where it didn't belong, getting too close.

Trying to learn too much about me.

He hadn't thought Mercer would pull in an outsider to hunt him.

He'd underestimated the bastard.

He hurried down the hallway. Other agents were working, barely glancing his way.

They knew that a killer was among them. Did they care?

No, because we're all killers.

Some just hid that truth a bit better than others.

He rounded the corner. His gaze cut to the office on the right.

She was there.

He sucked in a deep breath and walked closer to her door.

Then he heard her laugh.

Rachel Mancini wasn't alone, and there was only one man that ever made her laugh.

A few more steps and he saw that Dylan Foxx was leaning over her, putting his body too close to hers.

The fool gave away too much when he looked at Rachel. He made the same mistakes that Frank Malone had made with his Jessica.

His glances were too possessive, his posture too protective.

Rachel might not feel the same way that Dylan did, but what did that matter?

He needed a distraction, someone else for the profiler and Mercer to focus on.

He'd change the order of his game. Move his pieces around the board a bit.

Rachel glanced up then. The smile was still on her pretty face as she looked at him.

Time for my attack.

He stepped into her office.

COOPER BRACED HIS body in front of Gabrielle's. "You shouldn't be here," he said flatly.

Wait, who was he talking to? Gabrielle peered around his shoulder. The older man with the gray at his temples or Agent Evers?

Gabrielle pushed onto her tiptoes and tried to see a bit better.

"No." Cooper spun around and grabbed her shoulders. "The less you know about him, the better off you are."

Her heart slammed into her ribs. Just when she'd thought that things surely couldn't get any worse...

"Don't be so certain," the man replied. "I'm here to offer Ms. Harper a very special deal, one that I think she'll accept, if she wants to keep living."

She met that man's stare, feeling a wave of shock sweep over her. "Are you threatening me?"

The man was handsome, tall, fit...and dangerous. The danger clung to him like a second skin.

Noelle Evers stood beside him, and she kept glancing nervously at the fellow.

"I don't threaten," the man said simply. "Threats are a waste of time. It's actions that matter."

Cooper dropped his hold on her.

Gabrielle shook her head. "Who are you?"

"Let's just say I'm an old friend of your boss's."

Doubtful. "Are you the same 'friend' who convinced Hugh to take his little out-of-town trip?"

He flashed a grim smile. "Guilty."

Okay. Her breath was icy in her lungs. She wasn't

just looking at another agent. "You're the one in charge here, huh?"

His head inclined.

"You're in danger," Noelle said, her words sharp. "I think you're the killer's next victim."

Was that true? Or just the EOD's way of trying to keep Gabrielle in line?

"I believe that he's going to come after you—" Noelle advanced toward her "—in order to hurt Cooper."

Her temples were throbbing. "How would targeting me do anything to Cooper?"

Beside her, Cooper growled. Actually growled.

Her gaze shot to him.

"It would do plenty." He'd never looked at her quite that way before. The intensity in his eyes scorched through her.

For a moment, Gabrielle was at a loss.

"You need protection." The big boss seemed definite on this point. "The local cops can't handle this killer—"

"—because he's someone you trained, and now you can't control him?" Yep. There she went. Saying perhaps a wee bit too much to a man who could probably make her vanish in five seconds flat. Actually, he'd *already* made her vanish.

Mr. Mysterious stared at her.

Just stared.

She stared back, not about to let him think he was pushing her around—even if he was.

"I want this rogue stopped," he said clearly. "And I also want you to keep living. Despite what you may believe about me, my organization doesn't target innocents. We *save* them."

"The killer isn't saving anyone, and he's part of *your* organization."

Mr. Mysterious glowered at her.

Noelle focused on Gabrielle. "He's called you. He's broken into your house."

Gabrielle's eyes darted to Cooper, then back to Noelle. "There seems to be a lot of that going around."

Noelle's lips tightened. "The next move he makes could be to kill you."

She wasn't in the mood to die.

Cooper's boss straightened his, well, *already* ramrod-straight shoulders. "There are over two dozen of my agents currently working undercover missions. They are putting their lives on the line in order to protect innocents." That gaze of his was practically arctic. "Before we go any farther, I have to know that I can trust you, Ms. Harper."

Wait. He doubted *her?* "I'm not the one who's been pretending here!"

"Gabrielle," Cooper snapped out.

"Don't 'Gabrielle' me." She marched right up to Mr. Mysterious. "Look, I'm not interested in blowing the covers of your agents. I'm interested in stopping this killer. I made a promise to Kylie Archer's little brother. I told him I'd do everything possible to give his sister justice, and I mean to do exactly that."

"Even if the price you pay for that justice is your own life?" The man asked her. "Don't you think that price is too steep?" His gaze slid to Cooper. "I can already tell you, *he* thinks it's too high."

"I don't plan on dying," she managed to say. "I'm not blowing the covers of your agents, and I'm not winding up in a morgue." She paused. "Happy now? Can I go?"

"Once you agree to let Agent Marshall stick to your side—24/7—yes, then I'll be...happy."

She wasn't sure anything could truly make this guy happy. "Why are we even playing this game? You're going to stick me with your agent, no matter what I say."

His eyes seemed to warm as he studied her. "Cooper was right, you know. The two of you did make a good team."

Her gaze snapped to the mirror. She'd been in enough police stations to know how those two-way viewing mirrors worked. "I wondered how much of an audience we had."

Apparently, a pretty big one.

Gabrielle sighed. To get out of that place, she'd be ready to promise plenty. "I agree to the deal."

"You won't regret it," Cooper promised softly.

She already did. Actually, there were quite a few things she regretted concerning Cooper Marshall, but she'd shared enough with these folks.

"We're going to be monitoring your phone line. If he calls you again, we'll trace his call," the big boss said.

"I'm surprised you weren't already monitoring me," she muttered.

Cooper's cheeks flushed. "We were," he confessed. "After the first phone call—"

"Right, I got it." She shoved back her hair. "So I'm a target, the killer is coming, and I'm supposed to be the bait to lure him out. I think I'm up to speed now." Though she'd rather not be just then.

"You're not bait," Cooper immediately denied. His arm brushed against hers. "You're my partner. I keep telling you that. We're working together from here on out."

She wanted to believe him.

She couldn't.

"Cooper Marshall is the only EOD agent that you should trust," the boss told her.

Her eyebrows lifted at that warning.

"The others you've met—Rachel, Dylan—I don't want you alone with any of them. Cooper was out of the country when I first became aware of the rogue. Cooper is clear." Spoken flatly. "Trust him."

Noelle nodded. "And I'm going to finish working up my profile. Understanding why the rogue is killing is key. He's targeting the women first for a special reason. I—I think it's even possible that the man we're after lost some-one that he cared about, and now he's determined to take out his rage on the other agents. He wants them to feel the same pain, the same agony that he experienced."

Cooper frowned. "He's punishing *us?*"

"By taking away what you value most," the boss told him. "So remember the advice I gave you. Do whatever is necessary, Cooper, to protect what matters most."

GABRIELLE COULD ONLY see darkness. Another blindfold covered her eyes. Only this time, Cooper had been the one to blindfold her.

She might have gotten an audience with the mysterious EOD boss, but apparently she didn't have enough clear-ance to learn the EOD's address.

A door shut. Cooper took her hand, as he'd already done several times. A car engine growled, and then she heard the distinct sound of wheels rolling away.

Their ride—heading back to the EOD.

She waited, expecting Cooper to remove the blindfold. When he didn't, she tensed. *What's next?*

His fingers curled around her elbow, and he led her forward. He guided her up a set of steps.

A wind chime sounded. A familiar sound. It was *her* wind chime.

Her hands lifted, and Gabrielle ripped that blindfold away.

They were back at the brownstone.

So much for not being bait.

Cooper stood beside her. He stared at her with wary eyes. The guy was right to be wary. The darkness of the night surrounded him, and the only light spilled from the porch. In that harsh light, his face seemed carved from granite. The shadows and darkness surrounded him.

He opened the front door.

Right. They couldn't just stand out there. They'd no doubt make a perfect target if they did that.

She hurried inside and immediately went toward the stairs.

"Gabrielle." He caught her hand, stilling her before she could escape. "My place. Day and night, remember?"

Like she could forget.

Seething, she followed him. She understood why the EOD needed to be kept secret. She understood that he was doing his job.

But why did he make love to me?

That part, she didn't get it. The idea that he'd just been using her, trying to get close to her so that he could gather intel…that part hurt the most.

She made her way into his apartment, too aware of every move that he made. He shut the door behind her. She took five more steps—then froze. "Are we being watched?" The way she'd been watched back at the EOD?

"We could be under surveillance," he admitted as he came toward her.

Not what she wanted to hear. "Video equipment? Audio surveillance?" The whole place could be bugged. "Did they see what we did?" Her voice was a horrified whisper.

If he'd let the other agents watch them…she felt her cheeks burn.

Cooper gave a hard shake of his head. "Do you think I would let that happen? That was about me and you, and no one else."

Her breath rushed out in relief. She turned away.

"Don't treat me like a stranger."

Her hands trembled. She rubbed her fingers over her jean-clad thighs. "Isn't that what you are? I mean, I lay down next to my lover—a living, breathing man I trusted, but then I found out that he was some secret agent, and that he'd supposedly died on a mission in Afghanistan."

"I *should* have died. I was shot to hell and back—"

The image of his scars flashed through her mind.

"But somehow Mercer found out about me."

Mercer. She filed that name into her vault.

"I don't even know how I showed up on the guy's radar," Cooper continued. "He found out about me. He came for me. His Shadow Agents burst onto the scene, they dragged me out of that hell, and they brought me back to life." His shoulders rolled back as if he were trying to push away the memory. "But by that point, everyone on my original team already thought I was dead. And it wasn't like I had any family. I never knew my dad. Cancer took my mother when I was a teenager. Hell, I already felt like a ghost, so when Mercer made me an offer, I took it."

He turned on the lamp near him, and more light spilled across the room.

"I've worked with the EOD since then. The agents do their missions, and like Mercer said, we save lives."

It wasn't that simple. "One of the agents is taking lives."

He paced toward her. "And it's *our* job to stop him. I didn't expect you to get involved. You were my neighbor. The sexy girl who slipped into my fantasies. I'd known only blood and death until you." He swallowed. "Then you were in my world, looking so beautiful and smelling of lilacs."

She had lilac body lotion. A gift from Penelope.

"But then I found you at Lockwood's apartment. You

were in the wrong place. Hell, you almost walked *right* in on me."

Another piece of the puzzle snapped into place. *He'd been in Lockwood's apartment.* "That was why the door was open." He'd been there, first, before her. "You broke in to that apartment."

He nodded, and kept coming closer to her. "No one had heard from Lockwood in days. I knew something was wrong, and I had to get inside to him."

"How did you get out—" Gabrielle began, then stopped because she realized what he'd done. "You scaled the building."

Another nod. "The same way that the killer did."

Because they were the same—the same training, the same deadly instincts.

"Everything changed when you got involved," he said again. "Protecting you became a priority for me. I only called the EOD in because I didn't have a choice. I knew the killer had you in his sights—after that phone call, how could there be any doubt? It was too risky for you to go off alone."

"You thought I was going to blow your cover. You thought—"

"I thought that if anything happened to you, I'd go crazy." He was right in front of her. Not touching her, but seeming to surround her.

She shook her head. "You don't have to paint some fake story about how you feel, okay? You had orders. You had—"

"I'd had *you,*" he told her bluntly. The burn in her cheeks got even worse. "I'd had you, and there was no going back. It wasn't about one night—I want more than that from you. I want a hell of a lot more."

The first time she'd met him, Gabrielle had known that he was out of her league. Too intense. Too fierce.

And, damn him, too sexy.

"I'll have you again," Cooper said.

Her jaw dropped.

"Because you want me. You're angry, rightly so, but you still want me." He took her hand. Put it over his chest. Over the heart that she could feel racing so frantically. "And I want you. More than I've ever wanted another woman. The way I feel for you isn't about a mission. It's not about anything, but us."

Was he about to kiss her? She didn't want him to kiss her. Oh, dang it, she was the liar now. She wanted his mouth more than breath right then, but she was also scared.

Of him.

Of the way he made her feel.

Of making a mistake. *I'm already in too deep with him.*

"What do I need to do—" his words were a deep, sexy rumble "—to get you back again?"

"I don't want secrets." Her words surprised her. She'd meant to pull away from him.

Hadn't she?

So why was she edging closer? And why did she continue, saying, "I don't want any lies. I might not have your EOD clearance, but that doesn't mean you get to jerk me around." His heart was still racing beneath her touch. Only fair, considering her heart felt as if it would jump out of her chest. "And if we're partners, really partners, then that means you don't leave me behind. We work together. We share everything."

He was staring straight down at her.

She just didn't want…*secrets*.

"I should be running from you right now," Gabrielle

said. That would have been the smart thing to do, but her heart wasn't interested in smart. Her heart just wanted her to be close to him.

He'd gotten past her defenses. He'd gotten to her. She was afraid that she wouldn't be the same ever again.

"If you ran, I'd follow." His voice was deeper, sending a shiver over her spine. "I think I might just follow you any place you go."

Gabrielle couldn't pull her gaze from his. His stare burned. "Tell me...tell me that you didn't sleep with me for the case."

His hands lifted and curled around her hips. They seemed to singe her through her clothes. "I slept with you because you were driving me out of my mind. Fantasies weren't enough to keep me sane. What happened between us had nothing to do with the case."

That was good. That was— "If you ever have me handcuffed again, you are going to have some serious trouble on your hands."

He smiled at her. A smile that reached his eyes and made her heart ache. "Sweetheart, if I handcuff you again, you'll be in my bed—and trouble will be the last thing I get."

That was...*oh*. His mouth took hers. She let go of her fear and her anger because right then, they didn't matter.

She wasn't sure how much time they had left together. With the killer out there, there was no way to determine their future.

So she forgot about the future.

She let go of the past.

Gabrielle just held on to him.

His tongue thrust into her mouth. His hands curled around her hips and lifted her up against the hard bulge of his arousal. She met him, kissing him back with a fierce desire that grew and grew within her.

She'd never been the kind of girl to get swept off her feet...

Cooper raised her higher in his arms.

...until now.

He took a few steps, and her back hit the wall. He didn't release her. He kept her pinned there, and she twisted, arching against his hips.

Need rose to a feverish pitch within her as his mouth trailed down her neck. He licked her, kissed the curve of her throat. Had her gasping and digging her nails into his shoulders.

"I can't get enough of you." One of his hands yanked her shirt over her head. He held her easily. Sometimes, she forgot just how strong he was. He lifted her a few more inches, and his mouth pressed to the curve of her breast, right above the lace of her bra. "Your scent drives me *crazy.*"

He was driving *her* crazy. It hadn't been like this before. With Lane, the passion had been slow to build. She'd been hesitant, unsure.

There was no room for uncertainty with Cooper. He swept her up into a storm of need. Pleasure already pulsed through her. She wanted him naked. Wanted to wrap her body around him and hold on as tight as she could.

He'd gotten rid of her bra. Those fast fingers of his. His mouth closed around one breast, and desire pierced through her. She curled her legs around his hips.

She hated not being able to touch his skin, so Gabrielle yanked up his shirt.

He helped her toss it across the room. Heat radiated off him. Those hard, rippling muscles. So much power. But he was always so careful with her. So very careful.

And he was making her wait. *"Cooper..."*

His hand was at the snap of her jeans. The snap popped free, and her zipper hissed down. Then his fingers were pushing inside the material. Pleasure wasn't just close. He stroked her, caressing her sensitive folds. His fingers drove into her. Pleasure exploded within her at his touch. She jerked against him, caught off guard by the fast rush of her release.

"You're so damned beautiful." He carried her into the bedroom. The bed dipped beneath their weight. In moments, he'd finished stripping and their clothes were scattered across the floor.

He took care of the protection, then he came back toward her.

But this time, Gabrielle wanted her chance to explore him.

She pushed him back on the bed. Cooper hesitated, frowning at her.

She smiled at him, even as the desire rose once more. Bending forward, she put her knees on either side of Cooper's body. Her mouth pressed to his throat. When he groaned, and his hands flew up to hold her hips, Gabrielle knew that she'd just found Cooper's weak spot.

Her tongue licked over his skin. Then she slid down. She explored his chest. Those muscles that just begged to be—

Licked.

She kissed his scars. Gabrielle hated the pain that Cooper had suffered, and as she felt those scars with her fingers and lips, she realized just how close he truly had come to death.

What if he'd really died on that mission? What if I'd never met him?

Her eyes squeezed shut. She didn't want to think of a

world without him. He'd come to mean so much to her, so quickly.

She placed another kiss on his scar, on the one right above his hip. Her fingers slid down—

"Enough!" The word was growled. He tumbled her onto her back. Positioned himself between her legs. "Sweetheart, I can't take any more."

His fingers threaded through hers as he thrust into her.

She'd found release moments before, but the instant he drove into her, that wonderful friction from his body had her tensing.

Eagerly, she met him. Thrust for thrust. The need spiraled and built. The desire beat between them.

There were no more words. She didn't have the breath to talk. Their lovemaking was fast and raw and consuming.

Her hips rose to meet him. Her heart raced.

When her release hit her, Gabrielle's whole body tightened. The pleasure was so intense—rolling over her in endless waves.

Cooper kissed her. He shuddered against her then drove into her core once more.

A tear leaked from the corner of her eye. Nothing had been like that for her before.

Moments passed, and the only sound she heard was the ragged catch of their breaths.

Finally, Cooper's head lifted. His eyes held hers. "The case has nothing to do with what is happening between us. Right here, right now, it's only about you and it's about me."

She wished that things could stay this way.

Because as she gazed up at him, cloaked in the shadows of the room. Gabrielle realized just why his betrayal had hurt her so much.

And why, even despite the secrets he'd kept, she hadn't been able to turn away from him.

I'm falling in love with Cooper.

No, not falling.

She was already in love with her secret agent.

His mouth pressed to her cheek. He kissed the tear that she'd shed. And then he held her close.

Fear snaked through her because she liked the way his arms felt around her. She liked it too much.

The case had brought him to her.

Would the case also take him away?

RACHAEL MANCINI WAS exhausted. She'd just pulled a twenty-hour shift at the EOD's headquarters, and she was due back on duty at 0900. She shut her apartment door behind her, threw the lock and seriously thought about collapsing right there.

Into a very unglamorous puddle on her floor.

She lifted a weary hand and raked it through her hair. She'd crash in bed. After all, she was about 50 percent sure she could make it to the bedroom. After a few hours of refueling, she'd meet up with Dylan again.

He'd dropped her off, and the team leader had said he'd be back to pick her up so they could head in to the EOD together.

She shuffled away from the door.

Ten minutes later, she was just climbing into the haven of her bed when she heard knocking.

What the hell? She glanced at her clock. *No one* should be coming to her place at this hour.

Rachel grabbed her gun and padded, barefoot, for the door. She glanced through the peephole.

The Dragon waited on the other side of that door.

Her hands trembled around the weapon.

Thomas "Dragon" Anthony was a martial arts expert. He'd worked with the EOD since she'd been brought on board. The guy was quiet, dangerous—and he made her nervous. She'd heard too many tales about just how deadly he could be.

In the EOD, *all* of the agents were lethal. But Thomas was in a category all by himself.

She curled her fingers around the weapon and opened the door a few inches. Rachel kept her security chain in place, not that it would do any good at keeping someone like Thomas out.

Not if he wanted in.

"What are you doing here?" Rachel demanded as she kept her gun close.

His golden eyes glittered at her. "I was worried about you. I heard about the profile that's developing for the killer."

A profile that indicated the rogue was going after couples, killing one victim to make the other weaker.

"You don't need to worry about me." She and Thomas weren't close. Actually, as far as she knew, *no one* was close to the Dragon. He didn't let anyone close. But...

She'd saved his life. On a mission in the Middle East, Rachel had been on the team that pulled Thomas out of his prison. Sure, his captors had been dead by the time she arrived—courtesy of a weaponless Thomas—but he'd been bleeding out from the wounds he'd sustained.

She'd put pressure on the worst wound, had *kept* that wound closed all during the rough flight to freedom.

Not that Thomas knew about what she'd done. He'd lost consciousness right after takeoff.

"I think you and Dylan could be the next targets," Thomas said. His voice was deep, rumbling, and completely without any accent.

She blinked at his words, and she made sure her grip on the weapon remained steady. Thomas couldn't see her gun, but if he made a move toward her, she'd have it up in an instant.

After what had happened to the other EOD deaths, she wasn't going to trust anyone—

Except Dylan.

"You're wrong," she heard herself say. "We aren't a couple. We wouldn't come up on the guy's radar."

Thomas shook his head. "I see, so others see. I wanted to warn you."

Adrenaline pumped through her. She wasn't exactly feeling sleepy any longer. "You could have just called me."

His hands were fisted. A show of emotion, unusual for Thomas. "They're going to think it's me," he said softly.

Alarms were going off in her head.

"I lost her...my second mission. I lost her, and when the profiler digs through our files, she's going to think it's me." His breath heaved out. "It isn't."

"You need to talk to Noelle—"

"Warning you was priority."

But why hadn't he *called*?

His eyes glittered at her. "Can I come in?"

No way. "We can talk in the morning." They just had a bit of the waning night left. "I'll be at headquarters by 0900."

He leaned toward her. "You have to be careful—"

Rachel lifted her gun. "I am."

Every minute. Every moment.

"I'm going to ask you again," Rachel murmured. "Why didn't you just call me?"

He blinked. "I did. You didn't answer. That's why I was so worried. You fit the rogue's profile—I had to warn you."

She didn't buy his story. "You warned me. Now, we'll talk more tomorrow." Her immediate plans included a fast and frantic late-night call to Dylan. He needed to know about this little visit.

Thomas nodded. "Stay safe, Mancini." After one more long look at her, he turned away.

She didn't move. Not until she saw him head down the stairs.

Then she locked her door. Double-checked those locks. She put the gun down on the end table and hurried back into her bedroom to find her phone.

She grabbed it from her purse. Of course, it was working, it was—

Dead.

Rachel frowned. She'd charged the phone earlier. It should be fine. Damn it. She needed to contact Dylan, but she didn't have a landline, just her cell.

The floor creaked behind her.

Rachel froze.

She knew every inch of her apartment and just where to step for those familiar creaks and squeaks to sound. Because she knew the place so well, Rachel realized that someone was standing five feet behind her. Right inside the doorway.

The lights flashed off in her bedroom.

She didn't waste time screaming. Rachel turned and went in for the attack.

Chapter Eleven

Dylan Foxx knew that he shouldn't be hanging around Rachel's place.

He was starting to hit stalker territory.

He'd dropped her off thirty minutes ago. He'd left... but come back.

He'd learned about the profile that Agent Evers was working up—she thought the rogue was attacking couples. Eliminating the woman first then going after her lover.

That profile had made him worried.

He and Rachel weren't lovers, but...

...but I wish we were.

He'd wanted Rachel for years. Keeping his distance from her was impossible for him. He knew that he was too protective of her, that he got too close whenever she was near.

What if someone else had noticed that closeness, too?

What if the desire he felt for her caused Rachel to be put in danger?

His growing fear had driven him back to her place. It had made him lurk in the shadows of her apartment because he couldn't shake the feeling that something wasn't right.

He looked down at his phone. Maybe he should give her a call, just in case.

Then he heard the sound of footsteps coming quickly toward him.

He glanced up. The moonlight showed him the face of the man approaching—a familiar face.

Thomas Anthony.

In an instant, Dylan had grabbed the other man, jerking him to a stop. "What the hell are you doing here?" Dylan demanded.

He had his gun at the other man's throat.

Thomas stilled. "Easy…"

"Don't 'easy' me," Dylan snarled right back. Easy was the last thing he felt. "Why the hell are you coming out of Rachel's building at this damn time?"

The streetlight fell on Thomas's face. "That's why," he murmured. "I know how you feel, and I thought the killer might, too. I came to warn her."

Dylan thought he might be looking at the killer. Keeping his gun in place, he yanked up his phone with his left hand. He pressed the screen, instantly calling for Rachel.

"You're not going to get her," Thomas told him. "Her phone isn't working."

Rachel wasn't picking up.

He glanced up at her apartment on the top floor—the one on the far left end. All of her lights were off.

His back teeth ground together. "If you've hurt her…"
You're a dead man.

He wasn't scared of Thomas Anthony. No matter what stories circulated about the so-called Dragon, Dylan didn't care. He'd take the man down in an instant.

And if Thomas had hurt Rachel…*I'll tear him apart.*

"We're going upstairs," Dylan snapped. He'd see for himself that Rachel was fine.

Thomas turned around and headed toward the building. Dylan kept his gun at the man's back. They knew the rogue was EOD, and Thomas—an EOD agent with a shady past—*happened* to be at Rachel's place? To warn her? No way was he buying that story.

"I just left her," Thomas said. "She was very much alive, I assure you."

They climbed the stairs. No one else stirred in the apartment building.

Dylan's hands were sweating. He'd been in every hell-hole on earth during his time as a SEAL, and he'd been coolly calm during every single mission. Yet as he hurried toward Rachel's apartment, his stomach knotted and fear thickened his blood.

A few more steps and they were at her apartment. He pounded on the door.

No sound emerged from inside Rachel's home.

He reached for the knob. *Locked.*

"Rachel!" He called out her name. Her neighbors could just get angry with him for yelling. He had to see her. "Open the door!"

But there was still no response.

"Something's wrong," Thomas said. Fear flashed across his face. "She came to the door within minutes when I was here before."

Dylan lifted his foot and kicked that door in.

He ran inside. "Rachel!"

A faint moan reached his ears.

He tore through the house, flying to her bedroom. It was pitch-black in there. He hit the light switch.

Dylan saw her crumpled on the floor. Blood was all around her. She was so still. So still.

"No!" The roar burst from him, and, in the next instant, he was on his knees beside her. With shaking hands he turned Rachel over. Her dark hair fell over his arm.

Blood.

"She fought him," Thomas muttered from behind

Dylan. "Not like the others. She had a chance to fight for her life."

There were stab wounds on her chest, defensive wounds on her arms. And Dylan was afraid that she would die in his arms.

He yanked up his weapon, but didn't let her go. "You did this," he said as he took aim at the Dragon.

Thomas had his hands in front of him. No weapon, but that didn't mean the guy wasn't carrying a bloody knife. "It wasn't me, I swear! I came to warn her, just like I said before." He inched forward. "Let me help her. She helped me once, saved my life…"

"Take another step, and you'll have a bullet in your brain."

Rachel's blood was on his hands. Rachel was *dying* in his arms.

"I didn't do this," Thomas told him. "The apartment was locked from the inside."

And her bedroom window was wide open.

"I came out the front," Thomas continued doggedly. "I was with you, but whoever did this, *he's* getting away."

Thomas started to advance toward them.

Dylan fired his weapon.

THE RINGING PHONE woke Cooper, yanking him from a dream. He'd been running in that dream, desperately trying to get close to Gabrielle.

The loud ringing came again, and his eyes snapped open. The dream vanished.

Gabrielle was in his arms. *Safe.*

And the phone wasn't stopping.

"Cooper?" Her voice was husky, sexy. "Has something happened?"

A call at this hour *had* to mean something had gone wrong. He grabbed for the phone. "Marshall."

There was a murmur of voices. Then, "Rachel's hurt. The rogue went after her. *Her.*" Dylan's voice shook.

"She's alive." Cooper worried his clenched grip would shatter the phone. But Dylan had said *hurt,* not *dead.*

"Barely," was Dylan's low whisper. "We're in the ER, and I'm not leaving her. I found Thomas Anthony at her place."

The Dragon?

"She's bad," Dylan told him, and Cooper heard the pain and fear in the other man's voice. "I'm not sure she'll make it—"

"I'm on my way," Cooper promised.

"No! Don't come here—get to the EOD. Mercer took Thomas in for questioning after I shot the bastard."

Wait—Dylan had shot him?

"Get to the EOD." Dylan's voice grated over the line. "Find out the truth. Thomas swore he was innocent—"

But obviously Dylan hadn't bought that story, or he wouldn't have shot the guy.

"Prove his innocence or prove his guilt," Dylan ordered.

Cooper looked to the left. He found Gabrielle's wide eyes on him. "I will." He ended the call and just stared at Gabrielle for a moment.

"What is it?" Worry shone in her eyes.

Cooper swallowed. "We were wrong about you being the next target. The rogue attacked Rachel."

She inhaled on a sharp gasp.

"She's alive, but Dylan said she's badly hurt." He didn't tell her that Dylan wasn't sure if Rachel would survive.

She has to survive.

If she didn't, Cooper wasn't sure how Dylan would react.

He climbed from the bed and grabbed his clothes.

"There's a suspect in custody at the EOD. I'm going down for an interrogation."

"And I'm coming with you." She jumped out of bed, giving him one fine view of her body before she started yanking on clothes.

He hesitated. "Gabrielle, you know I can't just take you to the EOD office."

She shoved back her hair. "Then blindfold me. Do whatever you have to do." Gabrielle walked toward him with her gaze snapping. "But you aren't leaving me behind, *partner.*"

No, a partner wouldn't leave her behind.

He caught the back of her head and pulled her toward him. He kissed her, hard, fast and frantic, because he had to.

He knew Dylan must be in sheer hell right then.

And the thought of something like that happening to Gabrielle, of someone hurting her... "Damn straight you're coming with me," he said.

Twenty-four seven. That had been their deal. He wasn't going to break any more promises to Gabrielle. He needed her to know that she could count on him.

For now.

Forever.

Cooper didn't plan on leaving her when the mission was over. He'd found something special with Gabrielle, and he wasn't about to let her go.

She gave him a little nod. He finished dressing and grabbed his gun, then his fingers twined with hers.

He hurried to the door, yanked it open.

And found Deuce standing there. Deuce nodded when he saw Cooper. The guy gave Gabrielle a wan smile. "I'm here for guard duty," he said with a little shrug.

Cooper frowned at him. "What?"

"You're wanted at headquarters." Now Deuce was the one who frowned. "Didn't Dylan call you? Hell, I know he was messed up about Rachel, but Mercer wanted you to come in—"

"—for the interrogation," Cooper finished. "I know, we're going there now."

Deuce shook his head. "No, *you're* going." He glanced at Gabrielle. "Sorry, ma'am, but your clearance isn't high enough. The big boss sent me over to keep an eye on you until Cooper gets back."

Gabrielle stiffened. "Clearance or no clearance, I'm going with Cooper."

A long sigh came from Deuce. "Civilians never understand, do they, Coop?" He rolled back his shoulders. "Want me to give you two some privacy while you explain things to her? Make it fast, though, okay, buddy? Mercer isn't exactly patient."

Cooper hesitated.

"She'll be waiting when you come back," Deuce said as he turned away. "You know it. They're always waiting…"

No, they weren't. Sometimes you turned away—for a mission, for just a moment, and you looked back, and the one you loved was gone.

Loved.

His chest ached as Cooper stared down at Gabrielle. When had he started to love her? He hadn't loved anyone, or anything, not since he'd lost his mother.

Gone, in an instant.

The back of his hand brushed over Gabrielle's cheek.

"Cooper?" She gazed at him, waiting.

Did she think he'd leave her? That he'd break his promise to her?

"I want you to trust me," he said softly, needing her to understand. "I gave you my word. I won't go back on it, not ever again." Then he raised his voice, making sure Deuce could hear him as he said, "I'll call Mercer and let him know—"

The bullet hit Cooper, driving into his side and tearing through his body. Gabrielle screamed even as Cooper felt his body falling.

"You should've just left her," Deuce snapped. "Then I could have taken you out, one at a time, all nice and slow, just like I planned."

Cooper tried to pull his gun from the holster. Blood pumped from him, soaking the floor.

"Cooper!" Gabrielle reached for him.

He jerked out his weapon.

But Cooper didn't get the chance to fire that weapon. Because Deuce grabbed Gabrielle, and the man who'd worked side by side with Cooper pressed his gun to Gabrielle's temple.

"I don't like using a gun for my kills." Deuce's voice was low and hard, with a lethal edge. "It's just not personal enough. Death should be personal, don't you think?"

Cooper dragged himself to his feet. The bullet was still in him, and the wound burned as the blood dripped down his body.

He stared into Deuce's eyes.

Deuce smiled. "If you don't drop your weapon, I'll kill her right now."

Cooper let his weapon fall.

"Good," Deuce praised. The fingers of his left hand were wrapped tightly around Gabrielle's throat. Too tightly. "Now walk back into your apartment. Nice and slow."

Keeping his eyes on Deuce and ignoring the pain, Cooper retreated, walking backward into his apartment.

Deuce followed, still with that tight grip on Gabrielle.

When they were all inside Cooper's place, Deuce told Gabrielle, "Lock the door. We want to make sure we don't have any unwanted guests."

Cooper saw her fingers tremble as she obeyed.

He could barely contain his fury—and his fear. Deuce had been the one to kill Lockwood? McAdams? The one to attack Rachel?

"You know, perhaps I've been wrong all this time…" Now Deuce's voice was considering. Mild and calm— just the way the guy was when they were playing cards.

Only this wasn't some card game.

This was life. Gabrielle's life.

"I thought it was better to kill the women they loved, then let the agents suffer until I put them out of their misery." Deuce thrust the gun barrel harder against Gabrielle's temple. "But making you *watch* while I kill her, oh, I think that is going to be even better…"

MERCER GLARED AT Thomas Anthony. The agent was wounded, but they'd patched him up.

For the moment.

If Mercer found out that Thomas was the rogue in his group, he'd do more than just wound the guy.

I'll destroy him.

"I'm not changing my story, Mercer," Thomas said. The guy's voice was even. No sign of rage or fear darkened his face. "I went to warn Rachel because I thought she was a target. When I left her, she was *fine*."

"And why'd you think she was a target? That part, I just don't see…"

"Rachel hauled me out of that prison camp. She stayed with me, telling me I had to fight, that I had to live, for nearly eight hours straight." Thomas stared steadily back at Mercer. "I heard the docs saying I was a dead man.

And I heard her—telling me to live. The way I figure it, I owed her."

Mercer let his brows climb. "You owed her a knife to the chest? That was your way of saying thanks?"

Thomas's jaw tightened. "I owed her protection. When I heard about the profiler's theory, I knew I had to warn Rachel."

"Because you're in love with her…" He tossed this out, looking for a reaction from the agent.

"*No*. Because *Dylan Foxx* is. Why the hell else do you think the guy shot me? When he saw Rachel like that, on the floor and bleeding, he went crazy."

Mercer was well aware of Dylan's feelings for Rachel Mancini; he just wanted to see what Thomas would reveal.

"I was trying to help her." Thomas was repeating the same story, again and again. "Dylan thought I was attacking again, so he shot me. He wasn't about to let anyone but the doctors get close to his lady."

Mercer's eyes narrowed. "I find myself curious…just how did you learn of the profile that Agent Evers was developing? That profile *should* have been confidential."

Thomas shrugged. "Deuce told me about it. He said he'd heard the FBI agent talking to you."

Deuce?

Mercer kept his expression blank.

"Deuce said it looked like the killer was going after the people that the agents cared about, attacking the women they loved first, then taking out the agents." Thomas rocked forward in his chair. "That's when I thought of Rachel. I knew about how Dylan felt—hell, how could I not? Have you *seen* the way the guy watches her? And I thought, hell, if the rogue wants to hurt the EOD, he'd focus on them. He'd take out two agents all at once."

Only the rogue hadn't been able to take out Rachel. She'd fought back.

The rogue had been denied his victim.

Would he try to attack her again? Or would he focus on someone else?

Mercer stood and advanced toward the door.

"You believe me, right?" Thomas called out. "Mercer?"

Mercer didn't respond. He went into the observation room. Two other agents were there—agents whom he trusted: Gunner Ortez and Logan Quinn. "I want to know where Deuce Porter is," Mercer said. "And I want to know *now*."

RACHEL'S EYELIDS TWITCHED. A soft moan slipped from her lips.

Dylan's heart raced in his chest. "It's okay," he told her, aware that his voice was no more than a rough rasp of sound. "You're safe." She was headed into the OR. She shouldn't even be opening her eyes then.

Not with the drugs that the doctors had given her.

But Rachel was staring up at him. Fear and fury battled in her stare. "D-D…"

"Take it easy," he told her. "I won't let anyone hurt you. Not ever again."

She grabbed for his hand. Her grip was surprisingly strong. *"Deuce…"*

And as understanding sank into Dylan, her rage became his.

"WHY?" COOPER GROWLED. He kept his eyes on Deuce. If he looked at Gabrielle, if he saw her fear, he was afraid he'd lose control.

Deuce was hurting her. And Cooper knew that unless he stopped him, Deuce would take pleasure in killing Gabrielle.

That can't happen. Cooper didn't want to live in a world that didn't contain Gabrielle.

She was too important.

She was everything.

"Vivian," Deuce said softly. "My beautiful Vivian. She's why." He lifted the gun a few inches from Gabrielle's temple.

That's right. Get the gun off her. Focus on me.

"Do you remember her, Coop? You'd just joined the EOD on that mission."

Cooper's guts were twisted in knots. *Vivian. Vivian Donaldson.* "She was the blonde. She was—"

"Mine!" Deuce screamed at him. The gun went right back to Gabrielle's temple. "Vivian was mine, and I was hers. We met in the Marines. We joined the EOD together. Our lives *were* together." Deuce's breath heaved out. "Until that mission…that last damn mission that got screwed to hell and back."

"Did she die?" Gabrielle asked him softly.

"She jumped in front of me." Deuce was staring at Cooper, but Cooper wasn't sure the other man actually saw him in that moment. "She took the gunfire meant for me. The bullets—they tore through her body. She jerked and shuddered, and she died." His breath heaved. "I was holding her in my arms, and more bullets came flying. They hit me. I *should* have died with her—"

"But we pulled you out," Cooper said. They'd also taken Vivian. They'd tried to help her, but it had been too late.

And, once he'd recovered, Aaron Porter had become Deuce. The moniker was both for the fact that he could so easily assume the identity of another person…and because he'd been given a second chance.

A chance to kill?

"I lost her," Deuce whispered.

"So you wanted them to lose, too," Gabrielle said. She didn't sound afraid.

She sounded…sad.

Once again, that gun lifted from her head. "Why should they get the happy ending? The EOD *took* my life away. They didn't give me a second chance—they took her, and I had nothing." He smiled at Cooper. A chilling sight. "So I took from them. I took their hope. I let them see what it was like to have nothing, and then I killed them."

Cooper took a careful step toward him. "They were your friends."

"They were the men who should have saved Vivian. *You* were one of those men. You were there, too. If you weren't going to save her, then you should have let me die with her!"

Deuce wasn't sane. Not any longer. Too much grief and pain had twisted him. Broken the man he'd been.

Cooper's phone began to ring, vibrating in his pocket.

"Don't!" Deuce yelled. "Don't even think of answering it."

The phone kept ringing.

"Vivian wouldn't want you doing this," Cooper told him, trying to reach the man that Deuce had been. Was Aaron even still in there? "She was in the EOD to help people, not to hurt them."

But Deuce laughed. "The EOD isn't what you think. We're just Bruce Mercer's attack dogs, nothing more. Well, guess what? I'm attacking on my own. I'm getting my vengeance, and I'm showing the world what's really going on…"

Gabrielle pulled at the hand around her neck. "V-Van didn't leave that message in blood, did he?"

Another rough bark of laughter escaped from Deuce. "Now you're seeing things. That was me. All *me*."

"Because you wanted me to find out about the EOD," she whispered. Cooper still couldn't look in her eyes. He didn't want to see her fear. His body tensed as he took another step forward. He had to get close enough to attack.

"You wanted me…to write a story on them, didn't you?" Gabrielle's words were distracting Deuce, and Cooper needed the man to stay distracted. Distracted prey was easier to take down.

"You were supposed to show the world…but you didn't!" Spittle flew from Deuce's mouth. "Everyone should have learned the truth. At the EOD, we're all killers! They should fear *us*. But you didn't write the story. You just let him—" He pointed the gun at Cooper. "You let him seduce you, and you buried the story!" Red stained Deuce's cheeks, and, in the light of the apartment, Cooper could see the blood on the man's hand.

Rachel's blood.

"He was using you," Deuce snapped. "You were the assignment."

Cooper took another step forward. "She's *not* an assignment."

Deuce's smile chilled Cooper's blood. "What is she, then? Why don't you tell us both?"

"You already know." That was why the bastard was there. Why he planned to hurt Gabrielle. "That's the way your game works, right? You take the ones that the agents love, so we feel your pain." He lifted his hands, acting as if he were no threat. "Don't do it, man. *Don't*. I can't imagine what you went through when Vivian died—"

"No, you *can't!*" Deuce yelled at him. "But you will. Now why don't you tell her that you love her before she dies?"

"Cooper?" Her voice was a soft rasp.

Finally, he looked at her. Because this was it. The last moment. And he wanted her to know how he felt, no matter what else happened.

"I love you." He wasn't sure when it had happened. When she'd first started to slip into his fantasies? When she'd come smiling, to his doorstep, offering him her chocolate chip cookies?

Or when he'd seen her choke back her fear—and work to get justice for those lost?

Hell, the when didn't matter.

He just knew he loved her.

He also knew that he'd die for her.

And he'd *kill* before he let anyone hurt her.

Her lips trembled. "Don't...*don't*—"

Her warning came too late because he was already moving as Deuce started turning the gun back toward Gabrielle. That gun was *not* getting to her temple again. He lunged forward. His body slammed into Deuce's even as his hands fought for the gun.

They tumbled to the floor. Deuce still had a grip on Gabrielle, even though she was fighting him. Cooper grabbed for the weapon—and the gun exploded.

Chapter Twelve

The gunshot echoed like thunder in her ears.

It reminded her of another time, another blood-soaked night.

A night when she'd lost another man that she loved.

Cooper groaned, and his body sagged back.

"You weren't supposed to be first," Deuce snarled as he lifted the gun and took aim at Cooper's prone form. "But if that's the way you want it, old buddy…"

"No!" Gabrielle threw her body forward and wrapped her arms around Cooper. There was so much blood. The scent filled her nose and had her stomach turning. Cooper's body was slack. And…cold. His usual warmth seemed to be fading, and that chill terrified her.

"Get away from him!" Deuce rose to his feet. "Now!"

If she moved, he'd shoot Cooper again.

She hunched her body over Cooper's. His eyes were closed. She wanted them open. She needed to look into his gaze once more. He'd said that he loved her.

"I love you, too," she whispered, and tears had the words choking out of her. "I didn't… I didn't mean to love you, but it just happened." He'd gotten past her defenses. Gotten right to the heart that she'd tried to guard so carefully. "Don't do this, please, don't leave me."

"Don't worry." The gun pressed to her temple once more. "You'll be joining him soon enough."

Her head lifted, but she didn't move her body. She was half sprawled over Cooper, trying to shield him as much as she could. She gazed up at Deuce and saw a monster staring back at her. "Killing us won't give your Vivian any justice."

His lips tightened. "Revenge is better than justice any day of the week."

No, it wasn't. "I've done *nothing* to you! I didn't even know you until a few days ago."

"You've done nothing," he said, giving a little nod, "and you *are* nothing, to me." Then his gaze slid to Cooper. "But to him, you're everything."

She didn't have a weapon. His gun was jamming into her temple.

This was it, then.

Cooper was too badly hurt to help her. She didn't even think he was conscious.

She'd attack Deuce. She would fight—she would *try*. And if she failed, she'd die.

Her fingers squeezed Cooper's.

He didn't squeeze hers back, but his chest rose and fell. Cooper was still alive.

I'll keep him that way.

"It's over for you, Deuce," she said, speaking quickly. Distraction would be the key here. "Rachel survived your attack. She's at the hospital, and she's going to tell everyone that you were the one hurting her—"

Cooper's phone rang again.

Gabrielle flinched.

Luckily, Deuce didn't. If he had, his trigger finger might have squeezed and she could have died right then.

"Th-that could be Dylan. He was at the hospital with her. I bet they already know you're the D.C. Striker."

"Doesn't matter," he told her, sounding too confident and not at all distracted. "You think I don't know how to vanish? I'll just reappear in another city, with another face, another name, and I'll keep hunting. I won't stop until I destroy the EOD agents. The EOD took away Vivian, and I'll make Mercer and his attack dogs *pay.*"

Distract. Distract. "No one understands why you're doing this—the public just thinks you're a serial killer."

He grunted at that.

She licked her lips. "I can help you to make them all understand."

The pressure of the gun's barrel eased. "That's what you were *supposed* to do."

Keep him talking. "It's what I will do. L-let me get to a computer. I can write your story. I can publish it. I can make everyone understand about the EOD and what they cost you." If he'd just back away from Cooper, then she'd be able to breathe easier.

Getting him away from Cooper was priority one. Getting that gun away from her head? A definite priority number two for her.

"Yeah, yeah, they need to know," Deuce muttered. His eyes had narrowed to slits. "We're gonna tell them." He grabbed her arm and yanked her to her feet.

Then he drew back his foot and kicked Cooper as hard as he could, right in the wound on Cooper's side.

"No!" Gabrielle screamed.

Cooper didn't move.

"He's already dead," Deuce said and there was satisfaction on his face. "His heart just doesn't know it yet. A few more pumps, and he's gone." Then, seemingly certain that Cooper wasn't going to trouble him, he started pulling Gabrielle toward Cooper's computer.

The gun wasn't at her head.

And Cooper *wasn't* already dead.

His phone stopped ringing.

"Come on," Deuce demanded as he yanked harder on her arm. "It's time for the world to know—"

The front door smashed in.

Deuce whirled toward that door, shouting, and Gabrielle used that moment—*distraction!*—to slam into him as hard as she could. He staggered back, and tripped over Cooper's end table. He crashed to the floor, and, as he fell, Deuce yanked her down with him.

The gun flew from his fingers. Gabrielle scrambled for it, but he caught her around the waist and hauled her back against him. He flipped her over and his hands went right to her throat.

"Let her go."

That low, lethal voice came from just a few feet away. Deuce didn't let her go, but he turned his head and stared up at the man who'd just kicked in the door.

The EOD director—the guy Cooper had called Mercer—stood there, with a gun in his hand. A gun that was trained right on Deuce.

"I gave you an order," Mercer barked. "Get your hands off her and get to your feet, *now.*"

Deuce slowly freed her, and Gabrielle sucked in desperate gulps of air. Spots danced around her eyes.

"I didn't expect you to come," Deuce drawled. His hands weren't on Gabrielle's throat, but he hadn't moved back, either. Actually, his hand was dipping toward his waistband. "I mean, the big boss doesn't usually get his hands dirty."

"I made an exception this time." Mercer had a dead aim at the man's head. But even though Gabrielle saw that his aim hadn't wavered, Mercer's attention had. His gaze was on Cooper.

Deuce laughed. "You've always been making exceptions for him. You think I didn't notice? Hell, from the very beginning…that rescue mission was a suicide job, but you still sent us out to find him. You were desperate to get some jumper out of that hellhole, and I had to wonder…*why?*"

"I value all of my agents—"

"He wasn't an agent then," Deuce pointed out. "Not then, but you risked our lives for him."

Mercer was still looking at Cooper. A mistake. "Mercer!" She yelled her warning.

His gaze swung back, but Deuce had already pulled a backup weapon from his ankle holster. Deuce didn't hesitate—he fired on the director.

Even as Mercer fired at him.

The thunder blasted in Gabrielle's ears. Blood bloomed on Mercer's chest, and he staggered back.

Deuce fell to his knees. He'd been hit, too, and the blood covered his chest just as surely as it covered Mercer's.

But Deuce wasn't done. He turned his head, stared at her. Stared, smiled, and lifted his gun.

They were inches apart.

I won't go out without a fight.

"*No!*" A deep cry of fury and fear. Not her cry. Cooper's.

And—Cooper was there. He lunged at Deuce, with a knife gripped tightly in his hand.

Deuce tried to spin toward the new threat, but Cooper

had moved too swiftly. Cooper attacked with his knife, driving it into Deuce's body.

Gunfire didn't thunder again.

The gun fell to the floor. Deuce gasped. His hands fought for the knife.

Cooper shoved it even deeper into Deuce's chest. "It's… over…" Cooper growled. "Over."

And it was.

Gabrielle grabbed the gun. She pointed it right at Deuce.

But Deuce wasn't looking at her. Blood soaked the floor beneath him, and he lay there, staring at nothing.

Not anymore.

His gaze was open. Empty.

Gone.

"G-Gabrielle…" Cooper reached her for her.

Her wonderful, strong, *alive* Cooper. She hugged him and held on to him as tightly as she could.

More footsteps raced into the room.

"Mercer?" she heard one man demand sharply.

She didn't look over at the new arrivals. She was too busy holding tight to Cooper.

"I'm…fine," Mercer told them. "Get Cooper—he needs…hospital…"

Cooper was sagging in her arms. "Cooper?" Tears slipped from her eyes. No, no, he couldn't do this. The killer was dead. This was the point where everyone was supposed to be okay.

But Cooper was too pale. His clothes were soaked in blood, and he was so cold.

Too cold.

She held him, as tightly as she could.

When the EMTs rushed in, she was there.

So was Mercer.

Mercer's body trembled, but he glared at the EMTs. "You keep him alive. Keep him *alive*."

"And you damn well better follow his orders!" Gabrielle heard herself shout. Tears thickened her voice.

"Annalise's son won't go out like this. He won't," Mercer vowed.

Then they were in the ambulance rushing toward the hospital. Mercer was in the back of that ambulance with her. EMTs were trying to work on him and on Cooper, but Mercer kept shoving them away and demanding that they focus on Cooper's wounds.

"D-don't worry..." Cooper whispered.

She barely heard his words over the hum of the machines and the scream of the ambulance's siren.

"I'm not...leaving you," he said. His eyelids flickered then his eyes opened. The blue was hazy, weak, but he was looking straight at her. "Not...ever..."

"You'd better not," she told him, not able to hold back her tears. "Cooper, I've got plans for us. Do you hear me? Lots of plans. Spaghetti dinners and cherry pies and more breaking and entering. We're just getting started. I just found you." She could taste the salt of her own tears. "I don't want to lose you."

It almost looked as if he smiled. "Promise..." A bare breath of sound from him. "You won't."

He'd said that he wouldn't break any more promises to her. No more lies. No more secrets.

Only truth.

I won't lose him.

Hope began to grow inside of her.

Hope that her secret agent was as strong as she'd always thought. Strong enough to cheat death—and to stay with her.

Forever.

COOPER HATED BEING in the hospital. The place smelled too much of antiseptic, and the stark white walls hurt his eyes.

Not that the room was 100 percent white. To the left, right near his lone window, he had an explosion of color—twelve blue balloons, reaching for the ceiling.

The balloons were from Gabrielle.

His beautiful Gabrielle. She was beside him right then. Sleeping.

She'd been with him since the attack.

He'd woken a few times, seen her staring at him with fear and hope in her gaze. One time when he'd fought through the drugs, he'd opened his eyes and seen her holding those balloons.

She'd been trying to smile at him then.

She'd been crying, too.

Her fingers were entwined with his. He curled his around hers a little more, squeezing lightly.

Gabrielle gave a little gasp, and her eyes immediately flew open. "Cooper?"

He smiled at her.

In the next instant, Gabrielle was *in* that bed with him. She put her mouth to his and kissed him.

He loved having her mouth on his.

Her kiss was light and gentle, and the woman was out of her head if she thought that was enough to satisfy him. Her body was next to his, not touching him, and that wasn't good enough, either.

He pulled her closer, ignoring the burn of the IV in his arm.

"No!" Gabrielle said, pulling back. "You have to be careful. You need—"

"I have what...I need." He was staring right at her.

Her lips trembled.

"You said…you loved me…" His voice was raspy, and talking made his throat ache more, but he didn't care. The pain just meant that he was alive.

"I did," she whispered, searching his eyes.

"Say it again."

Her smile bloomed, full and beautiful. "I love you, Cooper Marshall."

"Again." His demand. He would never get tired of hearing those words from her.

Gabrielle pressed another too light kiss to his lips. "I love you."

This time, he was the one to tremble. Because, for an instant, he'd wondered what he would have done if Deuce *had* killed her.

I would have been lost.

"Cooper?"

He shoved the darkness away from his mind and focused on the light—on Gabrielle. "I think we need…to reevaluate our partnership," he managed to tell her.

Her brows lifted. "We do?"

"Um, I was thinking about something more…permanent." A whole lot more permanent.

She shifted against him, pushing herself up so that she could gaze down at him. "That had better not be the drugs talking."

A rough laugh escaped from him. That was his Gabrielle. Only she could get to him—could make him laugh, make him dream of a future. "It's not. It's me." But then his gaze fell on the white box that was perched on the table near his bed. A small, square box.

The kind that usually stored jewelry.

Gabrielle followed his gaze. "Mercer brought that by

for you. He said that he thought you'd be needing it."
Her fingers stroked his arm, an almost absent gesture. He
loved her touches. Her caresses.

Loved *her*.

"His wounds weren't nearly as bad as yours—no internal organs hit for him. He was cleared the next day, but
you…" Her hand stilled on him. "You scared me."

He caught her fingers, brought them to his lips and
pressed a hard kiss to her knuckles. "I'll do my…damnedest to never scare you again." He only wanted to make
her happy.

Some of the sadness eased from her eyes. "Rachel's
okay. She's still here, and Dylan's making sure that she
gets plenty of rest."

Cooper suspected that Dylan was too worried about
Rachel to let her out of his sight.

The little matter of a life-or-death situation could sure
change a man's perspective.

It had certainly changed his.

Gabrielle climbed from the bed. She picked up the
white box and handed it back to him.

Frowning, Cooper studied the box. He had no idea what
Mercer could be giving to him. "About…our partnership,"
Cooper began as he opened the box.

But then he fell silent.

A ring was inside the box.

Not just any ring. A ring with two diamonds, and a
twisted band of gold.

"Cooper?"

"This…this was my grandmother's ring." The memory
was there, in the back of his mind. His grandmother had
visited him when he'd been a kid, maybe four or five, and
he'd seen that ring. He'd played with it, tracing the dia-

monds and that braided twist while he'd sat in his grandmother's lap. He'd never forgotten that ring.

Then his grandparents had died. His mother had died.

He'd never seen the ring again.

So what in the hell was Mercer doing with it?

"It wasn't an enemy who took her." Mercer's words seemed to whisper through his mind. *"Cancer did that. It came in an instant. It took her from me too soon. I blinked, and she was just—gone."*

His fingers closed around the ring. He saw the small note that had been folded and tucked in the bottom of the box.

Gabrielle was at his bedside, watching him silently.

I always want her at my side. Wherever I go, whatever I do, I want Gabrielle there.

He opened up that folded piece of paper. A brief note had been written there. *Annalise would want you to give this to the woman you love.*

That was all it said.

But then, those few words said everything.

"Cooper?"

He had to swallow twice in order to clear his throat. "I should…I should be on my knees for this." He tried to climb out of the hospital bed.

Since he was still weak, he pretty much *did* fall to his knees.

Gabrielle grabbed him and staggered beneath his weight. "What are you doing?"

"Trying to…" He made it. His knees touched down. "Trying to ask you about our partnership. I told you, I want one…that lasts forever." He lifted the ring toward her.

Her lips were parted. He waited for her to speak. Gabrielle always had plenty to say.

Only she wasn't speaking at that moment.

And she was scaring him.

The man who'd never known fear was about to shake again.

"Gabrielle?" Cooper prompted.

She blinked. "Y-you were just shot."

Cooper nodded.

"You've been unconscious for forty-eight hours."

He didn't know how long he'd been out. Cooper didn't think it mattered.

"You wake up, and the first thing you do…" She swiped her hand over her cheek. Oh, wait, was she *crying?* He'd so messed up the proposal. "The first thing you do is ask me to marry you?"

Again, he nodded. "I love you."

Her arms flew around his neck. "Forever," she whispered in his ear.

He curled his arm around her. The IV jerked loose. So what? *The pain means I'm alive—alive with the woman I love.* "Forever," he told her.

She kissed him.

He hoped that kiss meant yes.

Gabrielle slowly lifted her mouth from his. "I'll take that new partnership." She also took the ring. He helped slide it onto her ring finger. The diamonds gleamed.

A part of his past.

He looked into her eyes.

His future.

For a man who'd never looked beyond the next mission, life had sure changed. Because in that moment, when he gazed into Gabrielle's eyes, Cooper saw every dream he'd ever had.

Love.

A family.

A real home.

Every single thing he wanted—it was right there.

He was going to grab tight to those dreams. No one—nothing—would ever take them away.

Cooper kissed Gabrielle once more, and he knew that he was tasting paradise.

Epilogue

"You *can't* go in there!" Judith's voice snapped. "Mercer is busy! He can't be—"

His office door flew open.

Mercer leaned back in his seat and studied the man who'd just fought his way past Judith, Mercer's determined assistant. Judith was currently glaring at Cooper Marshall.

Cooper was glaring at Mercer.

Ah, life was back to normal.

"It's all right," Mercer said as he waved Judith back. "I was planning to talk with him."

Judith narrowed her eyes on Cooper. "You've made my list, Marshall."

Cooper blinked at that. Surprise flashed briefly over his face.

"I won't be forgetting this," she added, then stalked away.

The door slammed behind her.

Mercer put his hands flat on the desk. "You're looking better. For a while there, agent, I thought you weren't as strong as I—"

"My mother had a brother," Cooper cut through Mercer's words. "She said that he was in the military. That he was a soldier who saved lives."

Mercer's fingers began to tap on the desk.

"She told me all kinds of stories about him when I was growing up. Stories that made me want to be like him. Hell, those stories are the reason I joined the service. I wanted to make a difference, just like he'd done."

Mercer's gaze swept over Cooper's face. "You have."

"My mother…she said her brother died."

Mercer swallowed.

"But then…" Cooper looked out the window at the busy streets of D.C. "I died, too, didn't I? I thought my 'death' was so I could help the EOD, but there was more to that, right? You were trying to cover my past, trying to protect me."

"I don't know what—"

"Your daughter has to be under constant guard because you don't want your enemies getting to her. I figure all of those enemies would go after your nephew just as easily."

Mercer's fingers stopped tapping. "Yes, they would."

Cooper nodded. "My mother…she sure loved her brother. At the end, she called for him."

Mercer's eyes burned.

"Just so you know," Cooper murmured. "She wanted Ben. Her big brother, Benjamin."

Benjamin Marshall. He'd been that man, in another life. Long before he'd become Bruce Mercer.

"I loved her," Mercer's words were rough with emotion.

"I know you did." Cooper took a step toward him. "You paid for my college. You've been the one in the background, all my life, watching me, haven't you?"

"Not all your life. I wasn't there when Annalise needed me most." His shoulders hunched at the memory.

Cooper walked around the desk. He put his hand on Mercer's shoulder. "My mother loved you," he said again. "And she wouldn't want you blaming yourself for the way things ended."

Annalise had been good. Such an open heart, a warm smile. "You have her eyes," Mercer whispered.

Cooper's hand tightened on his shoulder. "I gave Gabrielle the ring."

Mercer nodded. "Annalise…she would have liked Gabrielle." He found that he could smile. "Gabrielle's got a lot of fire in her. She's not afraid of anything. Just like you."

"Oh, I'm afraid," Cooper surprised him by saying. "Because of Gabrielle, I'm terrified. I'm afraid that if I don't grab on to her, if I don't take my chance with her, I'll lose out on the best thing that could have ever happened to me."

Mercer glanced up at him. "Hold her tight. Fight like hell for her, and *never* let your enemies get close."

Cooper nodded. He lifted his hand and turned to walk away.

Mercer stood. The chair rolled back.

Cooper glanced over his shoulder.

"And…if you ever need me," Mercer managed to say, "I'm here. I—I know I'm not much, not in terms of…" He trailed off because he didn't know what to say.

Not in terms of family.

He'd been a shadow in Cooper's life for so long. Mercer knew he didn't have the right to ask for anything more.

Not that he could. Not really. He'd made sure that no one would ever be able to trace his blood link to Cooper. That protection was his gift to the man.

Not that he expected Cooper to believe that.

Not that he had the right to expect anything of Cooper Marshall.

But…Cooper hadn't left yet.

"Gabrielle and I are talking about a wedding in the fall. We have to, uh, wait for her boss to get back in town." Cooper's lips twisted. "Seems someone sent Hugh to the Cayman Islands, and seeing as how he's the one who will be giving away the bride, Gabrielle wants to make sure the guy's back."

"I can make sure of that," Mercer promised softly.

Cooper nodded, but he still didn't leave. "You know, when Gabrielle found out that I was an agent, she could've kicked me out of her life. Told me that I was a liar and just walked away from me." He paused. "She didn't. She gave me a second chance. She's letting me prove myself to her. I'm going to show her that there's a whole lot more to me than she thought."

Mercer's fingers had started to tap against the desktop once more.

"I believe in second chances," Cooper said. "Deuce didn't. *I do.*" Then he exhaled slowly. "So don't make me regret this but…you'll be invited to the wedding, too. I'd like to learn more about you. About the soldier my mom loved so much."

Mercer's hand lifted and rubbed against his chest. It wasn't his new wound that was aching.

It was something that went much deeper.

"Maybe you can tell me about her, too," Cooper continued softly. "Because I'd like to share those stories. I'll have kids one day. They should know about her."

"Yes," Mercer's voice was too rough. He couldn't help that. "They should."

One more nod and Cooper slipped away.

The door shut behind him.

Mercer closed his eyes for a moment. *You have a good son, Annalise.*

His eyes opened.

And I'll damn well be worth the second chance that he's giving me.

He'd prove himself to Cooper. After all, he'd never failed a mission. *I won't fail him.*

A knock sounded at his door. "Mercer," Judith called.

Judith hated using the intercom. It wasn't personal enough for her.

She opened the door and poked her head inside. "Dylan Foxx is here to see you." A pause, then, "*He* has an appointment."

Mercer inclined his head. "Send him in."

She turned away.

Speaking of missions…

Dylan Foxx stalked inside Mercer's office. One glance and Mercer knew Dylan was different. Rachel's attack had changed the man, just as Mercer had feared.

The news Mercer was about to give him wasn't going to help the situation. In fact, it might just push Foxx over the edge.

Mercer motioned to the seat before him. "I'm afraid we have a problem," he said, as Dylan sat down.

Dylan stared back at him.

"It's seems Rachel Mancini's past isn't dead."

The agent turned to stone before him.

"And if we don't act to permanently bury that past, I'm afraid that Mancini will find herself in the crosshairs of a killer once more."

A muscle jerked along Dylan's jaw. "Tell me what I have to do."

Yes, that had rather been the response that Mercer expected.

He leaned forward and got to work.

* * * * *

"Don't tell me you haven't felt this heat between us," she said.

Stacy held her breath, waiting for Patrick to lie.

"I've felt it," he said, his voice rough with emotion.

She leaned back to look up at him. She wanted to see his face, to read all the emotion there.

"I am attracted to you. But duty doesn't always allow me to do the things I want."

Heaven save her from logical, steadfast men. "You'll be right here with me. You said yourself we can't do anything else until the morning." She took his hand and kissed his palm. "I need you tonight. And I think you need me."

Patrick's eyes met hers, the intensity of his gaze pinning her back against the pillows and stealing her breath. "If you're sure this is what you want," he said. "Because once this starts between us, I don't know if I can stop…"

ROCKY MOUNTAIN RESCUE

BY
CINDI MYERS

Published in Great Britain 2014
by Mills & Boon, an imprint of Harlequin (UK) Limited,
Eton House, 18-24 Paradise Road, Richmond, Surrey, TW9 1SR

© 2014 Cynthia Myers

ISBN: 978 0 263 91351 4

46-0314

Harlequin (UK) Limited's policy is to use papers that are natural, renewable and recyclable products and made from wood grown in sustainable forests. The logging and manufacturing processes conform to the legal environmental regulations of the country of origin.

Printed and bound in Spain
by Blackprint CPI, Barcelona

Cindi Myers is the author of more than fifty novels. When she's not crafting new romance plots, she enjoys skiing, gardening, cooking, crafting and daydreaming. A lover of small-town life, she lives with her husband and two spoiled dogs in the Colorado mountains.

To Delores Fossen — my friend,
cheerleader and best roommate ever.

Chapter One

When the first gunshots sounded, Stacy Giardino ran toward them. Not because she was eager to face gunfire, but because her three-year-old son, Carlo, had been playing in the front of the house, where the shots seemed to be coming from. "Carlo!" she screamed, and tore down the hallway toward the massive great room, where the boy liked to run his toy cars over the hills and valleys of the leather furniture and pretend he was racing in the mountains.

Men's voices shouted over one another between bursts of gunfire. One of the family's bodyguards ran past her, automatic weapon at the ready. Stacy barely registered his presence; she had to reach Carlo.

The living room of the luxurious Colorado vacation home was a wreck of overturned furniture. Stuffing poured from the cushions of one of the massive leather armchairs and a heavy crystal old-fashioned glass lay on its side in the middle of the rug, ice cubes scattered around it like glittering dice. But whatever had happened here, the combatants had moved on; the room was deserted, and the tattoo of automatic weapons fire sounded from deeper within the interior of the mansion.

"Carlo?" Stacy called, fighting panic. If any of those

stupid men had hurt her son, she would tear them apart with her bare hands.

"Mama?"

The frightened little voice almost buckled her knees. "Carlo? Where are you, honey?"

"Mama, I'm scared."

Stacy followed his voice to a dim corner under a built-in desk. She knelt and peered into the kneehole space—into the frightened brown eyes of her little boy.

She held out her arms and he came to her, his arms encircling her neck and his face buried against her shoulder. She patted his back and breathed in the little-boy smells of baby shampoo and peanut butter. "Who were those men, Mama?" he whispered. "They came running in, and they had guns."

"I don't know who they were, darling. And it doesn't matter." The attackers could have been law enforcement agents, members of a rival crime family or different factions of the Giardino family turned against one another. Stacy didn't care. They were all part of the cruel, violent world of men that she had to navigate through every day. That was what life was like when you married into the mob—always running and hiding, never knowing who you could trust.

The family had come to Colorado on vacation, but there was no getting away from the reality of their life, from the danger. Her father-in-law, Sam Giardino, had been at the top of the FBI's Ten Most Wanted list ever since his escape from prison the year before. Which was why they were staying here, on this remote mountain estate outside of Telluride, instead of in a condo near the resort like normal tourists.

And even while relaxing, Sam was directing the family "business," cutting deals, making threats and building up his evil empire. Putting everyone around him in more danger.

They could all do away with each other, for all she cared. The only other person who meant anything to her was Carlo.

She stood, straining to lift the boy, who was getting almost too big for her to carry. "I'm going to take you some place safe," she told him. "Just hang on to Mommy, okay?"

He nodded his agreement and she headed back down the hall, toward the stairs to the basement, where the safe room was located. The man who'd built this house—some billionaire who was a friend of Sam's, or who owed him a favor, since men like her father-in-law never had real friends—had built the concrete bunker and stocked it like those preppers she'd read about, people who were waiting for the end of the world.

Maybe this was the end of her world, she thought. Her husband, Sam's son, Sammy Giardino, had been battling his father for months now. Maybe those arguments had erupted into all-out war and Sammy was trying to wrest control of the family "business." She wouldn't bet against her father-in-law in that conflict; Sammy only thought he was tough. His father was the hardest, coldest man she'd ever known. He'd even pledged to kill his own daughter after she'd testified against him in federal court.

When she reached the top of the stairs, Carlo shifted against her. "They're not shooting anymore," he said.

Carlo was right; the gunfire had ceased. Muffled

voices came from the back of the house, but they sounded more like normal conversation than angry outbursts. Should she move toward them and try to find out what was going on?

She stroked her son's soft blond hair. "What did the men look like, Carlo? The ones with the guns?"

"They were really big, and they had helmets covering their faces."

Not any of the thugs Sam Giardino employed, then. She'd never known them to wear helmets. These men sounded like law enforcement, maybe a SWAT team. They'd found Sam's hiding place at last. Would they take Sammy away this time, too? She had no idea if federal agents could tie her husband to any of the Giardino family crimes. Women weren't supposed to concern themselves with the "business" side of things. In any case, Stacy never wanted to know.

She started down the stairs. She'd expected to meet others moving toward the safe room. Where was Sam's mistress, Veronica, and the cook, Angela, and the guards whose job it was to protect the women? Surely the cops wouldn't have gotten to them all.

But here she was, all alone with Carlo. Nothing new about that. Even in a room full of Giardinos she was the outsider, the one who wasn't one of them. They tolerated her and she tolerated them, but none of them would have been sorry to see the last of her.

How ironic to think she might be the one to survive this day. To escape. The thought made her heart beat faster. For four years, all she'd wanted was to get away from the hold the Giardinos had on her. She wanted to start over, somewhere safe with her son, where no one knew her and she knew no one. She didn't need other people in her life; she only needed Carlo.

As soon as the coast was clear—as soon as whoever had attacked the house had left—she'd find a car and drive as far away as she could. Maybe she'd even go overseas somewhere. She'd get a new identity, and a job. She'd rent an apartment, or maybe a little house. Carlo could go to school and they'd have a normal life. Just the two of them. Dreams like that had kept her sane all these years she'd been trapped. The idea that she might finally make them come true renewed her strength, and she all but ran toward the basement.

The basement was dark, but she didn't dare risk turning on the light. She groped along the wall, toward the hidden door at the back that led into the safe room. Inside, she'd be able to watch the other rooms in the house on closed-circuit television and see what was going on. The room had its own generator, its own ventilation, air-conditioning and heating system and enough food and water to sustain a whole family for a month. She and Carlo wouldn't need to leave until she was sure they would be safe.

She was halfway across the room, feeling her way around a stack of packing boxes, when she froze, heart climbing her throat at the sound of footsteps on the stairs. The tread was heavy—a big man—and he was moving slowly. Stealthily.

She cradled Carlo's face against her chest. "Shh," she whispered in his ear.

Light flooded the room. She pressed herself against the wall, hidden by the boxes, and blinked at the brightness. The scrape of a shoe against the concrete floor was as loud as a cannon shot to her attuned ears. She held her breath, and prayed Carlo would keep still. Her arms ached from carrying him, but she held on tighter still.

"Who's there?" The question came from a man, the voice deep and commanding. A voice she didn't recognize. "Come out and you won't get hurt."

She crouched lower and peered between a gap in the boxes at a man dressed in black fatigues and body armor. He carried an assault rifle at the ready, but had flipped up the visor on his helmet to scan the basement.

Carlo squirmed in her arms and whimpered. She patted his back. "Shh. Shh."

"Who's there?" the man demanded. He swung the gun toward her hiding place. The sight of the weapon aimed at her turned her blood to ice.

"Don't shoot!" she squeaked. Then with more assurance, "I have a child with me and I'm unarmed."

"Move out where I can see you. Slowly. And keep your hands where I can see them."

Holding Carlo firmly to her, she moved forward. The boy squirmed around to look, his little heart racing against her own.

The man kept his weapon trained on her as she moved out from behind the boxes. "Are you alone?"

"Yes."

He glanced around, as if expecting someone else to loom up behind her. Apparently satisfied she'd told the truth, he aimed the gun toward the floor. "Who are you?" he asked.

She met his gaze directly, letting him see she would not be bullied. "Who are you?"

"Marshal Patrick Thompson, U.S. Marshals Service," he said.

"Stacy Franklin," she said. Franklin was her maiden name, but she didn't have any desire to introduce herself to this lawman as one of the Giardinos. "And this is my son, Carlo."

"Hello, Carlo." He nodded to the boy. His expression was still wary, but he had kind eyes, blue, with lines fanning out from the corners, as if he'd spent a lot of time outdoors, squinting into the sun. Carlo stared at him, wide-eyed, his fingers in his mouth.

Thompson turned his attention back to Stacy. "I'll need you to come with me," he said.

"Come with you where?"

"First, upstairs. We'll take a preliminary statement from you, and then I'll need you to come with me to our headquarters in Telluride."

"Are you arresting me? I haven't done anything wrong."

"No, I'm not arresting you, but you are a witness, and we may need to take you into protective custody."

She had no intention of letting anyone take her into custody, but she kept that to herself. She knew the law; though Sammy had been the one with the law degree, Stacy had written all his papers and helped him study for all his tests. She'd read the textbooks and listened to the online lectures and studied alongside him for the bar exam. None of it was knowledge the Giardinos thought a woman needed to know, but she would use it to her advantage now.

"Why are you here?" she asked.

Marshal Thompson didn't answer. He motioned for

her to move ahead of him. "Come with me upstairs and we'll talk more."

She climbed the stairs, aware of him right behind her, a broad-shouldered, black-clad guardian who smelled strongly of cordite and hot steel from his weapon, which must have recently been fired.

He led her into the living room, where other men milled about, taking pictures and measurements. She sat. Carlo scrambled out of her arms and retrieved one of his toy cars and began driving it along the arm of the sofa.

Marshal Thompson removed his helmet and sat on the arm of the sofa, his weapon on the table beside him. He had short, light brown hair and he looked tired—as tired as Stacy suddenly felt. "What is your relationship to the Giardino family?" he asked.

She thought about lying, saying she was a maid. But they'd check her story and learn her real identity soon enough. She lifted her chin, defiant. "I'm married to Sammy Giardino."

His gaze shifted to Carlo, who was making motor noises, guiding the toy car along a seam in the leather upholstery. "This is Sammy's son?"

"Yes." She patted his chubby leg in the corduroy overalls he was already outgrowing. He was *her* son—Sammy had contributed half his DNA, but she had given the boy her heart and soul. He was the one thing that had kept her sane in this crazy household.

"How long have you been in this house?"

She should probably demand a lawyer, or refuse to answer his questions altogether. But she didn't really care about the answers. The sooner she told him what he wanted to know, the sooner he'd let her go. "We arrived on Sunday. Five days ago." Five days of unrelenting tension in which Sammy alternately sulked and sniped, while his father looked smug. Visitors came and went at all hours, and twice she'd awakened deep in the night to hear arguments between father and son, shouting matches she'd fully expected to end in a hail of bullets.

"Why did you come to Telluride?" Thompson asked.

Because I didn't have the option of staying behind, she thought. "We came on vacation," she said. "To ski." Carlo had loved the snow. He'd spent two half days in kiddie ski school, thrilled by the rare opportunity to hang out with boys and girls his own age. It was tough to arrange playdates when you lived with a mobster.

"Who else is in the house?"

"A lot of people. I don't even know all their names." This wasn't exactly true, but she was wary of telling Thompson anything he didn't already know, like the fact that her fugitive father-in-law had been here. If Sam had managed to escape, she didn't want him finding out she was the one who had betrayed him.

"Any other women?" Thompson asked.

Why did Thompson care about the women? "There was the cook, Angie. A woman named Veronica." No point explaining her role as Sam's latest mistress. "My sister-in-law, Elizabeth Giardino." Elizabeth had been a big surprise, showing up for lunch today as if her father had never threatened to murder her.

"That's all?"

She looked up at him through the fringe of her lashes. "All the women."

"And the men?"

She looked around the room, at the masculine furniture and big-screen television, at the black-clad men who dusted for fingerprints and took photographs from every angle. "There were a lot of men here. There always are." The women were merely ornaments. Accessories. Necessary for carrying on the family name, but otherwise in the way. They were kept in the background as much as possible.

"Was there anyone here who wasn't a member of the family?"

"You mean besides all the bodyguards?"

"Besides them, yes. Any visitors?"

"Elizabeth was a visitor. She doesn't live here."

"Anyone else?"

She shook her head. "But I don't keep track of everyone who comes and goes."

"Because you're not interested?"

"That, and because I don't want to know about the Giardino business."

"Sir, the M.E. says he's finished in the library," one of the black-clad officers addressed Thompson.

Thompson nodded. "All right. Then you can seal off the room."

"Where is everyone?" Stacy asked. The first shock of the invasion had worn off and uneasiness stole over her like a virus, making her feel sick and a little dizzy. "The other women and the rest of the family."

"They're being taken care of. You were the only one unaccounted for. Where were you when the shooting started?"

"In the bathroom, if that really makes any difference."

The double doors leading into the hall opened and

a man in black backed into the room, wheeling a gurney. Stacy stared at the figure on the gurney, covered by a white sheet. A bone-deep chill swept through her. "Who is that?" she asked, forcing the words out.

"Mrs. Giardino—" Thompson put out his arm to stop her, but she threw off his grasp and ran to the gurney.

The men wheeling it past stopped and looked at Thompson. "Sir?"

"It's all right." Thompson glanced at Carlo, who had crawled under the coffee table and was absorbed in orchestrating elaborate car crashes. "Let her look."

She hesitated, staring at the outline of a face under the white sheet, afraid of what she'd see there, yet knowing she had to look.

The man at the head of the gurney leaned over and flipped back the sheet.

Stacy gasped and covered her mouth with her hand. Thompson's hand rested heavy on her shoulder. "Can you identify this man for me, please?" he asked.

"That's my husband," she whispered. In death, he looked older than she remembered, his skin waxy and slack, the cruelty gone from his expression. "That's Sammy," she breathed, and staggered back into the marshal's arms.

Chapter Two

Marshal Patrick Thompson considered himself a good judge of character, but he wasn't sure what to make of Stacy Franklin Giardino. When he'd stepped into the basement of that backcountry mansion, the last person he'd expected to encounter was this woman who looked like a college girl or a rock star, not a mobster's wife. She was all of five foot two and probably weighed ninety pounds soaking wet. She had fine, sharp features and huge gray eyes, and her short, platinum blond hair only made her look more elfin and vulnerable.

Dressed in leggings, an oversize sweater and short leather boots, she looked more like the little boy's big sister or babysitter than his mother, but a double-check of the background files on the Giardino family confirmed she was indeed the wife—or make that, the widow—of the late Sam Giardino Junior, and the boy, Carlo, was the heir apparent of the Giardino mob family.

Patrick stood in a darkened office at the police station the feds were using as their temporary base in Telluride and studied Stacy and her son through a one-way mirror. The boy was eating cookies, painstakingly separating each cookie into two halves, licking all the filling out and then nibbling away the cookie portions. Stacy watched her son, scarcely moving except to occasionally cross and uncross her legs.

Nice legs, he thought, though he told himself he wasn't supposed to notice them. He wasn't supposed to think of the women he was assigned to protect that way. They were victims or suspects or witnesses. But he was a healthy, single man and sometimes...

"What do you think?"

Patrick flinched, and looked over his shoulder at the man who spoke, FBI special agent Tim Sullivan. Though his first impulse was to say that Stacy was a very appealing woman, he knew that wasn't what Sullivan wanted to know. "She says she doesn't know anything about the Giardinos' crimes—that the women were kept in the dark."

"Do you think she's telling the truth?"

"Maybe." Patrick turned to look at Stacy again. Beneath the carefully applied makeup he detected dark circles of fatigue beneath her eyes. Earlier, she'd been so fierce, like a mother bear protecting her cub. Now she looked more vulnerable. "What makes a woman align herself with a criminal like Sammy Giardino?" he asked.

Sullivan moved to stand beside him. "Maybe she didn't know he was a crook until it was too late."

"Then why not leave? Why stay in a marriage with a man like that?"

"That answer's easy. You don't divorce a mobster. You know enough about them to be dangerous, and as long as you're married, you can't be compelled to testify against them."

Had Stacy been trapped like that? The thought made

his stomach twist. "She had to have known what he was like before they married," he said. "The background report on her says her father is a shipping merchant who's suspected of having some shady dealings with the Giardino family."

As if sensing someone watching, she turned and looked directly into the mirror. Her eyes were hard and cold. So much for thinking she was vulnerable. He'd seen women like her before. They were hostile to law enforcement, uncooperative and difficult. But it was his job to protect her, so he would.

"You want me to talk to her?" Sullivan asked.

"No, I'll do it." Patrick picked up a file folder from the corner of the desk and stepped out into the hall.

Stacy looked up when he entered the room. Carlo had finished his cookies and lay stretched across two chairs, his head in his mother's lap. "When can we go?" she asked, her voice just above a whisper. "It's going to be Carlo's bedtime soon."

"I'll drive you to your hotel soon." He sat, one hip on the table beside her, a casual pose that was supposed to help her relax, but there was nothing at ease about the rigid set of her shoulders. With one hand she smoothed her son's hair, over and over. "We'll provide protection for you until we're sure you and your son are safe. If we decide to press charges against anyone else, you may be asked to testify, and in that case you'll be under our protection until the trial. After that, you'll have the option of going into Witness Security and assuming a new identity."

"No." The hand that had been stroking her son stilled. "I won't do that."

Not an unusual reaction to the idea of starting life over as someone else. It took time for most people to come around. "You and your son could be in danger," he said.

"I can take care of my son."

"We can talk about this more later. For now, you'll be assigned an agent for protection."

If looks really could kill, the hate-filled stare she directed at him would have felled him like a shot. He pretended not to notice. "Do you have family you want us to notify—parents, siblings?" he asked.

"I'm an only child."

"Your parents, then." He consulted the notes in the file. "Your mother and father, Debby and George Franklin, live in Queens?"

"I don't want to see them."

"Why not?" Had there been a rift when she married Giardino?

"That's none of your business."

He conceded the point and let his gaze drift to the boy. The key with a hostile witness was to find some point of connection. "How is your son?"

"He's tired and confused. He wants to go home." Her expression softened and she stroked the boy's hair again—a honey color several shades darker than her own. "I haven't told him about his father yet. I'm not sure he'd understand."

"And how are you doing?"

The hardness returned. "If you're worried I'm all torn up because my husband's dead, don't be."

"So you're not upset?"

"I'm not. I hated him."

"Then why did you marry him?"

She shook her head. "You wouldn't understand."

"Try me."

She pressed her lips together in a thin line. He thought she wasn't going to say anything, but he waited anyway. Had she really hated her husband, or was this a ploy to distance herself further from the Giardinos and their crimes? "My father and his father arranged for us to get married," she said. "I scarcely even knew him."

"Come on. This is the twenty-first century. And it's America, not the old country."

Her expression clouded. "I told you you wouldn't understand."

He let the words hang between them, hoping she'd elaborate, but she did not. She didn't look away from him either, but kept her gaze steady and challenging, unflinching.

He shifted, and his leg brushed against her arm. She flinched and he moved away. This wasn't right, him looming over her this way. He pulled up a chair and sat beside her, turned to face her. "I wanted to ask you a few more questions about today," he said.

"I can't tell you anything about the Giardinos."

"You were married to Sam Giardino's son for four years. You lived in the Giardino family home during all that time. I believe you know more than you think you know. Did people often come to the house to discuss business?"

She remained silent.

He removed a photograph from the folder—an eight-by-ten glossy used by Senator Greg Nordley in his campaign. "Have you seen this man before? At the house or with Sam or Sammy somewhere else?"

She scarcely glanced at the photo. "Where are the other women—Victoria and Elizabeth? Have you asked them these questions?"

The women were at this moment in other interrogation rooms, being questioned by other officers. "They're safe. And yes, we're talking to them."

"They'll tell you the same thing I will—we don't know anything. We weren't allowed to know anything. Women in the Giardino household were like furniture or children—to be seen and not heard."

"I'm surprised you put up with that kind of treatment."

Anger flared, putting color in her cheeks and life in her eyes. She looked more striking than ever. "You think I had a choice?"

"You strike me as an outspoken, independent young woman. Not someone who'd let herself be bullied." When she'd stepped out into the basement, the boy in her arms, she'd looked ready to take him on, despite the fact that she was unarmed.

She looked away, but not before he caught a glimpse of sadness—or was it despair?—in her eyes. "If you lived in a household with men who thought nothing of cutting a man's face off if he said something they didn't like, would you be so eager to speak up?"

"Are you saying the Giardinos threatened you?"

"They didn't think of them as threats. Call them promises."

"Did they physically abuse you?" His anger was a

sharp, heavy blade at the back of his throat, surprising in its intensity.

She shook her head. "It doesn't matter."

He shifted, wanting to put some distance between himself and this woman who unsettled him so. She was alternately cold and vulnerable, in turns innocent and calculating. He pretended to consult the file folder, though the words blurred before an image of Stacy, cowering before a faceless thug with a gun.

"Does the name Senator Nordley mean anything to you?" he asked, forcing the disturbing image away.

"He's a senator from New York. What is this, a civics test?"

"We believe the senator was at the house shortly before we broke in this afternoon."

"I didn't see him."

"Did you see Sam Giardino with anyone in the past few days who was not a regular part of the household?"

"No. I stayed as far away from Sam as I could."

"Why is that?"

"He and my husband were fighting. I didn't want to get caught in the cross fire. Literally."

"What were they fighting about?"

"Control of the family. Sammy wanted his father to give him more say in day-to-day operations, but Sam refused."

"But Sam was the natural successor to his father, wasn't he?"

"Supposedly. But Sam used to taunt him. He'd threaten to pass over Sam and hand the reins over to his brother, Sammy's Uncle Abel."

Patrick leafed through the folder. He found no mention of anyone named Abel. "Who was Uncle Abel?"

"Sam's younger brother. He was the black sheep no one ever talked about—because he wouldn't go into the family business."

"But Sam threatened to turn things over to him instead of to Sammy?"

"It was just his way of getting back at Sammy. Abel had nothing to do with the business and hadn't for years."

"Where is Abel now?"

"He and Sam's mother—Sammy's grandmother—live on a ranch somewhere in Colorado."

The hairs on the back of Patrick's neck stood up. There was something to this Abel Giardino. Maybe the Colorado connection they'd been looking for. "Did you ever meet Abel?"

"He and the grandmother came to our wedding. He looked like some old cowboy."

"And the mother?"

"The mother was scarier than either of her sons. She didn't approve of me and threatened to give me the evil eye if I wasn't good to her only grandson." Stacy shuddered, and rubbed her hands up and down her arms. "After meeting her, I know why Sam was so mean."

"All the more reason for us to offer you protection."

"I told you, I don't want your protection!"

At the sound of her raised voice, Carlo stirred and whimpered. She bent over him and made soothing noises. In that instance she transformed from cold and angry to warm and tender. The contrast struck him, made him feel sympathy for her, though he didn't want to. She was a member of a crime family, probably a criminal herself. She didn't deserve his sympathy.

When the boy had settled back to sleep, she looked at Patrick again. "Please, just let us leave," she said.

He stood. "I'll have someone take you to your hotel."

He left the room, shutting the door softly behind him. He found Sullivan in his office down the hall. "Have you heard of Abel Giardino?" Patrick asked.

Sullivan shook his head. "Who is he?"

"Sam's brother. He supposedly was never involved in the family's crimes. He lives with his mother somewhere in Colorado."

"Could he be the reason Sam was in the state?"

"It would be worth checking out. Stacy says Sam talked about choosing his brother to succeed him as head of the family, instead of Sam Junior."

Sullivan made a note. "Did you get anything else out of her?"

"Only that she apparently hated her husband's guts. And she doesn't appear to have fond feelings for any of the rest of the family."

"No confirmation on the senator?"

"She said she hadn't seen him around."

"Do you think she's telling the truth?"

"Hard to say. She's not one to give anything away. I'll ask Sergeant Robinson to take her and the boy to the hotel for the night and we'll try again in the morning."

He called the sergeant's extension and gave the officer his orders: take Mrs. Giardino and her son to the hotel they'd selected and stay on guard until someone else came to relieve him.

He returned to his office and sat back in his desk

chair. He liked to review a witness's answers while they were fresh in his mind. He looked for patterns and inconsistencies, for vulnerabilities he could exploit or new information he needed to explore further. Certainly, he wanted to know more about Abel. But he wanted to know more about Stacy, too, and how she fit into this sordid picture of a family of criminals.

Instead of thinking about what Stacy had said, his thoughts turned to everything she hadn't said. Why had her father and Sam arranged for her to marry Sammy—if that had indeed happened? What had the Giardinos done to make her so afraid? Was she really as ignorant of their dealings as she claimed?

And why did she get to him, making him forget himself and want to comfort her? Protect her? Was she just a good actress, accomplished at manipulating men, or was something else going on here? He needed to understand so he could avoid making a wrong move in the future.

A sharp knock sounded on the door. "Come in."

Sergeant Robinson, a thin, balding officer, leaned in. "Sir?"

"What is it, Sergeant? Why aren't you with Mrs. Giardino?"

The sergeant's gaze darted around the office, as if he expected to find Stacy Giardino standing in the corner. "She's not with you?"

"No. She's in interview room two. I told you that."

The sergeant swallowed, his Adam's apple bobbing. "The interview room is empty, sir. Mrs. Giardino is gone."

Chapter Three

Stacy wasn't about to wait around for Sergeant What's-his-name to haul her off to a hotel room that would be little better than a prison. She'd had enough of men telling her what she could and couldn't do and where she could and couldn't go. Now that Sammy was dead, she had a chance to start life over, but she was going to do it on her own terms.

She checked the hall to make sure the coast was clear, then woke Carlo. "Time to go, honey," she said, hoisting him onto one hip.

"Where are we going, Mama?" he asked.

"We're going to stay in a hotel. Won't that be fun?" She kept her voice to a whisper, but tried to sound excited for Carlo's sake. "They'll probably have a pool and you can go swimming."

"Will Daddy be there?"

His face was so serious—too serious for a little boy. "No, Daddy can't make it. But you and I will have a good time, won't we?" Soon, when things were more settled, she'd have to tell him about his father. Though Stacy had long ago ceased to like, much less love, her late husband, Carlo adored his daddy, even though Sammy had spent less and less time with the boy in the past months. She wasn't sure a three-year-old would understand death, but Carlo would be devastated once he accepted his father wasn't coming back. She'd postpone that pain for him a little longer.

Once in the hallway, she headed for the door marked Stairs. Less chance of running into anyone than if she risked the elevator. Fortunately, she only had to go down two floors and there was a back door. Probably where all the smokers went to sneak a cigarette, she thought, and slipped out, praying an alarm wouldn't sound.

The door opened into a parking lot at the back of the building. Only a few cars sat in the glow of overhead lights. A stiff breeze blew swirls of snow around her feet as she hurried across the concrete. She needed to find her way onto the main drag and lose herself in the crush of tourists.

She followed the sounds of voices and music to Telluride's main street, where she fell into step behind a crowd of adults and children—a big family group on vacation, she guessed. A quick check over her shoulder told her the brawny marshal wasn't following her—he was tall enough she'd have spotted him, even in this crowd. And he had the clean-cut good looks and alert attitude that pegged him as law enforcement from half a mile away.

She checked the shops along the street and spotted one that advertised children's clothing. A woman with a kid wouldn't stand out in there. She set Carlo down and pretended to look through the racks of clothing while he headed for the toy box against the wall. She needed a plan.

"Can I help you find something in particular?" an

older woman in a black wool skirt, pink blouse and boots asked.

"You have such great stuff here," Stacy gushed. "I wish I had more time to shop. I just ducked in here while I'm waiting for my husband. But I'll be back tomorrow when I have more time."

"Your son is adorable," the woman said, and she and Stacy both turned to watch Carlo fitting big foam blocks together.

"Thank you." Stacy offered her most dazzling smile. "He's going through that phase where he just loves trains and buses and airplanes. Does Telluride have a bus station?"

"Not really. Some of the hotels run shuttle buses to the airports, and there are buses to the ski area."

"Thanks. I was just curious." She could rent a car to get away, but that required a credit card and ID and would be easy to trace. She pulled out her phone and pretended to read a text. "Got to go. Come on, son, we have to go."

"But I want to stay here and play," Carlo said.

"We'll try to come back tomorrow and stay longer." She held out her hand and Carlo took it.

On the sidewalk once more, she tried to think of her next move. Maybe she could catch an airport shuttle. Anything to get out of town. She set off walking toward a high-rise on the corner where she could see several tour buses and a crowd of cars waiting for their turn to unload beneath the portico.

As she'd expected, the building was a hotel, and a busy one, crowded with people coming and going. Perfect. She'd just be one more anonymous woman in the crowd. She threaded her way through a line of tour-ists unloading luggage and skis from a shuttle bus and entered the lobby. She made her way to the front desk and turned on the charm for the clerk, a harried-looking young man with thinning blond hair. "What time is the airport shuttle?" she asked.

"Telluride, Montrose or Durango?" he asked, not even looking up from his computer screen.

She hesitated. "Um…"

"The bus to Durango leaves in ten minutes, but the one for Telluride will be right behind it."

"Great. Thanks." Durango it was.

She took a seat behind a potted plant and gave Carlo her phone to keep him occupied. She was showing him how to get to the games she'd downloaded for him when the phone rang, startling her.

She stared at the number. A 303 area code—Denver. Those marshals were probably based in Denver, weren't they? She hit the button to ignore the call, but a few seconds later, the chime sounded, indicating she had a message.

She hesitated, then decided to listen to the message. Maybe it wasn't the marshal at all.

Patrick Thompson's deep, velvety voice filled her ears. "Running away is not a good idea," he said. "Call me back at this number and I'll send someone to pick you up. I promise you'll be safe with us."

"Right." She was supposed to trust the people who had shot her husband. At least that was the story Thompson himself had given her. Apparently Sammy had killed his father, then turned the gun on his sister, but still, it was a federal agent who'd put the bullet in his back that killed Sammy. And though this Patrick Thompson guy had been nice enough when he was interviewing her, he was probably like all the rest—he thought she was like Sammy—a lowlife mobster, or even worse, his tramp of a wife. Why would they be so concerned about her safety? They really wanted her to tell all she knew so they could pin the Giardino family crimes on someone. But after today, no one was left to blame, except maybe for a few thugs who'd been following Sam and Sammy's orders.

She switched off the phone, hoping that would keep them from being able to trace its signal or GPS or whatever the feds used to keep tabs on people. She was tempted to leave the phone behind, but being that cut off from any resources felt too dangerous.

A deluxe passenger van pulled up and the driver announced the Durango airport shuttle. Stacy and Carlo joined the line of people climbing on board. "Name, miss?" The driver was checking off names on a list on a clipboard. He was a middle-aged man with a round face and an underdeveloped chin.

"I'm not on your list," she said. "I was hoping I could buy a ticket on board."

"I'm only supposed to take advance reservations."

Stacy shifted from foot to foot. Everyone was staring, the people behind her starting to grumble. She leaned toward the man, keeping her voice low, and at the same time giving him a look down the V-neck of her sweater—hey, she'd use whatever she had to pull this off. "Please," she said. "I just found out my mother is in the hospital and I was able to get a flight out of Durango to see her and I've got to get there. I can pay cash." And he could keep the cash and never tell anybody, if he was so inclined.

"Fifty dollars." He didn't even hesitate to bark out the sum.

She opened her purse and fished out two twenties and a ten. One thing about living with a mobster—they believed in paying cash and kept a lot around.

"Where's your luggage?" the driver asked.

"I already put it back there." She nodded toward the back of the bus, where a porter was loading suitcases.

On board the bus, she settled into a seat near the back, Carlo beside her. "Where are we going, Mama?" he asked.

"To that hotel I told you about." Once at the airport, she'd head to baggage claim and call one of the hotels that offered a free shuttle. She'd pay cash for a room and give a fake name. After dinner and a good night's sleep, she could decide what to do next.

Carlo settled with his face pressed to the glass, looking out the window. Stacy leaned her head back and closed her eyes. She was on her way. Not safe yet, but she would be soon.

"SHE'S HEADED TOWARD Durango."

Patrick leaned over the tech they'd assigned to trace Stacy's cell phone signal and studied the laptop screen and the little green dot that pinpointed her whereabouts. His last two calls to her had gone straight to voice mail, so he assumed she'd turned off her phone. Apparently she hadn't realized it still sent out a signal, even when switched off.

"What's in Durango?" Agent Sullivan asked.

"Maybe this Uncle Abel?" Stacy had said he had a ranch in Colorado, but she'd been vague about where.

"Someone else is in Durango today," Sullivan said. He held out his smartphone, which showed the front page of the Durango paper, with a story about Senator Nordley's speech to a political group in town.

Patrick's stomach churned. He'd wanted to believe Stacy's innocent victim act. Had everything she'd told them been a lie? "That's a little too convenient for coincidence," he said.

"Should we call Durango police and ask them to intercept her?" Sullivan asked.

"No. I'll go." He reached for his jacket. "I want to watch her, see what she does. And the fewer people who know about this, the better for security." He turned to the tech. "Keep tracking her. I'll stay in touch by phone."

The night was bitterly cold and blustery, big flakes of snow swirling in the parking lot security lights as he made his way to his Range Rover. He threaded the vehicle through the crowds on Main, then took the highway out of town, turning on the road up to the ski resort. This would take him over Lizard Head pass, through the small towns of Rico and Delores and into Durango. Stacy probably had a forty-minute head start on him, but he wasn't worried about following her too closely, not as long as she had her phone with her.

Provided she hadn't been smart enough to stash the phone, maybe in a bag that was now on board the shuttle while she ran the opposite direction. But he was going with his gut and the belief that she was headed to Durango herself.

He'd learned to trust his gut in his years with the U.S. Marshals, but things didn't always play out the way he wanted. Most recently, he'd agreed to allow Elizabeth Giardino, who'd been in Witness Security as Anne Gardiner, to go to the house where her father had been holed up with the rest of the family. The opportunity to catch a man on the FBI's Ten Most Wanted list after he'd been on the loose for over a year had been too tempting, especially since Elizabeth had been so determined to take the risk.

But her brother had almost killed her, and Patrick blamed himself.

He wasn't going to risk losing another woman in his care; he wouldn't let Stacy Giardino get the better of him.

When he reached the outskirts of Durango, he phoned the tech back in Telluride. "You still have her on radar?" he asked.

"Yes, sir. She was at the airport for a little bit. Then she was on the move for a bit, but she's stopped again. If you give me a moment, I can pinpoint an address."

"All right. I'll hold." He guided the car past well-lit shopping complexes down a main street lined with bars, restaurants and hotels. Like Telluride, Durango was filled with tourists celebrating after a day at the nearby ski area. It was the kind of place where it would be easy for a stranger to get lost in the crowd.

"Sir, I've got an address for you."

"Go ahead." Patrick leaned over and switched on his GPS.

The tech rattled off an address on Second Street. "I show it's a motel. Moose Head Lodge."

"Got it. Thanks." He hung up, keyed the address into his GPS then did a U-turn and headed back toward Second Street.

The Moose Head Lodge was a low-slung log-and-stone structure set back from the road. Two long wings stretched out from the central building, with doors for each room opening into the parking lot. Patrick parked the Range Rover across from the entrance and went into a lobby straight out of a Teddy Roosevelt nightmare, complete with a stuffed grizzly bear by the front counter.

"May I help you, sir?" asked the clerk, who looked scarcely old enough to shave.

"I'm looking for a young woman who just checked in. About five-two, short, pale blond hair. She probably had a little boy with her."

"I'm not allowed to give out information on our guests," he said.

"You can give me the information." Patrick flipped open his credentials on the counter.

The boy's eyes goggled. "Y-yes, sir. A woman like the one you described checked in about fifteen minutes ago. She's in Room 141—out back."

"What name did she register under?"

The boy turned to a computer and rapidly typed in some information. "She registered as Kathy Jackson. And she paid cash for her room."

"I need to reserve the closest vacant room to hers I can," Patrick said.

"That would be 142—right next door."

"I'll take it." He handed over his government credit card and filled out the reservation information.

"That room has two double beds and a microwave and minifridge," the clerk said as he handed over the card key.

"Is there someplace I can order in food?" He hadn't eaten since breakfast and it was beginning to catch up with him.

"There's a pizza place that delivers. The menu is in your room."

"That'll do." He drove the Rover around and parked in front of his room. There was no reason Stacy should recognize it, but in case she was looking out the window to see who had arrived, he kept the vehicle between him and her door and entered the room quickly.

Once inside, he made his way to the wall that separated his room from hers and pressed his ear against the sheetrock. The muffled music and voices from the television obscured any other sound at first, then he heard what he was sure was a child, and the unintelligible answer in a woman's voice.

They were there, probably in for the night, but he'd stay alert just in case. If anyone came to see her, or if she left to go out, he'd know. In the morning, he'd follow her and see where she went. Who she talked to.

He ordered pizza and listened to the sounds of splashing from the bathroom next door. Probably the boy getting a bath, but the disturbing image of Stacy in the shower drifted into his mind. Though she was petite, she had a good figure. Was he a creep for fantasizing about a woman he was supposed to protect? Or merely human for thinking about an attractive woman who was separated from him by only a wall?

And her own resistance to having anything to do

with him. Maybe her years with the Giardinos had made her wary of trusting anyone, especially those on the right side of the law. But he couldn't take the chance that some offshoot of the family—or their enemies— would come after her. The other women were in protective custody, and agents were busy tracking down everyone connected with the family and piecing together evidence for a multitude of crimes. Stacy was the only loose end at the moment.

After the pizza was delivered, he wedged the door open an inch, the better to hear any activity next door. He ate, then lay on the bed fully clothed, his weapon on the blanket beside him. All was quiet next door, even the TV silenced. He didn't expect to sleep much, if any, but he was used to long nights. He'd learned how to get through them and catch up on his rest later.

In spite of Patrick's resolve to stay awake, he must have drifted off. He woke to the sound of a woman screaming in the room next door.

Chapter Four

Instinct propelled Patrick out of bed, weapon drawn and ready. A dark sedan idled in front of the room next door, a bulky figure at the wheel. A woman's wails and the crying of a child shattered the predawn stillness and sent a jolt of adrenaline through the marshal.

He slipped out of his room, keeping to the shadows, out of reach of the parking lot lights. The door to Stacy's room stood open and just as he started to move toward it, a man ran out, Carlo clutched to his chest.

"Halt!" Patrick shouted, and shot wide, in front of the man. He didn't dare aim directly at him, too fearful of striking the child.

The kidnapper scarcely slowed as he returned fire, the shots muffled by a silencer. Patrick ducked into deeper shadow as bullets splintered the brick to his left, shards stinging the side of his face. The man tossed the boy into the backseat of the car and dived in after him and they took off, tires squealing.

Patrick fired, aiming for the vehicle's tires, but the car raced away too fast. Breathing hard, blood running down his face, he stared after the kidnappers, trying to make out the license plate number or any identifying marks on the car. But the plate had been obscured with mud, and the car was like a hundred other sedans in the city.

Heart pounding, he raced to Stacy's room. "Stacy?" he called when he reached the open doorway.

The silence that greeted him turned his blood to ice. He groped for the light switch and light illuminated chaos. The covers lay in a tangle, half off the bed, and a chair and a lamp were overturned.

"Stacy!" he called again. "It's me, Patrick Thompson. Are you all right?"

A whimper drew him to the bathroom. Weapon at the ready, he advanced toward the room. The overhead light glowed harsh on white tile and porcelain. He leaned into the doorway and found Stacy in the shower, fully clothed but slumped against the tile, blood running from a gash above her left eye. She moaned as he knelt beside her. "Stacy, can you hear me?"

She opened her eyes and stared at him, her expression blank. He knew the moment memory of all that had happened returned. Her eyes filled with tears and she struggled to stand. "Carlo! They've got Carlo!" she gasped, her voice ragged with terror and pain.

Patrick urged her back into a sitting position. "Tell me exactly what happened," he said.

"You have to go after them!" She gripped his arm, fingers digging painfully into his skin. "You have to get Carlo."

He gently pried her hand off his arm and cradled it in his own. Her fingers were ice-cold. "They drove away in a car," he said. "I promise I'll do everything I can to track them down, but I need your help. The more you can tell me, the more I'll have to use in my search."

The devastation in her eyes touched him. Gone was the cold, uncooperative woman he'd interviewed at the police station. Now she was a mother grieving for her child. She slipped her hand from his grasp and touched the cut on her head. "He hit me with the butt of his pistol."

Patrick found a washcloth and wet it from the tap, then pressed it against the gash. "Who was he? Did you recognize him?"

"No. I'm sure I never saw him before in my life. But he knew who I was. He called me Mrs. Giardino, and called Carlo by name, too."

"And you're sure you didn't know him?"

"Nothing about him was familiar, but it was dark and I was asleep when they burst in. Everything happened so fast." She slid her hand under his and took the washcloth. "What are you doing here? When did you get here?"

"I followed you here last night. I'm in the room next door."

"You were spying on me." Her eyes flashed with accusation—but that was better than the despair that had filled them seconds earlier.

"You ran away," he said. "I wanted to see where you were going. Who you talked to."

"How did you know where to find me? I didn't see anyone I knew...."

"Your phone gives off a tracking signal even when it's off." He sat back on his heels and studied her for signs she might be going into shock. But color was returning to her cheeks and she seemed more alert. "I'm surprised Sam Giardino let you have a standard phone like that."

"The men used throwaway phones, mostly, but they didn't care about the women. We weren't important enough for anyone to be concerned about where we were."

He took out his own phone. "I'll call the local police. They can put out an AMBER Alert. We might be able to stop them before they get very far."

"No!" She clutched at his arm again. "No police. He said if the police came after them they'd kill Carlo."

"If the police get to them quickly enough they won't have time to hurt the boy."

"No, please! I can't risk it. He said at the first sign of the cops they would cut Carlo's throat." She choked back a sob, struggling to keep it together. "Can't you go after them? You and I?"

"We'd have a much better chance of catching them with the police involved. An AMBER Alert will have everyone in the state looking for them."

"They'll see the notices on the news and Carlo will die!" Her voice rose, near hysterics.

He slid the phone back into his pocket. "I won't call them just yet. Tell me anything else you remember. Even little details might be important."

She nodded and scrubbed at her eyes with the back of her hands. She'd taken off her makeup, so that she looked much younger. More vulnerable.

A gentle tapping sounded on the door. "Ms. Jackson? Are you all right?" someone asked.

"I'll take care of this," Patrick said. He rose and moved quickly to the door and peered through the peephole. The desk clerk stood on the other side, looking around nervously.

Patrick opened the door. "Is something wrong?" he asked.

"Oh!" The clerk looked startled. "I, uh, I thought this was Ms. Jackson's room." He frowned at the number on the next door over—Patrick's room.

"Ms. Jackson is fine," Patrick said. "What did you need?"

"One of the guests called the front desk and said they heard gunshots coming from this room."

"They must have heard a car backfiring." The lie came easily; no need to involve this clerk until Patrick had made up his mind how to handle this.

"They sounded really certain."

"I think I'd know a gunshot, don't you?"

"Of course. Of course." He tried to see past Patrick, into the room. "And Ms. Jackson's okay?"

"She's fine. But she's not dressed for company." He winked and the clerk blushed red. No doubt the guy thought Patrick's story about conducting surveillance on Stacy had been an elaborate cover for an affair.

"I'll just, uh, get back to the front desk." The young man backed away. "If you need anything, just, uh, call."

Patrick shut the door and hooked the security chain, then returned to the bathroom. Stacy had moved from the shower to the toilet, where she sat on the closed lid, head in her hands. She looked up when he entered the room. "Who was that?"

"The front-desk clerk. Someone reported gunshots."

"What did you tell him?"

"I told him it was probably a car backfiring." He knelt in front of her. "Now tell me everything that happened."

She took a deep breath. "When I woke up, he was already in the room. He must have had a key or something, because I never heard a thing. Carlo was sleeping beside me and the guy already had hold of him, pulling him out of bed. That's what woke me."

She put the washcloth back over the gash, which had slowed its bleeding. "I screamed and he ordered me to shut up. I was terrified, finding a guy in my room like that. 'Who are you?' I asked. 'What are you doing with my son?'

"'Carlo is coming with me, Mrs. Giardino,' the guy said. 'If you know what's good for you, you won't interfere.'"

The guy might as well have told the sun not to shine. "Was there anything distinctive about his voice? An accent or anything like that?"

She frowned. "Not really. I mean, he sounded American, but not from anyplace in particular. He told me if I called the police he would kill Carlo—that if anyone followed them, they'd cut his throat." She bit her lip, fighting fresh tears.

"What did you do?" Patrick prompted.

"I tried to pull Carlo away from him. Carlo woke up and started crying. I wouldn't let go of Carlo, so the guy hit me." She winced, whether in real or remembered pain, Patrick couldn't say. "I staggered back and he grabbed me and threw me in here, then ran out with Carlo. I heard more shooting in the parking lot."

"He was firing at me. Your screaming woke me. I

tried to stop him, but he was using Carlo as a shield. I couldn't get off a good shot."

"He wore a mask," Stacy said. "A ski mask. I couldn't see his face. But his voice didn't sound familiar."

"There were two of them," Patrick said. "The driver was a big, bulky guy. The one who snatched Carlo was slighter. The car was a dark sedan with mud smeared across the license plate."

"You saw them! Then you could find them." Her eyes lit up with hope. "They won't suspect you—you're not in uniform, or driving a cop car. They probably don't even know you're here. I didn't, so why should they?"

"Except they shot at me. And I shot back."

"But they wouldn't have gotten a good look at you. Please, Patrick. Say you'll help me."

Only a colder man than him could have been immune to the pleading in her eyes. He wanted to promise her that he'd find Carlo, and soon. That he would protect them both from whoever was threatening them. He wanted to make that promise, but the knowledge that he might not be able to keep such a vow held back the words.

"Let's go back to my room and take care of that cut on your head," he said. "Then we'll decide what to do."

He found Stacy's coat and purse and draped them over her shoulders, then steadied her while she slipped into her boots. The gash had stopped bleeding and though she'd probably have a heck of a headache for a while, he hoped the damage wasn't more serious.

He led her to his room and shut the door behind them. She sat on the bed he hadn't slept in. "You'll be safer here with me," he said.

"I wasn't safe tonight. How did they find me?"

"If we can track you by your phone, they can, too."

She stared at the purse on the bed beside her. "Should I destroy the phone?"

"Not yet. The kidnappers may try to reach you through that number."

"Do they want money?" she asked. "Is that what this is about—ransom?"

"If they knew the Giardino family, they know Sam had money. Maybe they want to take advantage of his death to get their hands on some of it."

"Then maybe they won't hurt Carlo." Fresh tears filled her eyes and she covered her mouth with her hand, as if to hold back sobs.

Patrick squeezed her shoulder. "I know it's hard, but you need to pull yourself together. For Carlo's sake."

She nodded and made an effort to compose herself. He pulled out his phone again. "Who are you calling?" she asked.

"My office. I want to find out if anyone has noticed any unusual activity related to other people we're tracking in this investigation."

"You can't tell them. The kidnapper said—"

"I won't do anything I think will endanger Carlo. Why don't you go into the bathroom and clean the rest of the blood off your face while I make the call."

She glared at him, but stood and did as he asked. While she was out of the room, he'd talk to his supervisors about getting her into WITSEC right away—before the people who'd come after Carlo decided to come after her, too.

STACY STARED AT herself in the hotel bathroom mirror. She looked horrible—no makeup, blood matting her hair, an ugly bruise forming above her left eye. But what did it matter, with Carlo gone? Who would have taken him? Some enemy of the Giardinos, intent on revenge? Someone after money? She closed her eyes against the pounding in her head and tried to think, but her mind offered up no answers.

She debated eavesdropping on Marshal Thompson's phone call, but she didn't really want to hear what he had to say. And she needed to stay on his good side—he was the only one who could help her find Carlo. He'd seen the men who'd taken her boy, and he had weapons and a car and she presumed some training in tracking people. She wasn't going to do better right now.

She told herself she ought to be angry he'd followed her to Durango, but if he hadn't, she'd really be stuck with no one to turn to. And he'd been a decent enough guy. He'd listened to what she'd had to say and hadn't tried to order her around as if he automatically knew what was best. That was a change from the men she was used to dealing with.

Not that he wasn't all man. A woman would have to be half-dead not to notice those broad shoulders and muscular arms. He was taller and bigger than any of the Giardino men; she felt like a shrimp next to him. But that was okay. Being around him made her feel... safe. Something she hadn't felt in a long time.

He knocked on the door as she was washing the last of the blood out of her hair. She grabbed a towel and wrapped it around her head, turban fashion, and opened the door. "What did they say?" she asked.

"They agreed we shouldn't involve the local police. It might endanger the boy and it could jeopardize our investigation."

"What investigation? You keep using that word, but what are you investigating—me?"

"Not you. In fact, I want to move you into WIT-SEC right away. When we find Carlo, we'll bring him to you."

"No."

"I know you don't like the idea, but it's the best way to protect you and—"

"No. I'm not going anywhere until we know what happened to Carlo. When you find him, I'm going to be there."

"I can't track criminals with you in tow."

"I'm not going to get in your way, and I can help."

"How can you help?"

"I know how to shoot. I know how to keep quiet and stay out of the way and most of all—I know my child. In a tense situation, he'll come to me and I can keep him calm."

His mouth remained set in that stubborn line, his gaze boring into her, but she refused to let him intimidate her. She was through with men who tried to boss her around. "I won't go into WITSEC," she said. "If you don't let me go with you, I'll search for Carlo on my own." With no car, no gun and not even a clear picture of where she was, searching on her own wasn't a choice she wanted to make, but she could steal a car, buy a gun and read a map if she had to. She'd do whatever it took to find her boy.

"My first job is to protect you."

"Then you can do that by taking me with you to look for Carlo. Now come on. We're wasting time talking about it. We need to go after them."

She tried to push past him, but he stopped her, one hand on her shoulder. "You can't go out with wet hair. You'll freeze."

She pulled the towel from her head. "I don't care about my hair. It can dry in the car."

"You won't be any good to Carlo, or to me, if you catch pneumonia."

"Fine." She turned and grabbed the hair dryer that hung by the sink. "But as soon as my hair is dry, we leave."

She expected him to leave her to the task, but he remained in the doorway, reflected in the mirror, his gaze fixed on her. She tried to ignore him, but that was impossible; even if the mirror hadn't been there, she could feel his eyes on her, sense his big, brooding presence just over her shoulder. Why had he said that, about her not being any good to him if she got sick? Did he really think she was such as important witness in his mysterious "investigation"? He certainly didn't need her any other way.

Except maybe in the way men always seemed to need women, a traitorous voice in her head whispered. She shifted against an uncomfortable tightness in her lower abdomen, an awareness of herself not as mother, wife or daughter, but as a young, desirable woman. She'd buried that side of herself when she married Sammy Giardino—that it should resurface now astounded her. She'd heard of people who reacted to stress in inappropriate ways, for instance, by laughing at funerals. Was her response to tragedy and peril going to be this odd state of semiarousal? She couldn't think of anything less appropriate, especially if she was getting turned on by some big brute of a cop.

She switched off the hair dryer and whirled to face him. "What are you staring at?" she asked.

She expected him to say something about her looks—to tell her she was pretty or sexy or a similar come-on. It was the sort of thing men always said, especially when they wanted to talk you into their bed. Instead, he straightened and uncrossed his arms. "I was thinking how wrong the Giardinos were to take you for granted," he said, then, not waiting for an answer, he turned away.

She stared after him, confusion and pleasure warring in her. What some cop thought of her shouldn't matter, but she wasn't used to compliments—if, indeed, he'd meant the comment to be flattering. The fact that he saw past her physical presence to something in her character left her feeling off balance. She was used to people taking her for granted—not mattering to others was a kind of camouflage. It kept you safe. For this man to really see who she was past her skin felt daring and dangerous.

"Are you coming?" he called.

"Yes!" She grabbed up her coat and purse and followed him across the parking lot to his car—a black SUV that looked like something a rich tourist would drive, not a federal agent. If Carlo's kidnappers saw this vehicle behind them, they wouldn't be suspicious.

"Don't get your hopes up that this is going to work," he said as she buckled her seat belt. "If these guys are pros, they've already switched cars and headed out of town."

"But maybe they didn't," she said. "There isn't much traffic this time of night. Maybe we'll see them. They don't expect anyone to come after them, so maybe they'll be careless."

"That's a lot of maybes." He started the engine and put the vehicle in gear. "But criminals have done dumber things."

They turned onto the dark, deserted street and headed toward the highway. Streetlights shone on dirty snowbanks pushed up on the side of the road. They passed few cars; Stacy studied each one closely, but none contained anyone who looked like the man who had attacked her and taken Carlo.

They drove to the edge of town, then turned back and headed in the opposite direction. Patrick turned into a motel parking lot. "Look for a black sedan with mud on the plates," he said. "It's a long shot, but they may have holed up somewhere close."

Scarcely daring to breathe, she leaned close to the window and studied each vehicle they passed: old trucks, new SUVs, brightly colored sports cars. But no black sedan.

They checked four more motels with the same results. Patrick cruised through a silent shopping center. "I think they've left town," he said.

Profound weariness dragged at her. If she closed her eyes, she might fall asleep sitting up. Yet how could she sleep when Carlo was out there, frightened, held captive by strangers? "What do we do now?" she asked.

"We need a plan." He turned the car back toward their motel. "And we need more clues."

She took out her phone and stared at it, willing it to

ring. "If they'd just call and tell us what they want," she said.

"Maybe all they wanted was Carlo."

Carlo was all she wanted, too. He was all she had in this world. She couldn't accept that he'd disappear from her life this way. "He has to be out there somewhere," she said.

Patrick didn't answer. In the blue-white light of street lamps he looked grim and forbidding, shadows beneath his eyes and the golden glint of beard across his jaw. He looked like a man who wouldn't give up. She held on to that hope like a lifeline in a pitch-black sea.

Back at the hotel, she sank onto the edge of the bed. Her head throbbed and her eyes were scratchy from crying, but the physical discomfort was nothing compared with the pain of missing Carlo and feeling so helpless to do anything to protect him. "I'm going to look next door," Patrick said. "See if I can spot any clues. I'll need your key."

She fished the card from her purse, but didn't release her hold on it when he reached for it. "Give me your key," she said. "I'm going to the lobby for a soda. There's a vending machine there." The drink might settle her stomach and help her feel more alert.

They exchanged keys and she followed him out the door and walked past her room to the lobby. She kept out of view of the desk clerk, not wanting to explain the gash on her head, and found the vending machines in a back hallway. A handful of quarters later, she held a can of diet cola and a regular cola. Patrick didn't strike her as the diet type, but he'd probably appreciate the caffeine as much as she did.

Outside once more, she shivered in the cold that seemed to sink into her bones, despite the ski parka she hugged around herself. The parking lot was quiet and profoundly silent. Her footsteps on the concrete echoed in the stillness. The rooms she passed were dark and silent, as well. She and Patrick might have been the only ones here.

She hunched her shoulders and increased her pace. The sooner she was back with Patrick, the better she'd feel. And maybe he'd found something in her room that would lead them to Carlo.

She turned the corner of the building and strong arms grabbed her from behind. A man's thick fingers clamped over her mouth and a sharp blade pricked at her throat. "Make a sound and you're dead."

Chapter Five

The scent of Stacy's perfume—something expensive and floral—lingered in her hotel room. Patrick stood in the doorway and surveyed the scene, searching for anything that might provide a clue as to the identity of Carlo's kidnappers. The double bed still bore the indentations where mother and son had slept, and a single strand of white-blond hair glinted on the pillow. Patrick studied the hair and thought of the woman who had left it behind—such a compelling mix of strength and frailty, reserve and openness. She refused to cooperate in letting him protect her, and that only served to make him more determined to keep her from harm.

He turned away from the bed and examined the dull-brown carpeting, which was worn and matted, especially in front of the door. But a fresh smear of mud caught his eye. He knelt and with the tip of a pen, pried up a quarter-size fragment of the still-pliable clay. He sniffed it and caught the definite odor of manure—from horses? Cows?

He found an envelope in the desk drawer and slid the mud sample inside. He could have someone analyze it to narrow down the probable source, but dirt alone wouldn't be enough to find a man who didn't want to be found.

He searched the rest of the room and the bathroom and closet and came up empty-handed. Stacy had come here with nothing but the clothes on her back. What had she planned to do? Where would she have gone from here?

He would ask her, but he doubted she'd tell him. She definitely kept things to herself. *I know how to keep quiet and stay out of the way,* she'd said. Is that how she'd survived in the Giardino household — by being invisible? He'd known women like that, who suppressed every opinion and action and feeling in order to survive living with an abuser. In the end, they almost always ended up hurt anyway. Anger flared at the thought that Stacy had been forced to live that way.

He left the room, closing the door quietly behind him. He was turning toward his own room when a muffled sound made the hair on the back of his neck stand up. He waited and the sound came again, very faint, from up the walkway and around the corner.

The rough brick of the building scraped against his jacket as he flattened himself against it, his gun drawn and held upright against his chest. He moved sideways, one silent step at a time, toward the corner. A quick glance down this side of the motel revealed nothing incriminating. Then he spotted the darkened niche that held trash cans and a fire extinguisher. Nothing moved within that shadowed space, yet his heart raced in warning. He cocked his weapon, then slid a mini Maglite from his pocket and directed the beam into the darkest recesses of the alcove.

And into the terrified eyes of Stacy.

"Drop the gun or she's dead!" barked a man's voice.

Patrick carefully uncocked the weapon and let it fall to the sidewalk. "Who are you?" he asked. "What do you want?"

A man, middle-aged and bulky with muscle and layers of clothing, moved out of the niche, dragging Stacy with him. Her gray eyes were wide with fright, all color drained from her face. But the bright red blood that beaded where the blade of her captor's knife met her neck stood out against her pale skin. The wound made Patrick see red of a different kind, and he sucked in a deep breath, forcing himself to maintain calm.

"Stay there," the bulky man ordered. "My friend will be along in a minute to take care of you."

Patrick ignored the threat. Whether it was real or not, he needed to focus on the man in front of him and learn all he could about him in order to know how to defeat him. This guy didn't look like the one who'd taken Carlo; he was shorter and stockier. He wore dark slacks and a black overcoat and a stocking cap, but no mask.

"Where are you taking me?" Stacy asked, her voice quavering.

"Shut up!" the man said, and a fresh trickle of blood leaked from beneath the blade of the knife.

Stacy's eyes widened, but she kept talking. "Are you taking me to Carlo?" she asked. "If you're taking me to my son, I'll go willingly."

"My boss wants to see you." Like too many people, Stacy's captor apparently couldn't follow his own advice about keeping quiet.

"Who is your boss?" Patrick asked.

"One more word out of you and I cut her throat." He jerked Stacy more tightly against him and she gasped. Her eyes widened again, but not in pain this time. Patrick whirled around in time to see a second, thinner man move toward him. His knees slammed into the concrete walkway as he dropped to the ground and air reverberated with the sound of the shots that sailed over his head.

Stacy screamed and fought wildly against the man who held her. Patrick was torn between trying to save her and dealing with the second man, who had lowered his weapon to fire again. Stacy distracted them both as her heel connected hard with the stocky man's kneecap and sent him reeling. Patrick dived for his gun, rolled and came up firing as the second man let loose another volley of shots. The man fell back, shot in the chest, and Patrick leaped to his feet and pointed his weapon at the stocky man.

But Stacy's attacker was already running away across the parking lot. Patrick took off after him, pounding across the pavement, but the stocky man's bulk was deceiving; he quickly outpaced the marshal and was swallowed up in darkness.

Breathing hard from the exertion and the altitude, Patrick returned to Stacy. She stood with one hand to her throat, staring down at the wounded man, who lay inert, blood seeping from the chest wound. "Are you all right?" Patrick touched her shoulder and looked into her eyes. Some of the terror had receded, replaced by the weariness of someone who had seen too much to process.

"I'm okay." She took a deep breath. "I don't know about him, though." She indicated the man on the ground.

Patrick knelt beside him. "Who sent you?" he asked.

The man gave no answer; he appeared unconscious.

"I've called 911." The desk clerk, wide-eyed and breathless, raced up to them. "I heard the shots." He gaped at the man on the ground. "Who is he? Is he dead?"

Patrick searched the man's pockets and found a wallet and a driver's license. "This says his name is Nathan Forest."

"What happened?" The clerk turned to Stacy. "You're bleeding! I should have asked for an ambulance."

Patrick replaced Forest's wallet and stood. "This man and his companion tried to mug Ms. Jackson." He took Stacy's arm. "We'd better go."

She nodded, and didn't try to pull away when he turned her toward his room.

"Shouldn't you wait for the police?" the clerk asked.

"You can tell them everything they need to know." Patrick hurried with Stacy down the walkway and into his room, where he shut and locked the door. Then he led her into the brightly lit bathroom. "Tip your head back and let me have a look," he said, one finger under her chin.

She winced with the effort, but lifted her chin and let him examine the wound. "I imagine it hurts, but it's not very deep," he said. He grabbed a hand towel from a stack by the sink and handed it to her. "Put that around your neck to stop the bleeding, and then we've got to get out of here before the police show up. They'll ask a lot of questions we don't want to answer right now."

She pressed the towel to her neck. "Thank you," she said.

"For what?"

"For not involving the police."

"I'll have someone from my office contact them to see if they learn anything about Forest and his companion, but for now I don't want to waste any time with them. Get your things and let's go."

They passed the police cruiser and the ambulance on their way out of the parking lot. Stacy, the bloody towel in her lap, watched over her shoulder until the motel was out of sight, then faced forward once more. "Neither one of those men looked like the man who took Carlo," she said.

"I didn't think so, either," he said.

"So who were they? What did they want?"

He checked the mirror. So far, so good. They weren't being followed. "Two possibilities come to mind," he said. "Carlo was too much to handle, so whoever orchestrated the first kidnapping sent those two to get you."

"Then I would have gone with them. I could have helped Carlo."

"The other possibility is that the first two guys screwed up. They weren't supposed to leave you behind as a witness, so these two were supposed to finish the job."

She sucked in her breath and touched the cut on her neck. "What are we going to do now?"

"We need to find another place to stay. We need sleep and a shower and you need to take care of your wounds."

"I can't sleep, not when I could be out looking for Carlo."

"You can't help him if you're half-dead on your feet.

And we aren't going to find anything wandering around in the dark. Tomorrow morning we'll start fresh. I'm going to call my office and arrange to get another car. The desk clerk will tell the local police about this one and they'll probably be looking for it, to talk to us about Nathan Forest."

"I'll bet that's not his real name."

She was smart enough to figure that out, at least. "Nathan Bedford Forest was a Confederate general during the Civil War," he said. "Maybe this guy's mother or father was a history buff."

"Or maybe he made it up."

"Probably he made it up."

"And after we get a new car?"

"I think we'd better go see your Uncle Abel and find out if he knows anything about what's going on."

"Uncle Abel? Do you think he's behind this?"

"He's the closest living relative to Sam Giardino— the one Sam threatened to put in charge of the family business. And didn't you say he has a ranch somewhere around here?"

"Crested Butte. Do you think he has Carlo? Or knows who does?"

"The man who took Carlo had mud on his shoes— mud mixed with manure. The kind of thing you'd find on a ranch."

"But that could be anywhere—it doesn't have to be Abel's ranch."

"You're right. But it's the only clue we have right now. Talking to Abel seems a good place to start. If he doesn't know anything, maybe he can tell us who would be interested in the boy. You said Sam threatened to pass the family business on to Abel?"

"I don't think he was serious. Everyone always said the two brothers weren't on good terms."

"They might have patched up their differences and been in touch recently. Maybe that's why Sam decided to vacation in Colorado."

"Maybe." She sounded doubtful. "What if Abel doesn't know anything?"

"We'll worry about that when the time comes."

STACY WAS WORN out with worry by the time Patrick located a motel he thought suitable for their purposes. Set back from the road on a side street, the collection of 1950s-era cabins strung together in a row offered rooms for rent by the week and free local phone calls. "There's a light in the office, so we should be able to get a room," Patrick said as he cruised past the place. "I'll park the car a few blocks away and we'll walk back."

"Why do we have to do that?" she protested. The thought of walking even a few hundred yards in the dark and cold made her want to sink down into the seat and refuse to move.

"If the police spot the car, I don't want to make it easy for them to find us."

In the end, she made the walk leaning on Patrick. When he'd offered his support her first instinct had been to refuse, but she was so tired she was almost dizzy, and his arm around her was the only thing that felt safe and solid in the world.

Their room was cold and musty, with two double beds covered with green chenille spreads, and the kind of maple furniture Stacy remembered from visits to her grandmother's house when she was a little girl. She stretched out on the bed farthest from the door while Patrick made phone calls.

Though she would have sworn she was too worried to sleep, she was unconscious within seconds, despite the glare of the overhead light and the low murmur of Patrick's voice across the room. She woke some time later to darkness, and the sensation of someone slipping her boots from her feet, then tucking a blanket around her. She opened her eyes and stared up at Patrick. "I didn't want to wake you," he said, and settled the blanket around her shoulders.

She struggled back to consciousness. "What did your office say? Do they know anything about Nathan Forest?"

"Nothing yet. They're going to send someone with a new car for us. In the meantime, go back to sleep."

"You won't leave, will you?" Where had that question come from? She'd never wanted this lawman in her life, but now, with Carlo missing and after being attacked twice in one night by strangers, the thought of being left alone terrified her.

"No, I won't leave." He patted her shoulder. "I'm going to lie down in the other bed and try to get some sleep. You do the same."

"All right." But welcome oblivion didn't return easily. She lay in the darkness, listening to the hum and tick of the heater, and the creak of bedsprings as Patrick shifted on his own mattress. He definitely wasn't like any lawman she'd ever encountered—not that she'd known many. Along with the rest of the family, she'd attended Sam Giardino's trial a year and a half ago and seen the officers who surrounded him—cool, expressionless men and women in uniform who never glanced her way. She'd never bothered to differentiate one from the other. They were all simply "the law." The enemies of the Giardino family, and thus her enemies, too.

Patrick had that same erect bearing and devotion to duty. He'd regarded her with suspicion from the moment he found her hiding in the basement, and he'd followed her to Durango because he suspected her of some wrongdoing, she was sure.

But he'd also risked his own life to protect her, and he'd ignored at least some of the law to help search for Carlo without involving the local police. She was a stranger to him, yet he acted like he cared. Did he think she was such a valuable witness for his mysterious case, or was something else at work here?

Sleep finally overtook her, though she slept fitfully, haunted by dreams of shadowy figures who pursued her and glimpses of Carlo reaching for her, calling for her, his little face streaked with tears.

"Stacy, wake up. It's all right. You're safe."

She woke sobbing, the pillowcase wet from her tears. In the dim glow from the bedside lamp, she stared at Patrick. He'd removed his shirt, belt and shoes, and sat on the side of the bed dressed only in slacks. Light glinted on the dusting of hair across his muscular chest. Such an odd thing to notice at a time like this, she thought. It was such an intimate, masculine detail—maybe her mind's attempt to avoid thinking about the bad dreams, or the reality that her son had been taken from her.

"You had a bad dream," he said, one hand resting warm and heavy on her shoulder.

"I was dreaming of Carlo." Her voice broke, and she closed her eyes in a futile effort to hold back more tears.

"I really don't think the people who took him will hurt him," he said.

"How can you say that? I read in the paper about children who are kidnapped and suffer horrible things." She pressed her hand to her mouth to stop the words, though she couldn't keep back the thoughts behind them.

"This doesn't feel like that kind of crime," he said. "They wanted Carlo specifically, and I think they want him alive and unharmed."

"You can't know that," she said.

"No. But I have good instincts about these things."

She wanted to believe him. He sounded so calm and certain. So reassuring. "I'm scared to go back to sleep," she said. "Scared of the dreams."

"You need to rest." He looked at the clock beside the bed. It showed 3:19 a.m., though it seemed days since she'd gotten off the bus in Durango. So much had happened.

He reached to turn off the light again and she grabbed his wrist. "Please."

"You want me to leave the light on?"

With the light on the chances of either one of them getting more sleep would be less. And she needed him alert and ready for action tomorrow. Or later today, actually. But the thought of facing the darkness again unsettled her. "Maybe you could just…lie here beside me." She looked away as she spoke. He probably thought she was trying to come on to him; men always thought that. "Just lie here, nothing else," she added. "I'd feel safer that way."

He looked past her to the pillow on the other side of the bed. "All right." He got up and walked around the bed, then stretched out on top of the covers. "Will you cut the light out now?" he asked.

She reached up and switched off the lamp. The weight of his body made the mattress dip toward him. If she relaxed even a little, she'd probably slide down toward him. "You should get a blanket," she said. "You'll be cold."

He reached over and pulled the spread from the bed closest to the door. "I'll be fine now," he said. "Get some sleep."

She closed her eyes and tried to do as he'd said, but the awareness of him next to her kept her tense. She lay rigid, trying not to move or breathe, waiting for morning.

"What's wrong?" he asked, long after she was sure he'd fallen asleep.

You're what's wrong, she could have said. *I want you here and I don't want you here.* "I don't know," she said. "So much has happened."

"You've been through a lot," he said. "Too much."

"How do you deal with it?" she asked. "I mean, people shooting at you. Having to shoot other people."

"I try to stay focused on what's important."

"What's important," she repeated. Carlo was the only thing that was really important to her. "Do you have a family? Kids?" She knew so little about him.

"No family. No kids. My parents are still alive, but they retired to Florida. I don't see them a lot."

"So it's just you."

"I have a sister. She's in Denver, so I see her as much as I can."

"That's nice." She'd always wanted a sister or brother, someone who knew her and all about her life and loved her anyway. Unconditionally. At least, that was what she imagined having a sibling would be like. "No girlfriend?" She wished she could take the question back as soon as she asked it. She didn't want him thinking she was interested in him that way, not with him lying next to her in bed like this.

He was silent a long moment before answering. "This kind of job is hard on relationships."

"Life is hard on relationships." At least, the life she knew. Her parents had been together for years, but that was more out of stubbornness than anything else. The Giardinos stayed together because divorce was dangerous. Sammy had made it clear that if she tried to leave him she would lose everything—the money, Carlo and even her life.

She squeezed her eyes shut. She didn't want to think about Sammy or the Giardinos. She needed to stay focused on the present. Right here. Right now. Talking to Patrick was calming her down. She felt as if she could say anything to him here in the dark, knowing he was close, but not touching him. Not seeing his face to read whether he was judging her or not. Just laying it all out there. "Do you ever get lonely?" she asked.

"All the time."

"Yeah." She licked her lips, tasting the salt from her tears. "Me, too."

She gave up resisting then and let her body slide toward his. She lay alongside him, and rested her head in the hollow of his shoulder. He stiffened. "What are you doing?"

"Nothing," she said. "Just…hold me. That's all."

Gradually, he relaxed, and brought his arm up to cradle her close. "I just…don't want to feel so alone right now," she said. "Don't make a big deal out of it or anything."

She was prepared for him to argue, or to try to take advantage. If that happened, she'd have to move away. But he merely let out a long breath. "All right," he said. "Get some sleep."

But she was already sinking under, lulled by his warmth and strength, and the sensation that here was a man who could protect her, the way no man ever had.

Chapter Six

Patrick woke from restless sleep, aroused and all-too-aware of the woman nestled against him. Though Stacy was fully dressed, the soft fullness of her breast pressed against his side, and her hand, palm down, lay on his stomach, tantalizingly close to the erection that all but begged for her attention.

A lesser man—one who didn't have the job of protecting a witness in a federal case and tracking down her missing child—might have taken advantage of the situation. He could have rolled over and pulled her close and sought comfort and release for both of them in the act of lovemaking.

But even if Stacy Giardino had been open to the idea of sex with him—and considering her wariness of him the day before, that was doubtful—she was off-limits to him. She was his responsibility and his duty, not a potential lover.

Reminding himself of this didn't do a lot to quell his desire, but it enabled him to ease himself away from her and out of bed. He pulled on his shirt, then checked his phone on the way to the bathroom. A text from his office informed him a four-wheel-drive Jeep had been left for him in the parking lot, the keys under the driver's-side floor mat. Someone had picked up his other car from its parking place two blocks over, along with the sample of mud from Stacy's hotel room that he'd left on the backseat.

A second text informed him that Nathan Forest had died before regaining consciousness. So far nothing new had surfaced about his identity or his connections.

The bedsprings creaked as he stepped out of the bathroom and Stacy let out a soft moan. He moved to the side of the bed. "Stacy?" he asked softly.

She blinked up at him, confusion quickly replaced by the pain of remembering all that had happened. He tensed, prepared for her to break down, but she pulled herself together and shoved herself into a sitting position. "Have you heard any news?" she asked.

"We have a new car and Nathan Forest is dead. Nothing more."

She covered her eyes with one hand. The gash on her forehead was bruised around the edges, but it didn't look infected. She probably should have had stitches to prevent a scar, but it was too late for that now. The cuts on her neck glowed pink against the pale skin. "How are you feeling?" he asked.

"Everything hurts." She uncovered her eyes and looked around the room. "Is there coffee?"

A two-cup coffeemaker and supplies sat on a tray by the television. "I'll make some," he said. "Why don't you take a shower?"

"Good idea." She moved past him to the bathroom and a few seconds later he heard the water running. He started the coffee, then slipped out to the car.

The Jeep was several years old, the red paint faded

and the leather seats worn. But it was equipped with a new GPS and good tires. And in the backseat he found two plastic shopping bags filled with toiletries, snacks and a change of clothes for each of them. Somebody at headquarters deserved a commendation for that.

He carried the bags inside and tapped on the bathroom door. "Stacy, I've got a bag here with some clothes and other things for you," he said.

No answer. Maybe she couldn't hear him for the shower.

He tried the knob. The door wasn't locked. He eased the door open, keeping his eyes averted from the steaming shower, and set the bag just inside the door, then went to pour himself a cup of coffee and wait.

When she emerged from the bathroom half an hour later, damp hair curling around her face and smelling of floral soap, he was seated on the end of the bed, the television on and turned to the local news. "I've never been so grateful for clean underwear and toothpaste in my life," she said. "Where did they come from?"

"The agent who delivered the new car left them."

"Well, he—or she—deserves a raise." She smoothed a hand over the pink-and-white hoodie and matching yoga pants. "I'm betting it's a woman with good taste. She even thought to include a little face powder and lipstick. I feel almost human again."

She definitely looked like she was feeling better. The dark circles beneath her eyes had faded some, and she'd combed her hair to hide most of the gash on her forehead. In the casual clothing, with the lighter makeup, she looked younger and more vulnerable than she had when he'd first questioned her the day before.

He stood and rubbed his hand across the bristles on his chin. "I think I'll shower and shave," he said. "There are some snacks in that other bag there. Help yourself to breakfast."

She glanced at the television. "Any news?"

"Nothing of interest to us."

After a shower and shave, he dressed in the Nordic sweater and jeans he found in the bag and returned to the bedroom. The casual clothing made him and Stacy look more like tourists, or even locals. Stacy sat cross-legged on the end of the bed, eating peanut butter crackers and staring at the television. "They just did a promo about a shootout at a Durango hotel last night," she said. "I think that's us."

He sat beside her and waited through commercials for a used-car dealer, life insurance and dish detergent. Then a somber-faced reporter came on to report on an exclusive break in the story of a shooting at a local hotel. "Though the incident was at first reported to be a random mugging, we've since learned information that ties this killing to organized crime. The woman assaulted, who has since disappeared, was Stacy Giardino, daughter-in-law of fugitive Sam Giardino, head of one of the country's deadliest organized crime families, who was gunned down at a vacation home near Telluride yesterday morning. Ms. Giardino was accompanied by a man who identified himself as a U.S. Marshal. The two left the hotel shortly after the shooting before local police could question them. If you see either Ms. Giardino or her companion, please contact police immediately."

The reporter described Patrick as two inches shorter

than his true height, with brown hair. The screen then flashed a photograph of Stacy that had been taken at her wedding, almost five years before. She'd worn her hair long then and looked all of sixteen, swallowed up in yards of billowing tulle and satin.

Patrick punched the remote to turn off the television. "I don't think we have to worry about anyone tracking us down based on that description, but we shouldn't take any chances."

"How did they figure out who we are?" she asked. "I registered at the hotel under a fake name."

"I used my real name," Patrick said. "And I showed the clerk my U.S. Marshal's ID. He probably gave that information to police and someone made the connection to Sam Giardino. Nothing is really secret anymore."

"What are we going to do?" she asked.

"Keep moving and try not to attract attention."

"I'm ready to leave now." She stood and brushed crumbs from her lap. "You said we were going to Uncle Abel's ranch?"

"That's the plan. Do you know where it is?"

She shook her head. "Just Crested Butte. I don't think the town's that big. Maybe we could ask?"

"We could, but we'll have to be careful. We don't want to let them know we're on their trail, if they have Carlo."

"Do you think they do?"

"I don't know. But it's the only direction I can think to go at the moment. I asked my office to look for an Abel Giardino in Crested Butte, but they haven't turned up anything yet."

"Maybe he's using another name. The family story

was always that he didn't want anything to do with the business."

"That could be. I think the best thing for us to do now is to go to the town and see what we can find out."

"How long will it take us to get there?" she asked.

"About five hours, if the weather cooperates."

She glanced out the window. "It's gray out there, but it's not actually snowing."

"We should be fine. Come on."

They carried the supplies and their dirty clothes with them, not wanting to leave behind anything the authorities—or their enemies—could use to track them. Though not as comfortable as his Rover, the Jeep ran well, and the heater worked, blasting out heat to cut the frigid outside temperature.

They soon reached the outskirts of town and drove past empty snow-covered fields and expanses of evergreen woods and rocky outcroppings. Occasionally one or two houses sat back from the road, or small herds of horses or cattle gathered around hay that had been spread for them. "How do people live out here?" Stacy asked. "It's so remote."

"It is, but maybe you and I think that because we're city people."

"Where are you from?" she asked.

"New York. I grew up in Queens, just like you."

She hugged her arms across her chest. "I don't know if I like that you know so much about me. I'm not a criminal, you know. I've never had so much as a parking ticket."

"I know." At least, she hadn't actively participated

in any crimes that he knew of. "But you married into a criminal family."

"So that makes me guilty by association?"

"In a way, it does." Innocent, law-abiding people didn't have intimate connections to mob criminals, in his experience.

"Was that why you followed me to Durango? Because you thought I was going to commit a crime?"

"I wondered why you were running away from the protection we offered. I wanted to see what you would do."

"You call it protection—I call it another form of prison." She looked away. "I've had enough of that, thank you."

"Are you saying you were a prisoner of the Giardinos?"

"I might as well have been. I promised 'til death do us part, and Sammy made it clear I had to keep that promise."

"You told me your father and his father arranged the marriage, but you never told me why you agreed to it."

"My father owed Sam Giardino some kind of debt. I don't know what it was, but he made it clear that I had to marry Sammy in order to save his life."

So a wife for Sammy was the price for George Franklin's safety? From what Patrick knew of Sam Giardino, this kind of twisted plan was his specialty. "How old were you?"

"I was nineteen. I had a dead-end job at a boutique in the mall, but I wanted to go to college. I knew the Giardinos had money. I figured I'd marry Sammy, save my dad, go to school on Sammy's dime and divorce him after a few years. But it didn't work out that way."

The regret in her voice pulled at him. "No divorce."

"And no school. Sam thought educating women was a waste of money and what he said was the law. So Sammy went to law school and I read his books and wrote his papers."

"And you had Carlo."

"Yes." She picked at imaginary lint on her pants. "I love him more than anything, and I'm so glad I have him now, but I wasn't thrilled about becoming pregnant so quickly. Of course, by then I'd figured out that even without a kid, the Giardinos weren't going to let me leave. Once Carlo came along, I was really stuck."

"What will you do now that Sammy is dead?"

"I'd like to go back to school, if I can scrape up the money. I'll get a job, find a place to live. I figure after helping Sammy through law school getting my own law degree won't be too hard."

Simple dreams. Not the plans of a criminal mind. Of course, some criminals were very good actors. They could make people believe what they wanted them to. But he didn't think Stacy fell into that category. "What kind of law?"

"I don't know. I'd like to do something to help women and children."

"You'd make a good lawyer."

"You really think so?"

"You're calm under pressure. You're smart and you know how to think on your feet."

"Thanks. I really fooled you, because I don't feel

calm." She twisted her hands together. "Do you think we'll find Carlo?"

"We'll find him." He tightened his fingers around the steering wheel. He would get the boy back to his mother if it was the last thing he did.

The strains of an Alicia Keys song drifted up from the floorboards. Stacy stared at him, the color drained from her face. "My phone."

"Answer it." He pulled over to the side of the road, but left the engine running.

She fumbled in her purse and pulled out the phone. "Hello?"

"Put it on speaker," he said.

She did so, and a woman's soft, deep voice filled the Jeep. "Hello, Stacy."

"Who is this?"

"That's not important. But unless you want your son's death on your hands, you'll turn around now and go back to Durango or New York or Timbuktu, for all I care. Do that, and we'll let you both live. Keep on the course you're on and we'll kill the boy and then come after you again. And this time, you won't escape."

"Who are you? What have you done with my son?" She raised her voice. "Carlo, are you there? Can you hear me? It's Mommy."

"Mommy! Mommy, where are you? I'm scared. Mommy!"

The phone went dead. Stacy covered her mouth with one hand and stared at the phone.

Patrick gently pried the phone from her hand and scrolled back to the history. "Unknown number," he said. "I could try to have someone trace it, but they were probably smart enough to make the call from a throwaway phone, or even a pay phone. There's still a few of those around."

"What are we going to do?" Her voice shook, but she was holding it together. After hearing her son's voice in distress, that took a lot of guts. His job was to stay calm and make it as easy as he could for her.

"First, we get rid of the phone." He slid the cover off the back and popped out the SIM chip, dropped it to the floor of the Jeep and smashed it with his heel. Then he broke the rest of the phone into as many pieces as he could and tossed them out the window.

"You can't just throw them out the window," she protested.

"I'm sorry, but we can't risk keeping the phone when someone can use it to trace you."

"No, I mean, you're littering."

She looked so genuinely distressed, he bit back his laughter. "I'll write myself a ticket later. Come on. We have to get out of here." He put the Jeep in gear and made a U-turn, headed back the way they'd come.

STILL REELING FROM hearing Carlo crying for her, Stacy struggled to understand what was happening. "What are you doing?" she asked Patrick. "Where are you going?" Surely he wasn't giving up the plan to go to Crested Butte.

"That was in case anyone was watching. I want them to think we're acting on their threat and retreating. I looked at the map while you were in the shower this morning and we can get to Crested Butte another way, using back roads."

She sat back, though truly relaxing was impossible. Carlo had sounded so upset.... She swallowed a knot of tears. She couldn't break down now. She had to keep it together, for her little boy's sake.

Patrick patted her arm—though whether this was a gesture of reassurance or merely to get her attention, she wasn't sure. "Did you recognize the woman's voice?" he asked.

"No." There had been nothing familiar about the voice at all.

"Is Abel married?"

"He wasn't the last time I saw him, but that was five years ago."

"He was living with his mother then."

"Yes. And she didn't sound like that. She was old."

"How old?"

"Seventies? Abel is fifty, at least. Maybe we're on the wrong track." This new idea increased her agitation. "Maybe Abel doesn't have anything to do with this and we're wasting time, while whoever does have Carlo gets farther and farther away."

"That's possible. But whoever has him knew—probably from your phone—that we'd left Durango and were headed toward Crested Butte. And they wanted you to go away. That tells me we're headed in exactly the right direction."

"What if they do have someone watching us and he—or she—figures out we didn't really turn around?" She looked around, as if expecting to see someone spying on them. "They might hurt Carlo."

"I don't think so. They took the boy on purpose, for a specific reason. If they'd wanted to kill him, they could have done away with both of you in your hotel room before either of you woke up. They're making these threats to scare you and keep you away, but I think they want the boy alive."

"But why would they want him? He's just a baby." Her voice trembled on these last words, but she sucked in a deep breath and continued. "He can't tell them anything or give them anything."

"What about Sam Giardino's will? Does Carlo inherit anything now that Sammy is dead, too?"

"You'd know the answer to that better than I do. Doesn't the government confiscate ill-gotten gains?"

"If they can prove a link to a crime, yes."

"It's not as if Sammy had tons of cash and money in bank accounts. He lived well, but most of his money was in the business. And Elizabeth is still alive. She's bound to inherit something."

"But the majority would go to his son, or his son's son, I would think."

"Yeah. Sam was a chauvinist, all right. Though he'd have said he was following tradition." Women didn't rate as high as the family dog in the Giardino household. "But even if Sam had decided to leave his money to Carlo, he wouldn't just hand everything over to a three-year-old," she said. "There'd be a trust or something to tie the money up until Carlo was old enough to take control."

"Then maybe money isn't the driving force here. What else?"

"I can't think of any reason why anyone would want to take Carlo." He was her baby. No one loved him or cared for him more than she did—why would anyone else even notice him?

"I think this is our turnoff up here," he said, indicating a road that branched to the left. "It goes around the lake and doesn't get much use this time of year, but it's usually kept plowed."

"I'll take your word for it," she said.

The two-lane road was paved for the first mile, and then blacktop gave way to gravel. A thin layer of snow covered the rock, and banks of snow had been pushed up on either side. He had to slow his speed to about thirty around the many curves; no doubt it would take even longer to get to Crested Butte. She struggled to avoid fidgeting with impatience.

"I still can't believe anyone would want anything from Carlo," she said after half an hour of silence. Talking was better than letting her thoughts range out of control, and for a guy, Patrick was a decent listener. He didn't discount her ideas with every breath.

"Maybe we're looking at this wrong," Patrick said. "Maybe Carlo isn't the target at all—maybe it's you."

"Me?"

"If someone wanted to hurt you, what better way to do that than to take away the one person who matters most to you?"

She wrapped her arms across her stomach, his words like a physical blow. "If Sammy was still alive, I might believe he'd do something like this. He hated me enough."

"Why did he hate you?"

She'd spent most of her marriage trying to figure out the answer to that question. "I was one more thing his father forced on him. Left to his own devices, he'd have chosen a tall, long-legged, busty model type. Someone he could dress up and show off, who'd cling to his arm and look at him adoringly and pretend not to have a brain in her head."

"It's not as if you aren't attractive."

She winced. Did he feel sorry for her? Why else would he be handing out compliments? "He called me 'troll.'" Saying the hated nickname out loud still hurt. "And he said I was too smart for my own good." Though at least she was smart enough not to feel insulted by his acknowledgment of her brains.

Patrick's knuckles on the steering wheel whitened. "You're not a troll," he said. "And I'd rather be with a smart woman than ten supermodels who play dumb."

"I don't guess you get many chances to guard supermodels," she said. "You might change your mind if you did."

She didn't give him a chance to hand out more false compliments. She sat forward and peered at the road ahead. "Are you sure we're headed the right way? This doesn't look like much of a road."

The graveled two-track had narrowed further, trees closing in on either side. They'd seen no sign of houses or other traffic in miles. "The map showed this as an alternate route." He glanced at the screen on the GPS unit mounted on the dash. "And the GPS shows we're headed in the right direction."

"It just doesn't look as if anyone has traveled this way in a while."

"That's good. Whoever is threatening you won't think to check this route."

"Maybe not." But her expression remained clouded.

They rounded a curve and he had to slam on the brakes to avoid hitting a tree. The huge pine lay across the road, branches filling their field of vision, the needles almost black against the white snow. Patrick shifted into Park and stared at the tree. It completely blocked both lanes.

"What do we do now?" Stacy asked.

He slipped his gun from his holster, making sure it was loaded and ready to fire, then grasped the door handle. "Stay here while I check things out," he said. "If anyone starts shooting, stay down."

Chapter Seven

The tree was positioned perfectly for an ambush, lying in the arc of a narrow, uphill curve with thick woods on either side. Keeping low and using the car as a shield, Patrick examined the snow around them for tracks, but found only the prints of squirrels and birds. He froze and strained his ears, listening, but heard only the pinging of the cooling engine and his own labored breathing.

Slowly, he made his way along the tree to the trunk, and felt some of the tension ease out of him when he saw the bare roots stretching toward the sky. This tree hadn't been cut, as he'd first suspected, but had fallen, toppling over in a storm, or from the weight of snow and age.

He holstered his weapon and balanced on the tree trunk to peer over the branches at the road beyond. The snow on that side looked much deeper, the route barely discernible. The tree had probably been here awhile. He jumped down and tramped back toward the car.

Stacy climbed out of the passenger side and met him halfway. "What were you looking at up ahead?" she asked. "What did you see?"

"Looks like the tree blew over in the last storm. The

road's completely blocked. We'll have to turn around and go back the way we came."

"Couldn't we move the tree or something?"

"Even if we could, the road up ahead hasn't been plowed. We'd never make it through."

"I can't believe we've wasted so much time coming all this way only to have to backtrack," she said.

"Me, too. But it can't be helped. And maybe doing so convinced the kidnappers that we've given up."

"How could anyone believe a mother would ever give up looking for her child?"

"Maybe they don't have children." He reached for the door handle as the glass in the door shattered into a thousand glittering shards.

"Get down!" he shouted, as he dived beneath the car. The sharp report of gunfire echoed through the canyon, the sound folding in on itself until the crescendo crackled like thunder. Bullets slammed into the side and top of the vehicle, rocking it from side to side and shattering the front windshield and mirrors.

"Stacy!" He turned his head, searching for her, but nothing moved in the limited area he was able to see from his place beneath the car. He slid sideways on his stomach, gravel digging into his elbows and knees. The silence following the gunfire pressed down on him, the only sounds the pinging of the cooling engine and the scrape of his body as he dragged it across the gravel.

He emerged on the opposite side of the car, using the vehicle as a shield between himself and the shooter. "Stacy?" he called again.

"Over here."

He followed her voice to a narrow space between two

boulders on the side of the road, but when he started toward her, another barrage of gunfire sent him diving for the cover of the vehicle.

"Patrick?" Her voice rose in alarm. "Are you all right?"

"I'm fine. Are you okay?"

"I'm okay. What are we going to do?"

He levered himself up just enough to peer over the hood of the car at the opposite side of the canyon. Nothing stirred in the red-and-gold rock cliffs, but the shots had definitely come from that direction. But where, exactly?

He slipped out of his coat, then searched the side of the road until he found a broken tree branch. He draped the coat over the branch and raised it up above the hood of the car. Shots erupted from an outcropping of rock opposite. Was it his imagination, or were these shots from a lower trajectory than the previous barrage? Was the gunman working his way down to them? Or was he simply moving in closer for a better chance to pick them off?

He glanced back over his shoulder toward the niche where Stacy sheltered. He couldn't see her, and he couldn't risk crossing the open space between her and the car. "Stacy, can you hear me?" he asked, keeping his voice low.

"Yes."

"I'm going to try to climb up and come in behind the shooter. But I need you to distract him while I get away."

"How can I do that?"

"I'm going to give you my gun and I want you to shoot up at the canyon wall—just enough to draw their fire. While they're focused on you, I'll get on the other side of the fallen tree and start up the canyon on the other side. I should be far enough down there that they won't be able to see me."

"I don't think we should split up," she said. "What if they do see you and shoot you?"

"I won't let that happen. If I don't try this, they'll just keep us pinned down here until dark, then they'll move in and pick us off."

Silence. Had he frightened her so much she was unable to speak?

"All right," she said after a long moment. "Tell me what to do."

"When I tell you, move as fast as you can to my side. Stay low."

"All right."

He sighted in on the rock outcropping and steadied his pistol on the hood of the car. "Now!" he called, and squeezed off three quick shots.

Stacy hurtled out of her hiding place and dived into the snow beside him as another hail of bullets shook the car.

Patrick helped her to sit up. Blood streaked her face. "You're hurt," he said.

She shook her head. "Just some broken glass that nicked my cheek. I'm fine. Now tell me what to do."

He fit a fresh magazine to the weapon and handed it to her. "See that rock outcropping up there—the one where there's a slash of almost purple-colored stone, sort of shaped like an arrowhead?"

She nodded. "I see it."

"When I give the word, start shooting at that outcropping. Just hold down the trigger and empty the magazine at that spot."

"You can't go up there without a gun."

"I have another." He slid the SIG Sauer from the ankle holster and checked the load. "I'm going to leave you with an extra magazine." He didn't explain she was to use the other bullets if their assailants slipped past him and came after her, she was smart enough to figure that out on her own.

She clutched the gun in both hands, keeping the barrel pointed at the ground. "Be careful," she said

"I will." He rested his hand on her shoulder for a moment—she felt so small and fragile, yet she had more strength than some men he'd known. "Are you ready?"

She took a deep breath. "Yes."

He nodded and she took aim and began firing, splinters of rock exploding from the stone outcropping, the report of gunfire obliterating all other sound.

He ran, keeping low and moving in a zigzag pattern they'd drilled into him during training. The movement was supposed to make him a more difficult target to hit, but he doubted a spray of automatic weapons fire would miss. But his plan to focus the assailant's attention on Stacy seemed to have worked; he made it to the tree unharmed and dived over the trunk, landing in thick, soft snow on the other side.

Post holing through knee-deep drifts, he powered his way to the opposite bank and began making his way up the rocky slope. Ice, snow and loose rock made the climb difficult; for every foot he gained, he slid back six inches. The cold left his hands numb and penetrated his thin clothes until he shook from a bone-deep chill. Rocks tore at his clothing, cutting his skin, but he ignored the pain, pushing on.

When he judged himself to be a little above the outcropping where he'd spotted the shooter he began working his way sideways, scrambling over scrubby trees that clung to the side of the canyon, slipping in slush and loose gravel. Below, all was silent; even the echo of the gunfire had faded away.

His path intersected a narrow game trail, the hoofprints of deer clearly outlined in the snow along with the ridged soles of a man's hiking boots. Patrick examined the imprint; it was fresh and sharp, and similar prints led down the slope. The shooter had come this way to set up his post among the rocks.

He moved more slowly now, as soundlessly as possible, his pistol drawn and ready to fire. Soon he could look down into the niche formed by the outcropping of rock, a space just wide enough for a single man to crouch.

But the niche was empty. The snow around it was littered with spent bullet casings, the metal jackets glinting in the snow.

Patrick dropped into the niche and looked around. A search revealed an empty chip bag and sandwich wrapper, and the deep impression where someone had sat, possibly for a long time. Had someone staked out this area, just in case they'd decided to come this way? The idea that whoever was behind the kidnapping would have gone to such trouble—invested the manpower to cover even this remote route—disturbed him. Why was one little boy worth so much trouble and expense?

Whoever had been here wasn't here now. They'd

either anticipated his arrival and made their getaway while they had the chance—or they'd taken advantage of his absence to descend to the road, and Stacy. He'd heard no shots, but there were other ways of killing a person. The image of Stacy at the hotel, a knife to her throat, flashed through his mind, and a wave of sickness shook him.

"Stacy!" he shouted.

Stacy! echoed back to him from the canyon walls.

Half climbing, half sliding, he made his way down the side of the canyon. He tried to stay in cover, behind trees or boulders, but as he descended, no one shouted at him or fired at him or tried in any way to stop him. This indication that he was alone spurred him to move almost recklessly, stumbling down the steep embankment toward the car.

"Stacy!" he shouted again as he ran toward the vehicle. No answer came.

The car sagged in the roadway with three flat tires. Most of the windows were shattered, and bullet holes riddled the body. Patrick registered the damage as he made his way around the wreck, but there was no sign of Stacy. She wasn't underneath or inside, or back in the niche between the rocks where she'd initially sought shelter.

He examined the snow beside the car, but his own movements earlier had trampled it into slush. On his knees now, he studied the ground for the waffle-soled tread of the hiking boot he'd seen in the tracks on the opposite side of the canyon. He found a partial print that might have been a match, but he couldn't be sure. He started to stand, but a glint of something bright in the gravel caught his attention. He leaned forward and plucked a thin gold earring from the mud. His blood turned to ice as he recognized one of the hammered hoops Stacy had worn. She'd lost it here in the mud, in a struggle he hadn't been around to protect her from.

"No! LET ME GO!" Stacy tried to vent her rage on the man who held her in his unyielding grip, but he muffled her shouts with the sleeve of his jacket, shoving the fabric into her mouth until she was almost choking on the taste of dusty tweed. Thus silenced, she fought all the harder, kicking and scratching, but her struggles did nothing to slow his progress as he dragged her down the canyon. A second man trailed after them, an automatic weapon cradled in his arms as he scanned the embankments on either side of them.

Her heel connected hard with her captor's shin and he grunted and shifted his hold enough to uncover her mouth once more. "Let me go!" she screamed again.

The man with the gun was on her in two strides, punching her hard on the side of the face so that her vision blurred and her ears rang. "Shut up!" he commanded.

She blinked and his face returned to focus—a hard, lean face, skin stretched tight over wide cheekbones and a square jaw. His eyes were so pale they were almost colorless, like ice chips set in his face, and his expression was just as cold. It was a face she'd seen before, but the knowledge only confused her. This man had worked for Sam; she was sure of it. So why did he want to hurt her now?

He leaned close to speak to her, his breath smelling of stale coffee and cigarettes. "You make any more noise and I'll cut your tongue out." As if to demonstrate, he pulled a knife from his pocket and flicked open the blade.

She tried to swallow, but her mouth was dry. "What do you want with me?" she whispered.

His gaze swept over her, stripping her, reducing her to an object, not a person. "I want a lot of things," he said. "The question is, which do I want first?"

The man who was holding her laughed at this—an unpleasant, awful laugh without mirth.

The pale-eyed man touched the blade of the knife to her throat, to the soft space over her vocal cords. He made a flicking motion and she felt a stinging pain, then the trickle of blood against her skin. "Do you think you'll be more cooperative if I cut you first?" he asked.

She stared at him, terror rendering her speechless. "I think I'll have to cut you," he said. "For a start."

She stared into his eyes and saw her own death there—a slow, painful death. She had no idea why these men had taken her, but she knew she couldn't stay with them. She had to get away.

She closed her eyes and made herself go limp, pretending to faint. The bigger man who carried her laughed. "You scared her senseless," he crowed.

"She'll be easier to carry that way," the pale-eyed man said. "Hurry up. We're still a ways from the car."

"What about that marshal?" the big guy said.

"Someone will deal with him later. He won't get far with his car disabled."

The big man shifted her over his shoulder, carrying her with her head hanging down his back, one hand grasping her bottom obscenely. She kept her eyes shut and tried to review her options, but she didn't seem to have any. Except she believed she had to get away from them before they reached the car. Once inside a vehicle she would truly be at their mercy. They could knife her or shoot her or do whatever they wanted within the prison of a car. At least out here in the open she had a hope of outrunning them.

That was her first move, then. She had to find a way to make the big guy put her down before they reached the car. As soon as he lowered her to the ground, she'd take off running and take her chances. But what would make him want to put her down? She could be sick on him—except she'd never been able to throw up easily. Even when she was ill and emptying her stomach would have made her feel so much better, her body refused to vomit. Morning sickness for her had been constant nausea with little relief.

Being sick wasn't an option, so what did that leave?

It left her with no pride and no shame. In the battle between momentary embarrassment and saving her own life, she chose life. Taking a deep breath, she tensed her muscles. Here goes....

"What the hell!" The big man howled and loosened his hold on her.

"What is it?" the pale-eyed man said.

"She pissed on me!" The big man slung her to the ground. As soon as she was free of his grasp, she sprang to her feet and ran toward the cover of a copse of trees. The air around her exploded with gunfire. Bullets ricocheted off rocks and thudded into the dirt at her feet, but she refused to slow. Better to die in a hail of bullets than be cut to death by a knife.

She reached the trees and pushed into a deeper thicket, barbed vines cutting into her hands and face. She prayed she wouldn't be trapped in the underbrush, where Pale Eyes and his companion could easily pick her off. If she could push on through to more open ground she'd have a better chance of getting away, since the underbrush would slow the two big men even further.

What she would do then, she didn't know. Even if she could get back to the car, it wasn't drivable. Pale Eyes and his buddy had descended on her maybe fifteen minutes after Patrick had left her. Did this mean they'd met him on their way down and killed him? She had heard no shots, but Pale Eyes could have used his knife. She hoped somehow Patrick had survived, that he hadn't given his life in order to protect her.

Whatever had happened to him, though, she was on her own now. She was stranded in the wilderness, with no weapon, no transportation and not even a coat to keep her warm.

The idea that she might die of the cold after dodging bullets all afternoon brought tears to her eyes, but she pushed them away. She wasn't going to give up. Not when Carlo was waiting for her to come to him.

After what seemed like half an hour but was probably only a few minutes, she emerged into a clearing of tall grass and scattered boulders. She crouched behind one of the larger boulders, trying to catch her breath and listening for sounds of pursuit. But she heard nothing—no gunfire, no crashing through the underbrush, no running footsteps or shouts. Nothing but the rasp of her own breathing and the thud of her own heart.

"Stacy!"

Her name, shouted in the ringing silence, would have been startling enough, but the realization of who was calling for her made her jump up and push her way back through the underbrush toward the sound.

"Stacy!" Patrick shouted again. "It's all right. You can come out."

She emerged from the trees and stood on the side of the gravel road, looking back the way she'd come, at the two figures slumped in the gravel, at Patrick's feet. He held Pale Eyes's automatic weapon in one hand and his own pistol in the other. In the fading light she couldn't read the expression on his face, but the relief in his voice was clear as he called to her. "Stacy! Are you all right?"

"I'm okay." She began walking toward him. She was bleeding and wet and cold, and beginning to shake from the strain of it all. But she was alive, and Patrick hadn't given up on her. They were going to find Carlo. They were going to find her son, or die trying.

Chapter Eight

They found their attackers' car parked on the side of
the road a quarter mile away, the keys in the ignition.
A quick search of the backseat found ammunition for
the weapons, some rope, a roll of duct tape and a couple
blankets. The trunk contained two suitcases, an empty
gas can and a spare tire. "Looks like they planned to tie
you up and cover you with the blanket," Patrick said,
tossing her one of the coverlets. "Wrap yourself up in
this. You must be freezing."

"Maybe they were just going to wrap up my body
until they could dispose of it," she said.

"It would have been easier to leave you for dead back
on that deserted road." He slid into the driver's seat and
cranked the engine. The deeper they got into this, the
less sense it made. Kidnappers took the boy, but left
Stacy unharmed. Then different men came back for
Stacy. They hadn't killed her outright, which seemed to
indicate they had intended to take her somewhere alive.
The anonymous female caller threatened to kill Carlo if
Stacy and Patrick kept coming after them, yet someone
had set up an ambush on the most obvious secondary
route for them to take. Once again, the attackers hadn't
killed Stacy, but had seemed to want her alive.

When he'd come upon the two thugs they'd been firing into the underbrush, shouting for Stacy. He took up his position behind a rock and called to them and they turned their attention to him. He'd been close enough to pick them off before they killed him.

He turned the car around and set the heater to run full blast. By the time they reached the highway he was starting to feel his feet again.

Stacy stirred and rearranged the blanket more tightly around her. "I recognized one of those men back there," she said. "The tall one with the pale eyes. He worked for Sam."

He hadn't expected this; so far everyone they'd encountered had been a stranger to her. He slowed the car and glanced at her. "Are you sure?"

"Yes. I'd never forget a face like that." She pulled the blanket more tightly around her. "He creeped me out. He was always staring at me."

"What did he do for Sam? Do you know?"

"He was just another thug. Muscle. An enforcer."

"Was he at the house the day Sam was killed?"

"No. He didn't come to Colorado with us. He worked in New York. He wasn't one of the family bodyguards, or anyone who spent a lot of time around the house. He was just, you know, an employee. He came to the house a few times to meet with Sam."

"When was the last time you saw him?"

"A couple months ago?" She wrinkled her nose. "Maybe a little longer. Whenever he showed up I always left the room, so I have no idea why he was there."

"Who could he be working for now?"

"I have no idea about that, either."

"Do you remember his name?"

"No. I don't think I ever heard it. It's not like Sam introduced me to the people he worked with."

"My people will run his fingerprints—maybe they'll come up with a match. Did he say anything about why they wanted to kidnap you?"

Her face went a shade paler. "He said a lot of things about what he wanted to do to me but nothing beyond threats. I thought he wanted to kill me, though I think he planned to…to hurt me first." She swallowed, visibly gaining control of her emotions.

He covered her hand with his own. "I don't think they—or whoever they were working for—wanted you dead. If that was the case, it would have been so much easier to leave your body in the canyon. Safer, too."

"But the caller said I was to stay away, and I thought since we hadn't, they wanted to punish me."

"We don't even know if the caller and these guys are connected. Or maybe the call was just a ploy to get us to take a different route. There aren't that many ways to get to Crested Butte. Whoever wants you could have reasoned it would be easier to stop us and separate us in a remote canyon. Did either of those men say anything to let you know what they were up to? Or who they worked for?"

"No. They never mentioned Carlo or where they were taking me or who they were working for or anything useful."

"What about the other guy? Did you recognize him?"

"Not really. But I didn't pay a lot of attention to the men who came and went at the house. I only remember the one guy with the pale eyes because he was so creepy."

Her voice shook, all the fear and terror of her ordeal condensed in those few words. "You did great," he said, hoping to bolster her spirits. "You kept your head and you didn't stop fighting. You got away."

"Thanks to you. I was afraid they'd found you first and killed you."

"They never saw me until it was too late."

"Well…I'm glad you're okay. I'm glad I'm not trying to find Carlo on my own."

She slumped against the car door, weariness in every inch of her posture. Fatigue dragged at him as well, the long hours and constant tension catching up with him. "You look exhausted," he said. "Even if we make it to Crested Butte, there's no way we can locate the ranch tonight. I think we should stop and rest before we go on."

"No, we have to keep going. If we can just get some coffee, I'll feel better."

"All right." Maybe coffee would help. And something to eat, though he wasn't hungry.

Over an hour passed before he spotted the gas station/convenience store set back from the highway. A sign advertised Beer and Bait and Clean Restrooms. "I'll fill up the car while we're here," he said, pulling up to the gas pumps. "This looks like the only place for miles."

"All right. I'll get some coffee and try to clean up a little in the ladies' room." She started to open the door, but he put a hand out to stop her.

"Here." He slipped out of his coat. "Your jacket's torn and muddy. Put this on."

"It's miles too big."

"Then it will cover more of you."

She looked down at her clothes, which were all but in tatters after her dash through the briars in the canyon. "I guess I am a mess. All right. Thanks."

She tossed the blanket in the backseat and pulled on his coat. She pushed the sleeves up and wrapped it around her as tightly as she could. She looked like a high school girl wearing her boyfriend's letter jacket. Cute.

"What are you smiling about?" she asked.

He hadn't even realized he'd been smiling. "Nothing. You go in and get what you want. I'll be there as soon as I'm done filling the tank."

When he came inside she was adding cream and sugar to a large cup of coffee. "You should get something to eat, too," he said.

"I'm not hungry."

"I know. But we'll both feel better if we eat."

She selected a couple granola bars while he added a ham sandwich to their purchases. While he waited for the clerk to tell him the total, he suppressed a yawn.

"I know the feeling," the clerk said. "I come on shift at three this morning—I was supposed to get off at eleven, but the other woman didn't come in, so I had to work a double."

"I'm going to go on outside to wait," Stacy said, gathering up her coffee and snacks.

"I'll be right out," he said. He handed a twenty to the clerk. "When you were working this morning, did you see a little boy, about three years old, with blond hair? He was probably with a man."

She counted out his change. "Who wants to know?"

He took out his ID. Showing it was a risk; if she'd

seen the bulletins saying Durango police were wanting to question him, she might conclude he was a fraud or somehow on the wrong side of the law and contact the authorities. He didn't have time to waste straightening out this mess. But if she had seen Carlo and his captors it would confirm he was on the right track.

He decided to risk it, and flipped open the leather folder. She studied it and nodded. "Who is it you're looking for, again?"

He took out his phone and clicked on Carlo's picture. "This is the boy I'm looking for. His name is Carlo. He was taken from his mother last night. We think the men who took him headed this way."

She leaned close to study the picture, then nodded. "I saw him. At least I'm pretty sure it was him. He was crying, kind of throwing a temper tantrum, the way kids do when they're so tired. The man brought him in to go to the bathroom and the boy didn't want to go back out to the car. He sat down on the floor over there and the man had to drag him away. All the while he was crying and calling for his mommy." She looked stricken. "I wish I'd known. I thought he was just being a brat. I always watch for those AMBER Alerts and such. I haven't seen anything about this kid."

"It's a sensitive case. We're trying to keep it quiet for now. Can you describe the man he was with?"

She frowned, concentrating. "He was maybe six feet, kind of thin, dark clothes. He was bent over the boy, so I never really saw his face."

Patrick slid the phone back into his pocket and checked her name tag. "Thank you, Marne. You've been very helpful. Did you see what kind of car they were in?"

She shook her head. "Sorry. They parked around on the side and it was dark over there."

"If you remember anything else, call this number. Let them know you spoke to me." He handed her his card.

"I will. I hope you find him."

"Thank you."

He waited until he'd driven away to tell Stacy. "We're on the right track," he said. "The clerk back at the store thinks she saw Carlo early this morning. He was with a man who sounds like the one who snatched him from your room."

"She did? Why didn't you tell me before?" She turned to look back the way they'd come. "We have to go back. I have to talk to her."

"There's no need for that. She already told me all she knew."

"Turn this car around now! I want to talk to her."

The intensity of her anger hit him like a wave. He held on to the steering wheel more tightly, half believing she'd rip it from his hands. "Will talking to her really make you feel better, or only upset you more?" he asked, trying to make his voice as calming and gentle as possible. "It would definitely upset you. Isn't it enough to know we're on the right track?"

She wilted back against the seat. "Nothing will be enough until he's safe again. But if I could just talk to her…." She looked back again, twisting her hands in her lap.

Common sense and all his training told him turning

around to talk to the clerk again would be a waste of time they could better use finding the uncle's ranch. But her longing to cling to even this tenuous contact with her son tore at him. He slowed the car, then pulled to the side of the road and headed back the way they'd come.

He pulled up to the front of the building and Stacy had unhooked her seat belt and opened the door before he'd even shut off the engine. He followed her into the store, where a pasty-faced young man looked up from behind the front counter. "Where's the woman who was working here a few minutes ago?" Stacy asked.

The man shook his head. "There's no woman working here," he said.

"Her name was Marne." Patrick approached the counter and showed the clerk his marshal's ID. "She was working a double shift. I spoke to her for several minutes."

"You must have the wrong store," the clerk said. "I don't know any Marne, and I'm the only one working today. I came on at seven this morning."

"You're lying." Stacy gripped the edge of the counter-top and stood on tiptoe, leaning toward the taller young man. "We were just here and Marne was here. If this is your idea of a joke, it isn't funny."

"I swear, there's no one named Marne here. There's no one else here at all."

Patrick glanced at the camera mounted over the front camera. "You have security tapes. I want to see them."

"You'll have to talk to the manager about that. And he'll want a subpoena." The clerk raised his chin defiantly, but his gaze didn't meet the marshal's.

"Where's the manager?" Stacy asked. "I want to speak to him."

"He isn't here. He won't be in until tomorrow. But if you want to leave a name and number, I'll tell him to call you."

Patrick gently took Stacy's arm. "We're wasting our time here," he said. "Let's go."

"But he's lying! I know that woman was here. I saw her. You talked to her. Why is he lying?"

"Come on." Patrick urged her toward the door. "We'll figure this out, I promise."

Back in the car, he locked the doors, half-afraid Stacy would rush back into the store and physically attack the clerk. "He's lying," she repeated, sending a murderous look toward the clerk, who watched them with a sullen expression.

"Yes, he is." Patrick started the car and backed out of the parking space.

"Where are we going?" she asked. "Are you just going to let him get away with that? Maybe he's holding Marne hostage in a back room. Maybe she's in trouble because she talked to you."

"I think Marne is probably fine," he said. "Though her name likely isn't really Marne." He pulled out his phone and hit the speed dial button for his office.

"Who are you calling?" Stacy asked. "What are you going to do?"

"Give me Special Agent Sullivan." He pulled the car into a lay by about a mile from the store. "I'm going to get to the bottom of this," he said to Stacy. "Give me a little bit."

"Sullivan." The lieutenant's voice was brisk and confident.

"Thompson here. I need you to send a team out to Lakeside Grocery in Lakeside, Colorado, about two hours outside of Durango on Highway 50. Get a subpoena for the front counter surveillance tapes. I want to know the details and background on every clerk who worked there last night and today, and anyone who came in. I'm especially interested in an older female clerk with a name tag that says Marne, and a man who may have come in with the little boy we're looking for, Carlo Giardino. While you're at it, you should also get a team out to County Road 7N in the same area. We had a shootout with a couple guys who tried to kidnap Stacy."

"Any casualties?"

"Two."

Sullivan swore under his breath. "What is going on with this case?"

"That's what we're trying to find out. Focus on the gas station first—those guys in the canyon aren't going anywhere."

"Sure thing," Sullivan said. "What's up?"

"I talked to the clerk, Marne, a few minutes ago, and she told me she was working this morning when a man brought Carlo into the store to use the restroom. But when Stacy Giardino went back there to talk to her just now, there's a clerk—with no name tag—who swears there's no one named Marne there, and he's the only one on duty."

"You think someone set you up?"

"I do. See what you can find out and let me know."

"Where will you be?"

"We're headed to Crested Butte. I'm more and more convinced the boy is there."

"You could be headed into a trap," Sullivan said.

"It feels that way, but I'll be careful. Something big is going on here, and I want to know what."

"I'll get right on it."

He ended the call and slid the phone back into his pocket, then turned to Stacy. "You should have threatened that clerk," she said. "Made him tell you where Marne was."

"I'm sure that's what Sammy would have done."

She folded her arms across her chest. "It would have worked. The clerk would have talked."

"Maybe. Or someone watching in the back room would have opened fire and killed us all."

She pressed both palms to her forehead and moaned. "I don't understand what's happening," she said.

"I'm not sure," Patrick said. "But I think Marne was a plant. Someone told her to tell us about seeing Carlo and one of the kidnappers. Once she'd done her job, she was paid off and sent away."

"But why do that?"

"I don't know. Maybe to make sure we headed in the right direction. To lure us. All of this seems orchestrated to keep us eager to get to Crested Butte."

"But that doesn't make sense. Those men in the canyon tried to kill us. They must have been waiting to ambush us. And before that, we got the phone call warning us away."

"They tried to kill me. They wanted you alive. They tried to kidnap you. And maybe the warning was really to get me away—they still wanted you, but they needed to find a way to separate us."

"They threatened me. I think they wanted to take me away and torture you."

"Men like that think threats will make a captive more compliant and easier to handle. I'll admit, I'm impressed you got away from them."

"I'll do anything to save my son." She shifted in her seat and looked away.

"Since they couldn't kill me and they failed to bring you in, maybe plan B is to lure us to where they can try again."

"Are you saying the kidnappers want us to find them?"

"I think they want us where they can pick us off and shut us up," he said. "Whether or not Carlo is being held at his great-uncle's ranch, a remote property in a rural area sounds like an ideal place to get rid of the two people who have been interfering with the kidnappers' plans."

She pinched the bridge of her nose between her thumb and forefinger. "Are you saying the woman was lying, too—that she never saw Carlo?"

"I don't know. Maybe she saw him and maybe she didn't. Her job was to make us believe Carlo and the kidnapper passed through here so we'd keep following the trail of breadcrumbs."

"And are we going to keep following it?"

"I think we have to, but I want more information first."

"What kind of information?"

"I want to know who's behind this, for one thing."

"I thought we'd decided Uncle Abel was behind it. Isn't that why we're headed to Crested Butte?"

"But why would Abel want Carlo? He doesn't need him to step in and take control of the Giardino business. He's the only surviving Giardino male. He could just show up and start giving orders."

"I don't care why he's doing this—I just want my son."

"I want your son, too. But we can't go barging into an ambush. We need to know more about what we're dealing with."

"You're dealing with an old man who hasn't had anything to do with the family for years."

"But you said Sam threatened to turn the business over to him, passing over Sammy. That could mean the brothers had been in touch."

She shifted in her seat. "Maybe. Or maybe we're looking at this all wrong and Abel isn't the one behind this at all."

"If not Abel, who do you think it is?" he asked.

"I don't know. Maybe it's the old woman—his mother."

"You think Carlo's great-grandmother kidnapped him?"

"I think that woman is capable of anything." She shivered. "The one time I met her, she gave me the creeps. She was a regular witch, and she ordered everyone—including Sam—around like they were slaves."

"Maybe, but my instinct is that someone bigger is behind this." An eighteen-wheeler rocketed past on the highway, shaking the car.

"What do you mean, bigger?" Stacy asked.

"Think about it. Someone is going to a lot of trouble here—planting witnesses, tailing us. That takes manpower, and vehicles and weapons—all that adds up to a lot of money."

"Abel and his mother have money, I'm sure."

"Not that kind of money."

"So who do you think is behind this?"

"Do you remember I asked you about Senator Nordley?"

She nodded. "You think a senator masterminded all this? Why?"

"Power? Money? Because he has secrets he wants to stay secret?" Patrick shook his head. "I don't know, but word is that Nordley was behind Sam's escape from prison last year. And Anne—Elizabeth Giardino—said she saw him at the house right before our raid."

"But if Nordley was working with Sam, whatever secret he had died with Sam."

"Maybe. But maybe it's not about secrets. Maybe it's all about money. Politics is an expensive business. If an ambitious man like Nordley wanted to, say, run for president, he'd need a great deal of money to do so. The Giardinos have that kind of money. If he did a favor for the family, they would want to reward him."

She considered this. He was glad now he'd brought up the subject. He'd been a little worried she'd become hysterical, or more distraught, but he should have known better. She was sharp, and talking with her was helping him to organize his own thoughts and theories. She'd said she wanted to be a lawyer, but she would have made a good agent, too.

"So you think Nordley helped kidnap Carlo for Uncle Abel? But why? It still doesn't make sense."

"No, it's doesn't," he admitted. "But I'm going to keep working at it until it does make sense. After that, we'll know the best move to make." He put the car into gear.

"Where are we going?" she asked.

"We need to find a place to hole up for a while, to plan our next move."

"No!" The fierceness of her objection—the sudden change from calm to agitated—unsettled him. Yes, she'd been through a lot, and her emotions were on edge, but she'd never struck him as the hysterical type. He hesitated, his hand on the gearshift.

"The more we delay, the more danger Carlo may be in," she said. "We have to go to him now."

"We don't even know for sure he's at the ranch—or where the ranch is, exactly," he said. "We'll be putting him in greater danger if we barge in without a plan. And we'll be putting ourselves at risk, too." He turned his attention back to the road and prepared to pull the car out onto the highway.

"Stop!"

He groaned. This was not an argument he wanted to have. What had happened to the reasonable woman he'd been admiring only seconds before? "Look, Stacy—" He turned to her and the words died on his lips.

She held a gun in both hands and it was aimed right at him. "I won't let you keep me from my son," she said.

Chapter Nine

Patrick had faced down his share of desperate men and women with guns, but the sight of Stacy holding a weapon on him made his blood run cold. Her hands shook so badly she could scarcely keep the weapon still. He wasn't so worried that she'd deliberately shoot him, but that the gun would accidentally go off. At this close range she'd be unlikely to miss. "Stacy, put the gun down," he said, his words soft, each one carefully enunciated.

"No. Not until we're in Crested Butte. Drive."

"We're still hours away. Are you going to hold the gun on me the whole way?"

"If I have to." Her gaze met his, defiant—but he glimpsed the fear behind her bravado.

"Stacy, I don't believe you really want to kill me. I'm on your side, remember?"

"You say that, but why won't you take me to where you know Carlo is?" Her lip trembled. "Why are you keeping me from my son?"

"We don't know where he is. We still have to find the ranch and then we need to determine he's there. We can't just go barging in. He might be hurt. I know you don't want that."

"I just want my boy!" The words ended on a wail and the barrel of the gun dipped lower. Great. Now if she fired she'd blast him right in the crotch.

He shifted in his seat. "I want to find your son," he said. "I want to see the two of you safely together. But I won't do anything to jeopardize his life. Or yours."

"At least in Crested Butte we'd be closer. We could find him. I might see him on the street."

"Crested Butte is still two hours away, at least. We're both exhausted. We're dirty and cold and you're hurt."

"I'm fine."

"You've got cuts and scratches and bruises all over your face and hands. Your clothes are filthy and neither of us has had six hours of sleep in the past forty-eight. If we're going to help Carlo, we need to be strong and rested and sharp."

She looked away, the gun dipping farther. He kept his eyes on her, waiting. "When will I see him again?" she asked.

"Maybe as soon as tomorrow. It depends on what we learn."

"Then why can't we go to Crested Butte and look for him now?"

"That's what the people we're dealing with seem to want us to do. I think we'd be safer if we stopped somewhere more out of the way. We can rest and come up with a plan—one that will keep Carlo safe and alive."

She brought the gun up once more. "I just want this to be over," she said softly.

"So do I. But shooting me won't bring back your son. I really do want to help, if you'll trust me."

She wet her lips. "I haven't had a lot of people in my

life I could trust. You're a lawman. Why should you be any different?"

From what she'd told him, every man she'd ever known, from her father to her husband, had betrayed her. He wouldn't add his name to the list. "You can trust me because I haven't let you down so far. Have I lied to you or done anything to hurt you?"

She bit her lip, then shook her head.

He held out his hand. "Will you give me the gun?"

She hesitated, then nodded and let him take the weapon from her hand. Only when he held the gun did the tension drain from his shoulders. Exhaustion buffeted him and he had to fight to tuck the gun safely under the seat and put the car in gear. "Are you okay?" he asked.

"Yes." She closed her eyes and swayed a little in her seat. She was so pale, the scratches and bruises on her face standing out against her ivory skin. "As all right as I can be."

Twenty minutes later, he turned in at a blue neon sign that advertised Motel. The old-fashioned tourist court was a low-slung row of rooms with doors painted bright turquoise, opening onto a gravel lot. Patrick paid cash for a room to an older man who wore suspenders and a checked shirt. No more flashing his credentials unless it was absolutely necessary. He and Stacy needed to fly under the radar now.

"You want ice, it's a quarter," the man said.

Patrick fished a quarter from his pocket and slid it across the counter. The old man shuffled off to a back room and returned shortly with a plastic bucket of ice. He handed it over while frowning at Stacy, who'd insisted on coming inside. "You sure you're okay, miss?" he asked.

She gave him a wan smile. "I'm just tired."

"You look like somebody beat you up." The clerk scowled at Patrick.

"I was in a car wreck," Stacy said. She took Patrick's arm and leaned against him. "I'll be fine. My husband is taking good care of me."

He was aware of her warm body pressed against his all the way back to the car. He parked in front of the room and carried both suitcases and the weapons inside, wrapping the guns in the blankets to hide them from anyone who might be watching. "Why did you tell the clerk I was your husband?" he asked.

"I thought he'd be less suspicious if he thought we were married. He was looking at you like he wanted to call the police. I had to do something."

"A car wreck was quick thinking."

"I'm sorry about before," she said. "When I pulled the gun on you. I wasn't thinking. I—"

"It's all right. You've been through a lot. Come here and sit down." He motioned toward the bed.

She looked wary. "Why?"

"I want to take a look at those cuts. I found a first aid kit in the trunk."

She sat on the edge of the bed and he angled the lamp shade to give him a better view of her uptilted face. The gash on her forehead where Carlo's kidnapper had hit her had scabbed over, and the bruising around it was an ugly purple and yellow, the skin slightly puffy and raised. He cleaned it with a cotton ball dipped in antiseptic, then dabbed antibiotic ointment along it, before covering it with a gauze pad held in place with strips of surgical tape. "I should have done this before now," he said.

"We haven't exactly had a lot of free time," she said.

He began cleaning the dozens of other scratches on her cheeks and along her jaw. "You look like you ran through a rosebush," he said, pausing to pluck a thorn from alongside her ear.

"I didn't stop to identify the local flora. Maybe they were wild roses."

He dabbed ointment on the deepest of the scratches, then cradled her jaw in his hand and turned her head to study the bruise along the side of her face. "Which one of those thugs did this?" he asked.

She closed her eyes and swallowed. "The one with the pale eyes. He threatened to cut out my tongue."

He forced himself to relax his hold on her jaw, to continue tending to her wounds without comment. He was getting good at holding back his anger, but he couldn't hold back his memories of another hotel room and another woman whose cuts and bruises he'd nursed like this. His sister was safe and well now, long free of her abuser, but the years when she'd suffered and he'd been unable to help her had left their scars.

"Do they make you take first aid when you train to be a marshal?" she asked.

"I was a Boy Scout." He leaned back to study his handiwork. She was still a mess, but with luck none of her injuries would become infected, and she'd heal without any major scars.

"Let me guess—you were an Eagle Scout."

"Yes."

She looked triumphant. "I knew it. Eagle Scout to U.S. Marshal. I guess it makes sense."

"There was a stint in Iraq in between. College before that."

"Did you think when you were doing all that you'd end up babysitting a mafia wife?"

"It's a little more than that, don't you think?" Her eyes met his and he felt the jolt of connection, and the weight of emotions he didn't dare examine too closely.

He stepped back, and began packing up the first aid kit. "Why don't you take a shower? I'll see what I can find for dinner. I think we passed a café right before I turned in here."

He felt her gaze on him for a long moment before she stood and went into the bathroom. Only when he heard the door close behind her did he raise his head to stare after her. He was treading on shaky ground here. In his career with the U.S. Marshal's office, he'd shepherded half a dozen women through the Witness Security program, many of them single, beautiful and vulnerable. He'd never crossed the line that separated professional from personal. But Stacy had him tiptoeing across that line, contemplating how close he could get before he reached a point where he could never go back.

A SHOWER REVIVED Stacy somewhat. Afterward, she stood wrapped in a towel, contemplating her ruined clothing. Between the mud, brambles, blood and other bodily fluids to which the garments had been subjected, they were little better than rags, but, since she had nothing else to wear, she had no choice but to wash them. She dumped the rest of the bottle of hotel shampoo in the tub and added several inches of hot water, then dumped the clothing in to soak.

Patrick was gone—she assumed to get dinner—when she emerged from the bathroom. She spied the suitcases by the door and hefted one onto the bed. The two thugs were unlikely to have anything that would fit her, but even a T-shirt and boxers would do for sleeping. Fortunately, Pale Eyes or his buddy hadn't bothered to lock the bag. She unzipped it and breathed a sigh of relief when she spotted clean boxers and socks. No T-shirts, but she found a man's dress shirt, neatly folded and still in a bag from the cleaners.

By the time Patrick returned with two plastic bags, she'd changed into the borrowed clothing and sat cross-legged on the bed, rifling through the rest of the contents of the suitcase. The marshal paused in the doorway. "Feeling better?" he asked.

"Much. I'm washing my clothes, so I borrowed some from our two late friends. There's probably stuff in here that will fit you."

"Good idea." He set the bags on the table by the window. "Anything else interesting?"

"One of them liked science-fiction novels." She tossed a paperback onto the bed. "And one of them wore a night guard." She pointed to a case for the dental appliance. "Who knew?"

"What about the other case?" he asked.

"I haven't checked it yet."

"We'll take a look after we eat. I got a couple burgers. There wasn't much choice."

"I'm so hungry, I could eat almost anything."

She followed him to the table, where he unpacked

the food from one of the plastic bags. "What's in the other bag?" she asked.

"Since we had to leave everything back at the other car, I picked up a few things—toothbrush, toothpaste, a razor, things like that."

She peered into the bag, then reached in and pulled out a tube of lipstick and a powder compact. The lipstick was pink. "I'm guessing these aren't for you."

The tips of his ears turned almost as pink as the lipstick, though his face remained impassive. She suppressed the urge to giggle. There was something about an otherwise tough guy who got embarrassed about buying a girl makeup that was sweet—as was the purchase in the first place. "I notice you went to a lot of trouble to fix yourself up before," he said. "I thought it might help you feel better."

"You thought right. Thank you." She resisted the urge to kiss his cheek—just as a gesture of thanks. That might be taking things too far.

They sat across from each other at the little table, eating burgers and fries and drinking from bottles of water. The food tasted good, but as her hunger abated, the familiar anxiety about the future returned. "What do we do next?" she asked.

"In the morning I'll call my office again—see if they've come up with an address for Uncle Abel." He wiped mustard from the corner of his mouth with a paper napkin. "I also want to know if they've found out any more about Sam and Sammy's wills."

"So you still believe Carlo's kidnapping is related to the will?"

"People commit crimes for many different reasons,

but a lot of times they're motivated by what they stand to gain, such as money, power or revenge. A three-year-old doesn't have any power. Kidnapping him hurts you the most. Have you thought of anyone who would use Carlo to get back at you?"

She shook her head. "The only person who hated me that much is dead."

"Are you talking about Sammy?"

Yes, Sammy. Her not-so-dear departed spouse. "Don't tell me a husband can't hate his wife, because he can."

"Did you feel the same way about him?"

"Sometimes I thought I did…." She studied the remains of her hamburger, her appetite fading. "Other times… In the beginning, things between us were pretty good. Sammy was sweet on our honeymoon. He seemed to really like me, and we had fun. But later, after Carlo was born…" She shook her head. Nothing she'd done had pleased her husband, and he'd lost the desire to please her. After a while it felt safer to stop trying.

"Did he hit you?" Patrick's voice was low, his gaze boring into her, as if the answer to this question made a difference to him.

"No. He was proud of that. 'You can't say I'm cruel,' he used to tell me. 'I never hit you.' But there are worse things than being hit. Bruises and even broken bones can heal, but the things people say to you… Those wounds can go a lot deeper." She felt the pain from those injuries still—maybe some of them would never heal.

She waited for him to ask what Sammy had said to her, but he didn't. Maybe he respected her privacy too much—or maybe he didn't really care. Why should he? Though he'd seemed concerned about her welfare, maybe that was just part of doing his job. Mr. Eagle Scout would never shirk his duty.

She set aside the remains of her burger. "Why don't we see what's in the other suitcase?" she said. "Maybe there's some clothes you can wear."

He looked down at his mud-stained shirt and jeans. "You think I need new clothes?"

"I think it's a miracle the motel clerk didn't call the police. You look like a derelict."

He rubbed his hand over his chin, and the scrape of bristles against his palm sent a hot shiver up her spine. "I could probably do with a little sprucing up." He leaned over and grasped the handle of the second suitcase. "Let's see what my options are."

He tugged, but the case didn't budge. "I remember this one was heavy," he said. He stood and used both hands to heave the suitcase onto the bed.

Stacy stood beside him as he unzipped the top and folded it back. She let out a squeak, and covered her mouth with her closed fist. "Is that real?" she asked, her voice scarcely above a whisper.

Patrick nodded, and reached into the case and took out a stack of bills from the rows and rows of similar stacks filling the case. "It looks real to me," he said. "There must be thousands of dollars in here. But what were our two late friends doing with it?"

Chapter Ten

Stacy stared at the suitcase full of money. It didn't even look real, so much of it all together. "How much do you think is in there?" she asked.

Patrick rifled through the stacks of bills. "Looks like all twenties, in bundles of fifty—I'd guess fifty thousand dollars."

She sank onto the bed. "What were those two doing with that much money?"

He felt along the side of the case and in all the pockets. "There's nothing else in here—no notes or ID or anything like that."

"It's the kind of thing you see in those TV mysteries," she said. "The unmarked bag of bills, dropped off in the park to pay ransom. But ransom for whom? Have they kidnapped someone besides Carlo?"

Patrick pulled out his phone. "Let's see if headquarters knows anything."

While he waited on hold to speak to who knows who, Stacy looked through the other suitcase—the one with the clothes. She found another science-fiction novel, a phone charger (but no phone) and an open box of condoms. Nothing incriminating or even threatening. Except for the fact that they'd attacked her and Patrick with guns and knives, they might have been any traveling businessmen.

"Let me know what you find. I'll call back in the morning." Patrick ended his call and slid his phone back into his pocket. "They're going to do a trace for large sums of missing cash, but I'm not holding out much hope that that will turn up anything. A team is on its way to the canyon to see if they can ID the guys."

She studied the open suitcase. "Maybe we could trade the cash for Carlo."

"We could try—if we knew how to get in touch with whoever has him." He closed the suitcase and set it on the floor. "I'm going to take a shower. You should try to get some sleep. Maybe we'll be able to get more information in the morning."

He took some clothes from the other suitcase and carried them and the plastic bag of toiletries into the bathroom. In a few minutes, she heard the shower running.

Stacy lay back on the bed, on top of the covers. One bed. That was all right. Sleeping with Patrick last night had been nice—even if they were only sleeping. She'd never met a man like him. He could be hard, brutal even—he hadn't hesitated to kill three men to save their lives. But he'd been so gentle, too, when he was tending her wounds, or when he held her while she cried.

He was the kind of man she wished Sammy had been. But Sammy had never looked at her the way Patrick did—as if she was an intelligent person whose opinions mattered. As if she *counted*.

And she could never think of Sammy the way she thought of Patrick—that he was a good man who de-

served her respect and admiration. All the bad things
Sammy had done had blotted out any good that might
have remained, whereas the more she knew about Patrick, the more good there was to see.

She closed her eyes, the soothing rhythm of the water
in the shower beating against the tile lulling her to sleep.
She dreamed she was on a beach with Patrick, and they
were lying in the warm sun and he was smiling and taking her in his arms....

PATRICK LIFTED STACY and held her close, her head resting
against his chest, his heartbeat a steady, strong rhythm
in her ear. His hands caressed her back, and she slid
her arms around his neck and snuggled closer, pressing
her breasts against his bare chest, her nipples straining
against the thin fabric of the T-shirt.

He grew still, his heart beating harder in her ear. "I
didn't mean to wake you," he said softly. "I was just
trying to get you under the covers."

She opened her eyes, the fog of sleep clearing as she
stared up at him, at the jut of his chin and the masculine
plane of his freshly shaved cheek in profile. He smelled
of soap and shaving cream and warm male skin. This
wasn't a dream or a fantasy; he was really holding her
in his arms. And the thought of him releasing her and
moving away, as much as the memory of her erotic
dreams, made her brazen.

"I'll get under the covers if you'll get under there
with me," she said. She smoothed her palm down the
taut muscles of his chest to his flat abdomen, stopping
just short of the waistband of his boxers.

He took her by the upper arms and gently pushed

her away from him. "I'd better sleep on the floor tonight," he said.

She looked into his eyes, feeling bolder than she had in a long time. Maybe because she'd reached the point where she had nothing to lose. She'd given up everything—her name, her dignity, even her child. She had nothing left but the need to be honest with herself about what she really wanted, and right now, she wanted Patrick. "Don't sleep on the floor," she said. "I want you to sleep with me. To make love with me."

"I don't think that would be a good idea." He rubbed his hands up and down her arms, a gentle caress that negated his words.

"Because you think it would be unprofessional?" She trailed her hand along his jaw, enjoying the smooth coolness of the freshly shaved skin.

"I'm supposed to be protecting you," he said.

"No one's going to hurt me while you're this close." She kissed him just below the ear, then began feathering kisses along the path her hand had just traced.

"Stacy, no." He cradled the side of her head.

"Don't tell me you haven't felt this…this heat between us," she said. She held her breath, waiting for him to lie.

"I've felt it," he said, his voice rough with emotion.

She leaned back to look up at him. She wanted to see his face, to read all the emotion there. "We've been through hell the past couple days," she said. "I can't think of much worse. I've been terrified and hurt and my whole life right now feels like a nightmare. I can't think about the future and I don't want to relive the past. All I can do is hang on to this moment and focus on getting through the next day, the next hour, the next minute."

"You should sleep," he said. "We both should sleep."

"Or we could lie down together on this bed and forget about everything else for a while by focusing on each other. We could give in to that attraction we've both felt and create at least one good memory from this whole mess."

"I am attracted to you." He smoothed his hand down her shoulder, his thumb grazing the side of her breast and sending a tremor through her. "But duty doesn't always allow me to do the things I want."

Heaven save her from logical, steadfast men. She'd heard that men liked women who played hard to get, but apparently the reverse was true—the more Patrick resisted, the more she wanted him, and the more she was determined to persuade him. "You'll be right here with me. You said yourself we can't do anything else until the morning. We're stuck here in this room. In this bed." She took his hand and kissed his palm. "Please. I don't want to beg, but I need you tonight. And I think you need me."

"What about protection?"

She laughed. Even on the verge of giving in, he was still so calm and practical. "There's a box of condoms in the suitcase. More than enough, trust me."

"Then I guess we have everything we need." His eyes met hers, the intensity of his gaze pinning her back against the pillows and stealing her breath. "If you're sure this is what you want," he said. "Because once this starts between us, I don't know if I can stop."

He would stop if she asked; he was that kind of man.

But she wouldn't ask. "I want this, Patrick," she said. "I want you."

He leaned forward, covering her with his body, lips pressed to hers, chest flattening her breasts, stomach to stomach and thigh to thigh. He held himself up just enough to keep from crushing her, but the weight of him felt good. She wanted him close—even closer. She shifted to shape herself more firmly to him and opened her mouth to deepen the kiss. His tongue caressed and claimed her, and she reveled in the sensation.

He was such a contradiction—hard muscle and tender caresses, insistent pressure and whispered encouragement. He helped her out of the boxers, and then the shirt, so that she lay alongside him naked. She should have felt vulnerable—exposed. But seeing her reflection in his eyes, she felt more beautiful than ever.

He shaped his hand to her breast and dragged his thumb over the distended nipple, eliciting a gasp. "You're really special, did you know that?" Then, not waiting for an answer, he bent his head and covered her breast with his mouth.

She closed her eyes and surrendered to the heat and light he sent coursing through her. Waves of feeling she'd almost forgotten could exist washed over her. He turned his attention to her other breast, then moved lower, trailing kisses along her ribs and across her abdomen.

She arched to him and felt him smile against the curve of her thigh and press her down into the mattress. "Don't be impatient," he said.

"I feel as if we've waited so long," she said.

"We can wait a little longer. It will be worth it." As

if to prove his point, he ran his tongue along the sensitive folds of her sex. She bit back a moan and felt him smile again. He was normally so solemn; she liked the idea that she could make him smile this way.

ONE OF PATRICK'S former supervisors had labeled him single-minded—so intently focused on one task he failed to notice anything else. The man hadn't meant it as a compliment, but Patrick saw this talent for intense concentration as a gift sometimes.

At this moment, he wanted nothing more than to focus all his senses on the woman in his arms—on the silken feel of the skin of her thighs, on the intoxicating scent of her, on her sweet taste on his tongue. For these few minutes or hours he could lose himself in her, devote his full attention to pleasuring her and receiving pleasure in return.

She sighed and shifted beneath him, arching to him, a sweet offering and a silent plea. He rested his hand on her stomach, a gentling gesture. He was so tempted to bring her to release right away, but that would be cheating them both. Instead, he left her wanting, and moved away from her.

"Where are you going?" she asked.

He smiled and removed his boxers, his erection straining toward her. If she'd had any doubts about how much he wanted her, surely that would be erased now. He dug in the suitcase until he found the box of condoms. Whatever else the two thugs who attacked them had been up to, at least one of them had planned on getting lucky.

She sat up and reached out her hand. "Let me," she said.

"I don't think that would be a good idea." Even her gaze on him was enough to make him lose focus; at her touch he might go off like a rocket, spoiling this for them both.

He carefully rolled on the condom, then knelt on the bed beside her. "You're so beautiful," he said, caressing her breast. She was so petite and perfectly proportioned.

"Flattery will get you everywhere. Now come here, handsome." She reached for him and he moved between her legs. He didn't ask if she was sure or if she was ready; the answers to those questions were clear in her actions.

He was a man who lived his life by control. His survival and the survival of those he was assigned to protect relied on his vigilance. He had to always be on guard, aware, in charge. But with Stacy he was able to surrender, to lose himself in passion and pleasure.

She responded with similar abandon, opening to him fully, then wrapping her legs around him to keep him close, meeting him thrust for thrust. And all the while she looked into his eyes, holding him with her gaze, letting him see all her emotions—an offering as intimate and intense as the giving of her body.

He waited for her, feeling the tension within her build, doing whatever he could to coax her to her release. When at last she came with a loud cry he followed her quickly over the edge, holding her close, rocking together with her, moving as one, unable to tell where his pounding heart ended and hers began.

When at last he withdrew to lie beside her, she shocked him by bursting into sobs.

"Stacy, what is it?" He bent over her, alarmed. "Did I hurt you? What's wrong?"

"I'm sorry. I didn't mean…" She shook her head and tried to push him away. "I'm just being stupid, I—"

"You're not stupid." He pulled several tissues from the box by the bed and handed them to her. "What's happened to upset you?" he asked. "I really want to know."

"It wasn't you, I promise." She blew her nose. "I'm such a mess."

Maybe this was grief over her husband, finally hitting her. Or a memory of something else—the human mind was a funny thing, and emotions could sneak up on people. "Maybe it would help to talk about it," he said.

She nodded and dabbed at her eyes with a fresh tissue, then looked up at him through a fringe of lashes glittering with tears. "Being with you, just now, was so wonderful. I was afraid no man would ever want to touch me like that again." Her voice broke on a fresh sob.

He caressed her cheek. "It was wonderful for me, too. I've wanted you from that first night at the hotel."

She turned away from his touch, her shoulders hunched, and refused to look at him. "My husband—Sammy—hadn't touched me for at least two years. He told me no man would want a woman like me, that that was why my father had to sell me to the Giardinos, because he knew no other man would want me."

"If he wasn't already dead I'd make him wish he

was." Patrick closed his eyes against a surge of anger, the rage a physical thing that heated his blood and shook him. "He was lying. And he was a fool." He took a deep breath, struggling for calm. Sammy was gone now; there was nothing Patrick could do to hurt him. He needed to focus on Stacy. He gathered her close and kissed her—he kissed the top of her head and the side of her face and the tip of her nose before lingering at her lips, trying to tell her without words how worthy she was of all the love her monster of a husband had denied her.

She began crying again, the tears flowing silently down her cheeks. He tasted them, salty and sweet, the taste of his own mixed emotions of regret and longing.

He pulled her down beside him and held her, the covers pulled up over them, her head cradled against his chest, until her tears were spent, and she sighed again. "I'm sorry," she said. "That's not the reaction a man wants after making love to a woman."

"I'd rather you be honest with me than pretend," he said.

"That's one of the things I like about you. You don't lie, even when lying would be more convenient."

"You've had enough of lies. Including all the ones Sammy told you. Don't believe him."

"I try. But sometimes it's hard."

He squeezed her shoulder. "Maybe when this is all over it would be a good idea for you to talk to someone. A counselor. I could give you a name."

"Yeah. That probably would be a good idea." She snuggled down more tightly against him. "Thank you, for everything."

"Try to get some sleep," he said. "We've got a big day tomorrow."

"Maybe I'll get to see Carlo."

"Maybe you will." And maybe he'd figure out a way to say goodbye that wouldn't end up hurting them both.

POUNDING ON THE door woke them. The room was pitch-black and Patrick groped for his phone on the bedside table. The display showed 5:00 a.m.

"Who is it?" Stacy sat up beside him, the covers clutched to her chin.

Patrick reached for his pants as the pounding repeated. "Open up!" a deep voice demanded. "This is the police."

Chapter Eleven

Stacy stared at the door, heart pounding. Could she possibly have heard them right? "What are the police doing here?" she whispered to Patrick.

"I don't know." He zipped his pants and pulled on a shirt. "Hold on. I'm coming!" he called.

"I'd better get dressed, too," Stacy said. She looked around for the shirt she'd discarded last night, but realized Patrick was wearing it.

"Better stay put," he said, as the pounding rattled the door frame again.

"Open up or we're coming in!"

Patrick jerked open the door and a beefy uniformed officer all but fell inside. Patrick stepped back, keeping his hands in clear view. "Can I help you?" he asked.

A second, older officer followed the first one inside. "Are you driving the black sedan parked in front of this room?" he asked.

"Is something wrong with the car?" Patrick asked.

The older cop's eyes narrowed. "I need to see some ID, Mr...."

"United States Marshal Patrick Thompson." He handed over his credentials.

The officer's eyebrows rose as he studied the ID. He glanced at Stacy. "And this woman is?"

"A material witness in a federal case."

The officer took in the single bed, clothes scattered around it. "Riiight," he said, drawing out the word.

Stacy felt her face heat, then bristled. She'd done nothing to be ashamed of—the police were the ones who ought to be ashamed, barging in on them this way.

"We're going to need the two of you to come with us down to the station for questioning about the murder of two men on County Road 7N yesterday afternoon," the older officer said. He returned Patrick's ID to him.

"I killed those men," Patrick said. "They ambushed us in the canyon and attempted to kidnap this woman."

The younger officer spoke up for the first time. "Why didn't you report this to our office?"

"This is a federal case. I reported it to my office and they're sending investigators. How did you find out about it?" Patrick's face was impassive, but Stacy felt the temperature in the room drop a few degrees at his chilly tone.

"A couple out snowshoeing stumbled on the bodies," the older officer said. "Then the hotel owner called to report a couple suspicious customers." He glanced at Stacy again. She pulled the covers more tightly around her neck—not because she was ashamed, but because the draft from the open door was freezing.

The officer turned back to Patrick. "If you'll both get dressed and come with us, I'm sure we can get this all sorted out."

"I'm sure that won't be necessary," said a commanding voice from behind the officers.

The police moved aside to reveal a slender man in a dark suit and overcoat. He flashed an ID badge. "Special Investigator Tim Sullivan," he said. He nodded to Patrick, then to Stacy, as if he found naked women in the beds of his coworkers every day of the week.

"Agent Sullivan…" the older officer began.

"Thank you for your help, officers," Sullivan said. "We can handle things from here. We promise to send your office a full report of our investigation."

"The crime occurred in our jurisdiction," the younger officer protested. "I believe—"

"I believe you don't want to be charged with interfering with a federal case."

Agent Sullivan's tone, as much as his words, made the officer blanch. He turned to his companion. "We'll be going now."

"Good."

When the door had closed behind the two officers, Agent Sullivan turned and regarded Patrick and Stacy. "I think, Marshal Thompson, you might have a little explaining to do."

"And I think you two should continue your discussion outside," Stacy said, "so that I can get dressed."

Sullivan tilted his head, as if considering the question. Stacy was sure he was about to make an off-color remark, but the glower on Patrick's face apparently made him think better of it. "Of course," he said. He glanced at Patrick's bare feet and unbuttoned shirt. "I'll meet you outside."

Patrick retrieved his shoes, then fished a clean pair of socks from the suitcase and sat on the side of the bed to put them on. Stacy studied his back, trying to read his thoughts in the tension there. "What happens now?" she asked.

"Maybe he's learned something about the whereabouts of the ranch, or Carlo." He drew up one leg and began tying the laces of his shoe.

"They won't pull you off the case, will they?"

He stilled. "Maybe they should."

"No!" She leaned forward and rested one hand on his shoulder.

"I've broken pretty much every rule and behaved unprofessionally. They'd be justified in pulling me off the case."

"I won't let them," she said. "Not when we've come so far. You know me and you know the case. I trust you."

He turned his head to meet her gaze at last. "We've crossed the line. You're not just a stranger I'm duty bound to protect."

"Does that mean you'll be any less committed to keeping me safe or helping me?"

"It means I've lost my objectivity. That could affect my judgment."

"I won't let them take you away from me. I won't."

He turned his back to her again and finished tying his shoe. "That could be up to Sullivan." He straightened. "You'd better get dressed." He walked out the door, not looking at her again.

SULLIVAN STOOD IN the light from a single bulb that illuminated the stairwell several doors down from the room. Patrick moved toward him, zipping up his coat as he did so.

"You look like someone dragged you through the mud." Sullivan nodded at a smear of dirt on the sleeve of the jacket.

"Those two in the canyon ambushed us. I thought I'd sneak up behind them and they moved in and tried to kidnap Stacy."

"And you shot them."

"Yes."

"How gallant."

"I was doing my job. You would have done the same."

"Maybe."

"How did you end up here?" Patrick asked. "Your timing is uncanny, by the way. The local cops were ready to haul us off to jail."

"We had someone monitoring the scanner. They heard the call go out."

"You must have been close."

"We were at that convenience store. Nobody knows anything about anyone named Marne."

"What about the surveillance tapes?"

"What do you know—the machine had a malfunction and stopped working for half the day yesterday."

Patrick grunted and shoved both hands in his coat pockets. Neither man spoke for a long moment. An eighteen-wheeler sped by on the highway, Jake brakes rattling as it headed down the grade.

"Want to tell me what's going on with you and the Giardino woman?" Sullivan asked.

"No." He blew out a breath. "I know I screwed up. It just…happened."

"Sometimes it does. Is it going to affect your ability to do your job?"

"No." He faced the other man, surprised at the sympathy he found there. "I'm not some besotted schoolboy. I know how to handle myself."

"What about her?" He tipped his head toward the hotel room. "Women sometimes read more into these things."

"Stacy's concerned for her son. She knows what happened between us.... She knows there's no future there."

"Does she?"

"She's a lot stronger than she looks. Stronger than anyone I've known. Are you going to report us?"

"I don't work for the U.S. Marshal's office, do I?" His gaze slid past Patrick to the walkway beyond. "Hello, Mrs. Giardino. How are you doing?"

She nodded and stopped close, but not too close, to Patrick. "Have you found out anything about my son?"

"Maybe we should go inside to discuss this. Where it's warmer."

They trooped silently back to the room. In the men's absence, Stacy had made the bed and picked up the scattered clothes. Patrick relaxed a little. Not having the evidence of their indiscretion staring them all in the face helped a little. Stacy sat on the side of the bed and the two men took the chairs at the table. "Have you found my son?" she asked. "Have you found Carlo?"

Sullivan shook his head. "Marshal Thompson asked us to locate a ranch that belongs to Abel Giardino. We've found a place we think might be his and we've put it under surveillance."

"What have you seen? Have you seen a child?"

"We've only been watching the place a few hours at this point, and so far there's been nothing to see."

"Where is this place?" Stacy asked. "Can we go there?"

"That wouldn't be a good idea," Patrick said. "If they are holding Carlo and we go busting in, they might harm him—or carry him away to an even more remote location."

"As long as there aren't any signs that the boy is in danger, it's best to watch and figure out when to make our move," Sullivan said. "The first step is to verify that Carlo is even there."

"That's all you can tell me?" she asked. "We have to wait?"

"Maybe we'll know more later this morning, when people on the ranch wake up and start moving about. One of our spotters might see something then."

"You'll let me know right away?"

"We'll let you know as soon as it's safe to do so."

Patrick wanted to reach out, to squeeze her hand and offer her some sort of comfort. But with Sullivan looking on, he didn't dare. "Is there anything else you can tell us?" he asked.

"We did learn more about the wills," Sullivan said. "Both Sam's and Sam Junior's." He pulled a small notebook from his pocket and flipped through it. "We were able to get a judge to unseal the documents and they proved very interesting."

"How interesting?" Patrick asked. The hair on the back of his neck rose, a sure sign that the information was going to be good.

"Both Sammy and his father left everything to Carlo.

But it's tied up in a complicated trust. The manager of the trust directs the distribution of the money until Carlo is twenty-one."

"Who's the manager of the trust?" Stacy asked.

"You are." Sullivan closed the notebook and replaced it in his pocket. "You didn't know?"

She shook her head. "Why would Sam—or Sammy, for that matter—give me control over any of his money?"

"You're the boy's mother," Sullivan said. "Aren't you the most logical choice?"

"In the Giardino family, women never control the money," Stacy said.

"Was this one more way Sam was getting a dig in at Sammy?" Patrick asked. "It made sense that he'd die before his son, and then Sammy would have to watch while his son inherited everything—and you had control."

"Sammy would have hated that," Stacy said. "But Sammy had a will, too. Why didn't his will name someone else as administrator for the trust?"

"Maybe Sam forced him to agree to the same terms," Patrick said. "It seems to me that Sammy did what Sam told him to, at least some of the time." He'd married Stacy because his father had arranged it, hadn't he?

She nodded. "But this…"

"He may have had something else in mind," Sullivan said.

They both looked to him. He waited, clearly enjoying the suspense. "The terms of the trust make clear the custodian can do anything with the trust—including signing over control to a third party. Maybe Sammy figured he'd persuade you—or force you—to sign control over to him after his father died. And if he died first, his father could do the same."

"What happens to the trust if I die?" she asked.

"Control goes to Carlo's legal guardian."

"Do you have a will?" Patrick asked. "Have you named a guardian in the case of your death?"

She shook her head. "I'm only twenty-four. I never thought…"

Patrick did touch her hand then, moved by her distress. "It's all right," he said. "Of course you didn't."

"In lieu of a named guardian, it would be up to the court to decide," Sullivan said.

"Wouldn't the court give the boy to his next of kin?" Patrick asked.

"Maybe," Sullivan said. "Who would that be?"

"Not Uncle Abel," Stacy said. "I'd think it would be Elizabeth. She's his aunt."

"That could explain why the kidnappers decided they needed you alive," Patrick said. "Abel might have known enough about the will to know Carlo would receive everything. Later, he found out he'd need you to sign over control to him, so he sent his men back to get you."

"Why go to so much trouble?" she asked. "Abel has money of his own. And the government is liable to seize all of Sam's assets, aren't they?"

"The government can only seize assets they can link to crimes," Sullivan said. "And money we can get to and know about. Though we are still conducting our investigations, we suspect Sam had considerable amounts stashed in foreign accounts, in Switzerland and the Caymans, for example."

"So by gaining control of Carlo's trust, Abel Giardino could gain control of that money," Patrick said.

"Or someone else who is controlling Abel could gain control of the money," Sullivan said.

"But they need me alive, and they need Carlo alive, to do it," Stacy said. She didn't quite smile, but her eyes held a new light, and Patrick felt an easing of the tension within himself, also.

"So we can be reasonably sure the boy is safe for now," Sullivan said. "Which gives us more time to connect the dots between Giardino and our chief suspect."

"Senator Nordley," Patrick said.

Sullivan frowned and cut his eyes to Stacy. Clearly, he didn't approve of Stacy knowing of the government's interest in Nordley. "Yes, we would like to know more about the senator's involvement in this."

"Wait a minute." Stacy leaned toward him, her eyes blazing. "What exactly are you saying?"

Sullivan faced her, hands on his knees, his voice just this side of patronizing. "I'm saying we believe your son is safe with his uncle for the time being. The best thing for you to do is to go home and wait and we'll let you know when he can return to you."

Chapter Twelve

Stacy had heard of people seeing red, but she'd never experienced this red haze of anger clouding her vision. "My son is not *safe* with anyone but me. And you are insane if you think I'm going to go anywhere and wait until the government decides they can get around to returning him to me."

"He's in no danger," Sullivan said. "As long as he's safe…"

"How do you know that? You told me earlier you hadn't even seen him. Or was that a lie to try to shut me up?" She stood, and Patrick rose also, prepared to prevent her from launching herself at Sullivan. "He is away from his mother, with people he doesn't know. He's alone and afraid and you will not leave him there one *second* more than necessary."

"Mrs. Giardino, we are talking about a major investigation that has ramifications with the security of the United States," Sullivan said.

"What does Nordley have to do with national security?" Patrick asked.

"He's head of the Senate's committee on homeland security."

"I don't care if he's best friends with the head of the

Taliban," Stacy said. "You can investigate him *after* you rescue my son."

"We really can't do that." Sullivan looked to Patrick. "Explain to her how important this is."

"I can't." Patrick folded his arms over his chest. "You can't justify leaving a three-year-old in a dangerous situation for the convenience of an investigation."

"He's not in any danger."

"I don't agree. And I won't go along with any plan to delay his rescue."

"Then it's just as well the decision isn't up to you." Sullivan stood also and started for the door.

"Where are you going?" Stacy asked.

"Back to do my job. I'll be in touch."

"That's all you have to say?" Patrick asked.

"All that you need to know."

"Have you seen Carlo?" Stacy asked. "Is he really all right?"

Sullivan looked from one to the other. "I'm not going to discuss this investigation with you any further. Now, if you'll excuse me, I have a job to do."

"I have a job with this investigation, too," Patrick said. "The Bureau isn't running this show."

"It is now. But don't worry—you still have a role. Your job is to protect Mrs. Giardino." He smirked. "Obviously, you're taking that assignment very seriously." He opened the door. "I'll be in touch."

Sullivan left. Patrick moved to the window and watched the agent get into a black SUV and drive away.

Stacy watched over Patrick's shoulder. "Aren't you going to stop him?" she asked.

"I can't." He turned away from the window. "That

last dig about you was his way of letting me know he won't say anything to my supervisors about our relationship as long as I stay out of his way. If I make trouble, he'll have me reassigned. You'll get a new handler who'll have orders not to let you get near the investigation."

"I can't believe this is happening. What are we going to do?"

"At least if I stay with you we can work together." He put his arm around her and pulled her close. "We'll find Carlo."

"But he ordered you to stay away."

"It wouldn't be the first time I've bent the rules to help someone I was sworn to protect." He'd sent Elizabeth Giardino a gun, though doing so had been out of line. Directly disobeying orders to look for Carlo was a much more serious transgression; it could cost him his career.

"You'd risk your job for me?" she asked.

"Finding Carlo is the right thing to do," he said.

"How will we find him? We don't know where the ranch is."

"The same way Sullivan probably found him—we'll talk to people and listen to what they have to say. We will find him, Stacy. I promise." He squeezed her shoulder. And when they did, he'd do what he had to do to reunite the child with his mother, even if it meant defying his bosses and the government.

Stacy dressed in the clothes she'd worn the day before, which were at least a little cleaner after their soak in the tub and a night spent drying over a chair. Patrick wore clothes that had belonged to the pale-eyed man, though the shirt was a little tight across his broader shoulders. They packed their few belongings into Pale Eyes's suitcase and prepared to leave. They were on their way out the door when Stacy remembered the other suitcase. She put her hand on Patrick's arm to stop him. "Wait. What about the money?"

He nodded and went to retrieve the second case from under the bed. He unzipped the top and surveyed the neat stacks of bills inside, as if to reassure himself they were still there.

"We didn't tell Sullivan about this," she said.

"I never told my office, either." The oversight wasn't deliberate; he'd simply forgotten with everything else that had happened. He zipped up the case. "I'll be sure to report it the next time Sullivan bothers to get in touch. In the meantime, we might be able to use it as a bargaining chip."

"With the feds or with Uncle Abel?" she asked.

"Maybe both." He carried the case out to the car and locked it in the trunk. He didn't know if fifty thousand dollars was enough to persuade anyone involved in this case to act differently, but the money might link up some of the players. Had the two thugs been delivering or receiving the cash? Who had put it into that suitcase? He added these to the growing list of unanswered questions in this case.

LIGHT SNOW FELL as they drove toward Crested Butte. Stacy didn't ask what they'd do when they got there. Stacy trusted Patrick had a plan. All she could focus on was Carlo and praying that he was indeed all right. Maybe Abel and Willa liked little children and they'd be kind to him and do what they could to calm his fears. It wasn't the same as having his mother with him, but she wanted him to feel safe. To know he was loved. Wasn't that the best security of all, to know that someone cared about you and wanted to protect you?

"Do you think Agent Sullivan is right about the reason Carlo was kidnapped?" she asked. "To gain control of the money?"

"Greed motivates a lot of crimes. But you said Abel has money of his own?"

"Sam always said he did. He referred to him as 'my brother, the rich rancher.'"

"What kind of ranch does he have? Cattle?"

"Horses, I think. Maybe some cattle, too. I'm not sure. Sam always talked about Abel 'playing cowboy' and said he was rolling in the big bucks."

"Maybe he was being sarcastic."

"Maybe. An honest rancher probably doesn't have as much money as a mobster."

"We don't know that he's honest," Patrick said.

"Kidnapping isn't honest," she agreed. "And if he was the one who sent those two thugs after us in the canyon, how did he know to hire people who had worked for Sam, unless he and Sam had been in contact—even working together—all along?"

"I wonder if the cash in that suitcase was payment to the thugs for going after you—or if they were supposed to deliver it to Abel from someone else."

"From Senator Nordley?" she asked. "Was he fronting cash to Abel until he had the money from the will?"

Patrick shook his head. "It's all speculation. And we

could be completely wrong. We're still not certain Abel even has Carlo."

She slid down lower in the seat. "I hope he does. At least then we know where he is. If he isn't with Abel and Willa, then he's vanished." The thought made it difficult to breathe.

Patrick squeezed her hand. "We'll find him. I promise."

She nodded, too moved to speak. She believed he meant his words, but she also knew he couldn't guarantee that Carlo was safe. She wouldn't rest easy again until her son was safe in her arms, and far away from the people who wanted to hurt him or use him.

After two hours of driving, a highway sign informed them they had reached the outskirts of Crested Butte. Patrick turned off the highway at a complex of warehouses and industrial-supply businesses. "I'm headed to the airport," he said, before Stacy could ask. "We need to get rid of this car."

"Because Abel's men might recognize it?"

He glanced at her. "That, and because the feds know it."

She sat back in her seat. Right. If Sullivan and his bunch recognized that Stacy and Patrick were getting too close to their precious investigation, they'd do everything they could to stop them.

Patrick parked the car at Crested Butte's tiny airport, which was housed in a single terminal with two gates. He carried their suitcases inside and led the way to the rental car counter, where he rented a yellow Jeep Cherokee with a ski rack. "The snow is great right now," the clerk said as she handed over the keys. "Have a great vacation."

"Thanks." His eyes met Stacy's and she looked away. She only wished they were a happy couple on a relaxing vacation, instead of two people thrown together in a desperate search for her missing son.

From the airport they drove into the heart of Crested Butte, which proved to be a picturesque hamlet of Victorian-era wood-front buildings painted bright colors, clustered along a few streets against a backdrop of snow-covered mountains. Patrick found the courthouse, parked in front of it and went inside to the clerk's office. "We're doing some research and would like to look through the tax records," he told the middle-aged redhead behind the counter.

"You can use this computer." The clerk led them to a small workstation and pulled up the county records program. "You can search by the name of the owner or by address," she said. She started to type in an example, but the phone rang. "I'd better get that," she said. "If you have any questions, just ask."

Stacy sat in the chair in front of the terminal while Patrick pulled a second chair alongside her. "I guess I'll start with the obvious," she said. She typed the word *Giardino* in the space for last name and hit Enter.

"No records returned," Patrick said.

In quick succession she tried Abel, Willa, Sam and even Carlo. But nothing came up that looked remotely like the ranch Abel supposedly owned. "Try Nordley," Patrick suggested.

She tried the name. "Nothing."

Patrick sat back. "This isn't getting us anywhere.

Even in a county this small, there must be thousands
of properties. We can't research them all."

"You're right." She clicked back to the home page,
then pushed out her chair. "I have an idea. Just give
me a minute."

With her most friendly smile in place, she approached the clerk. "Maybe you can help me," she said.
"I'm doing a college thesis on historic ranches of Gun-
nison County. Do you know who might have a listing
of all the ranches in the area?"

The lines on the clerk's forehead deepened. "The
historical society might be able to help you," she said.

"So you don't maintain any kind of listing of ranches
or anything like that in this office?"

"We have a map the cattleman's society put together
a couple years back, but it won't tell you if the places
on it are historic or not."

"Could I see the map? It would be a great start."

"I think I have a copy around here somewhere." She
retreated to a back room and returned a few minutes
later with a yellowing scroll. "Here you go. Just return
it to me when you're done."

Resisting the urge to unfurl the scroll and examine
it right there at the counter, Stacy thanked the woman
and carried her prize back to the workstation. "This map
supposedly shows the ranches in the county," she said.

Patrick took hold of one end and helped her spread
out the documents, which proved to be an artistic rendering of the county, complete with mountain ranges,
miniature skiers and carefully sketched-in cattle and
forests. Stacy scanned the names of the ranches: Red
Hawk, Powderhorn Creek, Pogna Ranch. She stopped

when she came to a name affixed to a parcel not far from town. "Willing and Able," she read. "That has to be it. It's a play on their names—Willa and Abel."

Patrick pulled out a notebook and wrote down the general location of the ranch. Stacy typed the road number into the computer and came up with a listing of properties in the vicinity. Third from the top was the name A.G. Holdings. "Abel Giardino," she said.

Patrick nodded and replaced the notebook in his coat. "Let's drive out there and take a look."

Stacy returned the map to the clerk. "Did you find what you were looking for?" the woman asked.

"I think so. Thank you very much." She couldn't hold back her smile. Maybe in just a little while she'd be able to see her son.

"Hurry," she said to Patrick, and rushed past him toward the Jeep.

He followed at a slower pace. Once they were buckled in, he turned to her before he started the car. "Right now we're just going to drive by to make sure we have the right location—and to see if we spot any of the federal surveillance. I doubt we will—these guys are very good. But we won't be stopping and lingering. And we won't be driving up to the front door and demanding to see Carlo."

"Of course not." Though part of her had envisioned just such a scenario.

"I know it's hard for you, being this close and having to wait," he said. "But if we're going to retrieve Carlo safely, we have to have a plan. I'm hoping this drive will suggest a way to approach the ranch house without being seen by either the feds or Abel's guards. This is just a reconnaissance mission."

She nodded. "All right." She reached out and pressed down the door lock. She could do this—but if she actually saw Carlo, all bets were off.

Patrick consulted the map of the area the rental car company had given him, then drove out of town and turned onto a plowed gravel road that cut between expanses of snow-covered fields crisscrossed with sagging barbed-wire fencing. They passed herds of cattle eating hay that ranchers had spread for them that morning, the feed a dark green line against the pristine whiteness of the snow that rose above the animals' hocks.

Other pastures were vacant, the snow as smooth as buttercream frosting on a wedding cake, unmarred by even the tracks of deer. Stacy thought again of the remoteness and loneliness of this country. "I could never live here," she said. "So far from everything."

"Some people like it, I guess," he said. "No neighbors to see what you're up to."

No neighbors to notice a little boy who didn't belong there. "Our neighbors in New York probably saw plenty," she said. "But they knew to keep their mouths shut."

"Good point." Patrick shifted into a lower gear to climb a steep hill. "The Willing and Able should be up ahead, just around this curve."

Stacy looked, but saw nothing but the same empty fields and barbed wire. They drove for another five minutes before a driveway appeared, a simple W&A on the black iron gate, which was closed, though the packed snow showed signs of recent travel up the drive. Stacy craned her neck, but could see nothing past the line of trees that marked a bend in the driveway. She tried to suppress her disappointment. "I thought we'd at least see a house or something." A house with a little boy's face pressed to the window, watching for his mother.

"These ranch houses are set way off the road," Patrick said. "I figured the best we could do would be to get a sense of the layout and determine the most likely locations for federal agents."

"And what did you decide?" she asked.

"I think the feds probably have someone watching the gate," he said. "There's another drive across the road. My guess someone is set up in the trees."

"Do you think they recognized us?" Her stomach lurched.

"I ducked my head and yours was turned away. They might run a check on the Jeep's plate and they'll find out it's a rental, but I used a fake ID."

A surprised laugh escaped her lips. "You have a fake ID?"

The tips of his ears flushed red. "It comes in handy sometimes."

"And here I thought you were a strictly-by-the-book guy."

"I do what I have to to protect my charges."

She reached out and squeezed his hand. "Thank you for protecting me. And thank you for staying with me after Sullivan found out about us. I know you didn't have to do that."

"I won't leave you until I know you're safe."

But he would leave her then. The knowledge started an ache deep in her chest. When had this man, whom she had hated, even feared when they first met, become such an important part of her life? The shift in her attitude had happened long before they'd slept together; something in her had recognized Marshal Patrick Thompson as someone she could depend on. Someone she could trust with her deepest secrets.

With her heart.

She pushed the idea away. She had to think about Carlo now, to focus on him. Everything else, including worries about the future, was secondary to freeing Carlo and keeping him safe. "How are we going to get to the ranch house and find Carlo?" she asked.

"We'll have to find a back way in."

"How are we going to do that?"

"I have some ideas. But first, let's get out of here."

He turned onto another gravel road marked with a green Forest Service sign. After crawling along for what seemed to Stacy like an hour, they emerged onto the highway south of town. "We need to rent a hotel room," Patrick said. "We can talk there without being overheard and make plans."

"All right." Renting a room meant more delays, but so would arguing with him. And when they did find Carlo, it would be good to have a safe, warm room to bring him back to.

They found a vacancy at a small motel in town but didn't bother to bring their luggage inside. They did bring the map, which Patrick spread out on the table by the window. "This is the road we came in on," he showed her, tracing the route with his finger.

"There's the ranch." She pointed to the curve near the ranch gate.

"Right. Now, let's see…." He punched some buttons on his phone, then turned the screen so she could see.

She studied the photo of one large roof and several smaller ones grouped among some trees. "What am I looking at?" she asked.

"That's the Google Earth shot of the Willing and Able ranch house."

"You're kidding."

He shook his head. "Forget government satellites. Anyone can look at this stuff online."

"I wonder if Abel knows that."

"Even if he does, there's nothing he can do to prevent it." He laid the phone alongside the map and zoomed out. "This picture was taken in the summer. You can see this back drive that snakes behind the house and out this other direction." He pointed to a faint, broken line on the map. "That's this road here."

"It's not really a road," she said. "More of a trail."

"But it's a way in."

"Except it's probably not plowed in the winter."

"If it is, the feds will have it staked out. But if it isn't, they probably won't bother watching it too closely."

"But that doesn't help us. Even with four-wheel drive we won't get down a road that hasn't been plowed. You saw how deep the snow was."

"We can't drive down it. But we can walk. Or rather, snowshoe."

"Uncle Abel's men will spot us a mile off. It's not as if we can run in snowshoes."

"We'll wait until after dark. They won't see us. And we won't have to run."

"Carlo could never walk far through snow, and he's almost too big for me to carry."

"I could carry him."

She studied the image of the ranch house roof. Was Carlo really there? "I don't know. Can we really do this?"

"We can. I think it's the best way to get close and remain undetected. Once we determine where he is in the house, we'll sneak in and out with as little fuss as possible."

She regarded him more closely. "You talk as if you've done this kind of thing before."

"I was with Special Forces in the service."

"You're just full of surprises, aren't you?"

"Before long you're going to know all my secrets," he said. He didn't exactly smile, but the look he gave her sent a jolt of heat straight to her belly.

"How can I say no when you put it like that?" She took a deep breath. "What next?"

"We need better winter clothing, snowshoes and a few other supplies. Time to go shopping."

Good idea. Shopping was one thing she was good at, and searching through stores for the supplies they needed would eat up time and provide a welcome distraction from her worries about Carlo and the chances of this crazy plan succeeding.

At a backcountry outfitter around the corner from their hotel they purchased long underwear, snow pants and jackets, hats, mittens and snowshoes. "These have a narrower profile that make walking and even running easier than ever," the clerk, a young man with a goatee and two earrings, pointed out as he helped Stacy strap on the lightweight aluminum shoes. "And you'll want poles to help with your balance." He shortened a pair of aluminum poles and handed them to her.

She stood in the middle of the store, poles planted on either side of her, and looked over at Patrick. He was busy stuffing their purchases into a large backpack. "I think I can get the hang of this," she said.

"Trust me," the clerk said. "If you can walk, you can snowshoe."

From the outfitters, they walked down the sidewalk between walls of snow, past shops that sold everything from T-shirts to gourmet cookware. "Are we looking for anything in particular?" she asked.

"Right now we're just killing time," he said. "If you see anyplace you want to go into, say the word."

She stopped in front of a window that displayed a variety of toys from an old-fashioned sled to video games. "Let's go in here," she said.

The store was filled with items that would have delighted Carlo, but she settled on a ten-inch-high bear with thick brown fur and a blue bow around its neck. "I think he would like this," she said. When they took him back to the hotel later tonight—as she prayed they would—it would be good to give him this bear to comfort and distract him.

"I'm sure he would," Patrick said, and took out his wallet to pay for the purchase.

They ate pizza at a restaurant at one end of the street. "Do you think Sullivan was right, that Carlo is safe?" she asked as she nibbled a slice of pepperoni.

"I think he didn't want you to know at first that

they'd found the boy, but I think he is safe. Abel needs Carlo to have access to the money."

"How does Senator Nordley play into this?"

"Rumor has it he wants to run for president. That takes a lot of money. Maybe Abel promised Nordley a share of the cash if he'd help Abel get his hands on it."

"He can have every bit of it, for all I care. I just want my son safely back with me. I don't even want the Giardinos' ill-gotten gains."

"Seems to me you've earned your share of their wealth," he said. "It could make you and Carlo a lot more comfortable."

"I can look after Carlo myself," she said. "I'd rather be poor and free of the taint of that family. I'm even thinking of changing my name when this is all over."

"Back to your maiden name?" he asked.

She made a face. "It's my father's name, and he never did me any favors. I think I'll have to come up with something new. A fresh start."

"If you go into WITSEC, you can choose whatever name you like." At her frown, he held up his hand. "I know you don't want to go into the program, but I just thought I'd point out that it automatically comes with a name change, and a fresh start."

"I'll think about it." Maybe it wouldn't be so bad, letting the government help her out. And it might mean she'd get to continue to see Patrick, at least some of the time.

After lunch they slowly made their way up the other side of the street to the hotel. Back in their room, she flopped down on the bed. "This waiting is killing me. When can we leave?"

"It gets dark pretty early. We can start that way about four-thirty."

She checked the bedside clock. "Three hours."

"Try to get some sleep. It could be a long night."

"What are you going to do?"

"I'm going to organize our gear." Already he'd spread half their purchases on the table and was unwrapping items—a flashlight, energy bars, water bottles, first aid kit, emergency blanket and more things she couldn't remember.

"You can lie down on the bed and I promise I won't attack you," she said.

He looked startled. "What?"

"I know you feel bad about us sleeping together," she said. "Like you shirked your duty or betrayed an oath or something."

"You're wrong." He went back to wrestling with the wrapping on a small pair of binoculars. "I ought to feel bad about my unprofessional behavior, but I can't regret making love to you."

"Then why are you avoiding even touching me?"

He set aside the binoculars and looked at her. "Because if I touch you—if I come over there and lie down beside you—I won't be content with just a nap."

"Oh." His words—and the heated look in his eyes when he said them—sent a hot shiver down to her toes.

"You must be exhausted," he said. "You're worried about your son and nervous about tonight. Sex is probably the last thing on your mind. I'm trying to be a gentleman."

She was all those things he'd said, but none of that

mattered now. "I don't need a gentleman right now," she said. "I just need you."

His silence was like a vise around her chest, preventing her from breathing. Maybe she'd been wrong to be so frank, so open with him. Maybe he didn't really want her that way. He was trying to find a kind way to reject her.

He stood, his gaze still locked to hers, and unbuttoned the top button of his shirt. "I never was good at being a gentleman," he said.

Chapter Thirteen

Whereas their lovemaking before had been full of the uncertainties and hesitations of any new partners, Stacy felt more sure of herself with Patrick now—and more sure of him as a man who would welcome whatever she had to offer. When they lay together, naked under the covers, she allowed herself the luxury of exploring his body—of discovering the play of muscle beneath the smooth flesh of his back and shoulders, delighting in the ticklish spot just at his waist, thrilling to the feel of the shadow of beard along his jaw.

"What is this?" she asked, running her finger along a puckered scar across the top of one hip.

"Sniper round."

"And this?" She moved to a purple slash across his biceps.

"Bullet wound." He covered her hand with his. "If you start inventorying my scars, we'll be here all night."

His kiss cut off her response, but the kiss was response enough. She'd never known such kisses, deep and sweet, both insistent and tender, leaving her dizzy and breathless and feeling so…cherished. She opened her eyes and met his gaze.

"I like that you watch me when we make love," he said.

"I don't want to miss anything," he said. With Sammy—before he'd turned his back on her altogether—she'd kept her eyes closed to avoid seeing the disdain with which he so often regarded her. Patrick's eyes held none of that scorn—only lust and longing and something that felt, to her at least, like appreciation.

They made love languidly that afternoon, each giving and receiving pleasure, teasing out the moments until they could wait no longer. After he entered her, she urged him onto his back so that she rode atop him, directing the tempo and depth of his strokes, his hands guiding her hips, the increasing pace of his breathing and the glazed look in his eyes letting her know when he was near to losing control. But he turned the tables when he reached down to touch her, sending her over the edge with a cry of delight.

Afterward, they lay together, cocooned in warmth and satisfaction, the light showing through the crack between the curtains fading from gold to muddy gray. "No tears this time," he said.

"No tears." She had plenty to cry about in her life right now, but Patrick was not one of those things. She might weep later, when he left her. But not now. She wouldn't spoil the time they had together with sorrow.

PATRICK HADN'T INTENDED to fall asleep, but he must have. When he woke it was full dark, the only light the faint glow from the parking lot security lights. Stacy lay curled against him. He shook her gently. "Stacy. It's time to go."

She stirred and buried her head deeper under the covers. "Stacy!" He shook her harder. "It's time to get up and go find Carlo."

"Carlo." She looked up at him, then sat up, pushing off the covers. "What time is it?"

He checked the clock. "It's after six."

"Oh, no! We're late!" She scrambled out of bed and grabbed for her clothes.

"It's okay." He moved to the table and began searching through their purchases. "We have plenty of time. Waiting until later is probably better. Don't forget to dress warm."

"All of a sudden I'm so nervous," she said. "What if we can't find him? What if the feds stop us? Or Abel and his men?"

"Stacy, it's okay." He put his hand on her shoulder. "It will be all right. You can do this."

Her eyes met his and some of the panic faded. She nodded. "You're right. Together, we can do this."

Half an hour later, they were headed out of town in the Jeep, the headlights cutting through the darkness. He took a different route this time, one he'd plotted on the map to avoid the locations where federal agents were most likely to be posted. This meant traveling at slow speeds down narrow, winding back roads. Stacy didn't say a word, but she gripped the dashboard as they bumped over ruts, tension radiating from her.

After more than an hour, they passed a break in the fence. Patrick stopped, then backed up the Jeep and angled it until the headlights shone through the gap, illuminating the faint indentations of a snow-clogged track. He checked the GPS coordinates on his phone. "This is where we get out," he said.

"Are we just going to leave the Jeep here?" she asked.

"I think I can nose it under those trees ahead. I doubt anyone is going to come along at this time of night. There aren't any fresh tracks since the snow this morning."

He parked the car under the trees and they piled out and strapped on snowshoes. Stacy took a few experimental steps forward. "What do you think?" Patrick asked.

"Not bad," she said. "Hopefully I'll do as well in deep snow." She tilted her head to look up at the sky. The morning's clouds had vanished, leaving inky black sky dotted with a million stars and a thin sliver of moon. "It's beautiful," she said, her breath forming a cloud.

"Beautiful, but cold." He moved alongside her and handed her a pair of chemical heat packs. "Slip these into your mittens."

"Thanks." She added the hot packs to her mittens, then switched on the headlamp he'd also handed her. "We've got about a mile trek to the ranch house," he said. "We'll take it slow, and no talking. I don't think anyone's listening, but might as well be safe."

"What if they have dogs?"

"They aren't likely to be roaming around away from the house in this cold. We'll be on the lookout when we get closer. Are you ready?"

"Yes. Let's go."

He led the way down the snow-packed trail. Their tracks would have been clearly visible to anyone who passed by, but there was no way he could think of to hide their passage in the fresh snow. He set a brisk pace, but soon slowed as Stacy fell farther and farther behind. He stopped and waited for her to catch up. "I'm sorry," she whispered. "I—"

He put a finger to his lips and shook his head, then handed her a bottle of water. She drank, then he drank and replaced the bottle in the pack and patted her shoulder. *You're doing great,* he wanted to tell her. Instead, he gave her a thumbs-up and indicated they should move on.

He shortened his steps and she was better able to match his pace. The track emerged from the woods into open pasture and the drifts grew deeper, their shoes sinking into the soft, untrodden snow. Clearly, no one had passed this way in some time—a good indication that the feds had overlooked this route, too.

After about half an hour they saw the glow from the lights of the house, then they rounded a curve in the trail and spotted the house itself, surrounded by half a dozen outbuildings— horse stalls, a garage and storage sheds. Patrick stopped and she halted behind him, close enough he could hear her labored breathing.

He waited, listening for the barks of dogs or the rev of an engine, for shouts or voices or any indication that they'd been spotted. He pulled the binoculars from the inside of his jacket and scanned the area, wishing for the night-vision goggles he'd used in the military. Still, the outside security lights provided enough illumination for him to determine that the area was deserted.

They were going to have to get a lot closer to the

house to find the boy. He touched Stacy's shoulder and indicated they should remove their snowshoes.

Snowshoes discarded and poles laid aside, he started toward the house, keeping to the shadows, stepping in snow to his knees. Stacy literally followed in his footsteps. Though the snow made for slow going, it also muffled the sound of their approach. The house remained silent, undisturbed by their presence.

He stopped at the edge of the clearing, about a hundred yards from the side of the house, giving them a view of both the front and back yards. Nothing moved, and the only sounds were the hum of what must be a furnace and the rough inhalation and exhalation of their own breath.

Stacy tugged on his arm and he bent to her. She put her mouth against his ear. "The curtains are all closed," she said. "How are we going to know which room Carlo is in? And how are we going to get to him?"

His original plan had been to hunker down and watch the house until he had a feel for the layout, but arriving so late, they could sit here all night and be no better informed in the morning than they were now. And the longer they stayed, the greater the risk of someone spotting the Jeep or seeing their tracks heading toward the house.

He turned and led her back down the trail until they were far enough away from the house he was sure they wouldn't be heard. "We'll have to get inside," he said.

"How? The doors will be locked, and there will be guards."

"I can pick a lock. But I don't think there will be guards."

"Sam always had bodyguards," she said.

"But Abel isn't Sam. He's a rancher, not a mobster. And there aren't enough vehicles for very many people to be here. That garage holds two cars, at most, and the only other car is that old truck by the shed—and it's covered in snow, as if it hasn't been driven in weeks."

"Maybe they're parked somewhere else."

"Maybe so, but why go to all that trouble? This is Abel's home. He feels safe here. If he does have guards, they're probably up by the main gate—the only way in this time of year."

"It's still taking a huge risk."

"Would you rather we went away and left Carlo in there?"

"No. Of course not."

"Good. Then follow me inside. Stick close and don't make a sound. From what I could see, there's a front door, a side door opening to the walkway to the garage and a back door that probably opens into a kitchen or a mudroom."

"That's all I saw, too."

"We'll try the back door first. If we hear anything, we'll move to another door, or a window."

"What do we do when we find Carlo?"

"If he's alone, we'll sneak him out the same way we came in. If he isn't alone, I'll take care of the guard and you look after Carlo. If we're separated, meet up back at the Jeep."

"All right." She hesitated, then stood on tiptoe and kissed his cheek. "Thank you," she whispered. "For everything."

She should wait and thank him when her boy was

safe, but he didn't tell her that, merely patted her shoulder then turned to lead the way up to the house. He'd deliberately downplayed the risk of what they were about to do, in order not to frighten her, but he had no such delusions. It would take all his skills—and a great deal of luck—to come out of this unscathed.

STACY FOLLOWED PATRICK out of the shadows onto the pristine expanse of snow behind the ranch house. Their footsteps made dark holes in the snow, like a row of ellipses leading across the yard. At the bottom of the steps they halted and listened. The furnace shut off abruptly and she strained her ears, listening. From somewhere deep inside the house came the sound of voices, followed by the buzz of canned laughter—the television.

Patrick wiped his feet on the bottom steps and brushed the bottoms of his trousers, trying to remove as much snow as possible. She did the same. His eyes met hers and he nodded, then started up the steps.

The knob turned easily in his hand. Maybe he'd been right about Abel not thinking like a criminal; Sam would never have left a door unlocked, especially not at night.

Her heart hammered painfully as he eased open the door, then slipped inside, moving gracefully despite the bulky pack on his back. A few seconds later, he beckoned for her to follow.

A light over the stove cast a dim glow over scuffed red linoleum floors and white Formica countertops. A dish drainer with four plates, four forks, three glasses and a coffee cup sat beside the sink. She felt a jolt of elation as she counted the dishes. If one of the sets belonged to Carlo, that meant they had only three adults to deal with.

A door from the kitchen led into a darkened dining room. Patrick stopped to one side of the doorway and pulled her alongside him. From here they could look into the living room, where a man and an older woman sat in two armchairs in front of a large flat-screen television. She scanned the room for some sign of Carlo but found none.

They retreated to the kitchen and moved to a second door, which opened into a cramped hallway and a flight of stairs leading straight up. Patrick started up them, keeping close to the railing. She did the same, trying to make each step as light and soundless as possible.

At the top of the stairs they stopped again to listen. A commercial came on the television advertising a fast-food chain. "Is there any more of that ice cream?" a man's voice asked.

"In the freezer," a woman answered. "Get me a bowl, too."

Stacy clung to the stair railing, feeling dizzy. Floorboards creaked below them as the man moved from the living room into the kitchen, where only seconds before, he would have found them. Light poured out from the room as he flicked the switch and she couldn't breathe. Would he notice anything out of place in the room? Despite their best efforts, had they tracked snow inside?

Patrick's hand on her arm forced her attention back to him. He indicated they should continue down the hallway to the left of the stairs. On tiptoe, she followed, toward a door beneath which a light glowed.

The light in the kitchen went out as they reached the

doorway that must lead to a bedroom. Patrick put his ear to the door, and she moved past him to do the same.

A woman was speaking. Stacy gasped as she recognized *Where the Wild Things Are,* one of Carlo's favorite books. "'Oh, please don't go—we'll eat you up—we love you so!'"

"That's my favorite part," a little boy answered.

Stacy bit her thumb to keep from crying out. Patrick put a steadying hand on her shoulder. She nodded, though it took everything in her not to burst in and grab her child to her. She looked to Patrick, her eyes pleading. *What do we do?* she mouthed.

He gestured they should wait.

The minutes dragged as she listened to the woman finish reading the story. Had the book really been so long when she'd read it? When Max was finally safely home the woman pronounced, "The end."

"Read it again," Carlo said when she was done. The way he always did when Stacy read that story to him.

"It's time for you to go to sleep now," the woman said.

"Will I see Mommy tomorrow?" Carlo asked.

Stacy let out a moan—she couldn't help it. Patrick gripped her shoulder more tightly and she nodded.

"Maybe your mommy will come tomorrow," the woman said. "Now close your eyes and go to sleep."

"I want a drink of water first."

Patrick stiffened and moved to the other side of the door. Stacy stepped farther into the shadows on her side.

Steps crossed the room, then the doorknob turned and a shaft of light fell on the hallway floor. A short, middle-aged woman with long gray hair stepped out into the hallway. Before Stacy could even blink, Patrick clamped his hand over the woman's mouth and carried her into the bathroom across the hall. Stacy slipped into the bedroom.

"Mama!" Carlo shouted.

"Shh! Shh!" She put her fingers to her lips and rushed to him. "You have to be very quiet," she said. "I don't want Uncle Abel to know I'm here."

The boy frowned. "Why not?"

"It's a surprise." She tucked the blanket from his bed around him and gathered him into her arms. He wore blue flannel pajamas with little fire trucks on them and she could smell toothpaste on his breath. "I've missed you so much," she whispered, hugging him tightly.

"I've missed you, too. Where have you been?"

"Shh. We can't talk now. Now, promise me you'll be very, very quiet. A friend and I are going to take you snowshoeing in the woods. Won't that be fun?"

"But it's dark." He looked toward the window. "And it's cold."

"Please, baby, it will be all right, I promise. Just be quiet and do what Mommy tells you."

"Uncle Abel and Grandma Willa won't like it," he said.

She hesitated. How could she explain the danger to a three-year-old? "No, they won't like it," she said. "And if they catch Mommy here with you, they might hurt us both. So it's very important that we sneak away without them knowing."

Unfortunately, this information only confused the boy more. "But Uncle Abel told me you were coming to see me soon. And he promised to take me for a ride on one of his horses."

"Maybe you can do that soon." She tucked the blanket more firmly around him. "Do you have snow boots?"

"Downstairs."

They didn't have time to search downstairs for boots. She settled for pulling a pair of socks over his bare feet.

The bedroom door opened and Patrick stuck his head in. "We need to go," he whispered.

"Carlo, this is my friend, Patrick," Stacy said. "He's going snowshoeing with us."

Carlo's eyes widened. "He's big."

"Hello, Carlo," Patrick said. "Will you let me carry you?"

Carlo shook his head and clung to his mother.

"I'd better take him for now," she said.

He held the door open wider and motioned for her to go ahead of him.

The kitchen was still dark and the television still blared as they made their way down the stairs. Carlo squirmed and buried his head against Stacy's shoulder, but didn't say a word. She pulled the blanket up over his head and stepped carefully down the stairs. Only a few more steps and they'd be out of the house, halfway to safety.

At the bottom of the stairs, Patrick moved ahead of her. He kept one hand in his pocket and she was sure he was holding his gun. She wondered what he'd done with the babysitter but would have to wait to ask him.

They crossed the kitchen, but when he pulled on the

door, it refused to yield. He turned the knob back and forth, but the door wouldn't budge.

"I remembered to lock it this time," said a voice behind him. "Now turn around, slowly. And keep your hands where I can see them."

Chapter Fourteen

"Uncle Abel, you weren't supposed to see us." Carlo's childish voice broke the silence of the adults, reminding Patrick of all that was at stake here, far beyond his own safety.

"Your uncle Abel is smarter than some people think," the older man said. He was clearly cut from the same mold as Sam Giardino, with the same putty nose and jowly chin, more fleshy and older looking than his brother, who had relied on plastic surgery and expensive spa treatments to maintain his youthful looks.

Abel gestured with his pistol. "Young man, take that gun out of your pocket and lay it on the counter there."

Patrick did as he asked.

"I won't let you take my son." Stacy shifted Carlo to one hip and glared at the old man.

"Your son is a Giardino. He belongs with family." The old woman moved slowly into the kitchen, pushing a walker in front of her. Her sparse gray hair was cut short like a man's and her spine was bent thirty degrees, but her voice was strong and her eyes blazed with determination.

"He belongs with his mother," Stacy declared.

The old woman's mouth twisted into an expression

of disgust. "Sam never should have let his son marry you. I knew as soon as I saw you at the wedding that you had no respect for the family. You were trash he never should have bothered picking up."

Stacy drew herself up taller, eyes sparking. If not for the boy in her arms, Patrick thought she might have flown at the woman. "Your family doesn't deserve my respect," she said.

The old woman dismissed her with a wave and turned to her son. "Get rid of the man and we'll deal with her later."

"I want to know who he is first." Abel jabbed the gun at Patrick. "Who sent you?"

"Nobody sent me," Patrick said. "I agreed to help Stacy retrieve her son."

"I told you, I'm not stupid." He waved the gun threateningly. "You're that marshal assigned to protect her. Thompson."

Patrick didn't allow his expression to betray his surprise. No one was supposed to know where Stacy had been since Sammy's death—or who she was with. Though maybe he had heard the speculation in the news. "My job is to keep her and the boy safe," he said. "I don't care about anything else."

"As if I'd believe that. You work for the feds. Though you've got more nerve than most of them, coming right into my house."

"He's telling the truth," Stacy said. "He's only here to help me. Let us go and we'll leave you alone."

"Shut up," the old woman snapped. "I told you, we'll deal with you later."

"I have something that belongs to you," Patrick said.

"Maybe we can agree to an exchange—the boy and Stacy for what I have."

"What do you have that belongs to me?"

"I have the fifty thousand dollars."

The old man arched one eyebrow. "Fifty thousand dollars that belongs to me? And where did you get that?"

"The two men you sent after us in the canyon had it."

"Those two idiots," Willa said. "I told Abel that was a bad idea. He thought we should get you out of the way and bring Stacy here by herself. You were doing fine getting here on your own without those two interfering, and we could have dealt with you when you arrived. But he doesn't listen to his mother."

Stacy stared at the old woman. Patrick could read her thoughts from the expression on her face—was the old lady for real?

"You probably think fifty thousand dollars is a lot of money to a man like me," Abel said.

"Fifty thousand dollars is a lot of money to most people," Patrick said.

"Not to my brother. If you offered fifty thousand dollars to Sam, he'd take it as an insult."

"I'm not offering the money to your brother," Patrick said. "I'm offering it to you."

"What do you think, Mother? Are those two worth fifty thousand dollars?"

"She isn't worth fifty cents to me, but she's not getting the boy for any price."

"Carlo is my son," Stacy said. "You have no claim on him."

"Stacy," Patrick said. He gave her a warning look. They had nothing to gain by antagonizing these people.

She bit her lip and gave a single nod to show she understood, then rested her head against Carlo's. He whispered something to her and she replied, then smoothed her hand down his back.

"Give me the money," Abel demanded, a new, harder edge to his voice.

"It isn't here," Patrick said. "You let Stacy and Carlo go and once they're safely away, I'll take you to the money."

"And then what am I supposed to do with you?" Abel grinned, showing a missing incisor. "I could kill you, but then I could do that anyway."

"Patrick, no!" Stacy said. "I won't leave without you."

"So that's how it goes, is it?" Abel's expression darkened. "My nephew not cold in his grave and you've taken up with a fed."

Willa called Stacy an obscene name. Stacy cradled Carlo's head to her breast, covering his ears.

"I think I will kill you," Abel said.

"Not in front of the boy," Willa admonished, as if she was warning him against drinking or swearing or some other petty sin.

"No, not in front of the boy," Abel agreed. He motioned to Patrick again. "Take off that pack and turn and face the door, hands behind your back."

Patrick did as the old man asked, moving as slowly as possible, but quickly enough not to provoke his captor. Stacy kept her eyes on him, anger and fear doing battle in her expression. "So you don't care about the money?" Patrick said, when he was facing the door.

"I wondered what happened to it, but there's plenty

more where that came from. Fifty thousand is nothing compared to what I'm going to have as soon as Stacy here signs a few papers for me."

"I won't sign anything unless you let Carlo go," she said.

"Carlo will be fine here with Mother and me. We'll love him like the son and grandson we never had." He opened a drawer and took out a roll of duct tape. "You like it here, don't you, Carlo? You're going to learn to ride horses and be a cowboy."

Carlo said nothing. He stuck out his lower lip and watched his uncle wrap layer after layer of tape around Patrick's wrists.

Patrick's mind raced. He had to do whatever he could to stay here with Stacy, Carlo and the others. As soon as Abel got him alone, the man would most likely kill him. With his hands bound, Patrick had less chance of overpowering the older man. Years of ranch work had honed his muscles, and the weapon put the odds well in his favor. "Even if Stacy signs papers giving you control of the trust, you won't have legal custody of Carlo," he said.

"What, are you a lawyer, too?" Abel tore the last strip of tape, patted it into place and stepped back. "We've taken care of it."

"Stacy is going to sign over custody of Carlo to us," Willa said.

"I most certainly am not," Stacy said.

"You will unless you want to see the boy hurt." Willa smiled—a horrible grin, made more so by the unnaturally white false teeth that gleamed between her withered lips.

"Mommy, don't let them hurt me." Carlo clung tightly to Stacy, his arms around her neck.

"I won't let them hurt you." If looks really could kill, Willa would have been struck dead right then.

The old woman looked around. "Where's Justine?" she asked.

No one answered.

"Where is Justine?" Willa demanded again.

"What did you do with the nanny?" Abel asked.

"She's fine," Patrick said. "She's in the bathroom upstairs, tied up."

"Well, go untie her, Abel," Willa said.

"I'm a little busy right now, Mother."

"Oh, just shoot him and be done with it. But outside. You don't want to make a mess in here."

Patrick couldn't decide if Mother Giardino was off her rocker or playing the part to unnerve them. He suspected the latter. The old lady looked frail, but her eyes—as well as her tongue—were sharp.

Abel pressed the gun into Patrick's lower back. The hard metal barrel drove into one kidney, reminding him of the damage a bullet at this range would do. The older man grasped the doorknob and turned. Nothing happened. "It's locked," Patrick said.

Abel rewarded this answer with a harder jab of the gun. He unlocked the door and opened it.

"No!" Stacy, still holding Carlo, rushed toward them.

Patrick whirled around in time to see Abel, gun in hand, turn to face her. Her eyes widened in horror and the boy began to wail. "Stacy, hit the floor!" Patrick shouted.

She dropped, throwing her body over Carlo's at the

same time Patrick aimed a mighty kick at Abel's back. The old man went sprawling, the gun flying from his hand. A shot rang out, the bullet splintering the frame of the doorway that led into the hall as it sank into the wood. Stacy screamed, Carlo wailed and Willa shouted curses.

Patrick stepped over the old man on his way to retrieve the gun. Abel grabbed at his ankles and Willa headed toward him with surprising speed despite her walker. Stacy clambered to her feet and pulled Carlo up after her. "The gun!" Patrick called to her. "Get the gun."

She looked around, but apparently didn't see the gun. Patrick raced across the room, thinking he could kick the weapon toward her, but Willa intercepted him, banging him hard in the shins with her walker. Patrick leaned over to shove her aside, but a hard blow to his back knocked him off balance. He turned and Abel landed a solid punch to his chin. Patrick staggered back, trying to maintain his balance.

He heard Stacy coming before he saw her. "Nooo!" she bellowed, and ran at them. She jumped on Abel's back, hands flailing, clawing at his eyes and nose. The old man turned in circles like a rodeo bull trying to throw off a rider. Carlo, still wrapped in the blanket, huddled against the wall and watched the spectacle wide-eyed, his thumb in his mouth.

"Carlo, run!" Stacy shouted. "Run and hide."

The boy hesitated, then turned and raced out the open back door, the blanket trailing behind him like a cape.

Stacy drove her thumb into Abel's eye. With a howl

of rage, the old man grabbed her arm and slung her to the floor, where he began kicking her, his cowboy boots connecting with her ribs with a sickening thud.

Patrick shouted and rushed the old man. Hands still bound behind his back, he had little defense against Abel's fists, but at least the rancher had left Stacy alone. She crawled to the side of the room and leaned against the wall, clutching her side and moaning.

"Stop this! Stop this at once!" Willa shouted. But no one paid her any attention. Abel's fist connected with Patrick's nose and blood spurted. He blinked, trying hard to clear his head. To think. If Abel got hold of the gun again, Patrick was done for, but with his hands tied and Stacy helpless, the old man had the odds in his favor once more.

Abel rushed at him again. Patrick dodged the punch, but the old man still landed a glancing blow. Patrick staggered back.

"Don't let him get out the door!" Willa shouted.

Out of the corner of his eye, Patrick saw Stacy move. She was sliding sideways along the wall, still hunched over and nursing her ribs, or pretending to do so. But she was moving, ever so slowly, toward the handgun that lay in the doorway to the darkened dining room.

"Maybe we should take this outside," Patrick said loudly. "Untie my hands and fight like a man."

"As if insults from a fed mean anything to me." Abel hit him again, a hard blow that snapped his head to one side and sent him staggering again.

"Quit playing with him, Abel," Willa said. "Where is that gun?" She looked around and spotted Stacy. "What do you think you're doing?"

Stacy froze. "I think my ribs are broken." She looked around, as if only just now becoming aware of her surroundings. "Where's Carlo? What have you done with my son?"

"Abel, where is the boy?" Willa asked.

"We'll find him later," Abel said. "When I'm done with the fed here."

"Abel, we should find him now," Willa said.

"He's three years old. He can't drive and he can't walk far in this snow. We'll find him."

"If we lose that boy, we're done for," Willa wailed. "You know that, Abel."

Abel shook his head, looking more annoyed than ever. Patrick leaned back against the counter, stealthily stretching his fingers in search of a knife, a bottle, a frying pan—anything he could use as a weapon.

A heavy footfall on the back steps made them all freeze and look toward the still-open door. A dark figure filled the space, then moved into the room, followed by two burly men with guns drawn.

"What's going on here?" Senator Gary Nordley took in the two battered men, the young woman on the floor and the old one by her walker.

"We caught them trying to steal the boy away." Abel stood up straighter and wiped a smear of blood from his cheek.

"Where is the boy now?" Nordley asked.

"He ran out the door and is hiding somewhere." Abel motioned toward the landscape behind the senator and his bodyguards. "We'll find him. He can't have gone far."

Nordley shook his head. "Abel, you told me you could handle this. Was I wrong to put my faith in you?"

Abel walked over to the dining room and retrieved his gun. "I'm handling it. You don't have to worry."

Nordley scowled at Patrick. Behind him, the two guards focused their weapons on the marshal. "You must be Thompson. I heard you'd been giving my men trouble."

"Hello, Senator. My colleagues told me they suspected you were behind all of this. I had a hard time believing it at first."

"Why wouldn't you believe it? You don't think I'm capable of orchestrating a project like this?"

"A kidnapping is not a project," Stacy snapped. "Murdering people is not a project, you scum."

Nordley turned to her, his expression affable. "Mrs. Giardino. That's not any way to talk to someone to whom your family owes so much."

Stacy struggled to her feet, using the wall for support. Her face was pale, and she was clearly in pain, but her eyes never lost their expression of defiance. "I don't owe you anything."

"If not for me, Sam Giardino would have rotted in prison for the rest of his life."

"I wouldn't have been sorry to see it," Stacy said.

"Maybe not. But this way was so much better. He had a chance to settle his affairs before he died. To make a will giving everything to his only grandson, to be held in trust until the boy is old enough to appreciate the money. In the meantime, there are those of us who can advise him on how to put the funds to the best use."

"That's what this is all about, isn't it?" Patrick said. "You want control of the Giardino family fortune."

"Not for my own selfish aims," Nordley said. "For the good of this country."

"Right. You're a true patriot." Stacy didn't keep the scorn from her voice.

Nordley looked offended. "It takes millions of dollars to run a successful political campaign. In the past I've been obligated to corporate donors and special interests for their contributions. With the Giardino money, I'll be beholden to no one. I'll have the ultimate freedom and the political power to do what's right, without concern for the special interests. And the beautiful irony is that I'll be using corrupt mob money to do good for the American people. I hope Sam Giardino is spinning in his grave at the idea."

"You're crazy," Stacy said.

"Genius is often confused with insanity," Nordley said. "The founding fathers were willing to make sacrifices to turn their ideals into reality. I'm willing to do that, too."

"Killing us isn't some noble sacrifice," Stacy said. "It's murder."

"Who said anything about killing you? You're still useful to me." He turned back to Patrick. "But I have little use for a federal marshal who interfered with things that are none of his business."

"You don't think blood on your hands would look bad to the voters?" Patrick asked.

"There won't be any blood on my hands. If anything, you'll be a hero. An officer who died in the line of duty."

"What are you going to do?" Stacy asked.

The senator ignored her. "Abel, you and Stevie take Marshal Thompson out to one of the barns and take care of things." He motioned toward the door.

"Not the barn," Abel said. "It would upset the horses."

Nordley glowered.

"They're sensitive animals," Abel said.

"Take him to Timbuktu for all I care," Nordley growled. "I don't want to see him again."

"Don't you talk to my son that way," Willa snapped.

Nordley nodded to the old woman. "No disrespect intended."

"You can't kill him!" Stacy protested.

"I told you. I won't be killing anyone," Nordley said.

"You can't let anyone else kill him, either," she said.

"Why not?" Nordley arched one eyebrow, all skepticism.

"You brought me here to sign over control of Carlo's trust. But I already signed it over to Patrick—to Marshal Thompson."

The lines around Nordley's eyes deepened. "Why would you do that?"

"It's because I was going into witness protection," she said. "With a new identity, I couldn't control the trust, so I signed over control to Marshal Thompson. He'll handle things and see that Carlo and I have everything we need."

Patrick couldn't believe what he was hearing. It was a crazy idea, but she was doing a good job of selling it. Nordley turned to him. "Is this true?"

"Yes," he lied.

"What happens if you die?" Abel asked.

"Another agent will take over control of the trust on Carlo's behalf." Was that the right answer?

"You'll spend years in court trying to untangle this," Stacy said. "By the time you're done, Carlo will be grown and you'll be too old to run for president."

"I think you're lying," Nordley said.

"Do you want to take that chance?"

Nordley stuck out his lower lip, considering. "Stevie, you and Ray take these two out to the barn and lock them up," he said after a moment. "Then help the rest of us search for the boy. I'll put in a call to my legal team and get to the bottom of this."

One of the big bruisers grabbed Patrick roughly by the arm and dragged him toward the door. The other man followed with Stacy. Patrick looked into her eyes, intending to offer some reassurance. Instead, she was the one who buoyed his spirits, her eyes shining with triumph over the way she'd tricked the senator.

He wanted to tell her not to get overconfident. Their good luck couldn't last, and when Nordley figured out he'd been had he was liable to take his anger out on them. But no need to add to her worries now. Let her savor her little victory—she'd had few enough things to celebrate lately, and a little respite from worry would help her prepare for the danger ahead.

Chapter Fifteen

Though Stacy's every instinct was to struggle against the man who dragged her toward the barn, she forced herself to relax. Her side ached where Abel had kicked her; if he had broken one of her ribs, struggling would only make things worse. And Patrick wasn't fighting his captor. He had experience in these situations, didn't he? She should follow his lead.

The icy night air hit her like a slap across the face. A shiver convulsed her body and she clenched her teeth to keep them from chattering. As the two thugs led them across the snow she scanned the darkness for some sign of Carlo. He shouldn't be out in this cold. She prayed he'd find a warm place to hide and stay hidden. She didn't want any of these people laying so much as a finger on him ever again.

The barn was dimly lit, smelling of sweet hay and warm horse. One of the animals nickered from the horse boxes that lined both sides of a central passageway. Low-voltage lighting glowed along the floor in front of the boxes, but one of the thugs—Stevie, the senator had called him—flicked a switch and overhead fluorescent lighting flooded the space with a harsh white glow. Several of the horses stirred, their feet shifting on the concrete floor.

"Where should we put them?" the other thug, Ray, asked.

"Over there." Stevie jutted his chin toward a horse box whose door stood open. Half a bale of hay spilled onto the floor inside the box. Stevie led Patrick to an iron ring fastened to one wall in the box and pulled at it. "This should work." He spun Patrick around and wrapped a plastic zip tie around his already-bound wrists and cinched it tight. He wound a thick rope over this, then fastened the rope to the iron ring.

Ray fastened Stacy's wrists together behind her back with a plastic zip tie, then bound her ankles. "Sit on the hay," he told her. "You'll be more comfortable."

She doubted it, but did as he suggested. "Should I tie her to the wall, too?" he asked Stevie.

Stevie was fitting a zip tie around Patrick's ankles. "She won't go anywhere trussed up like a chicken," he said. He pulled the tie tight, then stood.

"Should we gag them?" Ray asked.

"Who's going to hear us if we yell?" Stacy asked.

Stevie looked around, as if searching for a gag, then shook his head. "Forget the gag. We need to go find the kid."

They left the stall, closing the door behind them. She strained her ears, listening as their steps receded. The overhead lights went out, then the barn door opened, creaking on its hinges. As the door closed again a horse across the aisle kicked at its stall, then whinnied.

Stacy looked at Patrick. His lip and one eye were swollen, and dried blood streaked one cheek. He had to be in pain, but the eyes that met hers were calm. Thoughtful. He wasn't panicking, so neither would she. "Now what?" she asked.

"Now we get out of these restraints, find Carlo and get out of Dodge," he said.

"Right. Piece of cake." She struggled against the plastic ties binding her wrists. "But how?"

He looked down at his bound ankles. "These are just plastic zip ties. They probably came out of Abel's garage. I can tell you how to get out of them, then you can free me. How are your ribs?"

She shifted on the hay bale gingerly. "A little sore, but I don't think they're broken, just bruised." Looking at his battered face where Abel had beat him, she felt like a wimp to complain. "Just tell me what I need to do and I'll do it."

"It'll be easier if you slide down until you're sitting on the floor."

She lowered herself to the floor. The concrete was cold, the chill quickly seeping into her. "Now what?"

"Now you've got to bring your arms under your body and around until they're in the front. It'll be easier for you because you're short. How flexible are you?"

"Pretty flexible. I do yoga."

"Then no problem. Take it slowly."

But moving slowly only made her ribs hurt worse, so she forced herself to push past the pain. Leaning back, she worked her wrists under her bottom, then scooted back, gritting her teeth as she contorted her spine into a C and worked her bound hands down the back of her thighs. Knees to chest, she made herself as small as possible. She kicked off her shoes and forced her arms down, ignored the protests from ribs and arm sockets. She sucked in her breath and slid her arms around her feet.

From there, the rest was easy. She eased her bound hands up until they rested at her waist in front of her.

"Good girl," Patrick said. "Now all you have to do is break the cuffs."

She almost sobbed. "How am I going to do that?"

"You're a lot stronger than you think. Raise your hands to about chest height and spread your wrists as far apart as you can. Point your elbows out."

She followed his directions, then looked to him for further instruction.

"Now thrust down with as much force as you can, pulling your arms apart as you do so. Deep breath in.... Now!"

She jerked her arms down, putting everything she had into it, and the plastic snapped apart. She gasped, then stifled a shout of triumph. If any of their captors was close enough to the barn to hear, she didn't want to give herself away. "It worked!"

"Now see if you can untie me. If not, we'll have to find something to use to cut me loose."

Her ankles still bound, she used the wall to push herself to her feet, then hopped awkwardly to him. "I can do this," she said as she fumbled with the rope. "They didn't tie it very well."

"They probably figured with the restraints it was overkill." He turned sideways to give her more room to work. She bit her lip, concentrating on threading the strands of the coarse rope back through the loops of the knot. "There," she said as she pulled the last of the knot loose. "The rope's gone, but what about the rest?"

"Now take off one of your earrings."

"My earring?" She put a hand to the thin gold hoops.

"Just one. And I can't promise this won't break it."

"It's just an earring." She unhooked the bauble and held it out to him.

"Take it and thread the end of the hook between the plastic strap and the little square lock on the zip tie." He turned his back to her and offered up his bound wrists. "It'll be a tight fit, but you should be able to force it in."

She grasped his hand to hold him steady, then wedged the tip of the earring wire into the lock on the cuffs. "I can't get it to go in without bending."

"Keep working at it. A little at a time."

She took a breath, let it out then tried again. This time she was able to ease the wire in a full inch. "What now?"

"Pull on the plastic. See if it will loosen."

She tugged hard on the plastic strap and it began to slide from the lock until it was loose enough for her to remove it from his hands. "What about the duct tape?" She studied the thick layers of silver tape wrapping his wrists.

"Find an end and rip it."

She picked at the tape with one nail, idly noting that she was overdue for a manicure. She almost laughed to be thinking of such things at a time like this.

"What are you smiling about?"

She looked up and found his eyes on her, the affection and tenderness in his expression sending warmth through her. To think she had resented him when they'd first met—been afraid of him, even. She looked away. "I was just thinking how different this is from the life I've been leading—about how sheltered I've been."

"You've done great. I don't know when I've met anyone braver—man or woman."

His praise made her feel about ten feet tall. She pulled the last of the tape from his wrists. He rubbed them, wincing. "Now the ankle bindings—do yours first."

Now that she knew how to use the earring to bypass the locking mechanism on the zip ties, she made short work of their ankle restraints. She was even able to slip her earring back into her ear when she was done. Patrick was still rubbing his wrists, grimacing. She took one of his hands between hers and smoothed the angry red flesh, still sticky with tape residue. "Does it hurt much?"

"I'll live."

She kissed his wrist, his pulse fluttering against her lips. He slid his hands up to cup her cheek and raised her mouth to his. Closing her eyes, she gave herself up to the kiss, all thoughts of danger and lost children and uncertain futures deliberately shoved aside for this one moment of sweetness.

A moment that ended too soon. Patrick pulled away, though he still cradled her face between his hands. "Whatever happens, I want you to know you're the most amazing woman I've ever met," he said.

"Only because I'm with you." She rested her hands on his chest, palms flat over his heart. "You make me believe I can do anything." No one—not her parents or old boyfriends or her husband—had ever had that kind of confidence in her. She could have loved him for that alone.

"That's because you can." He kissed her forehead, then turned toward the door. "Come on. We have to find Carlo before they do." He grasped the doorknob. It turned easily enough, but the door refused to budge. He shoved against it, but the heavy wooden door scarcely moved.

"What is it?" Stacy tried to see around him. "What's wrong?"

He turned back to her, his face grim. "There's a bolt thrown over the door from the outside. We can't get out."

CARLO WAS COLD. The night air cut through his thin pajamas and his socks were soaked from running through the snow. The snow was cold on his hands, but when he walked now, the snow burned his feet. How could the snow be both hot and cold?

He huddled between the water barrels on the side of the house and looked out at the darkness. He was afraid of the dark. Even in the daytime, he had never been far from the house alone. Uncle Abel said there were wild animals out there—coyotes and bears that would eat little boys.

He could hear people calling his name—Uncle Abel and other men he didn't know. He didn't answer them, and tried to make himself smaller in the narrow space between the two water barrels. He'd decided to hide here because he could see the lights of the yard from here. He could see the barn and the cars and other familiar things.

He was so cold. His teeth chattered and his whole body shook. Even with his knees drawn up to his chin and his arms wrapped around his legs, he was still cold. He had lost the blanket somewhere while he was running; he couldn't remember where. When he breathed out, his breath made little clouds in front of his face.

The voices had moved around to behind the house now. Would they come around here eventually? What would Uncle Abel and the men do if they found him? Uncle Abel was usually nice, but tonight he had looked angry. He'd been very angry at Mommy and the man with her. Carlo didn't like it when people were angry.

His daddy had been angry a lot, and had yelled at Mommy. Sometimes he'd made her cry, and that made Carlo sad and mad and afraid, all at the same time.

Where was Mommy now? She hadn't been here for so long, then tonight she had finally come, and then she'd told him to run away. None of it made sense.

He put his head on his knees and closed his eyes. Maybe if he went to sleep he'd dream about being some place warm.

The barn was warm. The horses made it warm. The horses were big, and they scared him a little, but he liked to watch them from a distance. The other day Uncle Abel had put him up in the saddle in front of him and walked the horse around the corral. Carlo had never been so high up before. He loved the feel of the horse rocking beneath him. Uncle Abel had promised to teach him to ride when he was bigger. Carlo would have his own pony and learn to be a cowboy.

He could go to the barn and hide. He'd be warm and if he couldn't sleep, he could watch the horses.

He stood and peered around the barrels. The yard was quiet and empty. He dashed across the wide strip of blackness between the house and the barn. When he reached the deeper shadows beside the barn, he was out of breath and his side hurt from running. His feet still burned, but the rest of him felt a little warmer.

He felt his way around the side of the building to the door to the feed room. Standing on tiptoe, he could just reach the doorknob. He opened it and went inside. The door from the feed room to the main barn stood open. Low-voltage lights illuminated the central walkway between the horse boxes. The barn cat, Matilda, came up and leaned against his legs. He ran his hand along the soft fur of her back and smiled. "Good kitty," he whispered. He didn't want to wake the horses, who were probably sleeping.

He pulled a saddle blanket from a pile by the door and lay down on a bale of hay beside the feed bins. The cat curled up against him. He was warmer now, and sleepy. Maybe in the morning, he'd see Mommy again.

Chapter Sixteen

Patrick studied the door on the horse box. It was made of heavy wood with forged iron hinges on the outside. It was built to contain animals weighing hundreds of pounds. But he couldn't accept that there wasn't some way out. "Stand back," he told Stacy.

When she'd moved out of the way, he took a few steps back, rushing the door. He slammed into the heavy wood, the impact reverberating through his already battered body, rattling his teeth and blurring his vision. The door didn't budge.

"I don't believe this!" Stacy wailed. "We've got to get out of here and find Carlo!" Her voice rose in a shout of frustration. Patrick felt like shouting with her. Instead, he looked around the bare stall for anything he could use to hack or pry at the door.

"Mommy? Mommy, where are you?"

He froze and looked to Stacy, whose eyes locked with his. "Carlo?" She ran to the door and stood on tiptoe, as close to the rectangular wooden vent at the top of the door as she could get. "Carlo, Mommy is here, in the horse box."

Shuffling sounds—small feet on concrete and hay—moved toward them. "Mommy, I want to see you."

"I'm in the horse box, baby. Someone locked the door and I can't get out. I need you to help me."

Small fists pounded on the door. "Come out, Mommy."

Stacy knelt now, making herself the height of a three-year-old. "I'll come out, baby. But I need your help. Look up, at the top of the door. Do you see the bolt?"

"Uh-huh."

"Can you climb on something and get to that bolt? Is there a feed bucket or something you can stand on?"

"There's a bucket in the feed room."

"Then be a good boy and get it and bring it over to the door."

He didn't answer, but Patrick thought he must have moved away. Stacy closed her eyes and pressed her forehead against the door. Patrick moved to put a hand to her shoulder. She must be exhausted, but they'd all be out of here soon, she and Carlo safe.

Something scraped on the concrete. "I got the bucket!" Carlo shouted.

"Good. Now turn it upside down and put it in front of the door. Climb on top of it, but be careful."

"Don't worry, Mommy. I'm a good climber."

"I'm sure you are. But be careful."

Patrick scarcely dared to breathe while they waited. The last thing they needed was the boy falling and busting his head on the concrete floor. The bucket rattled and the boy beat his fists against the door. "I made it!"

"Great," Stacy said. "Now reach up and pull back the bolt."

"I have to stand on tippy-toes." Scrabbling noises, accompanied by little grunts. "It's in there really hard."

"You're a strong boy. Pull hard."

A metallic *thunk* announced the bolt's moving. "I did it!" Carlo crowed. "I opened the door."

"That's wonderful, baby. Now climb down and move away from the door so I can come out."

More scraping and fumbling with the bucket. "You can come out now, Mommy."

Stacy eased open the door. Carlo hurtled into her arms. "What were you doing in there, Mommy?" he asked, his arms around her neck. "Were you hiding?"

"That's right, baby." She stroked his hair and kissed his cheek. "We were hiding, but not from you."

The boy looked over her shoulder at Patrick, eyes wide. "I was hiding," he said. "But I got cold, so I came into the barn."

"You did great." She hefted the boy onto her hip and turned to Patrick. "Can we go now?"

"In a minute." He scanned the passageway and the area around the stalls, then slipped into the feed room, looking for anything he could use as a weapon. He found a short-bladed knife on a shelf there and pocketed it. He picked up a horse blanket and took it to Stacy. "Wrap the boy up in this."

She tucked the blanket around her son. "When we get to the car, you'll be a lot warmer," she said.

One hand resting lightly on Stacy's shoulder, Patrick leaned in to address the little boy in her arms. "We're going to sneak past your uncle and his guards and go to my car, which is parked on the road through the woods. It's kind of a long way for your mom to carry a big guy like you. Would you let me carry you?"

Carlo put his thumb in his mouth and looked at his

mother. "It's all right," she said. "I'll be right here beside you."

The boy nodded, then held his arms out to Patrick. That simple gesture of trust brought a lump to his throat. He settled the boy against his chest; the weight felt good there. Right. Stacy's eyes met his across the top of the boy's head and she offered a weary smile. "Thanks," she whispered.

He should be thanking her. Until he'd met her, his life had revolved around work and duty. He still took those things seriously, but she made him see beyond the job, to other things that might matter to him. "Let's go," he said. "Stay close to me and keep to the shadows."

Once he'd determined the coast was clear, they left the barn. The yard was silent and still, not so much as a moth fluttering around the light over the back steps of the house. No one called Carlo's name or ran through the yard. Had they called off the search for now, or taken it farther afield?

He guided Stacy around the perimeter of the light, the knife clutched in one hand, ready to lash out at anyone who came near. Once they reached the pasture and the deeper darkness there, they'd retrieve their snowshoes and be able to move faster. They wouldn't stop again until they reached the car. In half an hour they'd be headed toward Denver, where he'd find a safe house for Stacy and her son until the task force had rounded up Nordley and Uncle Abel and everyone else involved.

They'd reached the edge of the yard when a woman's scream tore apart the night silence. He whirled and saw a woman racing across the yard, a man chasing after her. The man grabbed the woman by her long hair and dragged her back toward the house. "The babysitter," Stacy whispered.

"Why is he hurting Justine?" Carlo asked.

"I don't know, baby." Stacy rubbed his back and looked at Patrick with eyes full of questions.

"That was one of Nordley's thugs," Patrick said. "Maybe she panicked and threatened to go to the authorities."

"Maybe so." She continued rubbing Carlo's back. "Was Justine nice to you, honey?"

"She was real nice. So were Uncle Abel and Grandma." His lower lip trembled. "When will I see them again? Uncle Abel promised me a pony."

Before she could answer, the back door to the house flew open once more. This time a man rushed down the steps, followed by one of the thugs. "Is that Uncle Abel?" Stacy asked.

The first man was Abel. He and the younger, burlier man struggled, then three gunshots sounded, *Pop! Pop! Pop!* like firecrackers in the winter stillness. Abel slumped to the ground, and a dark stain formed on the snow. Patrick cradled Carlo's head against his shoulder, turned away so the boy wouldn't see.

"What's happening?" Stacy whispered, as she pulled the blanket over Carlo's head.

"Mo-om! What are you doing?" He tried to push the blanket away, but she held it in place.

"You don't have a hat. I don't want your head to get cold," she said.

The younger man dragged Abel back into the house. Patrick couldn't tell if the old man was alive or dead.

"Do you think Nordley turned on him?" Stacy asked. "We have to do something."

"You really want to help these people?"

"They were kind to Carlo. And they're the only relatives he has left. If the senator is attacking them…"

She was right. He couldn't abandon two old people and the babysitter to Nordley's thugs. "Let me get you and Carlo to the car, then I'll come back."

"No. I won't leave you. And two people against Nordley are better than one."

Not when one of the people was a woman with a little boy to look after, but he didn't bother to say it. He knew Stacy well enough by now to know he wouldn't be able to convince her to leave. "We need a way to draw them out," he said. "If we try to charge the house, they have the advantage."

"Let's find a safe place to leave Carlo." She looked around the compound. "I wish we had someplace warmer."

"That's it." Patrick felt the surge of excitement that accompanied a good idea, one he knew would succeed. "We need to start a fire. That will draw them out of the house, plus alert the agents who are watching the place."

"How are we going to start a fire?" she asked. "We don't have any matches."

"Leave that to me."

The building farthest from the house in the ranch compound was an open-sided shed half filled with hay. If Patrick could get the hay going, it would make a bright, hot fire with a lot of smoke, perfect for raising the alarm. He searched the feed room and grabbed a flashlight. Further searching among the supplies on the shelves produced a wad of steel wool. "What are you going to do with that?" Stacy asked.

"I'm going to start a fire. Come on. Let's get to the hay barn."

Two minutes later they crouched in the deep shadow of the barn. Patrick pulled hay loose from the bales until he had a foot-high pile in the open area at one end of the shed. Then he unscrewed the top from the flashlight and set the two batteries next to each other nestled in the hay. He tore off a piece of steel wool. "Take Carlo to the end of the shed," he told Stacy. "Just to be safe."

She did as he asked. He dropped the steel wool on top of the batteries, bridging the gap between the posts. The batteries sparked and the wool burst into flames. He nudged the burning wool onto the hay, which caught quickly. Within seconds a line of fire crept across the floor, toward the bulk of the hay stacked at the end of the shed.

Patrick joined Stacy and Carlo just outside the building. "Now we wait." He started toward the house. When Nordley or his thugs emerged, Patrick would be ready.

BY THE TIME they reached the house, flames had climbed to the roof of the hay shed. The fire crackled and popped like small-arms fire and smoke filled the air, stinging the nose. The agents watching the ranch would have seen the blaze by now, and the people in the house were bound to notice soon. Gaze fixed on the back door, Patrick saw the first movement and pulled Stacy and the boy into the deeper shadows beside the house as the door burst open and Senator Nordley, followed by

Stevie, ran out. "Get the hose," Nordley shouted. "I'll turn on the water!"

"Abel must be hurt badly," Stacy whispered, "if he's not coming to help."

Patrick nodded and started toward the steps, but Stacy rushed past him, Carlo in her arms. He grabbed her wrist and pulled her back. "Let me go in first," he said.

She nodded. "Of course." She stepped back to let him pass. "I'm just worried about Abel and Willa."

Right. The people who had kidnapped her child and threatened to kill her. But they'd been kind to the boy, and something about them had touched her. Despite her tough attitude, Stacy had a tender heart. Ordinary things—not littering and taking care of family—mattered to her. "Here's the plan," he said. "I go in first. We know there's just one guard. I'll overpower him. Don't come in until I give you the signal."

She frowned. "But—"

"You need to stay here with Carlo."

She nodded. "All right." She moved to the side of the door with the boy, into the shadows on the far side of the steps. Knife at the ready, Patrick opened the door and slipped inside.

The kitchen was deserted, though the sound of the television still drifted from the living room. He peered into the room and saw the two women seated side by side on the sofa. The coffee table had been shoved out of the way and Abel lay on the floor at the women's feet, his face pale, eyes closed.

The guard stood a few feet away, cradling an AR-15, his head turned so he could look out the window toward the blazing hay shed. To reach the guard, Patrick would have to approach from the kitchen, making him an easy target.

Someone moaned, low and painful. "He's awake," Willa said, and leaned toward her son.

So Abel wasn't dead, though from here Patrick couldn't tell how badly he was injured. The old man moaned again, louder.

"Don't move," the guard ordered.

But both women had already dropped to their knees and were fussing over the injured man. The guard turned from the window and came over to them, his back to Patrick.

Patrick charged. In three strides he crossed the room and drove the knife blade between the guard's ribs. The man screamed and loosened his grip on the rifle enough for Patrick to wrestle it from him. The man froze when the marshal pointed the gun at his chest. "Facedown on the floor," Patrick ordered.

"I'm bleeding." The guard looked at the blood seeping down his side.

"You'll bleed more if you don't do as I tell you."

The guard lowered himself to the floor and lay on his stomach. Patrick turned his attention to the women. "We need something to tie him up," he said.

The younger woman, Justine, who was near Abel's age, tugged a scarf from around her neck. "You can use this."

"You use it." Patrick motioned with the gun. "Tie his hands, then find something to tie his feet."

She nodded and knelt beside the guard while Patrick

turned his attention to Abel. Willa leaned over her son. "Do something," she pleaded. "You can't let him die."

Abel appeared to have been shot in the right shoulder, and again in the thigh. Blood pooled around him on the floor, but had started to clot. He was pale and his breathing was labored, but when Patrick checked his pulse, it beat steady and strong, if a little rapid. "What happened?" he asked.

"He overheard the senator tell one of his men that when they found Carlo they should just kill him," Willa said. "Then Abel, as next of kin, could petition the court to get the money. Abel couldn't let that happen. Justine ran out, thinking she would find the boy first and hide him. Abel tried to distract the senator. They got into an argument and one of the guards shot him. Then they ordered us all in here." She stroked her son's forehead. "We needed the money to help save the ranch, but we fell in love with Carlo. We couldn't let that man hurt him."

Justine had finished tying up the guard. "Let me get some things to clean his wounds," she said.

"Of course." Patrick stepped back. "If you have a first aid kit, we can bandage him up."

"Where is Carlo?" Justine asked. "Do you know?"

"He and his mother are waiting outside. I'll get them now."

He returned to the kitchen and opened the back door. "Stacy?" he called.

She stepped out of the shadows, Carlo in her arms. Relief filled him; though he'd only left her a short time, there'd been a chance Nordley or Stevie would find her. Knowing she was safe eased some of his tension.

"Come inside." He held the door wider. "Everyone is in the living room. Any sign of Nordley and Stevie?"

"No. They must still be at the hay barn."

He glanced toward the barn. The flames had climbed higher and illuminated the night. They must be visible for miles.

He did a quick check around the outside of house and saw nothing to alarm him, though shouts came from the direction of the hay barn. When he returned to the living room he found Abel sitting up, propped against the sofa. Justine and Willa sat on either side of him. Stacy sat in the chair opposite, Carlo in her lap. The boy stared at his uncle, eyes wide, thumb in his mouth.

"Give me a gun," Abel said when he saw Patrick. "I want to shoot Nordley myself when he comes back."

"I thought you and the senator were friends."

"Sure. A friend who shot me." His mouth twisted in disgust. "We were never friends."

"How did you get involved with him in the first place?" Patrick asked.

"Don't badger him," Willa said. "He's hurt."

"He needs to know what he's dealing with," Abel said. He shifted, as if trying to get comfortable when that was impossible. After a second, he spoke again. "Sam sent him to me. When the economy was good I took out a second mortgage on the ranch to expand the operation. Then things went south. The land wasn't worth what it was, people weren't buying expensive horses, but the stock still had to eat. The bank still wanted to be paid. I asked Sam to help me. I figured criminals were the one bunch that were still doing well no matter what the stock market was up to."

He coughed, and Willa patted his shoulder. "You shouldn't talk so much," she said, and glared at Patrick.

Abel waved her away. "Sam said he couldn't help me, but he said he knew someone who could. Nordley came to see me and said if I'd do him a few favors, he'd pay off the mortgage. All that debt, gone."

"What did he ask you to do?" Stacy asked.

"That was the thing. It was nothing. He sent a couple men to stay here a few days. They rode around, walked the property, didn't bother anybody. He said he wanted to use the place as a retreat. They stayed in the bunkhouse, didn't bother anybody. He bought the mortgage from the bank and said as long as I cooperated, I didn't have anything to worry about. I know now he was just setting me up. Playing me for a fool."

"He couldn't have known Sam would die," Stacy said.

"I think he planned a hit on Sam before the feds got involved and did the dirty work for him," Abel said. "Nordley has that kind of nerve. He thinks he's a genius and everyone else are fools."

"After Sam died, he asked if we would look after Carlo." Willa took up the story. "He told us the mother didn't want the boy and he needed to be with family."

"He lied." Stacy hugged Carlo closer.

Willa ignored her. "Of course we would look after my great-grandson. Two of the senator's men brought him here one night."

"That's when Nordley told me the rest of the plan," Abel said. "That we were supposed to use the boy to get control of the money. I knew about the will. One of the last times I talked to Sam, he bragged about how smart he was, giving the money to the boy and tying it up in a trust. I guess Sam told his buddy Nordley about the will, too, but not about the boy's mother having control of the trust. That's why he ordered his men to just bring the boy here. When I told Nordley the boy's mother had control, he was angry. He said we'd have to get Stacy here and force her to sign over everything." His shoulders sagged. "By then I was in too deep. I couldn't see a way out."

"You'd have let him kill me for money," Stacy said.

"He would have killed me. He would have killed all of us." Abel shook his head. "I never wanted anything to do with the family business. All I wanted was to ranch. Sam said I'd betrayed the family. I figured involving me with Nordley was his way of getting back at me."

"We love the boy." Willa addressed Stacy directly. "We never would have hurt him."

Stacy nodded. "He loves you, too. He said you were good to him." She stood as if to go to the old woman, just as the window next to Patrick's head exploded and a bullet thudded into the wall behind the sofa.

"Everyone down!" Patrick shouted. He crouched beside the window, trying to glimpse the shooter in the darkness. Willa and Justine sobbed and Abel muttered curses and pleaded again for someone to give him a gun. More shots hit the outside of the house around the window. Patrick decided there was just a single shooter, but he was determined to keep them pinned down. Where was the other man—probably Nordley—and what was he up to?

Stacy's scream rose above the other background

noise, accompanied by the sounds of a struggle. "He's got Carlo!"

Patrick whirled and found the senator, his face streaked with soot, hair in wild disarray, clutching the boy to his chest. He pressed the muzzle of a pistol against the child's temple. "Unless you want me to kill the boy now, you'll put down that rifle and let me leave," Nordley rasped.

The shooter outside had silenced his weapon, also. Now came the rev of an engine, very near the house. "I believe that's my ride," Nordley said.

Patrick carefully lowered the rifle to the floor, every muscle protesting as the senator dragged a terrified Carlo toward the door. He looked for a way—any way—to stop the abduction, but the risk was too great. He believed Nordley wouldn't hesitate to pull the trigger.

Nordley made it out the door and down the front steps. Patrick, Stacy and Willa followed, keeping their distance, but unable to look away as the senator walked backward toward the car. He was even with the back bumper when Carlo, who had hung limp in his arms, suddenly came to life. The boy bit down hard on Nordley's arm and flailed his legs, landing a hard kick in Nordley's crotch. Nordley cried out and the gun went off.

Stacy screamed and covered her eyes with her hands. "It's all right," Patrick told her. "Carlo's free." The boy raced toward them. Nordley, doubled over, tried to fire after him, but his aim was wild.

Patrick grabbed up the boy and swept him into the house, herding the women before him. He retrieved the rifle and raced to the door once more, but Nordley was already in the car, driving away. A siren screamed in the distance, approaching fast.

Stacy, Carlo in her arms, came to stand behind him. "Are you all right, buddy?" Patrick asked.

"I didn't want to go with that bad man."

"You did good, darling." Stacy kissed him. "So very good. You were so brave." She watched Nordley's car careen down the driveway. "He's going to get away."

"Maybe not." The sound of screeching tires, crushed metal and breaking glass punctuated this statement. Patrick raced down the drive, running hard, but by the time he reached the crash site at the entrance to the ranch, men swarmed over the wreckage of a government-issue SUV and Nordley's Jeep.

Two men dragged Stevie out of the driver's side. The guard was able to stand on his own, though blood ran from a cut on his head. The passenger side of the vehicle was crushed.

"We think the passenger is Nordley." Special Agent Sullivan, looking sharp in a black ballistics vest over his black suit, came to stand beside Patrick. "We'll know more once we've cut him out and loaded him into the ambulance."

"It's him," Patrick said. "Is he alive?"

"From the sound of it, he is," Sullivan said. "And cussing a blue streak." He glanced down the drive. "What's the situation at the house?"

"An older man, the ranch owner, Abel Giardino, is shot. He needs an ambulance. Three women and the boy are frightened, but okay."

"I'm not going to ask you right now why you're here after I told you to stay away."

Patrick met the other man's eyes, refusing to back down. "I had a job to do, just like you. I had to keep Stacy Giardino and her child safe."

"In doing so, you forced Nordley's hand." He looked back at the car, where emergency personnel were prying apart the passenger door to get to the senator. "He might not have been so careless if not for you."

"You were right—he's behind all of this. He intended to use the boy to gain control of the Giardino money. He blackmailed Abel and Willa into helping him."

"I'll need your full report as soon as possible. And we'll want to interview the Giardinos and anyone else who lives here."

"We can talk about all that later. I have to take care of Stacy and her son now." He turned to walk back to the house.

"You could lose your job over this," Sullivan said. "Or at least get a ding on your record."

Maybe so. But he'd done what he knew was right, and he could live with that. "I guess we'll see."

"Do you think she's worth all this trouble?"

He smiled, though his back was to Sullivan. "Yes," he said. "Yes, she is." He walked faster, back to the house and back to Stacy. The sooner this was over and they were together, the better.

STACY REMAINED IN the house with Carlo while Willa and Justine followed the emergency personnel who carried the stretcher on which Abel lay. The old man was responsive and the EMTs pronounced him stable. "Will Uncle Abel be okay?" Carlo asked.

"He will." She forced a smile for her son's sake. "Tomorrow or the next day, we'll see if we can visit him in the hospital. I know he'd like that."

"Okay." Carlo buried his head against her chest and closed his eyes. He must be exhausted; she was. But too many things remained unsettled for her to rest easily.

As the EMTs and the two older women exited the house, Patrick squeezed past them. He still carried the weapon, though it was slung at his side. Dark blood smeared his shoulder and dark half-moons ringed his eyes. Yet she'd never seen a better sight. "You doing okay?" he asked.

She nodded. "Just tired. And I need to get Carlo to bed."

"I'll find someone to give us a ride to my Jeep and take you back to the hotel."

"I don't have to go to some police station and answer a bunch of questions about what happened?"

"There'll be time enough for that later. Right now you two need your rest."

"What will you do?"

"I'm still in charge of keeping you safe."

"Then you won't leave us." Relief surged through her. She'd been afraid that now that she and Carlo were out of danger, he'd be anxious to be rid of them. Sure, he'd said and done a lot of things over the past few days to make her think he cared for her, but maybe that had all been part of him gaining her confidence. Maybe now that he didn't have to be with her, he'd feel differently. "What will happen now?" she asked—the question she had repeatedly asked him throughout this ordeal. He always had an answer that reassured her and kept her going.

"Senator Nordley will face charges—kidnapping, attempted murder, aiding a felon.... I'm sure there are others. Abel could be charged, too, but I'm betting he can work a plea deal if he agrees to testify against Nordley. Especially if you don't press the issue."

She shook her head. "I believe his story about being caught up in Nordley's schemes. I meant, what will happen to me? Do I have to remain in custody?"

"No. But I'll help you get settled."

"I still don't want to be in WITSEC. There's no reason for that now."

"I wasn't talking about WITSEC."

"You mean I'm on my own?"

"Only if you want to be."

The warmth was gone from his voice, replaced by an anxious tone. He shifted nervously and studied her face, as if trying to decipher her thoughts. The man who was always so confident and sure of himself looked lost. "What's wrong?" she asked. "Why are you acting so weird?"

"Because I don't know how else to act." He touched her shoulder, a tentative brush of two fingers against her collarbone. "Would you think I was crazy if I told you I loved you?"

"That is crazy talk," she said, even as her heart raced.

He ran a hand through his hair so that the blond strands stood on end. "I know we've only known each other a few days. But in that time I feel I've gotten to know you and...I've never felt about anyone the way I feel about you. I think you're amazing—smart and brave and strong, and a great mother, a beautiful, sexy lover.... I just... I can't deal with the idea of losing you."

"You don't have to lose me."

His eyes searched hers again. "What are you saying?"

She shifted Carlo, who had fallen asleep, to her other side. "You live in Denver, right?"

He nodded.

"I could move to Denver," she said. "I can find a job, maybe even go back to school. We could see each other—see how we do together in the real world."

"I'd like that."

She almost laughed. "That's all you can say?"

In answer, he pulled her close and kissed her. Lips locked to hers, he lifted both her and Carlo off the ground. When their lips parted, they were both breathless. "I'd love that, Stacy Giardino," he said. "I love you."

"I love you, too, Patrick Thompson. As crazy as we both are—I love you."

Epilogue

One year later

Stacy looked out the window of the courthouse at the crowd of reporters waiting at the bottom of the steps. News vans lined the street and the microphones and cameras were three deep. "I can't believe they all want to talk to me," she said.

Patrick, looking more handsome than ever in a suit and tie, put a reassuring hand to her back. "Your testimony was crucial in convicting Senator Nordley, not to mention the human-interest angle of an ordinary woman being caught up in a mob family, then having to fight to save her child—the public loves you."

"I'll be happy when things settle down and I'm no longer in the spotlight." She straightened the jacket of her chic suit. The bold purple-and-black colors made her stand out in the sea of lawyerly gray. "Guess we'd better get this over with."

The door to the anteroom where she and Patrick had retreated opened and Carlo raced in. "Mama, we're going to be on TV!" he said.

"Looks like it." She knelt to smooth his tie. "You

remember what I told you? Mind your manners and don't speak unless someone asks you a question."

He nodded. "Aunt Deborah already told me all that."

Stacy looked up at the woman who had followed Carlo into the room. Deborah Thompson had the same blond hair and blue eyes as her brother, but she was petite and delicate. She smiled at Stacy. "Are you ready?"

Stacy stood and took a deep breath. "I think so."

Deborah came and slipped her arm around Stacy's shoulder. "You're going to do great. Just remember all we talked about."

Stacy nodded. For almost a year now she'd been seeing Deborah once a week for counseling sessions. It turned out Patrick's sister was a psychologist. A former battered wife herself, she specialized in helping other women who'd been in abusive situations.

With brother and sister on either side of her and Carlo running ahead, Stacy made her way out to the reporters. Camera flashes flared and voices shouted questions. She read the statement she'd prepared, thanking federal agents and prosecutors for bringing a serious predator and criminal to justice.

"What are your plans now that the trial is over?" a reporter asked.

"I've been accepted into University of Denver law school," she said. "I'll start classes there in a few weeks."

"Are the rumors about you and Marshal Thompson true?" another voice shouted.

"Is that an engagement ring you're wearing?" asked someone else.

Stacy smiled down at the diamond solitaire on the

third finger of her left hand. Patrick had given it to her at dinner last night, when they'd known for sure the trial would end today. His proposal hadn't been a surprise; they'd been inseparable for the past year. So her answer hadn't been unexpected, either.

"Stacy has done me the honor of agreeing to be my wife." Patrick had stepped up to the mic beside her.

"What do you think of that, Carlo?" someone asked.

Patrick lifted the little boy to the microphone so he could answer. "I think he'll be a good dad," Carlo said. When some in the crowd laughed, he buried his face in Patrick's shoulder, suddenly shy.

"That's all the time we have for questions." The chief prosecutor stepped in to guide them away from the microphones. They retreated back into the courthouse. Patrick's car was parked in the underground garage, making a discreet getaway easier.

"You did great." Deborah patted her shoulder. "I'll see you two later." She kissed Stacy's cheek, then repeated the gesture with Patrick and Carlo.

"How do you feel?" Patrick asked Stacy, after he'd set Carlo down. The little boy ran ahead to the elevator. "Are you relieved it's all over?"

"I'm relieved the trial is behind us. As for the rest…" She smiled and took his arm. "I feel like my life is finally beginning. I have school to look forward to, and the wedding, and us being together as a family. A real family, full of love and support. That's a first for me."

"Me, too." He stopped walking and turned toward her. "Have I told you lately how much I love you?"

"Not in the past half hour."

He kissed her lightly. "It's true." Then he deepened the kiss, pulling her close.

"You're embarrassing me!" Carlo's voice rang through the lobby.

"Better get used to it," Patrick called. "Your mother and I plan to spend the rest of our lives embarrassing you."

Stacy rested her forehead against Patrick's shoulder, laughing. A year ago, she wouldn't have believed she could be so happy. One man—and love—had made all the difference.

* * * * *